ATTACK
THE CHOHISH WARS

Copyright © 2022 by G. J. Moses

All rights reserved. No part of this publication may be reproduced, distributed, or transmitted in any form or by any means, including photocopying, recording, or other electronic or mechanical methods, without the prior written permission of the publisher, except in the case of brief quotations embodied in critical reviews and specific other noncommercial uses permitted by copyright law.

ISBN: 978-1-7341152-2-2 (Digital)
ISBN: 978-1-7341152-3-9 (Paperback)

10 9 8 7 6 5 4 3 2
Second Edition 2023
Front cover image by Damonza.com
Book design by Damonza.com

ATTACK
THE CHOHISH WARS

G.J. Moses

WAR IS SENSELESS. Death and destruction of the innocent must be prevented. Diplomacy has its place in the order of the galaxy. But it is much more robust with a strong military behind them. The Royal Galactic Navy prefers peace but is ready for war.

Signed:
Admiral Vyncis Rythey III
Year 4227

PROLOGUE

SAILING THROUGH SPACE, Captain Faustina Mcnamara of the Frigate Immortalite sat in her captain's chair in deep thought. She was sipping a cup of hot coffee wrapped in her two hands, trying to keep sleep away. She was a tea drinker in normal conditions, but now, she needed something with a bit more caffeine. She had been in her chair for over ten hours straight.

The main screen showed one of the slipstreams that bordered the Foisa System. Near the slipstream were a few dozen warships. The warships belonged to the Chohish empire, which had attacked the two occupied planets in this system without warning. The Chohish were a race unknown to humans at the time of the attack. The Chohish had killed indiscriminately without warning or provocation. Men, women, and children had died cruelly at their hands with no compassion.

The Chohish had finally been driven off but only after the extensive loss of life. The two RGN Frigates, Cameleon and Immortalite, had been assigned to monitor their movements in a forward observation position.

A human reinforcement fleet had arrived over the pair of planets in the Pandora system. Still, until additional units came, they hesitated to chase after the Chohish. They did not want to leave the two worlds undefended until the RGN could finish building their defensive platforms.

Both frigates were in stealth mode, with several more frigates further back monitoring them with even more behind them. Probes, which had been placed strategically around the entire system, were suitable for some things but not all. Having a human added as part of the monitoring process significantly increased the accuracy of the data obtained.

It had taken close to a month to get the Immortalite in its current position to relieve another frigate that had developed engine problems.

Up until a day ago, the activity had been minimal. Bland would be more accurate. The Chohish would rarely move, and even then, not far, and would return to their original location after a short timeframe. Faustina believed the movement had been for engine maintenance, something they would have done typically too. The frigates had nothing new to report, and most crewmembers were bored senseless, having been assigned here for the last three months. They were close to rotating out when it happened.

Faustina had been sleeping when the alert went off. Springing out of her bunk, she raced to the bridge without taking time to change out of her sleepwear. The bridge was a madhouse but organized nonetheless.

"Status" yelled Faustina while racing to her command chair.

Suddenly, the lights overhead changed to red. The alarm sounded an alert until the ensign turned it off as a signal from the captain.

"We are detecting half a dozen destroyer-sized ships heading in our direction. Their speed is increasing rapidly," a now anxious yet eager Lieutenant Brandt responded.

If the situation were not dire, the captain would have laughed.

Times like these are what personnel in frigates dreamed on. Dangerous as all hell, but usually the first to see action. They were not here to fight; they could, as they were not defenseless. But that was not their primary purpose. They were the eyes and ears of the fleet. When attacked, they ran. And few ships could outrace them.

"Move to starboard, slowly now, and stay within the speed required to maintain stealth protocol. Let's see if they actually know we are here or just fishing. And someone, please get some coffee delivered."

Hours later, they had moved hundreds of thousands of miles away from their original location and the path of the Chohish warships. Faustina knew this was not as far as she liked, but moving faster would have compromised their stealth protocol.

They sat motionless for nine hours while the Chohish warships flew past and around the area they had been near. It was apparent the Chohish had suspicions someone had been in the area.

"*Could the earlier frigate be detected because of their engine problems? They had not sent any ships to the area the Chameleon was occupying. I will bet they detected some leakage. Unfortunately, this area was the best for monitoring the slipstream section where the Chohish were patrolling,*" thought Faustina. "*We did not need to be this close to monitor the present ships. The probes would have sufficed for them; it is what may show up that we need to be here for.*"

Sipping on her hot coffee, she was glad she had taken the time to change out of her sleepwear and clean up. Still, she could feel the oil buildup on the skin of her face and the bitter taste in her mouth from all the coffee she had consumed. No matter how much she rubbed her tongue on her teeth, they felt grimy. She could have asked for stimulants from medical, but she did not want to use them until necessary. She always believed the drugs caused some loss of clarity even though medical denied that assumption. Then again, the coffee had a limited impact at this stage.

She had a question: *"If the Chohish suspected or knew we were here, why were they now trying to find us? What has changed?"* Or, as her heart pounded as she believed she knew, *"what was going to happen?"*

"Sensors, keep them locked on the slipstream. I suspect we will get visitors in a bit, " the caffeine-jittery captain ordered.

The bridge that had grown quiet now became a flurry of activity. The bridge crew came to the same realization as the captain from the tone in her voice. Some grinned, some laughed, but all dealt with the tension. But none were frightened.

The crew on a frigate rarely got involved in an actual battle, but it did not mean they liked it. Only in situations like this made it all worthwhile—the fear of being detected and possibly seeing something monumental in the ongoing war.

They were not disappointed. A few hours later, another alert sounded. This one was much quieter as it was only for the scanning station.

"We are detecting incoming ship transitions. We have identified three new Chohish men of war who have transitioned through the slipstream. Power indications that additional ships are still incoming," responded first mate Lieutenant Felton Brandt.

"Breakout of new ships?" asked Faustina.

"All the same so far, matching what we identify as Destroyers," responded the lieutenant.

"Notification been sent? Chameleon reporting same?" asked Faustina as she nervously watched more ships arrive.

"Notification sent with a point-to-point linkup. Cameleon reports they see the same. They have relayed the information to command," reported Ensign Floy Dale.

"More ships are transitioning. They are flooding through now, Captain; I am recording at least thirty additional, with more still arriving. Breakdown forthcoming. Numbers are constantly changing," an excited Lieutenant Brandt yelled while turning to look at the captain.

"Easy, Lieutenant, easy. We are all excited. Stay focused," ordered Faustina calmly.

Watching her crew, she could see they were all excited. But she needed to make sure they were paying attention to their surroundings.

"Where are the original destroyers?' she quietly asked. Usually, she would have to raise her voice to ensure she had their attention, but now, everyone was waiting on her orders. She could have whispered it, and they would have heard.

"They are still circling our original location. There was no longer any doubt the Chohish knew we were there. If they search hard enough, they will pick up our lendolium trail. No matter how good we try to contain it, some escapes," responded the sensor technician.

"Then let's move further back. Lieutenant Commander, if you would," ordered Faustina.

The feeling of the ship moving was the only response given. Faustina smiled as she expected no less. Lieutenant Commander Bobby Rhodes had been her first mate for years and only spoke when he felt it was necessary. Moving the ship was his response. She would miss him when he got a command of his own. He deserved it as he was very good at his job and well-liked by the crew.

But that was something to worry about in the future. The Chohish destroyers had picked up their trail. They had changed directions toward where Frigate Immortalite lay in hiding before the sensor technician gave her the expected update. "Captain, we are going to have company. Several Chohish destroyers have split off from the main group and moving toward us."

"Sound battle stations and red alert. Take us out of here at maximum speed, Commander; it looks like it's time to show our speed." Faustina ordered. "Evasive maneuver, maximum thrust. I expect they will fire upon us once detection is confirmed."

The red alert signal flashed throughout the ship. All personnel hastened to battle stations or where they would lock themselves down. They had been through this drill so often that it was like second nature.

The sudden movement starboard came as a shock to her system even though she expected it. Evasive maneuvers never gave a warning about which direction they would move next, as it was all determined by the ship's AI, and their bodies paid the penalty. Especially in a small frigate.

And none too soon. "Missile launch, wide dispersal" announcement went throughout the ship.

"Well, the warning and data on the new Chohish ships went out. Now, our job is to survive," thought Faustina.

THE RETURN

STANDING BEFORE THE enormous galley window, he heard the click-clack of high heel boots descending the hall. He knew his guest by the perfume that preceded her without turning. It was just as appealing now as when he first smelled it so long ago.

"I knew you would be here. Command pinged the room with notification the ships were near." Jeanne de Clisson, Captain in the Irracan Navy, said as she sidled beside him.

"I got the notification a few hours ago. Sorry, I did not want to wake you. Just because I could not sleep did not mean I should ruin it for you. I knew they would notify you when the ships were closer. And it was obvious where I would be, given our discussions the last several days. I had to see if it still showed the scars and resembled anything like the ship I once knew. I was astonished they didn't scrap it, delighted, but still surprised. It looked unsalvageable when they towed it away."

"The bones were still good. And it has something that few ships have, which makes it worth the extra cost to repair."

Turning, Captain Zeke Kinsley of the Royal Galactic Navy looked at her, puzzled. "And what would that be?"

Grabbing his right arm with both hands, Jeanne rested her left cheek against his shoulder. "Besides having a great warship reputation, it is now a symbol of what lengths the Royal Galactic Navy will go to for its people. The video of what the Lucky Strike looked like when they towed it away made every news broadcast on every human and Sorath world. Along with the story and sacrifice of the brave crew that staffed it. And that was after they sent a detailed video of the death and destruction on the two planets. You cannot just junk a symbol like that. Either of the two ships."

Smiling, she pointed out the window. "Now, that is one beautiful ship."

Startled, Zeke swung back to look at two ships barely visible in the distance. Slow, agonizingly slow, they enlarged. He watched as a ship he had once feared lost came closer and closer.

Pulling Jeanne in close, he moved her to wrap his arms around her waist with his chin on the back of her head. Whispering... "They, like you, are so beautiful, aren't they?"

Grasping Zeke's right hand, Jeanne pulled it up to her lips, kissing it softly before whispering. "They? You only have eyes for one particular ship, my dear. But yes, they are beautiful."

Both were startled when they heard a soft cough behind them. "Good afternoon; I hope I am not interrupting?" a smiling Governor Titus Muldane asked. "I was informed the task force was getting close and knew you two would be here. I hope you do not mind if I share this moment with you? Those are the Lucky Strike and Fox, no?"

"Not at all, and yes, that is them. It has been so long that I wondered if I would recognize my ship," said Zeke.

Moving to stand beside Zeke, as the two ships get closer, Titus acknowledges that Zeke might not. "My cousin is part of the command group at Vro. When Roger heard both ships were coming to his shipyard, he made sure they prioritized their repair. As you know, a lot of changes went into both. It is a possibility you may not recognize them."

Breathing in the fragrance that wafted from Jeanne's hair, Zeke muttered in reply. "I believe I will recognize her no matter the changes made."

Stepping back, Zeke exclaimed, "Wait a moment, your cousin? Oh, that explains how the Fox came into your possession. When we sent him our suggestions, I was unaware he was your cousin."

The sound of a chuckle answered his statement.

The word of the ship's pending arrival must have spread because the galley quickly became crowded with the crew from both ships as the minutes passed. All were watching in awe at the two warships that finally parked a short distance from them just over an hour later.

"You know, I never thought they could have put her back together after what she had been through, but from what I see on the outside, they did an awesome job. Look at her; she is gorgeous!"

The chatter picked up as the minutes went by. Just as some started asking if they could go aboard, Titus said they might want to wait.

At first, they were puzzled by Titus's comment when Lieutenant Isolde Iverson uttered, "Will you look at that?" in an awe-struck voice. They all turned to see where she was looking. Additional warships were now coming into view.

Zeke and Jeanne had seen large fleets before but never anything near the size of the one on display. Ship after ship kept appearing, and it was soon quite apparent that the RGN was not the only one to send a significant task force. Intermixed in the massive flotilla were Sorath ships of the line and many escort ships.

When the Sorath warships appeared, Hawke worked his way forward to stand next to Jeanne, gazing in pride at the sight of the Sorath ships. All knew why the Sorath would want to see this clearly as Sorath's fleets leaving their home systems were rare and did not begrudge him the least bit. Many smiled when they saw the wonder on his face.

"I knew they would be a part of this, but this? They mean business, don't they?" asked a proud Hawke.

"Yes, my friend, they sure do. And I am glad the RGN is not holding back either. And Jeanne, do you see the small contingent near the center?" asked Zeke. "Those are Irracan ships unless I am misreading their ship insignia."

Hugging his hand even tighter, Jeanne answered with pride. "You are not mistaken; those are Irracan ships. They will join my brother's ships, who will be part of this task force. We have payback due us."

"Do not forget Niflhel or Nocuous. Major Khaleesi Richards has been training thousands of our army personnel for the past half-year. Your Lieutenant Commander Jamie Chandler has been doing the same for hundreds of fighter pilots and support crew. A good many will be joining this task force under their command. Most will be left behind to continue the training on recruits, but everyone demanded to go with you. Most here lost someone or all they had. Now the survivors ask for an opportunity to right the wrong done them." Titus reminded Zeke and Jeanne.

Zeke nodded before looking at Titus and putting his hand on his shoulder. "We remembered Titus." Glancing over Titus's shoulder, he pointed to Khaleesi leaning against the bulkhead where she had a commanding view. "The Major already has her officers going through organizing the supplies the group joining us will need. If I know the Major, it is near completion by now."

The view from the gallery was one to behold. There were ships that many of those present had never seen in person. Carriers, Battlecruisers, Battleships, Troopships, Tenders, Heavy Cruisers, and

Cruisers were here. Smaller vessels like Destroyers and Frigates were so numerous; that it was impossible to count.

And finally, there was a type that was rarely seen this far from the primary industrialized planets—those being gigantic Dreadnaughts.

Dreadnaughts were dedicated to either Missile or Beam weaponry to maximize firepower. These ships were more than twice the size of Carriers, and the firepower they provided was intimidating. But they paid for all their size and firepower in speed as they were very slow relative to the other ships in the fleet. But they were not meant to be fast but have enough speed to get out of the way of missiles shot at them from a distance beyond the missile's fuel range. Adversaries had to get within the Dreadnaughts missile and beam envelope long before they could open fire. Rarely did they travel with a fleet, but here they were, a full dozen, six of both varieties.

It was Hawke who saw the markings on these gigantic ships first. Howling in pride, he slammed his palms against the window. "*AAaiiee Chohish*, soon you will meet my brothers and sisters. They have not forgotten you!"

Without warning, both communicators for Zeke and Jeanne buzzed. Both looked at each other in surprise before tapping to acknowledge.

"Captains, you and your command staff are to report to the main conference room at the top of the hour. We recommend that your crews start boarding their ships to familiarize themselves with the new systems as quickly as possible."

Looking at her timepiece, Jeanne laughed. "Well, that gives us a good eighteen minutes. So much for getting changed."

Sighing, Zeke tapped Hawke on his shoulder and indicated Will to join them. "We were asked to meet in the main conference room in eighteen minutes with both command groups. Can you two head that up? I will head there with Jeanne now and try and save some seats for us."

Looking at Hawke, Will nodded while tilting his head in Hawke's direction. "Getting him pulled away from the window may be the most difficult part of your request. But we will get it done."

With Jeanne's arm hooked in his, Zeke pinged Ensign Caspian Raske and Ensign Selena Bonilla. "Ensigns Raske and Bonilla, can you please get the crews headed over to our two ships? The command staff wants our command group to join a meeting."

He finished with a chuckle. "And if you can, make sure they do not break anything. You know Jax and his engineering crew; they will want to take apart everything they do not recognize."

Zeke and Jeanne made their way to the conference room without waiting for a response. They knew where to go as they had attended meetings in the same room for several months.

Entering the conference room, it was apparent something significant was happening. Attendees were rushing in, still tucking shirts in their pants or jackets hanging on just one arm.

Finding enough contiguous seats for such a large group was always an issue. Zeke and Jeanne went down the aisles, searching for a free section. They were surprised when they found the entire front row open. It had to be reserved for guests or top-tiered officers.

Resigned to standing, they were walking away when stopped by an attendant. The attendant asked for their names. The attendant smiled and told them the empty seats were for their group. Sitting in the middle, they were soon joined by the rest, who looked at them in puzzlement as they took their seats.

The doors were closed precisely at the top of the hour.

The chatter in the room rose suddenly when a small group of

admirals, a mixture of both races, entered from a side entrance to sit down at a table on the raised dais facing the attendees.

Silence quickly descended in the room, where a massive 4D video stream popped up over the admirals without a word. The images showed warships appearing through a slipstream, joining an already present fleet.

Gasps of astonishment sounded throughout the room as the number of ships appearing kept increasing until a flood of warships was transitioning through the slipstream. It finally ended, but not until dozens upon dozens of ships were now present.

Admiral Katinka Chadsey, in charge of the combined fleets, stood and raised her hands to quiet the low murmur that had emerged. The feet admiral stars on her shoulders, the only one wearing them, let everyone know who was in charge of the combined RGN fleets.

"No need to tell you what we just viewed. You are looking at the data supplied by the RGN Frigates Cameleon and Immortalite. The Chohish have reinforced their fleet to well over two hundred ships. Breakdown on the ship makeup you can all guess based on prior deployments. They are consistent."

"Fortunately, our joint task force arrived at this time. So one on one, we should be able to manage this new force. But if we have to split the force, we would be at a disadvantage numerically. But this is all pure conjecture; this is an unknown enemy. Unknown weapons, unknown tactics."

The Admiral stepped forward until she stood before Zeke and Jeanne. "So I would like to call upon Captains Kinsley and De Clisson. Captains, if you would. You are the only ones that have extensive experience fighting this adversary."

Surprised at the request, they looked at each other before replying; Jeanne smiled and asked Zeke to respond first.

Zeke took a few seconds to gather his thoughts while looking around to get an idea of who his audience was. What he saw would have been intimidating without Jeanne's presence; she looked at him confidently.

Standing, Zeke stood at ease with his arms crossed behind him. "Admiral, Captain Jeanne de Clisson, and I have run simulations and discussed this at length. We always believed the Chohish, no different than us, would send a large force to fight over this system."

Zeke nodded to Jeanne, who had risen to stand beside him. "Our simulations were set up using the Chohish weapons and fleet arrangement we dealt with here. Since we had no concrete data on the size or makeup of either force, we started with a small number to work out data specifics. Once we had that, we increased numbers and changed makeup. Some had us outnumbering them, some same size, and others where they outnumber us."

Zeke continued his report. "Our simulations show we should be able to defeat a similar-sized Chohish fleet. Our technology is to our advantage. This would be true, even if we split our forces to cover both planets. That is only because of the heavy defensive platforms recently installed on the moons and planets."

Pausing, Zeke took a breath to gather his thoughts. "But if the Chohish does not split their forces, the fleet that has to fight the Chohish would take a beating. With a good chance, those ships would become ineffective for the foreseeable future."

Jeanne picked up the conversation without any delay. "If so, that one battle could lead to unacceptable losses. That would potentially stop your plans to force your way through any blockading Chohish fleet into the next-door system with a large enough force to take the fight to the Chohish."

"Captain Kinsley and I believe we should not split our forces. Instead, we should send the fleet through the asteroid tunnel."

Jeanne raised her hand to point at a planet displayed in the paused 4D video. "Toward Nocuous, now that it has been made safe for travel again. I will let Captain Kinsley finish on what our recommendations are."

"The citizens of Niflhel are still living underground; the majority will continue doing that for the foreseeable future. It will take years before they can rebuild their cities. We recommend leaving a small defensive force around Niflhel if the Chohish sends some of their forces there."

"But our calculated guess is that the Chohish will stay in one group and head to Nocuous. Especially since they have confirmed that Nocuous has the lendolium reserves they require."

"Your recommendation then is to position ourselves around Nocuous?" asked Admiral Chadsey.

"No, it is not. Waiting there puts us at a disadvantage. What we recommend is meeting head-on. We had a plan in mind, but some vessels we just saw a few minutes ago have us rethinking those. So I would like to run some new simulations adding the new vessels in the mix before voicing them to this group."

Pausing to look at the Admiral directly, he changed his tone from reporting to his command voice. "I do not believe the Chohish will change their tactics now. Every time they met us has been head-on, a slugfest, no special tactics involved. From everything I have experienced, that is the way they prefer it. There is no reason not to meet them head-on; let's give it to them. They have not yet met our larger warships; we should use that to our advantage. We may only get this one opportunity to hurt them big time."

The silence that followed was palpable. Still standing, Zeke and Jeanne waited patiently while the officers on the dais discussed what they heard.

A few moments later, Admiral Chadsey signaled quietly to silence the whispers that had started.

"Captains, we agree with you." With emphasis, the Admiral resumed. "We listened when you spoke these past several months.

The data we retrieved from your two ships' computers on the prior engagements support what you just told us. We have been running our own scenarios with this in mind. That is also why the Sorath high command sent the '*vessels*' you mentioned if I am correctly guessing, that you saw earlier."

"I recommend that you, Captain de Clisson, and whomever you recommend join us in our strategy session to review our plans. With the arrival of the additional Chohish forces, we expect they will be making their move once they have had a chance to regroup. We will want to be underway before then."

"As for the rest of you, get to your ships and prepare for immediate departure. Make sure your crews know this is not a drill. We will send orders within the next several hours. All capital ships are to be ready to leave in two hours."

With that, the Admiral announced the meeting was over. Chaos erupted as everyone started contacting their ships while running out of the room.

Turning to their command crews, Zeke and Jeanne ordered them to board the ships and verify the readiness of the two warships. Jax interrupted them to notify them his engineers had already started running system checks. Finally, with a big smile, he finished. "Oh, and Captain Kinsley, LS1 said to let you know that he is '*impressed*' with the repaired ship. The Lucky Strike is cleared for service, just waiting on its Captain. Captain de Clisson, he said to tell you....."

After waiting a few seconds while Jax stood quietly, Jeanne frustratingly blurted out, "*What?*"

"Nothing else, that was it. LS1 said you would understand." They all started laughing upon seeing Jeanne roll her eyes.

LS1 was the name given to the Lucky Strikes ship's primary artificial intelligence (AI) by Zeke that everyone had found out in the past year had a wicked sense of humor.

Everyone was still chuckling when Admiral Chadsey joined them. "Did I miss something?" she asked with a questioning look.

"Just something from long ago," Jeanne responded while waving the crew away.

"Good, follow me, please." Admiral Chadsey led Zeke and Jeanne out of the large conference room, only to enter another room next door.

This room, tiny in comparison, consisted of a vast display table surrounded by workstations. Swivel chairs swung out from under the table on command.

A dozen officers stood around the table looking at a substantial 4D Halo. Meanwhile, the chairs were occupied by technicians speaking into headgear, simultaneously working an array of gear balanced in their laps while entering commands one-handed into the workstations.

A huge man, a good six and a half feet tall, with a shaved head topped by a body Zeke doubted had an ounce of fat. Huge muscles flexed in anger as he turned to frown upon their entrance. From the expression on his face, it was apparent the admiral was going to yell a reprimand for disturbing them. That was until he saw the fleet admiral. At that point, he nodded in recognition but did not relax his frown.

In a deep gruff voice, he asked. "Admiral, we were going over our plans one final time before we sent out the orders. Do you care to join us?"

"I do, thank you. I brought the two captains that I spoke to you about earlier. I want to get their opinion and recommendations before signing off on our plan. Let me introduce Captains Zeke Kinsley and Jeanne de Clisson. Captains, this is Admiral Nkosana Okeke. He brought the task force that had just arrived. Per my request, he jumped onto a Destroyer and arrived this morning. That was so we could work out our final plan, incorporating any changes if needed, now that we know all the resources that will be available to us. I doubt we have much time before the Chohish fleet starts deploying."

Making his way gingerly around the other officers surrounding the table, Zeke extended his hand out for a handshake. "Admiral Okeke, it is a pleasure. I have served under you several times in the past. It is my honor to finally meet you in person. Although I must admit, you are much smaller in person than has been rumored. The rumor has you over ten feet tall."

The bellow of the laughter that came from the throat of Admiral Okeke matched the breadth of his chest. "I see that the captain lives up to the description you gave me, Admiral; he has some spunk. I like that." drawled the Admiral as he grabbed Zeke's hand in an energetic handshake.

Silently groaning in pain as his hand was slowly mashed, Zeke stared into dark brown eyes that sparkled with an intensity he rarely saw. "Upon further review, I may have been mistaken, and you may live up to the rumors." visibly wincing as the Admiral released his hand.

"Make room at the table for our guests and the fleet admiral." Admiral Okeke ordered while he cleared a place for himself halfway down the table.

"Admiral Chadsey, this is what we came developed. Only a few minor changes from what you saw before your meeting."

Over the table now appeared a huge 4D Halo image of the entire system with all planets and opposing fleets. The simulation started with the RGN task force leaving the vicinity of Nocuous en masse. The Dreadnaughts followed behind the main fleet in a defensive arrangement. The rest of the fleet headed directly toward the Chohish armada, which had left the vicinity of the slipstream except for the original guard force of several dozen ships.

It took several minutes, even fast-forwarding, until the opposing forces were in range. Other than a few ships repositioning, it became a slugfest between the two fleets. The RGN won only due to their superior technology making the final difference.

Admiral Okeke looked around before he spoke. "Our best strategists confirm they believe this is the best plan for dealing with the Chohish fleet. Fancy flying took those forces out of the engagement window for the duration of the conflict, impacting our overall effectiveness. Our main concern is that if we do not meet them head-on, the Chohish will get around us and head to either of the planets while we turn around, giving them plenty of time to cause untold damage. Comments, anyone?"

Seeing none, he then commanded. "No? Alright then, let's pass the following orders on to…" when the Admiral was interrupted by a cough.

Turning, he saw that Fleet Admiral Chadsey had raised her hand, gesturing for quiet. "Nkosana, one moment, please. I asked the captains here to get their viewpoint."

"Well, Captains, is this similar to your simulations? Any suggestions?" she asked.

"Our simulations were severely limited as we did not know the extent of the forces we would have nor face. Like yours, we did many simulations based on different fleet sizes for both forces. I do have several questions I would need answering before I can answer your question with any degree of accuracy."

"We do not have time for this, Admiral. We need to leave now if we want to get positioned with some time to spare." a visibly angry Admiral Okeke exclaimed. "We have been running simulations since we put together this task force months ago using the information these captains supplied. The captains even confirmed the basics of our plan just minutes ago."

Fleet Admiral Chadsey turned on Admiral Okeke with authority dripping from her words with steel in her voice. "I will not repeat myself, Admiral Okeke; you will wait as long as I tell you to. Now let my guests ask their questions so they can respond properly."

Sighing, Admiral Okeke nodded his acceptance with a smile on the corners of his lips. "As you wish, Admiral."

Glancing at Admiral Chadsey to confirm it was okay to start asking his questions, Zeke took a moment to review the RGN task force layout. Pointing to the RGN fleet, he asked no one in particular. "What speed are they making?"

One of the technicians behind Zeke replied. "A bit under normal half speed for a capital ship. That is the maximum speed the Sorath Dreadnaughts can make."

Nodding his thanks, he then asked out loud. "Can anyone tell me how much time we have to deploy near Nocuous if we leave within the next several hours? Please confirm that we will travel through the tunnel now that it is functional."

"We will have half a day at a minimum, maybe more. It all depends on when the Chohish moves, which we expect to be within the next few hours. And yes, we will be moving through the tunnel." Admiral Okeke looked at them thoughtfully.

Everyone watched as Zeke grabbed the image of the fleets and moved them around so he could see them from all aspects. Then, turning toward Jeanne, he whispered and pointed here and there without indicating what they were discussing.

It was undeniable that the two had worked together before. Zeke would move the image in one direction while Jeanne would grab it to move it in another direction without asking. Both whispered for long moments before Zeke looked at Jeanne and said aloud. "You agree?"

Zeke slowly studied the personnel around the table upon her affirmative nod before he paused to stare pointedly at the fleet admiral before settling his gaze on Admiral Okeke.

20

"Admiral, if you let Jeanne grab a terminal, she will program a simulation we would like you to view before running it through the AIs for feasibility confirmation. If we may?"

Upon a glance from the Admiral, a technician allows her access to his workstation. Jeanne stopped beside him and had him answer a few questions before she sat down. "Wish we had Isolde here; she is much better at this than I am. But give me a few moments, ahh, there is your simulation file, now I need to change this, and this."

The tension rose as the minutes passed. Zeke looked at Admiral Chadsey to try and gauge how long her patience would last. He was relieved to see she showed no indication of losing her patience. That was not true for Admiral Okeke, who looked redder in the face as the minutes passed.

Finally, he heard from Jeanne what he was expecting. "OK, one more tweak… here we go… that should do it. Zeke, whenever you are ready."

Zeke could feel the tension radiate throughout his body. Then, trying to regain his composure, he took a deep breath. Zeke was in a room full of superior officers. He was about to suggest something different from what they had spent months planning. Then, letting the air out of his lungs slowly, he closed his eyes to let the stress leak away.

"Before this morning, I would have agreed with your plan. But now, Captain de Clisson and I believe a better option exists. Jeanne, if you would…"

The simulation Jeanne put together ran for over ten minutes. As the seconds slowly slid by, Zeke could feel the tension in the room rising. Then, glancing around at Jeanne, he could see she was just as nervous as he was.

Then, he was surprised when he heard support from the last person he expected. Admiral Okeke, now in a tone of respect, exclaimed. "Admiral Chadsey, now I see why you asked these captains to be here. I apologize for my earlier abruptness. I like this plan. Risky, but if it all goes as we just saw, well worth it."

"I concur. Admiral Timeti, what do the Soraths think of this plan?"

The voice that came back from the only Sorath in the room had an odd mechanical sound that he had never heard before. Still, Zeke knew that was because each Sorath adjusted to the translator embedded in their thorax differently. Hawke's had no mechanical sound at all. But the translation was understandable.

Zeke looked at the Sorath, who stood tall at the far end of the table with his wings pulled tightly against his back. He was surprised by the decoration displayed on his severely cropped shirt. Sorath did not believe in elaborate rank decorations, but this one had a small patch high on his left shoulder that left Zeke close to gawking.

The admiral stars on his shoulders, a decoration he only wore so any RGN forces knew his rank, were giant in comparison. But that tiny patch identified this Sorath as a member of the Supreme Council that ruled over all Sorath worlds. Only someone who knew Sorath's history would see the significance. There was only one council member for each populated planet in the Sorath empire.

Zeke doubted this Sorath had left his home world in decades; Sorath Council Members were very territorial. Yet, here he was, leading a task force. And even more surprising was the interest Zeke saw in the admirals' eyes, who stared intensely at himself and Jeanne. And something nagged at his memory, almost like he had met this Sorath somewhere before. Newscast?

"I like this plan better than the other, a lot more. Even though it puts my forces at severe exposure, this one has potentially much better results. So we Soraths are willing to take these risks. You have our approval."

"Ok then, let's run it through the AI while we transit through the tunnel and make a final call when we reach Nocuous. We can always return to the original plan if the AI recommendations return negative."

Zeke and Jeanne looked at each other in concern, as they would be responsible for an untold number of deaths if this failed.

CHANGE

STANDING ON THE bridge of the Lucky Strike, Zeke marveled at all changes. The bridge, once resembling a war zone, now had that brand-new look again, although it sure did not look the same. The bridge was not how he remembered it. Even his command chair had modifications. But there was one thing he was glad they had not changed. The bridge still had the soft colors of blue and white intermingled with the silver metal alloy he loved.

The crew had trained extensively for several months to get used to the new interfaces and controls, but that could not compare with working the actual units. The excitement that was prevalent on the Bridge was universal throughout the ship.

The bridge crew was mirroring Jax's reaction when he finally shuttled over. The happy smile on Jax's usually stern face was something to see when Zeke stepped off the shuttle. Jax was doing a jig in the middle of the bay with several of his maintenance crew. It had more than himself laughing.

Both first officer Lieutenant Commander William Farren and Hawke were hotly chattering over the new missile systems and the updated lendolium and Fusion-powered lasers. Isolde and Caspian were another pair excitedly testing the new scanners. But then again, he knew he felt the same. It was like the Lucky Strike had risen from the grave.

And now, here they were, heading away from Nocuous at half speed. They had exited from the asteroid tunnel one more time a good twelve hours ago. But this time, amid a fleet, the makeup he never dreamed would exist, let alone be a part of. Next to him, Admiral Timeti stood stiffly with his wings pulled tight against his back.

"Captain Kinsley, I appreciate you allowing me to ride with you. The reports we received from Hawke spoke of your crew's impressive skill and dedication. I wanted to see this for myself, to see if Sorath's training needs to be modified."

"Admiral, we are honored. A little surprised, though, that you will stay with us through the oncoming action and not onboard one of your dreadnaughts." Zeke could not hold back a little chuckle as he finished with, "Some of your ships are a bit safer than mine while being quite a bit larger."

"Each ship has an expert captain; I would be just in the way. Now is the time to see how they perform before we get too far from home. So don't you think that would be wise?" The Admiral turned to look at Zeke directly with no amusement in his voice. "All the while, I can watch your crew simultaneously, seeing how my people integrate with the RGN. Training together is one thing, actual combat being another."

Turning back to watch the main screens, Admiral Timeti continued. "Captain, my people have not forgotten the atrocities heaped on us. Death and destruction were on a scale that few today in your Empire could even conceptualize or believe. As bad as the atrocities in this system were, and I have seen the reports and halos of the destruction wrought here, they are only a microcosm of what happened to us. Even after several millennia, huge scars from the Chohish wars exist on most of our planets."

"We remember though, oh, how we remember. Now is the time to remind the Chohish how much we have not forgotten what they did to us," the admiral declared.

The admiral turned again to look directly at Zeke. "While we have time, do you have any more cocoa? I must get some for myself after all this is through."

The comment on the cocoa did not lighten the mood as he was sure the admiral intended. Zeke saw something he recognized in the admiral's eyes once he had turned to look directly at him. Zeke's eyes had looked the same as when he found the children inside the bus. When Zeke had picked up the little girl's body to cradle her in his arms, he felt a shudder run down his spine at the look he now saw: hate, pure unadulterated hate.

Breaking the gaze, Zeke tapped a button on his command chair's arm. Immediately, a voice came from the back of the chair. "Galley here, Captain. How may we help you?"

"Admiral Timeti would like a large cup of hot cocoa, and I would like some black coffee. While you are at it, you might want to see about checking on what everyone else on the ship wants. They will not have this opportunity again for a long time."

"Yes, sir, will do. Refreshments will be up in just a few." at which the connection ended.

As they waited, they monitored the main screens. The center screen displayed the icons of the fleet as it progressed. A dozen symbols have colored a mixture of purple and blue, a color no one on the ship had ever seen used.

A person from the galley entered bearing the requested coffee and cocoa.

Suddenly, just as he started sipping his coffee, the fleet broke up. Zeke loved the smell of coffee as the steam tickled his nose. He slowly sipped the hot coffee, which did nothing to calm his nerves. Then, as he watched the fleet head to the positions he and

Jeanne had suggested, he reviewed the plan in his mind again for the thousandth time.

"It is a good plan, Captain, relax." observed a remarkably relaxed Admiral Timeti. "We are committed and cannot change the plan now, regardless. The Chohish are on the move, heading straight for Nocuous, as you expected. We have been busy since they last visited. Mines protect both planets along with defensive platforms. Again, I say, relax."

"Captain, we are getting a request from Captain Meghan Kennedy for a conference call," reported Isolde.

"Put her up the left screen and on the ship speakers, thanks," responded Zeke.

Within seconds the bridge came alive with the sounds from the Fox. The left screen lit up with Captain Kennedy surrounded by her standard crew. Jeanne's sister Anne Dieu-Le-Veut is leaning on her husband's shoulder, Masson Dieu-Le-Veut, Sergeant at Arms Jan de Bouff, standing behind the captain's chair.

"Hello friends, good to see you again," came Meghan's voice over the loudspeakers.

"Hold on one second, Meghan; I want Isolde to bring the Jackal onto our call. Isolde?"

"Anticipated that would be your request when the request from Fox came in. Bringing on the Jackal now," answered Isolde.

"Hello, Zeke, Lance here. We are on full-ship speakers per Isolde's request. It is good to be part of the team again. Isolde informed us we are on with the Fox as well."

Lance and the Bridge of the Jackal appeared on the right-hand screen.

"Captain Kinsley, we have received and reviewed our orders. We want to confirm that they are now final and that there are no more changes before execution. True?" asked Meghan.

"They are. There will be no changes unless, of course, an

unplanned disaster happens. Which is a good possibility given our track record." responded Zeke with a shrug of his shoulders. A smattering of laughter followed his comment.

Walking to the center of the Bridge, Zeke looked around the room to scan each crew member before responding. "It is good to have you with us this time, Jackal. As you all know, we have a special role in the oncoming action. We will see some serious action if the Chohish does as Captain de Clisson and I anticipate. You know what to do. You have the skills, commitment, and, more than anything else, the bravery to do this. I know this, your Captains know this, *YOU know this!*"

Walking around the Bridge, Zeke stopped between two staffed workstations to put his hand on the shoulders of two of the crew. "As rough as it may get, do not forget, you are not alone. Many thousands of your fellow RGN shipmates, our new family members in the Irracan Navy, and our close allies and friends, the Soraths, are here with you. They will be counting on you to do your job as you will be counting on them to do theirs."

Now walking back to stand by Admiral Timeti, he looked at the center screen with a crooked smile. "I don't know about you? But the Admiral here is looking for some payback for what the Chohish did to his people. What say you? Do we show the Admiral that they are not alone in this quest? That we also have some payback due us?"

With that, all three ships erupted in noise as the crews shouted their support. It took Meghan and Lance a few minutes for their forces to quiet down. Meanwhile, Will only raised and lowered his hands to stop the noise on the Lucky Strike.

"Meghan, Lance, we will be one of several point defense teams for the Griffin. You know our main function; nothing gets through us. We have trained together these last several months; you know what to do. We are a team, do not separate unless necessary."

"Commander Farren, the ship is yours; let's get this ship positioned."

The warning lights came on, signaling lockdown. As everyone buckled in, the ship turned to port, followed by the Jackal and the Fox. After half an hour, they slowed until they came to a halt.

All three screens now showed the icons of the fleet. The fleet positioning is complete. Would it work? Many lives depended on it.

"Captain, the Chohish fleet continues on its projected course. Remote probes indicate they are staying grouped with Cruisers out front, followed by the Destroyers around the Battleships. I do not detect any Carriers nor any other types of ships than what we have already encountered." reported Isolde, with Caspian nodding in confirmation.

"Hawke, do they have Carriers? Or other types of ships?"

Hawke held up his hand, speaking into his computer interface, asking for a moment. Finally, sighing, he replied. "Yes, but very rarely used that we could see. There was no rhyme or reason when they showed up—our records of the ships held around fifty to seventy-five fighters. Our records indicate they rely mostly on the fighters from their Battleships and Cruisers. They have huge Beam ships with around a dozen of the Battleship's main weapons used against planetary defenses."

"Isolde, pass that info onto fleet command. Ok, people, we know what we are facing. The Chohish force heading toward us is massive, but we are not to be trifled with, as we have shown them before. You know what you need to do; you have done it before. So lets you and I do it again. Battle stations, people, battle stations!"

The three ships sat there quietly amid twelve gigantic ships facing the surge of the Chohish armada. Around them were scores of similar groupings, cruisers paired with two destroyers.

Then they did what was universally hated by all military

29

personnel. Waiting, where your mind could imagine all kinds of scenarios, some realistic, some bizarre, but all unsettling.

The hours ticked by slowly until it was time, but it was not lost on anyone when the battle started nearing them. He was patched into one of the Battlecruisers that, with the other larger capital ships, were fleeing ahead of the Chohish fleet, firing their missiles behind them nonstop.

Soon, the green icons came flashing directly toward them. Heading toward them were their Capital warships, followed by hell on wings. Missiles were pounding the Chohish while they waited. Unfortunately, the mines the Irracans had supplied on the last go-around were unavailable. The Chohish Cruisers were taking a beating, with red icons dropping motionless or disappearing altogether.

But the Chohish Destroyers and Battleships were coming on primarily unscathed. As they got closer, new icons were now appearing; hundreds and hundreds of them were appearing like a swarm of mosquitoes, fighters!

Without warning, the gigantic Missile ships opened fire. Over forty missiles from each ship raced away. Counting the seconds until the subsequent firing, Zeke could deduce that these ships did not have the new updated missile systems the Lucky Strike possessed. But that was to be expected as retrofitting the huge missile tubes that handled the much larger missiles would take much more effort than redoing a cruiser.

The noise in his ears silenced as Isolde replaced it with the communications between the three ships. "Meghan, Will, Lance, looks like we are about to get busy here… let's do it as we reviewed… stay together… watch out for the other ships……."

Pointing to Will, "All yours, Will. It's time to get us moving. Hawke, power up the shields and all weapon systems."

The ship reverberated with the whine of the power fluctuating as the ship's shields and weapons systems came fully online. Within several minutes they started moving with the two Destroyers moving in tandem.

As their speed picked up, the ships started to turn to port going into a large circle. It was only a minute before they passed between a pair of dreadnaughts continuing the circling maneuver. Then, as they passed out into the area behind the vessel, they could see the space filled with many similar groups of ships replicating the trick.

The green icons racing away from the Chohish now swarmed toward them. In long minutes, they finally flew past at full speed.

Shortly, they completed a half circle and passed the huge ships from the other side. The gigantic Beam ships let loose with firepower few on the Cruiser had ever seen live. The Beams from the ships were many times more powerful than their lendolium lasers. Dozens of lasers stabbed out at the Chohish with devasting impact.

The circling maneuver allowed them to attain full speed before heading toward the Chohish. What they saw was chaos. Explosions occurred everywhere, many from missiles, but others were Chohish ship's final gasps of life.

They raced toward the enemy. "Remember, Captains, our primary function is to protect the Dreadnaughts. We are not to engage the enemy directly unless no other option is present. Stay out of the energy weapons range. Will, Hawke, fire missiles when in range."

It was only another minute before the ship rocked from launched missiles, adding their rockets to the current chaos. The line of Chohish Cruisers was a shadow of when they had started. Most of the remaining ships bore damage that leaked flames and debris.

The line of Chohish Destroyers and Battleships was now the target of the enormous missiles fired by the Dreadnaughts. The rockets used by the Sorath's warships packed destruction magnitudes above what a missile of the next largest ship, a Battlecruiser, carried. And it was taking a heavy toll.

The Dreadnaught Beam ships concentrated their fire on the Cruisers, now in their range. When a lendolium laser from one of those ships hit an enemy Cruiser, sections of the vessel would disintegrate, shield or no shield, if not destroyed outright.

But now, the missiles from the enemy were in range. The trio of ships went into a defensive zigzag mode. At first, the number of rockets was manageable, but this lasted only a short time. Soon they were using everything the ships possessed to take down as many missiles as possible.

As the ship turned sharply to starboard to put their point defense in the path of several missiles, Zeke confirmed his belief that the rockets were targeting the dreadnaught.

"Isolde, notify Meghan and Lance to execute the spinning top in fifteen seconds," ordered Zeke. "Pass that info onto all the other Captains of the guardian group. Would you please pass on my recommendations for them to mirror our maneuver? Will, all yours."

As preplanned, Will had the Lucky Strike stop zigzagging and go into a tight spiral. Both the Fox and Jackal mirrored their new course. This maneuver allowed all three ships' defensive fire to be concentrated and not scattered due to individual course changes.

Still, many missiles got through; there were just too many to stop. Watching the humongous ships, Zeke saw they also had defense armaments. They were impressive but not complete. He watched as several missiles caused heavy damage to the Majestic, one of the missile ships.

Zeke glanced at Admiral Timeti and saw no expression change, despite losing many lives. This lack of concern was almost a clone copy of what he saw on Hawke's expression, who must also be aware by now. Why the lack of respect?

The Lucky Strike slammed hard backward before Zeke heard.

WWWHHHHOOOOMMMPPPP... Zeke heard deep groans as the crew was pressed hard against their restraints.

The lights dimmed to emergency lights for a few seconds before the Lucky Strike was violently shoved sideways again. *WWWHH-HHOOOOMMMPPPP...* again, more groans.

"*STOP* the spinning top immediately, back to evasive maneuvers. Pass the word," yelled Zeke grabbing his chair arms as the ship catapulted to port a third time from another near miss. "They are now targeting the protecting fleet."

Within seconds, the maneuver had ended. It became apparent they were now being targeted by the number of missiles exploding around them. Their ship was being jerked around like a toy.

Suddenly, the ship smoothed out and ran straight with no enemy missiles exploding around them.

Looking at the screens, Zeke knew why. Hundreds of Chohish fighters were heading directly toward them, only minutes away.

The screens then showed something new. Thousands of green icons appeared behind the missile and beam ships heading toward the enemy fighters.

Shortly, the green icons passed the gigantic ships, and soon after that, they passed by the Cruisers and Destroyers. One group stood out with a blue dot in the center of their green icon—another icon within this particular group of markers tinged with black and red at the edges. The cheering sound from the Fox let Zeke know they knew where Jeanne was, leading the Irracan fighters.

The Irracans were not alone. The monitors showed another group tinged in blue. The Lucky Strike also erupted in cheers of their own, mirrored by those on the Jackal.

Zeke knew Isolde had changed the markers, smiling, so they stood out. These were the fighters from the Lucky Strike and the Jackal. One of those icons had a black dot in the middle, Gunner's ship. Knowing this, he was surprised when new cheers erupted on the Bridge.

"Ok, Will, move us back to the front of the big boys and let the fighters have their go at them. Isolde, keep a close eye on the Chohish Battleships. When they hit the coordinates we discussed, let me know."

"Yes, sir, LS1 concurs with my estimate. The Chohish fleet is under five minutes from when they will reach a point where any deviation from their present course will not matter."

"Meghan, Lance, you catch that? Do your technicians and AIs concur?"

"Aye, Aye, Captain, they do," responded Meghan with a heavy long-drawn-out drawl. The Fox, along with the Jackal, erupted in laughter. The crew on the lucky Strike were barely holding back their laughter.

Admiral Timeti seemed startled by the response. Glancing at Zeke, he was about to say something when Zeke headed him off. Whispering, he explained. "Captain Kennedy is defusing a tight crew. The drawl is one they use when teasing visitors to their planet. You have to admit, it is pretty effective."

The smile that appeared on the admiral's face showed he concurred.

The battle between the fighters did not last long. The numerical advantage of the RGN and their allies would have been enough. Still, the skill difference made it a foregone conclusion. The red icons disappeared at a staggering rate.

When only a few red fighter icons remained, missile alarms sounded again. Meanwhile, the RGN fighters broke off and left the engagement area to the sides. The remaining red fighter icons regrouped and continued onward toward them without pause.

"The Chohish are firing on us while their ships remain in

range?" Admiral Timeti asked with horror. The tone let Zeke know the admiral was not expecting a response.

"Captain, ten seconds to go."

"Admiral, will you do the honors? Isolde, please connect us with Sorath command."

The Admiral, who had not demonstrated emotion before, now clutched his knees so tightly that Zeke could hear his knuckles popping. Zeke heard the admiral drawing a heavy indrawn breath before releasing was so loud that he heard it over the noise on the busy bridge.

"Admiral, you are now connected. The Chohish are about to reach......."

"FIRE! I repeat, FIRE all weapons!" yelled Admiral Timeti.

And then the crew on the Lucky Strike, the Fox, and the Jackal saw the Dreadnaughts let loose a barrage like fire coming from hell. All now realized that the ships had only used a small portion of their available firepower, a tiny part. Several hundred missiles raced away from each ship while the beams quadrupled their output.

The Chohish may have recognized the new danger but did not change their trajectory or speed. It would not have mattered anyway.

The missiles first picked off the remaining Chohish Cruisers before being redirected against the Chohish Battleships. At the same time, the lasers concentrated on the Chohish Destroyers. The Destroyer's shields were virtually ineffective against the power directed against them. Destroyer icons were blinking out regularly.

The Chohish were not going down without a fight; they still fought them. The Lucky Strike sensors showed all the ships releasing their missiles in a coordinated targeting, the damaged Majestic.

"Will, get us in there. We need to knock out as many of those Missiles as we can. Isolde, ask for assistance from the nearby groups." ordered Zeke.

Within a few moments, the three RGN ships and other RGN

warships took out dozens and dozens of enemy missiles. When hope started to rise, they were flung around like a spinning top as missiles detonated. Green icons began disappearing from the screens. Of course, not all rockets were targeting the Majestic.

They watched as many missile icons raced past them, headed directly toward the Majestic. At this point, all those on the Lucky Strike gasped when they saw the true defensive capabilities of one of these ships. There are several thousand defensive laser platforms, hundreds of antimissile missiles, and ECMs. No Chohish missile survived for long.

Upon the curious look from Zeke, the Admiral calmly explained. "Your plan required the Chohish to continue on a direct path to the planet through the Dreadnaughts. They could have gone around if they knew the ship's true capabilities. Our ships would have never been able to keep up. It would end up being the slugfest we all wanted to avoid, but now without the Dreadnaughts."

"You had worked out what we had to do offensively to draw them in. The Soraths knew we had to match our defensive capabilities with the limited offensive ones we needed to show the Chohish. Otherwise, they would know we were hiding something."

It was apparent that the Chohish finally understood what they now faced. They turned hard to starboard or port, trying to get out of range of the deadly lasers now targeting them.

Sighing in relief, Zeke was about to say something to the admiral when he saw what the admiral had not shown earlier, sorrow. The admiral leaned over to hug his knees in pain, not physical pain, written all through his body.

Upon straightening and seeing Zeke's concern, he remarked. "We knew we would take casualties to complete the surprise; it was acceptable. Captain, understand this; we would have sacrificed all the ships and lives they hold if that is what it would take to eradicate this force. All on those ships are volunteers and knew the risks." Closing his eyes, the Admiral finished with anger in his voice. "This war has only started, and my people will make sure the Chohish never get a chance to repeat what they did before. We will be taking the war to them this time around."

It looked like some Chohish ships would manage to escape the trap when, suddenly, another presence made itself known. From both sides of the engagement field, the main RGN fleet racing away from the Chohish fleet rejoined the fight.

Within another dozen minutes, the fleet eliminated the remaining Chohish active warships. Attempting to capture the Chohish still surviving in destroyed ships proved fruitless as the Chohish attacked any rescue attempt. An RGN task force was left behind to ensure the Chohish did not repair any vessel.

"Isolde, are we still connected to the Fox and Jackal?" Upon seeing her nod affirmative, he continued. "Lance, Meghan, any casualties, damage?"

"Fox here, minor damages and injuries, no fatalities. We can thank the redo they did; it is a lot tougher ship."

"Lance reporting. The Jackal took a hit on the stern, where we lost several personnel and injuries. The damage is not severe enough to require a naval yard. It will not impact our effectiveness."

"Lance, sorry to hear of the casualties; let us know if you need assistance. The Lucky Strike, from what monitors I can see, also took some damage that will require minimal downtime. Thankfully, no casualties yet, but many injuries from a hit on the starboard side, over half of those severe. Doc and his staff are overwhelmed, so Meghan, if you can spare some medical staff, we could use them."

"Can do, Zeke; I will have them shipped ASAP."

"Thanks, Meghan. Isolde, check with the other ships in the area on their status and if any need assistance. Especially the Majestic. And please, all, remember that we lost many ships here. Many of our people died here, so there is no celebrating. Do not forget to deploy all shuttles to assist with recovering escape pods."

Everyone on the Bridge visibly stood down and relaxed from a war footing. They watched as Hawke rose from his seat to approach Admiral Timeti, who had also risen from his chair. When Hawke reached the Admiral, his wings slowly spread before he knelt, his head bent down with his hands on the floor.

"Uncle, I hope my actions have met with your approval. I ask your permission to continue to serve on this ship with my friends. Even though our people have joined the war against our ancient enemies."

Taking a step, he stood over Hawke; the Admiral put his hand on Hawke's head, where he said with pride evident in his voice. "I was doubtful about the accuracy of your reports when I first read them about your time on this ship. My concern was that they were prejudiced because of your love for your friend, Captain Kinsley. And the fine crew on this ship. I was concerned your emotions were swaying you. I am pleased to find that the unparalleled dedication, expertise, and bravery of all on this ship and the Fox match the glowing reports you provided to the high council. I would be amiss if I ordered you to serve on another ship. Here you will stay, so ordered. Stand nephew, you have honored my brother, your father, your family, and all Soraths with your bravery and service."

With that, Hawke stood with his head held high while closing his wings. The Admiral spread his wings to wrap them around Hawke. Once completed, both leaned in until their foreheads touched each other. Both then started humming a strange soft tune.

A startled Will and Zeke looked at each other and mouthed the same question. *"Uncle? The Admiral is his uncle?"*

If they had looked at Isolde, they would have seen her smile. As she went about her duties, she thought. *"Really? You believed the Admiral in charge of all the Sorath's forces in this system would jeopardize his life and command just because he wanted to see how one ship performed. Captain, you should have known better and asked me, not the Admiral. You forgot, to the Soraths, family is everything. That is why the last war with the Chohish was so devasting to them. Almost every family lost someone, if not more. A good many family lines ceased to exist altogether. And Zeke, you should have recognized him; the Admiral was present when Hawke graduated from the Academy. He is in the graduation picture hanging on Hawke's bedroom wall that you must have seen thousands of times."*

Chuckling to herself, she spared another glance at the two Soraths. *"We would have missed you greatly, my friend; I am glad to know you will be staying."*

"Do you know what they are humming?" Will quietly asked Zeke.

"Every family has a unique song that they hum when one or more are going into harm's way, and the odds are; they will not return. The closest we humans come to this is a funeral dirge. Admiral Timeti is saying goodbye to his nephew. I imagine neither expects to return home." Zeke replied while looking at his friend embraced within the admiral's wings.

Turning with a frown, Zeke gestured for Isolde to join them. "We should find a song of our own, the way our luck is going. But let's finish up here first. First, check with Jamie on the status of recovery and resupply operations. We must prepare for the next phase of some damn idiot's plan."

"Wasn't that part of yours and Jeanne's overall plan?" asked Will, with puzzlement written all over his facial expressions.

"Yup, as I said, two frigging idiots. Speaking of idiots, we need Jeanne to join us." an exasperated Zeke responded.

Laughing, Will headed toward his workstation. "You're just pissed because Jeanne got to fly a fighter while you were stuck here."

UNEXPECTED GUEST

IN JUST A few hours, they were on the move again. The principal officers for the three ships were in a conference room on the Lucky Strike. A video conference call was in progress between the admirals and the Governors.

As Fleet Admiral Katinka Chadsey and Admiral Nkosana Okeke reviewed the battle results, the fleet, minus the Dreadnaughts and anything smaller than a destroyer, headed toward the slipstream. The smaller ships followed far behind as they would not be part of any battle. It would be many hours before the fleet came to contest the area with the several dozen Chohish ships still present. Still, it was apparent from the movements that the Chohish knew what was coming.

"Captains Kinsley and de Clisson, we would like to congratulate you on the success of the battle plan. Our casualties were relatively light, considering the size of the enemy task force we took on. Do you still believe we should proceed with the next stage?" asked Admiral Chadsey.

"Yes, Admiral, we do. The next Star System, Foisa, has been explored extensively. It is empty of planets but has some large asteroid fields. More importantly, it has several slipstreams to adjoining

Star Systems, two others than the one we will be entering. There were surveys in the past, but nothing extensive. One, Aheikrays, contains four planets, and the other, Vashai, has seven planets, all uninhabitable in their present state. There were no indications of indigenous life forms or presence in either system. Neither Star System has any useable quantities of lendolium present.

"These Star Systems have multiple slipstreams that we will need to check. Surveys are expensive, and with so many star systems closer to the home systems still unexplored, they take priority. Too expensive for the Governors to do on their own.

"Then you still want to go with your proposed plan calling for multiple task forces. Each task force is made up of two Destroyers and one Cruiser. Their task is to explore the nearby star systems until we find a slipstream that leads to a Chohish Star System?" asked Admiral Okeke.

"Affirmative Admiral. Anything smaller would reduce the survivability of any force if they met the known Chohish force groups. From what I can determine from the Sorath records, the Chohish do not regularly use any larger fighting ships other than what we have already faced. Having three ships would allow two to delay any force long enough for one to escape before they tried to return themselves. That is my hope, anyway. Although to increase the odds, it would be nice if all the ships involved have the updated firing systems."

"That will limit the number of groups we can put together. A half dozen groups at most. What if we doubled the size of the group? Would that suffice?" asked Admiral Okeke.

"Taking that many ships would negatively impact the remaining force. Without knowing the size of the Chohish forces, it would be foolish not to prepare for them to put together a force much larger than the one we just fought." Zeke said while shaking his head.

Sighing, he looked at Jeanne with sorrow written on his face. "The Chohish know what they are facing now. They will not make the same mistake again. I'm not saying they will change their tactics, but I expect they will, just that they may also return with a task force large enough to absorb that type of punishment and shrug it off."

Grabbing Zeke's hand, Jeanne squeezed it in reassurance. "We sure hope you have additional forces, a considerable force on the way."

The deep voice of Admiral Okeke overrode all others when he spoke up. "Governors, we recommend you evacuate as many civilians as possible. That may be the best option until you can rebuild the cities and we can ensure the system's safety."

The split view of the two Governors showed both of them rising quickly from their seats. Governor Muldane leaned over a large conference table and pounded on the table to get their attention. Both of their faces reflected the passion they felt. Governor Reynold's eyes were narrow slits that intensely looked at the screens.

"No, we will not leave." Governor Muldane announced with vehemence. "We refuse to give up our homes without a fight. Our citizens have made that quite clear to us. We will die here before......."

Admiral Timeti, who had relocated to the Majestic, interrupted them before they could finish their sentence. Seated in a colossal command center, surrounded by organized chaos, the Admiral smiled at the screen while lifting his right hand with his palm out.

"Governors, we are not abandoning you. Let your people know that they are not alone. I will be staying with a large contingent of my people to watch over our new friends of the Pandora System. Make sure they understand; we share their pain."

Taking a deep breath that he let out in a long sigh, the Admiral continued only after mumbling in his native language for a moment. When he did continue, sorrow could be in his voice.

"My people also refused to leave their home on the planet Ollebos when attacked those many years ago. Many millions died before the fleet could drive the Chohish away. Less than a quarter of the population survived in a world engulfed in flame and destruction. The survivors, like you, refused to leave when ordered by the high command. The few operational ships left in the orbiting fleet could not hold off the Chohish if they returned in any sizable force. The survivors knew the fleet would not even try since it would waste lives amid desperately needed resources. But they would not give up their homes without a fight. And no one on Ollebos would leave if faced with the same situation today. I know, believe me, Governors, I know. Ollebos is my home world."

Turning to look at Hawke, Zeke saw his friend, with closed eyes and tightly gripped fists, shaking his head in confirmation. He knew that Hawke had also been born on Ollebos.

Now, Admiral Timeti, speaking with deep anger and firmness evident even through the translator in his thorax. "My friends, the Soraths, have prepared for this day for thousands of years. The RGN may need additional time to assemble the resources to take this fight to the Chohish. Not so the Soraths. My people have already dispatched another large fleet. That fleet will be here within the month. The force coming is much larger than the contingent currently present. We have only started mobilizing; more fleets will arrive in the coming months."

"The RGN will also be responding. I expect another fleet to arrive in the same period, size unknown at this time, but it will be considerable." Admiral Chadsey added. "If we can figure out where the Chohish is coming from, we intend to take the fight to them. Based on this news, we will leave a large protection force around the planets while seeding the area more heavily with mines. The moons and planets are in the process of being even more heavily fortified with defensive platforms. We will do what we can to ensure the planet's safety, Governors, but we cannot make any guarantees."

Governor Muldane put his palms face down on the table in front of him before he replied. It was evident to all he was trying to control his emotions. But Zeke, having spent a reasonable amount of time with him in the last six months, knew that this was not the first request to abandon the planets. "We appreciate the concern, Admiral, but we will take our chances. The only thing we ask for is ground armaments. We will not go quietly."

It was Admiral Timeti who responded. "Governors, I am glad to hear we share the same feelings about what we call home. We will help you with that request. The coming fleet has all the armaments you will need for your people to defend themselves."

"We can review the planet's defenses later; right now, we need to concentrate on finding out where the Chohish are. Captains, while we decide who will be in the other five teams, what is the status of your ships, and how long before you can leave?" Admiral Chadsey asked.

"All our ships sustained damage in the preceding action, but not enough to impact us leaving immediately. We are ready to go once the slipstream is open," answered Zeke.

"The Chohish abandoned the slipstream just under an hour ago. Several frigates are en route to transit through the slipstream. Energy trails should tell us what slipstream the Chohish use in the adjacent system if they are gone. We should have an update in eight to ten hours." Admiral Chadsey informed the group.

"We will not wait, Admiral. If they get back before we reach the slipstream, they can transmit the data. But time is of the essence, and I want to see the Chohish fleet's actions before they exit the other system, if possible. So the Lucky Strike group will lead the way, and the rest can follow. I will let the other groups know where to proceed once they enter the system." declared Zeke.

A soft chuckle preceded the Admiral's response. "I had a feeling you would want to do that. Your prior commanders told me you were impulsive. I have three boosters on the way to your position. They will considerably shorten the time your ships arrive at the slipstream."

"Boosters?" asked a surprised Zeke.

"A temporary ship addon that mirrors the Irracan fighter shuttle booster setup used effectively in your last action. We took it one step further using blueprints supplied by the Irracans. The boosters are heavy and burn a tremendous amount of lendolium but are good for a temporary burn that will more than triple your speed for a few hours. Your ships had the feature to install the booster connection when being rebuilt. We also did the Jackal when it was sidelined for several months, figuring your group would need it first."

The Vice-Admiral started laughing at that point. "These boosters are all we have, period. I had them rush manufacturing these three anticipating this type of situation."

Now it was Jeanne that started laughing before speaking. "Admiral Chadsey, Captain Kinsley has often told me how insightful and cunning you are. I am glad to see that he was not exaggerating. With your last comment, I am taking it that these boosters have had minimal testing. We may be in for the ride of our lives with these '*boosters*.' Well…".

It was the sound of sudden excitement from the Fox that interrupted Jeanne. Over the din, they could hear betting.

Jeanne continued moving her right hand to cover her mouth, trying hard not to laugh. "As I was saying, Admiral, before my relatives rudely interrupted. Less than a year ago, I would have thought only Irracans would be crazy enough to look forward to testing these new, unproven engines in this manner. But now I am unsure as I look around the Lucky Strike and the Jackal. They confirm my belief that the personnel on all three ships share some of that same attribute; most, if not all, are a bit psychotic."

Stopping, she was unsure if she should be making the following request to an Admiral. "I do have one request, though. I was asked if you could assign someone to hold their betting slips in case we do not survive; that way, their relatives can settle the debts. Odd, I know. But as I said earlier Admiral, they are not all there."

Admiral Nkosana Okeke joined in with a booming voice tinged with laughter. "Captains, I have a unique request. I want to join your little group as an observer only, that I promise. Admiral Timeti would have liked to stay onboard, but he has to be here to coordinate the arriving Sorath's contingents. But I do not."

"I want to learn as much as possible about the Chohish and their origins. I believe that I can best be satisfied by going with you. And yes, I understand your reluctance; I would have had the same feelings when I was Captain. But I am telling you and all on this call you and your Captains have complete authority to do as you will. I will be along only for the ride."

Silence descended as all four captains nervously looked at each through the monitors. Then, after a few moments of complete silence, the Admiral added. "I have been told I am a bit crazy, too, if that helps your decision."

The smiles and nods of the captains preceded Zeke's answering. "You are welcome to join us, Admiral; we will be honored to have your presence. We will have use of your knowledge and vast skills. I will make my quarters available for you. Just be aware that you may have to share it with some fighter and shuttle pilots, as we will be housing many more fighters and marine shuttles than normal for our type of ship. We found they were instrumental last time around. Although, as a possible bonus because of that, you will have plenty of hot cocoa as that seems to be the pilot's favorite drink along with a certain unnamed admiral."

That unnamed admiral lifted his mug in salute before taking a slow sip. At the same time, his wings fluttered in a sign of contentment.

"Understood, Captain, thanks; a shuttle is prepping to take me over now. I expect to be on board when the boosters are attached."

"Well then, unless someone has anything else to discuss, I will adjourn this call." Admiral Chadsey announced. After waiting a moment and hearing nothing, the Admiral said, "Best of luck, captains and crew. You will need it."

With that, the connection ended. Hawke, silently standing a few feet from Zeke, raised his wings until several top feathers covered his mouth. Zeke, seeing this, glared at him. "Oh, stop, like I could have said no to that request. And yes, I know what that gesture means."

Jeanne looked at Will inquisitively. "A Sorath expression for calling someone a wuss. A big fat wimp. As a lady is present, I had to tone the rhetoric down quite a lot." Will replied with a huge grin.

Upon Jeanne looking at him in mock surprise, pointing to herself, Will shook his head negatively and pointed to Isolde over his shoulder. Isolde, who had been watching the whole exchange, started laughing as Will took a soft punch in the shoulder from Jeanne.

SLIPSTREAM

THE SHIP WAS shaking and filled with noise as the boosters were attached when Admiral Okeke walked onto the bridge. The loud chatter that had been present gradually silenced as they became aware of his presence.

Hearing the silence, Zeke smiled as he knew why without turning around. An admiral entering a Bridge always got the same response. Then, turning to see the Admiral, he could tell from the quick raising of the shoulders that the Admiral was familiar with this reaction. Unfortunately, that reaction came with the title when attached to a greatly admired person.

Zeke waved his left hand to signal hello while he finished a conversation with Jax, and he waved the Admiral over with his right. As the Admiral arrived by his chair, he ended his call with Jax.

"Sorry, Admiral, I would have met you when you arrived, but the installation of these boosters has all working overtime. I just got off with the head of engineering, who said we are minutes away from completion. Jeanne is getting the extra Irracan pilots situated but should be here soon. She has made her seat over there available for you as she rarely uses it."

It was Will who surprised the Admiral when he spoke just

behind him. "That is because Jeanne prefers the seat in her fighter. The Irracans are more open to their commanders fighting on the front lines than we are. Although our Captain here has been taking huge liberties with that particular item, as I am sure you know, Admiral."

The Admiral glanced at the Commander before looking around the bridge discreetly when he heard a swell of light laughter. He knew already that this was an excellent crew; he had seen most of the records and videos of the prior action, along with documents from the previous year. The comment made by the Commander, followed by good-natured laughter from the crew, spoke volumes about the respect they held for the command staff, especially their Captain.

Well, then again, that is part of why he was here. His excuse for joining this voyage was valid but not the only reason. Admiral Chadsey wanted to promote Captain Kinsley to Rear Admiral. The RGN needed fleet officers of this caliber in what she feared would be a long-drawn-out war. But Zeke had recently been promoted to Captain way ahead of standard protocol. But, as he would be here anyway, he had been ordered to observe Zeke in action. Admiral Chadsey needed to be sure before she had to fight through all the mountains of paperwork to support the request.

Anyone observing the interactions between himself and Admiral Chadsey would think they had a contentious relationship. They would be surprised to find out they had great fondness and respect for each other. If one ever really looked into it, they would find that wherever Admiral Chadsey went, he followed shortly afterward. Then, as Admiral Chadsey told him once over a glass of port, a commanding officer needed an asshole. One they could count on now and then, and being a giant brilliant asshole was a bonus.

The Admiral saw that the crew handled the new interfaces with the boosters calmly and expertly. They were quick learners and had done their homework in the past few hours. He remembered the severe doubts when suggested. It was a lot to take on in such a short timeframe with potentially catastrophic results, yet here they went about their tasks with little sign of concern. But an experienced eye could see it, and he did; they were nervous. And from what he could tell, the other ship's crew mirrored what he saw here.

Unexpectedly, Captain de Clisson strolled in, only to stop after just a few feet with her hands on her hips. "Howdy, my fellow Mateys, are we ready for the ride of our lives?" a loud but pleasant voice announced. The effect felt around the bridge was infectious. Smiles popped up on most faces even though only one person paused in what they were doing.

"Glad you could join us, Jeanne; we were afraid you would have to watch our exhaust from the Fox if you took much longer." rejoined Zeke. "And yes, we know about the bets between ships with the Fox."

"And did you make any bets?" asked Jeanne, her hands crossed under her breasts.

Sheepishly, Zeke replied. "I have bet Captain Kennedy a case of my Cocoa mix against some good Irracan coffee that we would be at the slipstream first. Captain Henry passed on any betting. He claimed he did not think it right that the Jackal took something from his new friends and commanding officer when there could be no doubt of the outcome. So Lance was kind enough to remind Meghan and me that their warship is named the "Jackal" for a good reason. They are deadly vicious but also fast, much faster than either of us."

At which both started laughing. Jeanne shook her hair loose after removing her trademark hat and slowly went to Zeke. She sidled up close, only to duck under his outstretched arms to sit at a workstation beside Isolde. Leaning over to Isolde while looking at Zeke, Jeanne nonchalantly asked. "How long do you think he will stand there with his mouth agape?"

Even the Admiral laughed with most of the Bridge crew when they saw the deep blush rush to Zeke's face. Hanging his head, Zeke muttered loud enough for all to hear. "I would retaliate, but she is much better at this than I am. I am still getting over the dye in the underwear event." at which the laughter became full-throated.

Only someone closely watching would notice the glance and slight nod between the two Captains. "*Ah, you two are good, really good,*" the Admiral thought. "*That got them relaxed.*"

At that moment, Isolde reported that Jax said the hookups were complete.

"Well, here we go, Will; please ensure all personnel wears safety harnesses. Admiral, that includes you. Jax, you online?" queried Zeke.

"Yes, Captain, the ship's AI is waiting on your command to initiate the boosters' firing. Bridge and engineering are hard-wired into the interfaces for monitoring and control. The booster controls on all ships will respond to the Lucky Strikes AI to ensure that they all fire at the exact same nanosecond. The boosters will disengage and disconnect automatically from the vessel once we reach your identified area. We will enter the slipstream without pause using the hostile emergent security protocol."

"The Jackal has volunteered for the forward position. Captain Henry said he understood you and Captain Kennedy wanted the fastest ship designated to that function."

Laughter came through the loudspeakers, but it did not take a genius to know who or where that laughter originated.

Turning to the Admiral, Zeke commented dryly. "You see what I have to work with?" But it is evident to the Admiral that Captain Henry, even removed as he was, was an integral part of this group. "*I am starting to see what Katinka saw in this young man. Besides*

*his tactical expertise, he can fuse multiple ship crews to work as one.
I hope this is not just a one-off; we will see. I expect this trip will test
everyone's abilities to the utmost if we are to survive."*

At a signal from Will, Zeke scanned the harness on the Admiral before announcing. "Ok, people, we are about to look for our enemy's home. Based on what we have learned, I expect they reside in multiple systems with many fleets of undetermined size, which will not take kindly to our trespass."

Walking toward the main screen, Zeke glanced around at the anxious faces. Then, just feet away from the colossal monitor, he slowly closed his eyes, at which point he visibly took a deep breath. He spoke in a calm, loud voice without opening his eyes while he raised his hands shoulder-high and clenched them into tight fists.

"Do I wish we did not have to go? Yes, without a doubt. Couldn't they have picked someone else? Yes, many others volunteered. Is this going to be dangerous? Yes, very much so. The odds are not good. Am I frightened? You better believe it."

Opening his eyes, he looked at each of his fists before continuing. "But who is best to send? Someone that does not know what the enemy truly is? Someone who has seen the horror inflicted on innocents but did not experience it?" Lowering his fists, he sighed.

Zeke unclenched them before he continued with a powerful voice that rang with command, simultaneously filled with anguish. "Or do you send those that have experienced the pain? Who personally witnessed the death and devastation wrought upon several worlds without justification? Who knows that what they witnessed may occur in many other worlds without them?"

Walking back to his chair, Zeke stood there for a few seconds, visibly drawing a breath. Sitting, he buckled his harness firmly around his body with steady hands. No one on the bridge moved nor turned their attention away from him. The monitors that showed the bridges on the other ships showed the same was occurring there. They all knew Zeke had not finished speaking.

With hard vehemence now present in every syllable as he looked around with anger in his eyes, the voice they now heard was barely recognizable. "Of all those that should go, we deserve that honor. We *DEMAND* that right. We have faced the enemy once, twice, thrice, and more. We know how they operate and have no regard for life or *honor*. Niflhelian's, Nocuousian's, Irracans, Soraths, and finally, RGN make up this little force. I intend to show the Chohish they should not piss us off. And we are pissed! We will fight until they no longer threaten innocent people who want to live in peace. There are two options for them. First, that can be unconditional surrender; I will leave the second option to your imagination."

Reverting to his normal command voice, Zeke announced, "Brace yourselves, everyone, LS1, initiate in thirty seconds."

"LS1?" asked a puzzled Admiral as a countdown and hurried activity sounded through all the ships. Before he got a response, a roar and intense pressure against his whole body cut off his desire for an answer. Breathing was his main concern now. If he survived, he would have to tell the engineers they needed to work on the inertia dampers; this was not good for a frail person.

The pressure was intense for a good minute before the inertia dampers could adjust to the sudden increase. Little by little, the tension eased. The Admiral watched as several crew members slumped in their seats, their heads lolling loosely. Others were gasping, trying to get a decent breath in their lungs. Only Hawke seemed unaffected; he smiled as if he enjoyed it.

Surprised, Zeke brought up the speedometer reading on his side chair panel. They were going over five times the max speed for a Cruiser. Computer simulations never went above three times.

The bridge was relatively quiet, with only an occasional whisper or seat adjustment to break the silence for the next few hours.

Finally, just a short distance from the slipstream, the boosters stopped automatically before disconnecting with a loud bang and shaking.

There was a message that appeared scrolling on the main screen. "What took you so long? Signed, the Jackal."

While raising both hands, Will signaled with a positive head shake. Will used his fingers to tell how many seconds the Jackal had arrived first, an outstanding margin if Zeke was reading the hand signals correctly.

"Will, when we can, send Lance a case of my special cocoa. Also, you better remind me to tell my mother to send several pallets of that stuff. Admiral Timeti was gifted a case, and the pilots in my quarters are going through it like candy. Thank heaven I saved several cases for Jeanne and my...."

The ship warning that they were about to enter the slipstream sounded and cut off whatever else Zeke said. Then, without any speed reduction, the three warships quietly entered the slipstream.

There was a lot of speculation on what comprises a slipstream. Was it a stationary variance of the wormhole with an entrance and exit? Or, as most believed, was it a rip in the fabric of space connecting two remote locations? No one knew for sure. But without them, travel to the far reaches of outer space would never have been possible. And each one was different in some fashion.

This one was no exception. The Admiral could feel his stomach turning over despite having made hundreds of slipstream transitions. And then the headache, the blinding pain behind the eyes, was something new. Still, then again, there was no consistency when traveling through slipstreams.

It was obvious this one was a lot rougher than usual. Maybe that was due to how fast they were going, but who knew? He watched as several of the crew retched up their last meal while hearing many moaning in pain. It took everything he had not to join them; unfortunately, admirals showing weakness were frowned on by the RGN.

With most of the crew incapacitated at times like this, a ship's AI proved its worth many times over. Besides running all the necessary calculations to do the actual transit, the AI monitored all the crew's health statistics, reporting any issues to the medical team.

Captains needed to maintain their composure during transitions, which was why the Admiral watched how the captain responded. It was not obvious, but he could see Zeke was affected by the twitching of his eyes and the grip of his hands on his armrests. But none of this reflected on his facial features, only concentrating on what the main ship screens showed, a blackness that would only change when they exited the slipstream.

A glance at Captain de Clisson confirmed what he expected. The only difference he saw between the two Captains was the slight quirk of Jeanne's bottom lip. He would swear she was trying not to laugh. Then, following her gaze, he quickly understood why.

Due to Sorath's physical makeup, Hawke was not nearly as affected as a human. Hawke was sitting sideways with his legs resting over his chair's arms while, at the same time, his arms were twirling to a tune that he was softly whistling.

It was apparent what Hawke was doing, even though he violated every RGN and Sorath safety protocol while transitioning a slipstream. There was nothing for the crew to do while transitioning except dwell on the pain they were feeling. Hawke was giving them something else to concentrate on, him. And he had to admit, it was working. In addition to all the strained but smiling faces he saw watching Hawke, he could feel his mouth start twisting into a smile.

As sharply as it started, it ended. Soft cursing mixed in with the loud gasps. They exited the slipstream running silent. Gradually the Jackal started falling further ahead, using minor undetectable side thrusts to move off to the right side, where they preceded the other two ships.

The three ships silently moved into the Foisa system, still advancing with the extra boost provided by the boosters; their main engines were powered up but not used. Using them at this time would not give any additional thrust. Slowly, the crew emerged from their stupor more quickly as time passed; within minutes, all were alert enough to resume their duties.

FOISA SYSTEM

"JACKAL IS IN position, Captain. We held off on normal emergent protocol probe deployment based on your orders. A full suite of probes from all three ships is ready to be deployed upon your command. The AI reports no unidentified objects within scanning range; however, there is a trail of a large group of ships passage." reported Isolde.

The last ended in a surprised tone that caused Zeke to look at Isolde, where he saw her glancing between several of her monitors while entering commands feverishly.

"Isolde? Is there an issue? "

Without pausing in her activity, Isolde responded, and she was apparently puzzled. "I cannot identify any scanning or probes directed toward us. I expected probes to be abundant through a good portion of this system. They have had plenty of time to lay down as many as they wanted. It makes no sense. Why none? It is possible; they do not even know we are here."

"That was one thing that puzzled me too when we entered the Pandora system," responded Zeke. "There were no probes there either. Only after we attempted to contact the planets did the Chohish know we were in the system. Maybe they do not normally carry probes, although that is hard to believe. Then again, everything about the Chohish has been puzzling since we encountered them. Can you tell me the direction of the ships?"

"All indications are they are all headed toward the slipstream that connects to the Vashai system, Captain."

Pausing, Zeke rubbed his palms on his pants to remove the sweat from the transition before replying. "Isolde, can you tell what speed they are making."

"Hmmm... that is a little difficult without the probes, but a rough calculation on their exhaust trail indicates they are making about half speed. The ions left behind indicate some of the ships may be damaged. I can be more precise once the probes are launched and deeper into the system." Turning to look at Zeke with a question mark on her face. "Can I launch the probes? Is there an issue I should be aware of?"

"Working on a hunch. Hold off on launching the probes for now. Drop a few local ones, so I know if anyone transits through. Use no propulsion. I do have a few questions for you. If the Chohish had gone to the maximum for the entire time while in this system, how far in-system would you guess they would be?"

Turning back to her workstation, Isolde spent a few moments running some calculations. Then, without taking her eyes off her screen, she verbalized the results. "If they had gone to maximum speed and maintained that speed when they entered the Foisa system, they would only be an hour or two from the Vashai system. Oh, and FYI, I dropped two local probes." Then, turning to look at Zeke, Isolde asked. "Anything else?"

"If we had entered at normal max speed, would the Chohish ships still have been in this system if they had not slowed down?"

Turning back to her console, Isolde started muttering into her interface to execute one of her preset programs. It took a few moments for the program to produce a report. "Based on the speeds we know of, I would say no. The two slipstreams are close." Then, after moving a strand of hair that had fallen over her left eye, Isolde paused in response.

She was evidently in deep thought before her eyes lit up in astonishment. "Oh, I see what you are getting at," she exclaimed in surprise.

It was Jeanne that broke the silence that followed. "Well, me bucko, what is it that devilish mind of yours is chewing on. Could you not keep us all in suspense? I would normally sit in my fighter with the rest of my crew but thought it was better to stay here for the moment, to see what we were running into."

Turning to face Jeanne, it looked like Zeke was about to respond to her query. Still, to everyone's disappointment, he sat silently, looking at her.

Getting frustrated, Jeanne raised her hand to point at Zeke when she paused, half lifted. The smile on Zeke's face let her know he had decided on something.

"Will, turn us toward the Aheikrays slipstream. Isolde, do not, I repeat, do not deploy any additional probes. I do not want our presence made known, no matter how slight it would be. Pass those orders onto the other ships. Make sure we do the turn altogether." ordered Zeke. "Isolde, leave a communication pod with a data dump telling the scouts following us where we have gone and to split up accordingly.

"Yes, Sir, changing ship's direction to bear toward Aheikrays," responded Will. Even so, it was apparent that he was clueless about why Zeke made that call.

"The Jackal and Fox have been updated and changing direction in coordination with us. All ships remained silent, following hostile protocols. Pod dropped." Isolde reported.

"Captain, may I ask why Aheikrays?" asked Will aloud, even though he was facing away to enter commands into his console.

The Admiral believed he knew why, as he would have made the same call, but stayed quiet as he was curious to see if it would match Zeke's explanation.

Sighing while rubbing at a leftover pain in his left shoulder from the slipstream transit, Zeke looked at Will silently until he could complete his activity. Only when Will stopped what he was doing and turned toward Zeke with undivided attention did Zeke answer Will's question.

"One of the main reasons I wanted to get here without delay was to see what the Chohish fleet would do. The Chohish have watched our ships for a good time now, so they know their capabilities. Based on what Isolde told us, they are trying to time it so that we see them entering the Vashai system. Hopefully, they want us to follow them with our main force. Hence, all the ships are together even though their trail looks like some are experiencing engine problems. The boosters were a new wrinkle that they, nor us for that matter, did not know existed. But they helped tremendously in showing us their intentions; I believe that is their intention. I could be wrong; we will find out."

It was Hawke who next spoke up. "Now I am mystified. What difference does it make that they stayed together?"

"I base this on their prior actions. Their past actions have not shown they care about any damaged ship or crew. Remember the fighter action? And then the pair of Destroyers after we left the tunnel? The question then is, why now?"

Jeanne answered with a whisper but loud enough to be heard by most. "The War of Nazuc Electorate."

Now it was the Admiral to be startled. "You know of that war, Captain? I am surprised."

Twirling her seat so she faced the Admiral, Jeanne looked at the Admiral with a devilish grin as her lengthy hair flipped over her right shoulder. "Know thy enemies, Admiral, know thy enemies."

Upon a nod from Captain Kinsley in his direction, the Admiral explained.

"Only a few teachers teach the War of Nazuc Electorate in the Naval Academy. I always thought it should be mandatory for all. It was a small action compared to others, but it was one for the books."

Looking at Jeanne with new admiration, the Admiral resumed the explanation. "When the RGN was young, several minor member systems, the Las Atryn and Nazuc Electorate, went to war. Their issue was over control of a huge asteroid field brimming with rare mineral deposits hard to find anywhere else at the time. Both knew they needed to resolve the war quickly, as the fledgling RGN, though much smaller than it is today, would send a force larger than theirs to resolve the conflict."

Stopping to take a sip of water from a flask, Nkosana continued. "Neither side wanted to take the risk that they either lost access to or had to share those resources. It should have been a one-sided war as the Nazuc Electorate forces were much smaller than the Las Atryn's. The Las Atryn was surprised when a small Nazuc Electorate Destroyer force brazenly attacked their home world. Even though surprised, the force was not near large enough to be a serious threat. The Nazuc were forced away after just a short battle with few casualties on either side. But the audacity scared the Las Atryn population tremendously, demanding immediate action from the civilian government."

"Against military recommendations, the Las Atryn main fleet was ordered to hunt down the Nazuc Electorate's fleet and destroy them. When the Las Atryn fleet entered the adjoining system, their probes indicated the Nazuc Electorate ships were now accompanied by another fleet of larger vessels. The ships were heading away from the Las Atryn slipstream. Probes revealed the Nazuc Electorate's main fleet had joined tother with the attacking fleet. There were now fleeing to the nearest slipstream. Even though it was relatively close, they should have made it through long before. Exhaust trails indicated damage to several destroyers, slowing them down.

Sitting straighter, he rocked in his seat, remembering listening to the instructor on the same subject. How best to explain it? "The slipstream that the Nazuc Electorate ships were approaching would take them to a system with no other slipstream. The Las Atryn forces gave chase at maximum speed, expecting to trap and overwhelm the Nazuc Electorate fleet, ending the war quickly."

"They followed through the slipstream and chased them to the farthest end. All of this took just over a week. Only as Las Atryn forces were about to attack the Nazuc Electorate fleet did they understand the full scope of the dupe. Their primitive probes, compared to today's, were now close enough to identify that the large ships were container ships, not one was a warship. And to make it even more embarrassing, they now knew that none of the ships they had been following were showing any signs of damage. Not only that, but the container ships had been busy. A massive minefield surrounded the relatively small area the Nazuc Electorate fleet was in."

It was Jeanne who finished the story upon a nod from the Admiral. "The Las Atryn Admiral in charge knew they could, in time, get through the minefield and destroy the Aris fleet. But time was not something they had much of, not if the Admiral had analyzed the situation correctly; he doubted they had any time. So it took a week to rush back to their home system, only to discover that their home world had surrendered unconditionally several days prior. They had surrendered to a Nazuc Electorate fleet of capital ships that were now circling the planet."

Isolde took everyone's attention away from the history lesson with a shout.

"Captain, I am detecting an abnormality near the Aheikrays

slipstream. I picked up a communication signal of some sort. Request permission to have several probes sent to the area I detected it in." an anxious Isolde reported.

Calmly he denied Isolde's request. "Permission denied on the probes, Lieutenant. Can you determine what was broadcast? Is it scrambled?"

"Negative, Sir, too much interference without a probe to strengthen the ship's scanning capabilities. But from what little I got, it is encrypted. No translation possible at this time."

Waving his hand in acknowledgment, Zeke settled back in his chair. "Relax, everyone; it will be many hours before we get to the Aheikrays slipstream. Isolde put your staff on hourly rotations. We must have your team at their best if something shows up unexpectedly. Add Hawke and whomever you believe can ensure your team gets the rest they need. Here's a thought, get with Jamie and see if she has some available staff. If I remember right, she has one or two that may fit the bill."

It did not get past the Admiral, the pink blush that swept up Isolde's neck, nor the smiles that many others tried to hide behind their hands. He knew of the relationship between Lieutenant Isolde Iverson and Lieutenant Gunner Morison. Anyone who watched the prior action videos could not miss their connection. Not that it bothered the Admiral. He was a big believer that to try banning relationships on a ship gone for many months, if not years, was impossible.

And he should know, as he met his wife on a ship that both had served on together years ago. His wife, a Commander in RGN intelligence, usually accompanied him on all his missions. She was not here now because she was squirreled away in sector command headquarters, reviewing all the data the Soraths had on the Chohish. Part of his delay in reporting to the Lucky Strike was recording a goodbye to her if he did not return, as he had grave doubts they would.

Silently, the three ships flew further into the Foisa system. Gunner and another of Jamie's technicians had long since joined Isolde's rotation. As time progressed and the hours passed, the crew relaxed more and more. Soon, mixed in with the sound of the workstation's activity, more and more casual conversations could be heard. That is until heavy boots marching down the hall overrode all other sounds.

Silence reigned when Major Richards marched onto the Bridge, followed by three other Marines. What took most by surprise was that even though the Major was in dress fatigues, the three Marines following her were dressed in their Marine armor. Their helmets were connected to a hook on their side. Most alarming, they carried their plasma rifles with a plasma pistol holstered to their upper thigh.

While Major Richards stopped inside the Bridge, the three Marines walked around her without pause. Two went to stand by the captains and one next to the Admiral. The Admiral was a little startled and was about to demand an exclamation until he heard Captain Kinsley sigh in exasperation, and Captain de Clisson started snickering.

Even more surprising was that once all the Marines were in position, everyone could hear their boots lock magnetically on the floor. Once the boots were locked, a wire ejected from the back of their armor toward the ceiling. Then, before the wire hit the top, a slot opened, upon which the wire snapped into a hole barely visible before it closed. A slight whirring sound occurred where the wire went taught, which caused the Marine to become immobile and secure.

Admiral Okeke was sidetracked again from asking what the hell was going on when Captain de Clisson started laughing. Seeing her unbuckle her harness so she could stand to hug the Marine next to her was a bit unsettling.

"Hello Michale, I have missed you." Jeanne paused while she gasped for air from laughing. "How have you been? I gather the Major is making sure we do not go anywhere unescorted. Not very trusting, is she?"

Grinning, Zeke did a fist bump with the Marine next to him. "Hi Shon, it's good to see you too. Who's your friend by the Admiral?"

Shon did not have time to answer Zeke before Major Richards did. "You are correct, Captain de Clisson; I do not trust you two at all in that matter. As we enter dangerous territory, I have again brought some babysitters for you two with revised instructions. And since the Admiral will probably be with you most of the time, I have brought Lance Corporal Marianne Chavez to be his shadow." There was no humor in her voice, but that had no impact on Jeanne as she continued laughing as she pointed to the dismay on the Admiral's face.

The Admiral, unused to someone laughing at him, turned to look at the Marine standing next to him. The Marine had long dark black hair wrapped into a tight braid dressed in a circle pinned tightly to the top of her head. The rich caramel skin did not grab his attention; it was the unusual violet eyes. They would have complimented her beautiful features if they did not mirror the severe line of her lips. Her facial expression unquestionably let him know that she meant business.

"Hello?" he offered. Seeing no response would be given, he turned toward Zeke, only to be met by a shake of his head.

"Sorry, Admiral, I was reminded that Marines have a separate command structure. It is my fault, though; Jeanne and I take liberties sometimes that we should not, so I cannot blame Major Richards." Turning to look at Shon, Zeke continued. "And to be honest, it is comforting to have them around. The Marines under the Major are the best in the RGN, hands down."

Looking at the hookup that the Marines were using, Zeke remarked. "Something new? I do not remember this on the old configuration."

"Yes, it was added during the rebuild to allow Marines to be stationed securely on the Bridge. The idea is to not increase the square footage while increasing security." answered a bored-sounding Khaleesi.

"I like it. The repair dockyards must have some very talented engineers to devise such a simple, ingenious method in so short of time," exclaimed Zeke.

"Thank you, I appreciate the compliment," replied Khaleesi sarcastically.

Turning to look at Khaleesi, a surprised Zeke pointed to the ceiling and mouthed, "You?".

Suddenly, the lights went red before starting to blink. The bridge went from relaxed to agitated in just a few seconds. Everyone checked and rechecked their systems to make sure nothing changed.

"Captain, the probes we dropped at the slipstream detect movement coming from the Pandora System. It looks like… one sec; more ships are arriving. I read ten Destroyers and five Cruisers. It looks like the other RGN scout groups have arrived," reported Isolde.

Entering quick commands, Isolde exclaimed excitedly, "They are not following stealth protocol; they are showering the system with lendolium exhaust. No way the Chohish cannot see them."

"As I requested them to, Isolde, when we learned of the boosters. I want to see how the Chohish reacts," replied Zeke calmly. "My mistake, I should have told you. I did let the other captains know."

Turning to look at Zeke, Isolde asked, "Orders?"

"I need you to let me know if there…" was all Zeke got out before Hawke interrupted.

"Isolde, I need your help here. I think there is a new communication from the Chohish ships that are not encrypted. Can you confirm?"

"You are correct, Hawke. Ship AI is interpreting, putting on loudspeaker……."

"… al… retu… Ae… orders of the Ghad Supreme Council. Attention all Sovereigns, you are to return to the Aether base station immediately, no delay. By order of the Ghad Supreme Council. Attention all Sovereigns…"

"Message repeats itself repeatedly, Captain; I will let you know if it changes."

While the Bridge crew stayed focused on their workstations, Zeke knew they all had their ears perked to see what he would do. He felt like stamping his foot while yelling 'HA' to see how many jumped but resisted his devilish impulse. He knew Jeanne would tell him to go for it; hell, she would have done it herself if she had thought of it. But the RGN command structure was a little more reserved, and they would not appreciate it.

Zeke disclosed his thoughts by seeing the Admiral looking at him with a questioning look. "If we had probes in-system, I am sure they would confirm my belief that this message is coming from the ships heading toward the Vashai system. And if so, why would they need to signal themselves? They don't. Why is it not encrypted?"

"I believe the original communications that Isolde intercepted is the actual command. The second communication is for us. It is all a misdirection. They did not expect us to be in-system to catch the first one. Not that they reside in the Aheikrays System, but use it to get to the Pandora System."

Without waiting for a question, Zeke turned to Will. "Speed?"

"We are steadily losing speed. We are barely above two and

a half times our normal maximum. I compute that we will be just over our normal maximum when we enter the slipstream for Aheikrays in close to four hours. There is a lot of dust around the slipstream, which may impact us more than I projected. At that time, I recommend we start using our engines again."

"I agree. Until then, Will, we all need to get some rest. Once we enter the Aheikrays System, who knows when we will get any? Have everyone get what they can, and have the primary staff meet back in two. I will cover the last two hours; can you cover me until then?" ordered Zeke unbuckling his harness upon the nod from Will.

Glancing at Jeanne with a raised eyebrow, "Want to get something to eat?"

Before Jeanne, unbuckling her harness, had a chance to answer, the Admiral responded. "Why yes, I would. Thank you, Captain; I did not think anyone would ask." The Admiral pointed to the startled expression on Jeanne's face and started laughing boisterously.

At which, many of the faces in the room mirrored the startlement on Jeanne's face. An admiral making a joke? Who ever heard of an Admiral laughing?

SHIP CHANGES

THE ADMIRAL MADE his way directly to the main cafeteria to monitor the crew's morale and where better than where they gathered to eat. Walking in, he was not surprised by how busy it was. Everyone would want to get something to eat and drink while they had a chance.

Sitting down at a large table near the far back bulkhead, he hoped he would remain unnoticed for a while anyway.

It was a good ten minutes or more that he saw Zeke and Jeanne enter. He waved them over when he saw them looking around. A large group of people surrounded the captains. The Admiral recognized most of the group from the videos even if he had not met them personally.

But what he did not recognize were the uniforms they were all wearing. They were a dark blue with thin white trim swirling around the outfit that got a bit wider on the arms, legs, and neckline. As they got closer, more details stood out. The entire uniform had a sheen like it had some metal inlaid. But most surprising of all was the weapons hanging around each of their waists, plasma pistols in a hip holster belt.

The group sat down in what he assumed was their preferred

seating arrangement. Jeanne grabbed the seat on his left while Isolde sat on his right. He was about to say hi to Jeanne when he noticed the intense scrutiny of the mammoth of a man sitting directly across from him. It took a few seconds for him to recognize Sergeant de Bouff from the videos. The man was close to his size, if not more significant.

On the other side to the Sergeant's left was a woman he did not know immediately. It was only the close resemblance to Jeanne; the same dark hair and bright green eyes he guessed correctly was Commander Anne Dieu-Le-Veut. That meant that the person to her left was Lieutenant Masson Dieu-Le-Veut, whom he did recognize.

There were others, but he did not have time to check them all out as Major Richards threw a large bag at him with force. Barely catching it in time, he was surprised by the weight. It was heavy, and one of the items inside had to be a weapon.

"Here is your uniform and weapon. It matches what you see the rest of us wearing. I recommend you put this on before rejoining us on the bridge." Khaleesi stated with force.

At the Admiral's curious look at Khaleesi, Zeke updated him. "After meeting the Chohish in combat, we realized we needed something better than our lasers for hand weapons. It is an experimental uniform that the Irracans whipped up for us with input from our engineers on the three ships and the miners from Niflhel and Nocuous. The miners were the main contributors since they deal with a treacherous atmosphere."

Seeing no indication that answered his puzzlement, Masson explained further. "The suits have armor and gyros built into them to give us more strength and protection while allowing us to use the plasma pistols. Normally, the kick from one of those babies could break your wrist. The suits also have a sensor that will quickly deploy a soft helmet around your head if they detect a loss of oxygen. In addition, compressed air packets around the suit will allow up to thirty minutes of normal breathing."

It was Jeanne who finished the explanation. "Besides the physical differences, we realized that the Chohish would not be hesitant to open a ship to space if that would kill any of their enemies. Even if it killed many more of their own. So we went to the miners asking for suggestions; our engineers worked with them to send blueprints to my home planet to rush producing the uniforms. Enough for all three ships with several hundred spares. The uniforms and plasma pistols arrived just hours before our departure."

Throwing her head back, Anne pounded the table before wheezing the rest through laughter. "Like the boosters, testing was minimal. As I was informed, *'It was tested using the highly rated Irracan testing protocols and standard,'* which means none. They offered no guarantees. There is a label on the inside of your uniform, where your butt sits, with the standard Irracan disclaimer *'Use at your own risk, we sure as hell would not.'* You have got to love it; now that's funny."

If the Admiral thought any here would be concerned, he would have been hugely surprised. All either smiled or laughed outright. But after seeing the videos, he believed he had a good read on the personnel around the table, brave and noble, every one of them. After what they had been through already, this was just another acceptable risk.

About to say something, the Admiral was startled to see the marines Shon, Michale, and Marianne, standing at attention just behind them. He had to talk to Khaleesi about how they did that without being noticed. None of his bodyguards were ever that quiet or invisible. Then again, maybe that was on purpose.

Regaining his composure, "Based on the lines over there, we may not make it through in time," pointed out the Admiral.

"Admiral Okeke, I..." was all Zeke got out before the Admiral raised his hand for him to stop.

"Please call me Nkosana. We do not have time to keep using titles. You know who I am just as I know who you all are. You do not use them when you converse among yourselves, and I would like to be considered a part of the group. Agreed?"

"Ok, Adm... err Nkosana. That is going to take a bit to get used to using. But as I was going to say, well, never mind, here they are now."

Waiters appeared from the mob and headed toward their table with trays stacked with food and drink. "Hate to do it, but there are times we cannot delay while waiting for food, this being one."

"Chance!" exclaimed Jeanne. "It is so good to see you again."

"Ah, it is the specialty lady; it is good to see you too! Unfortunately, I still do not have any salmagundi, whatever the hell that is. But I do have the grapes and melon you liked before. You and the captain will have to manage the specialties on your own as you did before."

With that, the waiters laid out meals in front of everyone while Zeke and Jeanne had to wave off the many asking about the specialties mentioned.

"Hey Chance, how are you here? I mean, this is not your normal station," asked Zeke.

"The ship's AI contacted me half an hour ago with the menu for everyone and asked if I was available to help. I felt honored the request came to me." With that, Chance started walking away. "And I am looking forward to having Captain de Clisson wait on me when all this is over, as the AI said she would."

The sputtering from Jeanne drew laughter from her sister Anne. "Now that I would like to see myself."

"Chance!" yelled Jeanne.

Stopping, Chance returned to the table with his head bent forward in a question pose. "Lady?"

"I just wanted to know if you have been able to talk with your wife and child? How are they doing?"

"They are doing great, my Lady. She and my son arrived in Niflhel months ago. She is helping with the medical teams. Before joining the Navy, she was a nurse with some surgery experience. So I got to spend four wonderful months with them. We are going to be parents again." said Chance proudly.

"Wow, that is great news. Any idea if it will be a girl or boy?" asked Zeke.

"Yes, it is going to be a girl. We will name her Jeanne Annette Friedell, after two extraordinary ladies." Chance said as he turned to leave one more.

It was Masson who caught everyone's attention when he burst out laughing. "Blow me down! I have never seen both Anne and Jeanne caught speechless. Chance, I think you have accomplished what I, and all on my planet, thought was impossible."

Everyone looked at Jeanne and Anne, who looked at Chance in amazement.

"Will it make a difference if I tell you that my wife's mother's name is Jeanne and my mother's name is Annette?" asked Chance before disappearing.

That only set Masson off even louder as he pointed to the two ladies whose faces were now a deep crimson.

As they ate, they chatted lightly about their family and friends. Anything to keep their mind off the upcoming passage through the slipstream into unknown territory, one that may be short-lived. Up to now, the risks have been minimum. But in a few hours, they would enter an enemy system with unknown results.

While he had time, Nkosana checked out the personnel entering the cafeteria. Most entered in groups, and very few entered alone. Good sign; it showed good crew cohesion.

While watching the crew, he noticed the lines that he thought would take forever to clear through were gone. The cafeteria was operating at an exceptional efficiency. The lines, now short, are moving fast, with most of the crew taking their meal and drinks outside. Unfortunately, there was not enough seating to accommodate the numbers present.

But his puzzlement was short-lived. As he kept his gaze on one, then another, he saw that they picked up the tray and drink in front of them without pause as they walked up to the belt. "*Ahh... somehow the fabricators know who wants what and when they are about to enter the cafeteria.*"

Noticing where Nkosana was looking, Zeke guessed what he was puzzling over. "Nkosana, all crew members have a list of meals they like entered into the cafeteria computers. In situations like this, once the crew member is near the cafeteria, the computers use his top choice, then move that to the bottom. The computers then track what line they are getting into, their placement in line, and voila, a meal to the right person with no fanfare. A few, though, will try and confuse the computers by changing places at the last second with personnel just before or behind them."

Pausing to look at Jeanne with a condescending look, Zeke continued. "The Irracans seem to get great pleasure from trying to break the mold. But the computer tracking systems have worked around those individuals with little difficulty. But they try again and again. They are even getting some of the RGN to join them in their antics."

"I have no idea what you mean. I am sure you are mistaken. My people would never do such a thing." Jeanne responded with false anger written on her facial expression.

A short time after they finished their meals, some in the group said their goodbyes and made their way out. Nkosana did the same as he wanted to change before rejoining them on the Bridge.

As he walked into Captain Kinsley's quarters, he was surprised at how small it was. There was a small office area, but it was magnitudes more minor than the standard size allowed for a ship's captain, even on a vessel much smaller than a cruiser.

As he changed, he had the ship's computer bring up the warship's blueprint on the bulkhead monitor. The display shocked him as he realized he was looking at a ship design that was not familiar, and he knew them all.

Quickly sealing his suit, he surprisingly found it quite comfortable even though it was more armor and electronics than fabric. "*Not bad,*" Nkosana thought as he examined the ship's layout more closely.

A few changes from other ships were immediately noticeable. Instead of the usual two to three fighter and shuttle bays on board a vessel of this size or larger, Nkosana was looking at six scattered evenly around the warship. And instead of being located next to the ship's hull, they were found inside midway to the center.

Puzzled about how the fighters and shuttles exited the ship, he tapped the display to communicate with the Ships AI verbally. "AI, can you explain how the fighters and shuttles exit the ship? How are they refueled and resupplied? Why are they located where they are?"

"Admiral, I have highlighted in red the magnetic rail systems used to eject ships from each bay. Returning ships are brought back in the same way by reverse using the computers on both the ship and the rail system. There are multiple rails systems for each bay. The rails are spaced at a precalculated distance to limit exposure to enemy activity. The yellow highlights are the refueling lines and resupply areas. You will notice that each bay's ordinance and fuel storage are behind the bay in armored bulkheads. All bays are connected by a rail system of a similar design so they can support each other at any time."

"How do they handle damaged ships? Or ships of different dimensions?"

"There are three small bays around the ship's outside perimeter. Damaged or other ships can land but relocate by rail to the previously mentioned areas. The bays AI are set to auto spray fire retardant on any damaged ship. Technicians are behind armored walls and only appear if needed."

Whistling in amazement, Nkosana asked. "Am I reading this right? There are fifty fighters with a dozen Marine shuttles on this ship?"

"You are incorrect, Admiral; ninety fighters with eighteen Marine shuttles are located in and on this ship. Besides the ones you mentioned, another forty fighters and six shuttles are on the ship's skin. All are under the ship's skin, which opens in less than a minute. The fighters are raised and pushed out to allow takeoff. They get their supplies by a rail system like we already discussed."

"Is this a new design? Have these been tested? How do you know they will work?" asked Nkosana with concern.

"Yes, they are. Governor Titus Muldane's cousin, Commander Roger Brooks, tested them successfully at the Naval base Vro. Hence the delay in their return by a month. Lieutenant Commander Jamie Chandler ran her tests, more extensively than those done at Vro, I may add, in what little time we had before entering this system. They worked out very well during the recent engagement. Same for the Fox, which was modified to match this design. Unfortunately, the Jackal could not have all the updates applied as some updates could only be done at the Naval shipyard. So I analyzed all the data, confirming that the intended object should work."

"Object intended?"

"Protection of fighter pilots and engineers while maximizing offensive firepower. I believe this also answers your other question about the location of the fighters. Moving them further inside the warships allowed the pilots and technicians to be under more armor during a battle."

Nkosana stopped to ask a question with his finger pointing to a section that described a significant change but was interrupted by the Ships AI before he could ask.

"The new hull, I believe that is what you were about to ask about, is honeycombed. Testing by Lieutenant Commander Jax Andrews and his engineers showed that using the new hull process to reduce space between molecules increased the strength tenfold. You cannot see the honeycombing without magnification equipment. Still, it satisfied Commander Brooks enough to incorporate it into the Lucky Strike, and the Fox rebuild. Commander Brooks is the one that added the second hull."

"Damn… all the improvements I see must have taken up a lot of space. Even though the two ships are much larger than their original configuration, I cannot see where they would have acquired that much. Look at the supplies; they are taking up three times the norm. And that cannot be correct… forty spare fighters and several shuttles in cases? And am I reading that correctly? Where did they get all that space?"

He glanced at the ceiling when he thought he heard a chuckle coming from the speakers just before getting a response. "The captains on all three ships held many meetings with their crews on the Majestic, asking for suggestions on improving safety while maintaining or increasing battle efficiency."

"Admiral, do you know the skills available on these ships? Sergeant Garcia, to name just one. His family has been in construction for generations. He grew up learning about the construction of all types of ships every day of his life before he joined the Navy. He is the one who Lieutenant Commander Andrews asked to confirm his theories. Every crew member had to be part of the process as the ship size would double, if not triple if they incorporated all the changes. But, of course, that would not be possible. The crew, including the officers, told the captains to cut the size of living quarters, anything necessary to make it happen."

Whistling as it was hard to believe that anyone would suggest cutting the size of living spaces on a man of war, Nkosana asked with admiration. "They volunteered to cut the size of their quarters? They were small already. I am surprised they allowed the captain's quarters to be as big as there are if they cut their own to what I am seeing."

Again, a hint of laughter drifted through the speakers before he got a response. "I think you already noticed that the captains' quarters are smaller than normal. Per the captains' requests, they were supposed to be even smaller, half their current size."

The speakers were quiet for a few seconds. Long enough that Nkosana wondered if the AI had finished. But before he could ask another question, the AI continued.

"The crew on these ships know their captains well. They had me change the original blueprints to what you are sitting in without their knowledge. They believed that the captains required the extra space as they always have crew members in their quarters for planning sessions. And in special cases, hosting visiting officers and dignitaries, such as yourself. That is what they told everyone anyway."

"They didn't want the captain to know what I heard them tell the Lieutenant Commander. They had determined anything smaller may force a cancellation of a routine they did not want to end. That routine is where Captain Kinsley invites crew members into his room for some of his hot cocoa. Which he did, does, regularly. So ending that was unacceptable, just not happening."

Again, the sound of a soft laugh echoed through the speakers.

With a sigh, Nkosana shook his head. "I am finding all this amazing, unheard of; I am impressed."

Faintly, barely heard above the sound of the air handlers, Nkosana heard. "So am I."

The Ships AI resumed with its report just as Nkosana was about to ask who that was. "The results of those meetings are the blueprints you are now viewing. These were sent onto Commander Brooks before the two ships arrived at Vro. As you can see, he approved most of the changes, improving a few and adding several of his own. To incorporate all the changes at the Naval Yard necessary to make this happen was only possible because of what these ships represent to all at Vro, if not this whole quadrant."

"You are telling me all the offensive and defensive capabilities listed here are accurate? What I see is close to what exists on a Battleship, more in many areas. How is this possible?"

"The massive size reduction of the lendolium reactors enabled adding more and a good deal larger than prior designs. Commander Brooks has sent these blueprints to the home office, where they are under review. The RGN will also use them in a few months after fully testing several items, such as hull strength. The Soraths have already started constructing new ships using this new design and updating the ones still under construction."

He then saw something odd but quickly realized what it was, the engines. There were more than usual. Smaller in size but three times the number. Everything about this ship was different. The capabilities he saw amazed him.

But as good as it looked, he knew it would probably not be enough for them. No one knew what they were facing. Seeing the Chohish throw away several hundred ships with abandon, he knew they must have enormous resources.

AHEIKRAYS SYSTEM

SILENCE REIGNED ON the Bridge, only marred by the sound of heavy breathing as the Lucky Strike was about to enter the slipstream to enter the Aheikrays System.

Dust around the slipstream was much heavier than expected and had reduced all their speeds to just over half speed. But even at this reduced speed, he did not want to risk detection by the Chohish. Instead, Zeke had all the ships continue into the slipstream with the engines sitting idle.

This transition was rough on some, but nothing like the prior one. Most were able to recover almost immediately after exiting the slipstream. And that was none too soon as far as Zeke was concerned.

Watching Isolde intently, waiting for her report on what the scanners were picking up, he was surprised when Hawke pinged him.

Glancing over, he saw Hawke pointing to the Admiral. Then, turning quickly, he was surprised to see blood dripping from the Admiral's right ear down the side of his neck.

As Zeke started rising from his seat while unbuckling his harness, the Admiral waved him off, seeing Zeke's movement. "An old war wound that bleeds occasionally. I am good; you have more important work to do."

Settling back down in his seat, Zeke re-buckled his harness. Looking back at Isolde, he saw she was waiting to give him a report.

"Captain, I am picking up some signal signals near a decent size asteroid field. But I need probes to get particulars."

"Send the probes; I want to know everything stationary, moving, or communicating in this system."

Turning back to her workstation, Isolde executed some commands while speaking into her headset.

"Probes away from all three ships. We doubled the normal deployment. So I sent a different group to enter the asteroid field to track down what the ship's scanners are crowing about."

Nodding his acknowledgment, Zeke settled in his command chair while waiting on the probe's reports. Looking at the sidebar on his chair, he saw the indication that their shields were up and the weapons hot. He knew that he did not have to check with Will and Hawke managing these together, but it was a habit ingrained from his fighter days. Without shields and weapons, a fighter was just a flying coffin in any fight.

If he had looked back at Nkosana again, he would have seen him smile when Zeke checked the weapon's status. It was a habit that both could not change nor want to.

Zeke looked longingly at the empty chair Jeanne used. Jeanne had left a little earlier to join her fellow Irracans sitting in their fighters, waiting to deploy if needed.

Even though she was a Captain in the Irracan Navy, Jeanne refused to give up being a fighter pilot when she had the opportunity. But, as she told Zeke, some of her fondest childhood memories were when she and her father would spend the day flying. Her father would take her around the large container ships orbiting her planet in whatever fighter her father could collar. She would sit on her father's lap in her custom-made spacesuit for hours, captivated by watching the stars and enormous ships flash.

He smiled as he thought about how happy Jeanne sounded as she relayed fondly how mad her mother was on Jeanne's first of many flights. Her mother lectured her father severely at length upon their return from an all-day and most of the night adventure she would never forget. They both looked like they had been in a wind storm with tangled hair, grease-streaked faces, sweat-stained clothes, and smelling like an oil pit. Jeanne took the steam out of her mother's chastisement with a giant grin on her face while cradled in her father's arms during the entire lecture. That lecture lasted until her mother, seeing the never-ending grin, could not keep from laughing, after which she ruffled Jeanne's hair in resignation. Jeanne was just over three years old at the time.

And Jeanne swore that when she was flying her fighter in the heat of combat, she could feel her father's presence next to her. And all that knew her father, including Jeanne herself, said that as good as a fighter pilot Jeanne was, her father was even better.

Slowly, reports started coming in from the probes. Again, nothing unless the Chohish used some undetectable scanning method. "*Could it be they only used them on ships?*" wondered Zeke. "*Odd makes no sense; I must be missing something. Or, thinking about it, it may make sense. They would not want someone stumbling on the probes during a normal survey system scan. Then it would be obvious someone was here.*"

More and more data came in. No sign of anyone else being in the system. Not until the probes entered the area where Isolde had reported signals from earlier.

"Captain, I am picking up an odd signature, matching a Chohish Battleship, inside the asteroid field. But the odd part is that I am not getting any energy readings from it. It seems to be alone there as I am not detecting any other craft now. Orders?" reported radar technician Ensign Caspian Raske.

"Ensign, pay particular attention to that asteroid field, no telling what is in there. Let me know if you detect anything, no matter how small."

"Will, take us toward that Battleship. Get Commander Chandler to send out all the fighters. They are to stay with the fleet until we know what we are facing. Keep the fighters in the communications loop to be updated on anything that may pop up. Jeanne, Gunner, you hear that?"

"Gunner here; we are patched in and will be ready when you need us, Captain."

"Jeanne here. Savvy that me, Matey. My Buckos will keep their ears and eyes open but muted. They are a chatty group."

Without missing a beat, Zeke continued as soon as Jeanne finished. "Hawke, work with Meghan and Lance's crew in preparing several firing solutions. No idea how many ships are in there, one for sure. We want to end this as quickly as possible before something else shows up, so get creative."

"Lance, Meghan, it is time to use the maneuvers we practiced for in a scenario like this. Lance, take point to starboard, and Meghan, you have the port side. Execute on Will's signal. Will, whenever you are ready."

"One moment Captain, the fighters have started exiting the ship. I am waiting for the fighters to finish deploying. Once they are in position, we will begin execution."

Nkosana was curious to see the new process, so he pinged Isolde. "Isolde, can you show me the outer skin of an area where the fighters will be deploying? I would like to see your new setup at work."

Nodding in acknowledgment, Isolde changed the feed on one of the side monitors, showing a section of the ship's skin.

In amazement, Nkosana watched as ships came flying out of the new bay, then again, as he thought on it, forcibly ejected out of the warship. *"They are traveling a lot faster than when they normally come out of a fighter bay."* he thought.

Not only flying faster but leaving the ship one after the other with no slowdown. And these did not include the vessels located on the skin. Instead, the skin receded into the warship, popping up a fighter ready to be decoupled from the locks holding it down. It was one of these fighters that drew Nkosana's close attention. Unless Nkosana was mistaken, it was not a fighter but a bomber. Curious, he brought up the blueprint for the area. They showed an access hatch hidden by the covering that the pilot and engineers used to access the fighter or, in this case, a bomber.

It was rare that he ever saw a bomber, and they were never on a cruiser. Bombers, along with all their specialized ordinance and maintenance, just took too much space. Bombers were usually deployed on carriers as they required fighters in overwhelming numbers to protect them. But when they were, they were to be feared. Bombers usually had only one task, deliver their heavy payload and leave. Bombers were slow compared to fighters, with heavy armor, some excellent defensive armament, and shields.

Only a few moments later, Will signaled that all ships were now in position. Even with the vastly improved inertia dampers, it was apparent when the vessel increased speed. The pressure on their bodies forced them deep into their seats.

The ships made a wide loop to come at the Battleship directly. The probes showed the Chohish Battleship sitting motionless inside the edge of the asteroid field.

"Captain, I am still not detecting any energy from the Battleship. Almost like they are powered down," reported Isolde.

"Gunner, take a couple of your crew for a quick pass. I want to see if they fire on you. I only want you to see if the Battleship is playing possum, so no need to get too close." ordered Zeke.

Before Zeke finished his orders, Gunner's ship and two others pulled away, heading toward the Battleship.

The Lucky Strike and the other ships continued with their fighter escort toward the Battleship.

"Isolde, can you determine if battle damage on the Battleship exists? Any other ships present?" asked Will.

"We cannot detect any exterior damage, although I notice something odd. There are locations on the Battleship; I think these are their fighter bays; they are wide open. No doors, no energy field. Almost like the Chohish left and did not close the doors behind them."

Gunner and the other two fighters headed straight toward the Battleship with no deviation—none of the regular zig-zag or twisting of the fighters.

"Isolde, any indication of weapons going hot?" Gunner's voice came through the speakers.

"Nothing Gunner, Caspian, nor Selena are detecting any energy change. Everything still quiet," responded Isolde.

Two fighters broke off, with just one continuing straight toward the Battleship. Just as the fighter reached missile range, it fired two missiles and did a hard port turn where they hit their afterburners.

Everyone watched as the two missiles raced on. Just before impact, they detonated, causing no damage to the Battleship.

Waiting on an update from Isolde, Zeke pinged Major Richards.

"Major Richards here, Captain?"

"Khalessi, put a team together to go board the Chohish Battleship. It is not showing any signs of life or energy readings. Capturing one intact will go a long way in researching this species."

"Already done, I anticipated this listening to Isolde give status reports. I do not recommend more than an eight-man squad. That should be enough for reconnaissance while limiting casualties if it is a trap. If needed, I had prepositioned multiple squads in Marine shuttles, so we are ready to go once you give the ok."

Before Zeke could respond, Isolde gave her an update. "No change on the Chohish Battleship, no movement, life signs, nor power readings."

"Major Richards, Captain Kinsley here; I concur with your plans; you have my ok. One stipulation, though, is that you are not to be part of this squad. That is an order, Major, not open to discussion."

Silence reigned for a few tense seconds, and Zeke could imagine the cursing on the other end. Then, glancing at Shon, who was back in his protection position, he could see Shon's eyes cringe in apprehension.

"Captain, Sergeants Dexton Kyler, and Evaline Miya will lead the mission. They will be taking two shuttles, four Marines assigned to each, with one shuttle going to each of the open bays. I have patched the Sergeants up with Isolde so she can monitor them or any of their team's cameras." None on the bridge could miss the tone of controlled anger in her voice. Several looked at Zeke in surprise. No one who knew the Major wanted to be on her wrong side.

Nkosana, mindful of the Marines stationed on the Bridge, discretely monitored Zeke and the Bridge crew to see their response to the Majors' reply. He was a little taken aback when Zeke spoke up on the matter.

Preceding his remarks with a soft chuckle, Zeke spoke loud enough for all on the Bridge to hear him. "The Major does not like to send her personnel off without her, especially into unknown or dangerous situations. Not because she does not trust her officers, she most assuredly does, but because she came up through the ranks. Khalessi experienced too many officers willing to throw away the lives of their men based on what they learned in a classroom.

There is no better class for an officer than experiencing the horrors of war or direct battle themselves. She, as I believe that experience trumps book learning."

Turning to look at the Nkosana, Zeke continued. "Same as the Admiral sitting on this Bridge right now when he could be back at headquarters safe and sound."

"If I know Khalessi, based on prior experience, she had already assigned the Sergeants to lead the expedition while she trailed along to gain her own experience and knowledge. To improve her ability to lead her men and women as we are now in a new warfare territory. Also, as she once told me, '*It is nice just to be a regular Marine once in a while.*' But unfortunately for the Major, I do not believe this is the time to risk our top Marine officer so early in the game. So she'll get over it. There is not one Marine or soldier on board our ships who will think less of her for it."

Looking at Lance Corporal Chavez, Nkosana saw the slight smile that confirmed what Zeke said was true. Glancing at the other two Marines, he saw they mirrored the expression on the Lance Corporal. Again, he was impressed with the leadership on this ship.

"Captain, Major Richards here. I ask you to reconsider the order stating I am not to be part of the mission. The battleship presents me with the perfect opportunity to see my marines in action and possibly explore an empty enemy vessel. The experience here will be invaluable later down the line."

Sighing, Zeke took a moment to think it over. He knew Khalessi was right but still had hesitations about letting her go. Losing her now could be disastrous later on. Then again, stopping Khalessi from leading, as usual, may cause even more harm. He was either going to trust her leadership or not.

"Major, you have my permission to go. But I want you and the entire team to beat a hasty retreat at the first sign of any trouble. Got that?"

"Sir, Yes Sir, Major Richards out."

"Shuttles are leaving the ship, Captain. Estimated time to arrival is twelve minutes," reported Isolde.

"Well, that didn't take long. Major Richards must still have been on the shuttle during her request." Nkosana thought.

Will gave a slight whistle. "Wow, these new shuttles are much faster than the old ones. I am watching their speed; they are already moving over half as fast as the old ones. Does anyone know their top speed?"

Before anyone could answer, Jeanne's voice came through the speakers. "Permission to escort the shuttles to their destination, Captain."

"Permission granted for four fighters for each shuttle. I want to keep the rest on alert for any surprises."

"Understood. I will be leading one group, Mason another. Gunner will assume overall command once he rejoins the group. Jeanne out."

"And before you ask, Admiral, Jeanne would not pay any attention if the captain ordered her not to go. All you would hear is laughter from her and all the Irracan pilots, who happen to make up most of our fighter crew. And maybe a few, if not most of our pilots, have come to know and respect her." Hawke explained. 'She works with the RGN and is deferring command to the captain. Jeanne does not have to take orders she does not like from them, even if she is romantically involved with one of their officers. She is in charge of all the Irracan forces assigned to us."

Nkosana looked at Zeke, only to see him shrug as if it was no big deal. Hmm... maybe he needed to adjust his opinion on Zeke even higher.

In short order, the shuttles with their fighter escorts reached the Chohish Battleship. The shuttles entered and landed on the landing bays while the fighters peeled off.

PUZZLE

SITTING IN THE Marine shuttle, Khalessi watched one of the monitors opposite her. The passenger compartment of the shuttle had no windows. Large monitors enabled the passengers to view outside as if the bulkheads were not even there.

Khalessi was awestruck at the size of the Chohish landing bay. The bay was full of fighters with several shuttles sitting nearby. It would have looked like a standard fighter bay if not for the most disturbing aspect, dozens of Chohish bodies lying haphazardly around.

It was evident from the few Chohish near where their shuttle landed what killed them, the sudden loss of air. Most showed signs of tissue swelling and bruising. The lack of suits on the bodies indicated that there had to have been a force field to contain the atmosphere at one time. Why it failed was a mystery at present. There should be multiple redundancies if their force field was like theirs.

It would not be an issue for the Marines as their armor supplied oxygen for breathing. But seeing so many frozen bodies was still disconcerting.

"Time to move, Marines, move, move... "ordered Dexton

Kyler with a commanding voice as the rear door dropped. The four Marines rushed out to defensive positions around the shuttle. The turrets on top of the shuttle silently cycle, looking for any potential threat.

"Vincenzo, you and Khalessi, take that airlock I see on the left. Imran and I will check out the larger entrance straight ahead of us. Stay in touch, people, slow and easy, stay safe. Retreat to the shuttle if you encounter any enemy forces. The pilots will provide covering fire if needed. Remember, this is a scouting mission, nothing more, understand? Move out."

Smiling, Khalessi took point leading. PCF Vincenzo Randall was one of the team's newer members and was assigned to this mission to get real experience. He was too green to lead a team, but since Khalessi insisted on coming, Sergeant Kyler would let the private tag along with her.

Cautiously, the two made their way toward the airlock, utilizing the fighters as cover, passing dead Chohish. As they got closer, it became apparent the airlock was several times standard size. They had come prepared to blast their way in, but Khalessi was surprised and delighted to see the airlock door ajar as she got closer.

Wary of a trap, she used hand signals to Vincenzo, or Vinnie as he preferred, to signal to come in from the backside while she went around where she could peek in. Seeing nothing to raise the alarm, Khalessi slowly walked along the bulkhead. She calmly walked up the sidewall until she was hanging from the ceiling using the magnetic soles on her boots.

Slinging her rifle onto her back, Khalessi pulled her plasma pistol. Seeing the rifle hanging upside down was odd until you realized that the armor had grabbed it magnetically. Then, walking toward the opening, she scrunched toward the ceiling until she could peer in. Not seeing any danger, she moved the tip of her pistol to push the door open. Only it did not move. Khalessi would have chuckled if it was not such a stupid mistake. The door would be very cumbersome to open without power.

Sliding to the floor, Khalessi, hiding behind the door for protection, opened it wide using the strength provided by her armor. Cautiously, Khalessi peered around the edge of the door. She could not detect any motion, so after taking a half dozen steps backward, she ran forward, grabbing the edge of the door where she flung herself inside. Then, rolling, she rose with her pistol raised and ready.

What Khaleesi saw would have made a newbie gag. Her career stopped sights like this from affecting her while in combat mode. She had seen death in all forms, many of which still gave her nightmares. The long hallway she was in branched in a T layout. At the top of the T was a large pile of Chohish bodies, a vast horrific-looking pile. It looked like they had been trying to access a secure access hatch. However, what was so horrific was that the Chohish had fought each other before the end; body parts and blood were everywhere.

"Sergeant Kyler, Khalessi here, sending you a feed on what we found. Orders?"

"Feed received. Ouch, that is a mess. Any sign of life?"

"Negative, we have encountered no movement of any kind."

"Continue. We have to blast our way in here. The door is massive, so it will take a bit to set up the charges. Blast ETA is five to seven minutes. Your armor will get the warning. Stay alert for any response. Kyler out."

"Khalessi, this is Captain Kinsley. I did not see any weapons on the Chohish. Can you check on that?"

"Request received; I will check when we get closer, Khalessi out."

While Khalessi was on the link to the captain, Vinnie entered and took point. Hugging the bulkhead, Vinnie slowly approached the T intersection while Khalessi mirrored his actions on her side.

Working in tandem, Vinnie moved a few feet and crouched, Khalessi moved a few feet and crouched, and so on, until they reached the end of the hallway.

"Captain, I can confirm; the only weapons I see are edged weapons, no phasers or pulsars."

"Message received, puzzling, Captain out."

The video feeds showed the Marines looking down both ends of the T where both ends of the T had closed access hatches, but no bodies, just in front of the one.

"Well, Vinnie, tell me what...."

Before she could answer, the armor signaled a ten-second warning until detonation. Flattening against the bulkhead, both Marines could feel the explosion through the bulkheads and floor.

"Access gained, moving on, Kyler out."

"Ok, Vinnie, to continue with our discussion. Thoughts on why the Chohish are gathered only here and not also at the other hallways?"

"Several thoughts come to mind. The ship shields failed in multiple areas, and the doors opened, causing a sudden full atmospheric loss and decompression. They were trying to access what they thought was the closest escape hatch; time was not available to go down either of the two halls. The Chohish did not know what was happening and tried to get on the other side of the emergency doors. The only option for safety they had"

"Excellent, my thoughts exactly. But something tells me that this was no accident. There should be too many safeguards, even for the Chohish, I believe anyway, for this to happen. So let's go see if you are correct."

With that, they walked through the bodies to the secure access hatch. Thankfully they had powered armor as the bodies were stacked high, and the Chohish were large and heavy. They had to spend a few moments clearing away bodies before they could try opening the hatch. Afterward, both looked like a nightmare, with blood and body parts plastered on their armor. Vinnie yanked on the hatch, thus confirming their suspicions about being locked. No easy access this way.

Without a word, Vinnie started placing charges around the hatch while Khalessi stood guard.

"Khalessi here, setting up a charge, detonation in two to three minutes, Khalessi out."

"Kyler here, copy that, Kyler out."

Watching Vinnie, Khalessi was impressed with his charge layout. Vinnie's layout took into consideration the areas reinforced on the hatch. It took a good eye to do this right the first time on a hatch never seen before.

With a nod, Vinnie let Khalessi know he was ready. Khalessi sent out the ten-second warnings. Both leaned against the bulkhead, shielded a bit behind several large bodies. The blast was powerful with lots of flame, vibration, smoke, and debris, but no sound; the suit ensured that.

Before the smoke cleared, both had sprinted through the hatch, only to pile into bodies stacked high on the other side. The bloody bodies added to the horror already coating their armor.

"Sergeant, Khalessi here; see the video I am sending you. Chohish casualties on both sides of the hatch. Chohish was trying to open the hatch to get away from something. Thoughts?"

"Kyler here. We have not encountered what you found beyond the bodies in the fighter bay. I would say a major AI malfunction, but I find that hard to believe. I am not even sure they have an AI. Based on your video, it looks like they fought each other to get through the hatch, unaware there was another group on the other side doing the same thing to get to their side. Maybe they believed, or were notified, that one hatch was the only area not failing."

"Hmmm… matches my thoughts exactly. Orders?" responded Khalessi.

"Make your way toward where we believe the Bridge to be. We need to get a data dump and hope it will tell us what happened here. Hopefully, the ship's AI may be able to interpret their database. Kyler out."

Video feeds from the Marines were being sent to the Lucky Strike and the rest of the small fleet as they slowed down not to overshoot the Battleship.

Zeke had Isolde bring the feed from Khalessi on the right-side screen, showing several dozen feet wide hallways with ceilings to match. The video was jerky from Khalessi taking evasive steps as she made her way down the hall. Zeke almost laughed when the video turned upside down as Khalessi made her way to the ceiling. The footage from the other three Marines mirrored her maneuvers.

Nkosana quietly whispered as he watched. "They are not taking any chances, are they?"

It was Will who responded to the admiral's comment. "I took a course that the Major provided for all that wanted it. Well, it was more like a demand for all personnel on this ship, but one we mostly agreed would be beneficial. Doc is one of the few exceptions. It was comical watching him trying to talk his way out of it as if that would change the major's mind. Even Doc admitted after the two months of pure hell; it was well worth it. One thing Khalessi and her Marines drilled into us, over and over again, was never let your guard down while in enemy territory. The enemy may be able to see your maneuvers, but it still takes some skill to make full use of it."

As Khalessi passed a room with no door, glancing inside before continuing, Zeke yelled for her to stop. "Back up, Major; I want a more detailed look inside that room."

The video stopped and backed up, where the feed entered the

room. It was a storage room that looked like a storm had come through. Equipment, blankets, and clothes were strewn all over the room.

"Captain, anything in particular?" asked Khalessi.

"I am looking at the mess. It looks like a rapid decompression, meaning it was from multiple vents. But, as Sergeant Kyler said, we need that database, in whatever form it may exist. I have a theory but need that database for confirmation."

"Will do, Khalessi out."

The video continued to show bodies scattered through the hall.

"Isolde, show me the Sergeant's video feed next to the Majors."

The feed from Khalessi split horizontally to show the two video feeds together, one on top of the other. Kyler's feed showed him making his way down a huge passageway. The contrast was startling, one littered with bodies, the other showing a vacant corridor.

They watched as both groups made their way to where they presumed the Bridge would be. Gradually, they made their way toward each other. Then, shortly, they met in front of a colossal hatch that stood ajar.

Sergeant Kyler, giving hand indications where he wanted the other three positioned, plastered himself next to the door where he started a countdown on his fingers. Holding his left hand up with five fingers extended, he started a countdown matched by pulling in one finger. "Five, four, three…." He then jumped through the hatch.

No one seemed surprised at the sergeants' actions except Nkosana.

Hawke quietly explained to Nkosana as they watched the video feed from Kyler's armor. It showed a massive Bridge with Chohish bodies scattered haphazardly around. "Again, part of the training. Never do anything expected. You may want to enquire about taking a course upon the Majors' return." Hawke smiled at the Admiral before turning back to watch the feeds.

Kyler moved around the edges of the Bridge with his pulsar rifle at the ready. He made no sly movements this time around, just sure and steady. In short order, he was standing next to the slumped-over body of one larger than all the rest. One they had come to recognize due to its size and apparel, a Sovereign.

The Sovereign was slumped over the shoulders of a Chohish that they also knew to be an officer. It appeared they had been looking at something on their screen when they expired.

"Kyler, Captain here. Unless I am mistaken, that has to be the central console that may house the database we need."

They watched as Kyler moved next to the console in question, pushing two bodies, none too gently, out of the way. They tumbled to the ground, frozen in the postures they had died.

Signaling Imran over, he moved away to give Imran room to work. Signaling Khalessi to the center of the Bridge next to the command chair, which seemed prevalent on all race's warships, they went into a private mode of communication.

Puzzled, the Admiral looked at the captain for an explanation. But Zeke either did not see the Admirals glance his way or just ignored him.

It was Imran's exclamation that came across the speakers next. They watched as he, now on his back under the workstation, tore out a section and threw it. What they saw from his viewpoint looked like a mass of what they assumed were wires.

"I believe I have an access point, maybe the database itself. I need the ship's AI assistance here." It looked like a data port similar to what they had connected to a large round metal cylinder.

"LS1 here. You are correct. Based on where the Sovereign and officer were, along with the research on the debris we found on other Chohish ships, that would be the local database. There should be a larger one in another section of the Battleship, but it would be too large to remove with your current resources. You should be able to remove the one in question with another individual. Look for three connections. Gently pry them from their fittings before your tear the database from its mounts. Second, you will not have the time to disconnect them properly as you do not have the correct tools to accomplish that. Third, Lieutenant Commander Andrews will have interfaces allowing me to query the database. LS1 out."

It was not lost on Zeke the puzzlement on Nkosana's face when he heard the ship's AI sign out, but he did not have time to worry about that now.

"Captain here, Sergeant, now that you know how to retrieve the database, I need you to speed things up. I do not like sitting around here; we are too exposed."

"Understood, Captain, will comply," responded Kyler, pointing to Vinnie to assist Imran. Meanwhile, it was apparent he was still in discussion with Khalessi.

Zeke broke the silence on the bridge of the Lucky Strike by stepping off his command chair to walk over to Isolde. He and Isolde held a quiet discussion, squatting until Zeke finally nodded while looking at what Isolde had displayed on her screen. After Zeke returned to his chair, he continued watching the action on the Chohish battleship.

The two Marines had yanked the database out and started lugging it toward the entrance. Meanwhile, the Sergeant and Major had rolled the Sovereign over and were tearing into his clothing. Not as easy as it looked as the body was frozen solid, not only from cold but also from rigor mortis. They removed items that they stored in little compartments on their armor.

Within another half hour, they were back on the shuttle and headed back toward the Lucky Strike.

ONWARD

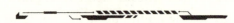

IT WAS OVER a dozen hours before the small fleet left the Chohish Battleship behind, marines and fighters back onboard each ship except for a dozen fighters leading the way.

The time delay was to enable the Marines time to plant explosives throughout the Chohish Battleship. Since the following fleet should be coming this way, getting an enemy ship intact was worth the risk. Warning probes were installed nearby with codes necessary to disarm the explosives.

"Is it wise to have Captain de Clisson leading the way?" asked the Admiral.

"Wise, maybe not, but that is her way. And one that her Irracans admire and respect greatly. They would follow her into hell and back." Zeke answered with pride. "And if I were still piloting a fighter, I would too."

Silence fell on the Bridge as everyone resumed their tasks. It was obvious where they were going after what one of their probes had picked up; a stale trail leading to a previously unknown slipstream.

The fighters spread out in an arrowhead formation, with the three Men of War following a short distance behind. The three warship's spread out in a straight line with the Lucky Strike in the middle.

As the hours passed, the rotation of crews happened faster than usual as Zeke wanted the first shift back on since they were about to enter the slipstream. He wanted the more experienced at the helm as they passed through. Who knew what they would encounter? Now was not the time for training. No one complained, though; all were professionals.

Looking around the Bridge, he could tell they were getting tense. Still, he could also see their conviction and confidence as they entered critical commands. Seeing this makes any captain proud; this was a crew he admired and respected. One, he was honored to have the privilege of being a member.

"Slipstream transition in five minutes, again, slipstream transition in fifteen minutes. Emergent level one stealth protocol was now in place." announced throughout the ship. Because of their last action, Zeke almost smiled as they now have half a dozen new protocols throughout the RGN.

"Will, if you would please…" ordered Zeke.

Working with Hawke, they sent half a dozen probes through the slipstream.

The probes returned as the warning went out for the five-minute notice for the slipstream emergence. Isolde and Caspian uploaded the data frantically while Will and Hawke retrieved the probes.

Patiently waiting for the report from Isolde, Zeke checked on the position of the ships one last time. "Commander Chandler, we have all the fighters on hot standby?"

"That is an affirmative, Captain. All fighters are idling on standby. We can start getting fighters deployed twenty seconds after notification." replied Jamie.

Turning his attention back to Isolde, he saw it was just in time as she looked up, ready to give her report.

"Probes indicate nothing in the immediate proximity of the slipstream. But they are picking up latent trails that lead to a huge stationary oblong structure that could be a space station. Not sure, as the size is multiple times the size of one of ours. That is our conjecture at this time without a closer examination," reported Isolde.

"Conjecture noted... Jeanne, lead your group in; we will be right behind you," ordered Zeke

"Aye Aye Me Capitano. Ok, you bunch of fleabags, let's see what is waiting for us on the other side.... get them shields up once through with your weapons hot. Yahooo....here we go.... follow me in boys and girls..." responded Jeanne.

The Admiral was about to say something when he heard a chorus of shouting coming through the speakers.

"Jeanne does have a different way of motivating her crew. Noisy and boisterous, but very effective. If you look at the captain, he is itching to get in his fighter and follow the lass himself." Chuckling, Hawke smacked the armrest on his chair. "Hell, so am I, so am I...."

And then, in less than a few seconds, all twelve fighters disappeared as they entered the slipstream.

Within another minute, it was their turn. As the Lucky Strike exited the slipstream, they saw they could not take a moment to recover from any effect of the transition. Instead, there was a full-fledged fighter battle raging. Hundreds of Chohish fighters had been waiting on them.

"Launch all fighters and get us the hell in there," ordered Zeke. "How long before we can fire?"

"We will be in range in twenty-six seconds, Captain," responded Hawke. "With your permission, I can fire some anti-fighter missiles now, hoping they grab their attention. May even pull some toward us."

"Good plan; execute at your discretion. Confirm all defensive arrays are powered up and available. If Hawke's method works, we will need all of them. "

Hurump, hurump, hurump sounded immediately, with a slight shudder felt throughout the bridge.

"Damn, what have they done to these missiles?" exclaimed Hawke.

"What's the matter?" asked a concerned Zeke.

"Nothing Sir, it's just that the missiles are moving at twice the speed while using only two-thirds the fuel. Based on the fuel expenditure, we are in range now! And just as impressive, we are firing twice as fast and half as many again. I cannot wait to see what the guidance system is like." a now very excited Hawke responded.

"I hope we are in time; our fighters are severely overwhelmed. Several ships have already gone red. Any idea if they were able to eject?" a worried Will asked.

"One made it, but two others did not," a sorrowful Caspian answered. "Just lost another ship; pilot ejected successfully."

Minutes passed along with two more fighters before the missiles became known. And they did so spectacularly. The rockets kicked into another gear for the last stage, taking the enemy fighters by surprise. Then, the enemy fighters were blinking out in quick order, one by one, two by two, three by three. There were no survivors after being hit by these missiles.

The remaining Irracan fighters broke off and headed back toward the ships. The Chohish came in hot pursuit after a brief pause to regroup. The missiles were still chasing them, but now that they knew the missile's abilities, they could evade more successfully.

Will observed, "The Chohish regrouped; they are changing their tactics. We knew their headlong rush to battle would not last, but I hoped we could see several more."

But the Chohish's pause gave another force a chance to enter the engagement window. And they made their presence known in short order. They were fresh with a full complement of missiles and used them with devastating effects.

Even though still vastly outnumbered, the RGN fighters showed that numbers were not always the determining factor; skill could sometimes count for more. And this was one of those times.

Dozens of the Chohish fighters died upon their initial meeting.

Flying in pairs, they swerved up, down, fast braking, and using their afterburners; they showed that to make the grade of an RGN and Irracan fighter pilot took great skill. Chohish fighter after Chohish fighter died in flames.

But it was not all one-sided. Here and there, an RGN pilot went up in flames. It almost seemed like the Chohish numbers would win until one special event determined the outcome.

A lone fighter reentered the fray, marked by a red and black icon. That fighter flew circles around the Chohish, taking them out. It soon became apparent the Chohish tried avoiding this fighter. No matter, though, the Irracan or RGN pilots were heartened by this unique fighter and renewed their attack with enthusiasm.

Monitoring the Chohish icons, Zeke noticed an odd pattern emerging. The Chohish fighters were starting to avoid engagement. Were they losing confidence? In the beginning, they had vast superiority, and there was no doubt who would be the victor. Now though, they were quickly losing that advantage.

But you had to give it to them; none retreated; they fought until no one remained. Unfortunately, the Chohish did not go out without causing additional deaths for the RGN force.

Without stopping, Zeke moved the Lucky Strike and her companion warships toward what all were assuming was a space station. The fighters spread out into a protective half-sphere while half a dozen shuttles started picking up the pilots who had to eject.

As they got closer, tensions rose. Were there more fighters? Usually, space station defenses worked in conjunction with men of war.

Attack Chohish War

But no large warships had been detected; were they possibly behind the station? When would the defensive armament start firing?

It was Hawke who broke the tension. "I think I know what we are looking at, Captain. I did not want to say anything until I could check my data to confirm. During our war with the Chohish, we ran into several stations very similar to this one. We found one after it had lost all power from a few lucky shots. We captured the Chohish station after we surprised them with a superior force."

"Enough with the history lesson Hawke. We are getting close. What is it?" said an exasperated Will.

"It is a warehouse station. The one we found contained all types of spare parts, fighters, food, clothes, etc."

"What were the station's defenses like?" asked Zeke.

"None that I know of beyond fighters. The one we examined had a large fighter bay in the rear of the station that could contain hundreds of fighters and bays for restocking men of war. The battle to retake that system was one of the largest battles of the entire war. I would not be surprised if the larger ships normally stationed at this station were part of the force we dealt with in the Pandora system."

Cradling his chin in his, "Well, I am not going to stop to try and board it. Who knows how many Chohish are on that huge thing? Nor am I going to leave it intact. I am sure they have some decent shields for something so large. So let's see how good these new missiles are."

"Jeanne, you listening?"

"That I am Zeke; what's up?" replied Jeanne.

"Get all the fighters that can manage another fight resupplied. I thought to concentrate the fire from our larger ships on one area and hope we could take out the shields for that area. Thought?"

"I like the plan. I will work with Gunner, Jamie, Meghan, and Lance on scheduling the fighters to get resupplied. I expect it will be three hours before we will be ready. Will that work in your timeline?"

Zeke scratched the left side of his temple to remove an itch and contemplated what waiting would mean. Should he go in with less fighter support? "I do not think I have any choice. We are still recovering pilots, and they get top priority. I doubt the Chohish sent out all their fighters, but they have some in reserve. How many is anybody's guess? I will have Will coordinate with the other ships to get an opening through their shields. Let me know when you are ready. And Jeanne, time is of the essence here. I am sure they sent out a distress call. Zeke out."

Unbuckling his harness, Zeke made his way over to Will and Hawke.

Will and Hawke had moved to hover over the large situation table. Floating above the table was a four-dimensional image of the Chohish station. The Admiral, unbidden, joined them.

Pointing to Isolde, Zeke indicated for her to join them. Isolde tapped Caspian on his shoulder and waved for him to tag along.

Upon reaching the small group, Zeke asked Isolde to conference in the command group from the other two ships. Within seconds, all were on the call.

"Everyone present? Good, you heard my conversation with Jeanne. We must figure out how to get past their shields and what location to try it on first—at the same time, doing this while trying not to get blown up. I would send the Jackal or Fox around the back, but I am afraid of separating forces. Does anyone have any suggestions?"

The awkward silence that followed was a good indicator that no one had a clear idea of how. The Chohish station offensive or defensive armament was an unknown quantity.

Looking around, Zeke asked again, but differently.

"How about going to where the fighter bays were and trying

there? We could also stop them from launching any additional fighters."

"I would bet that is where they have the heaviest shields. That would be the first area I would strengthen. I suggest we go after either of the sides as that is the minimal amount of space available to house shielding, " said Meghan over the link.

"Lance here, Zeke. Do you remember the carrier Infinity where we were in the same fighter squadron? It was similar in design, only a lot smaller than this Titan. Do you remember what their weak point was? The corners. The carrier had some powerful shields, but the shielding on the corners was minimally covered. We almost lost that ship due to that deficiency."

"You're right; I forgot all about that. Anyone else? No, let's give Lance's suggestion a go. Jeanne, keep all fighters waiting for resupply available as a protection shield against a possible fighter attack. Can you send a few around to check the backside? Isolde, you and Caspian, I need you two to watch out for any Chohish fighters and assess our attack's damaging impact."

"Meghan, Lance, have your technicians monitor the probes for any activity from all directions. As I said, the Chohish must have sent a mayday. Any response is going to be dependent on what is available. They may have stripped the immediate area to beef up the large force we dealt with, but I doubt they stripped it bare. Keep your eyes open. Send out any additional probes you may feel are needed. We do not want any surprises."

"Ok, people, we have a plan; let's see if Lance is right. Lance, you have the lead on this. Coordinate with each ship on when and where to fire. Based on what Hawke's history notes tell us, let's get close enough to add energy weapons if possible. Lance, the Lucky Strike is to go in first, and if we do not get any harsh response, the Jackal and Fox will close in. All yours, my friend."

They would have seen the Bridge crews pick up their activity if anyone was watching, but nothing else changed. The fighters were already in the process of repair, rearming, and refueling. Engineers were working feverishly on any damage and checking over the status of all sections of every ship. Shuttles were flying around, picking up pilots that had ejected. Everyone was already busy with a thousand and one different things—all, that is, except for the Marines.

The Marines were already in their shuttles. Three-quarters of these were calmly sitting in their armor, playing games, or monitoring the communication channels. The rest were dozing as they stood in their Battleoids connected to the ship's hull. Meanwhile, all in armor, their compatriots were stationed strategically around the three warships. These Marines were magnetically attached to a wall or stairwell to minimize their obstruction to others. Most, not all, were sleeping as no idle Marine wasted an opportunity to get some decent rest when going into battle.

And finally, three Marines stood on the Bridge in their armor, calmly watching as the Nkosana glanced at them in amusement before nudging Zeke. Nkosana would have sworn Lance Corporal Chavez smiled, but maybe not. He wasn't sure the Lance Corporal knew how to smile based on his experience so far.

"Captain, a question for you. Why Captain Henry?"

"Because Lance is one of the best intuitive officers I know. And that is what we need now. Don't get me wrong, Lance does not ignore hard data when making his decisions, but when that data is lacking, I do not know anyone else; I would rather be in charge. He is more often right than naught. Lance will be able to see what happens with our attack and adjust accordingly on the fly. Of that, I am sure. I do not want to get tied down directing this part."

No sooner had he finished responding to the Admiral than the vibration and sound of the missiles firing made itself known. The ship jerked, to a sudden increase in speed followed.

The screens showed the ship moving toward the Chohish station at an angle. They all watched as the icons for missiles got closer and closer to the station while the ship kept firing repeatedly. Suddenly, one detonated. Then another. One more. The remaining missiles never made it to the station.

"Looks like the station has some decent defenses. Those were missile interceptors. We will find out soon what other types they have shortly." remarked Will, who was entering commands furiously into his workstation.

"We are about to enter our energy range... Lance is using all three ships' AIs to coordinate the missiles, and soon, our energy fire." Hawke informed everyone.

The ship rocked as their different energy weapons let loose in several staggered intervals, all coordinated to hit one specific location simultaneously. The gaps allowed the different types of firearms the required time to reach the target together. Lance used LS1 to make the delicate calculations. And not just once but again and again.

The ship, while still moving at top speed, continued firing. And then they hit. Not the station's hull, but a shield flared brightly amid the energy and destruction that rained upon it. Not one of the first missiles nor energy salvo got through.

But that was only the first. The second had the same result. Same for the third. But one energy blast got through on the fourth. Then, unexpectedly, two other energy sources hit with the fifth strike. They all watched as the shields glowed hotly for a few seconds before it became dark again.

The sixth salvo of energy and missiles impacted the hull with no impediment. Considering the size of the station, it was minuscule. But it was a start. Again and again, they pounded away at the opening before they could tell the AIs targeting had moved to another hull section. Not a lot, but enough to double the width of

107

the breach. The new target section could not hold back so much destruction without the additional support of the destroyed shields.

Again and again, the AI's target moved. The breach opened broader and broader.

Then, several hundred Chohish fighters heading straight for the Lucky Strike came from around the back of the Titan platform.

The resupplied RGN fighters went to meet them. They took out dozens of the Chohish fighters, who did not evade or fire in return but kept going. The RGN fighters, having made their pass, had to make a wide turn before they could race after them. The Chohish force remained very formidable.

Watching this, Zeke paled as he understood what was happening.

"Evasive maneuvers. Get us as far away as possible from those fighters. Lance, Meghan, I believe those fighters plan to ram us."

All three men of war swung wide to head away from that station at maximum speed. So even though the new engines gave them hell-for-leather momentum, there was no way they could outrun a fighter. On that, there was no doubt in anybody's mind.

There was only a small force of fighters that stood in their way. These were the fighters waiting to get resupplied or repaired.

"Ok, me buccko's, you know what the oncoming fighters plan to do. Undoubtedly, they have loaded up each ship with all the bombs they can hold, then ram our ships. We cannot allow that. We need to stop them at all costs. So are you with me?" yelled Jeanne.

Having no missiles, these fighters had to get close to use their energy weapons. Which they did to make sure it counted. Heading straight toward the Chohish, they slowed down to maximize the chances of their first shots, even though it put them at a significant disadvantage, almost suicidal when attacked. It wasn't very likely they would get another opportunity.

No unique flying, just straight ahead. And the tactic paid off. Because of the reduced speed, they could get off multiple shots at different targets. Chohish fighters after Chohish fighters were destroyed. What surprised them all was that there was no return fire. The Chohish were flying with no change in direction at full speed.

"Zeke, I bet the Chohish removed their weapons and shields to make the fighters lighter and faster if they ever had any. With all the bombs they probably carry, they needed to reduce weight if they wanted any speed increase."

"I agree, Jeanne. Those fighters came that way to allow them to send out so many in such a short time. You cannot do anything for us now; watch our back in case anymore show up."

Now there was nothing between the fighters and the RGN fleet. The distance closed slowly. The three RGN ships ran together with over a hundred Chohish suicide bombs hot on their tail.

"Meghan, Lance, get your ships away from the Lucky Strike. Let's see if we can split them into more manageable sizes, " a worried Zeke ordered.

The two destroyers split to either side of the cruiser without an acknowledgment; none was needed.

All on the Bridge watched the Chohish on what they would do, hoping they would split up, only to see the Chohish fighters continue following the Lucky Strike.

"It is as I thought; they know we are the true threat to their station. The Destroyers do not have the firepower to destroy the station." Zeke said out loud for all to hear.

Turning to Will, Hawke, and the Nkosana, Zeke questioned if they had any recommendations.

"We will get some of the fighters when they get closer, a good many, but there are just too many. Odds are a dozen or two will get through no matter what we do." Will commented.

"Dropping ordinance behind us will not work; we are going too fast, and they will be monitoring for that." offered Nkosana.

"I wish I could help, Captain, but you rarely fight suicidal maniacs like this group. I do not have any brilliant last-minute suggestions I can make, sorry."

Hawke shrugged his shoulders as he had nothing to add, shaking his head negatively.

Zeke stared at the screen displaying a simulation of the positions of the Chohish fighters. He knew any change of direction would not help. Even with the upgraded defenses, the odds were way against them. Many would die. The cruiser could even be disabled. But even if they weren't, the damage would likely be severe enough that the mission would end.

It was like time flew by when he heard the first of their layer of defensive fire. The ship did not rock from these missiles. They were much smaller than the ones they used for combat against Men of War. These were for fighters; though much smaller, they were much faster. Hitting something relatively small with a missile while moving at maximum speed was like hitting the bullseye in a game of darts.

The crew knew. You could see it in the slump of the shoulders, the muted whispering, the haunted eyes. Even though they knew this mission was against survival, they never expected it to end so soon.

And when the point defense started firing, they were all startled by a sound they never expected to hear again.

"Captain, this is Gunner, we are..." was all he got out before he was cut off by another overstepping him.

"Yahooooo.... Ahoy, me hearties, time to heave-ho! Let's go hang 'em from the Yardarm," could be heard screaming across the speakers. Most here knew that voice; it was Masson from the Fox. What the hell was he doing on the Lucky Strike? Why the yelling?

The sound of fighters being launched continuously took them all by surprise.

The feeling of hope swept through the Bridge like a storm. Zeke would swear he even heard someone laugh and mimic Masson.

It was Jamie who came across the speakers seconds later that explained what was happening.

"Jamie here, Captain; we are launching the fighters that landed to be resupplied or repaired. I expect to get close to two dozen fighters out within the next minute. Half do not have missiles, but all are functional. We are working on another half dozen we hope to get out before the fighters can reach us. It will be close."

"Jamie, you and your boys are miracle workers; keep me updated."

The fighters did not immediately turn toward the ship's rear to go after the enemy. Surprisingly, as they came out of the side ejection tubes, they hit their afterburners to go into a wide loop where they went at the enemy fighters from the side.

They made their presence known—Chohish after Chohish died. Still, the Chohish came on. And then it became apparent why the loop. Never taking their foot off the afterburner, the fighters came flying back in one more pass before the enemy fighters would reach the Lucky Strike. Even more, RGN fighters joined the action.

But Zeke could see it would not be enough. Even with the point defense helping the fighters, he could see that a few enemy fighters would probably make it.

Hitting the general alarm, Zeke yelled, "Brace yourselves, everyone, this is gonna hurt, really hurt."

The next few moments went by agonizingly slowly. Bracing himself for impact, Zeke heard the proximity alarms. Then, unexpectedly, giant balls of flame appeared on the monitors. Before anyone could say anything, the Lucky Strike rocked wildly from other large objects racing by so close they brushed the ship's shields. Belatedly, the imminent collision alarm sounded, screaming a warning.

Startled, he was surprised to hear, "Ha! I told you, Captain Kennedy, the Jackal, is faster."

Meghan's reply was overwhelmed by the cheering from the Bridge.

His relief made him sit back while putting his head in his hands. He had so many questions that needed answering. *How did they do it? Why weren't the two ships flagged on the screen?* All he wanted to do now was the time to catch his breath and let his racing heart settle down.

And if he was not the captain of this ship, he might have been able to take that time, but he was.

"Ok, people, we need to stay on our toes. We left our brothers and sisters back near the enemy station unprotected. Let's go pick them up. Will, get us turned around and headed back. We have a station to destroy."

UNKNOWN

THE THREE SHIPS moved on toward a previously unknown slipstream. The probes sent out earlier had identified a pair of them. They were following a very faint trail that they were not even sure was the passage of a ship. It was a gamble, but what else could they go on?

Behind them was still-burning wreckage that used to be a Chohish Supply Station. And the fires lent support to that theory some credence as only an ample supply of oxygen would enable it to continue burning so long in the vacuum of space.

They had delayed another twenty hours to allow for refueling and rearming. Repairs were in progress. Some of their fighters had to be scrapped and destroyed to ensure minimal possible technology capture. Then there had to be some rest after what they had just gone through.

The lousy part also had to be done without delay, holding funeral services for lost pilots. Several recovered pilots succumbed to their injuries adding to the total loss. Services were held for all three ships so any could participate.

Jeanne landed her fighter on the Fox so she could attend the services there. Zeke led the service for all three warships from the Lucky Strike with a heavy heart.

They resumed their travel to the slipstream identified as a possible Chohish route with a solemn heart. It was going to take another fifteen hours before they reached the slipstream. Until then, all fighters were landed to allow the pilots additional rest.

"Captain, you want me to send a communication module back to the fleet on status?" asked Will.

"Send two modules, Will; we need to ensure the information gets through," Zeke answered.

With that, Zeke ordered a rotation of the shifts as they still had a way to go with no indication of immediate danger.

Everyone was exhausted from either the non-stop activity or stress. When in battle, there were no downtimes for anyone. Backups were either sent to the bunker backup command station in the middle of the ship or assisted their counterparts.

Like Ensign Selena Bonilla, Isolde's backup. Selena had been stationed in the backup command station and assisted Isolde remotely. If remotely is the proper term considering they were both on the same ship. And it was Selena who caught the anomaly. Isolde was in the process of leaving the Bridge to grab something to eat when Selena pinged her.

Rushing back toward her workstation, she grabbed Caspian by his arm to drag him along. Jumping into her seat, Isolde, still talking with Selena, searched the sensor logs from the probes for the data that had caught Selena's attention.

It took quite a few moments to find it, and it was fleeting. The probe had returned a shrouded image that disappeared within seconds just before it stopped responding.

Hawke noticed Isolde was back at her station in a heated conversation with Caspian. She had someone else on her link as he could see Isolde signal Caspian to hold one second while she spoke while keeping her finger to her ear.

Tapping Will, Hawke signaled toward Isolde.

Will, responding, coughed to get Zeke's attention, who had been in a quiet conversation with Nkosana.

Seeing Will pointing at Isolde, Zeke paused his conversation to rise from his command chair and walked over to Isolde's workstation. Standing behind her, he listened quietly for a moment before speaking.

"Something up, Isolde? What's going on?"

Without turning from her screen, Isolde brought up the image that caught Selena's attention.

"Selena noticed a quick blip of the image seen here just before the probe that sent that image went offline. Unfortunately, we have not been able to reestablish communication with that probe. That is not unheard of, as we lose them occasionally due to the probes having only minor shields to protect against dust."

"We can usually check with other probes in the same general area to see what happened. No other probe reported anything wrong or suspicious in the area. Nor were they able to capture any image like this one. Selena sent out a couple more probes to check this area out, but they have not reached that area yet."

Moving the image to one of her larger screens, Isolde enlarged the image to take up the whole screen.

"Normal process is for the probe that caught something it cannot immediately identify to signal another probe. Hopefully, other probes nearby will get an image from a different angle to update the original image into something the ship AI can recognize. But since the probe stopped immediately afterward, that did not occur."

" Selena noticed that the probe stopped sending us data, so she went through the last data section. Captain, I doubt Caspian nor

I would have seen it. Selena saw this and notified me immediately since she had no idea what it could be. The ship's AI could not identify it either."

A very faint set of images was on the screen at the nebula's edge. It was almost like they were oblong in structure, massive when appropriately scaled, but too vague to be sure. Could it be just a large grouping of dust? Then, when the image moved to the next frame, it disappeared.

"Put that up on the main screen. Let's see if that helps anyone guess what it could be?" ordered Zeke.

Many crew members stood to glance at the image once displayed on the main screen, but no one knew what it was.

As Zeke stared at the picture, that itch that he was missing, something started up.

It was then that Jeanne showed up. Zeke was looking at the image so intensely that he did not notice Jeanne was on the bridge until she sidled up next to him and put her hand in the crook of his arm. Jeanne stood there in silence, seeing Zeke entranced with whatever was on the screen.

"Whatcha looking at, my dear?" asked Jeanne after five minutes. Silently standing while waiting on someone else was not one of Jeanne's best traits. It was a miracle she had waited as long as she had.

"Hello, my love, something Selena found from a now nonfunctioning probe. Nebula distorts images regularly, so we are trying to figure out what that image could be."

Zeke stood staring at the screen as something kept telling him he should know what he was looking at.

Sighing, Zeke turned finally to hug Jeanne. "You had me scared for a while there, my dear. I should have known they would put up a fight somehow. We lost a good number of pilots."

Rubbing Zeke's arm, Jeanne looked up at him as she replied.

"It took all of us by surprise. Who would have known they still had hundreds of fighters just sitting there after losing so many? The fighter bay in that station must have been incredibly massive."

That's when it clicked. Twirling, almost throwing Jeanne away from him in haste, he stared at the screen and whispered in startlement. "*Carriers.*"

"What did he say?" asked Nkosana, who had moved next to Zeke when Jeanne had arrived.

"Carriers. I bet they are Carriers," answered Zeke, still in a whisper.

Everyone looked to Zeke as it was clear he had figured something out. Jeanne was puzzled over what he said until she caught him whispering it again. It took a few seconds before comprehension hit her.

"Of course... that is how they did it. The Chohish knew we were coming this way, so they unloaded multiple Carriers a short distance back from the slipstream to sit and wait for us powered down. The probes did not see them as it was looking for power signatures. So when the probes came through, that told them it was time to power up. They saved the fighters in the station as another surprise option that almost worked." explained Jeanne.

"Yes, they are changing their tactics. We suspected that would happen. The real question is, do they have other ships in the nebula besides Carriers? I have doubts they do, or they would have had them with the fighters when you came in, Jeanne." offered Zeke.

"Nebula, it's a good place where to hide. All that dust and gas affects scanning so much that it becomes almost useless. Are you thinking about going after them? Those Carriers could stay there for days on end, and we would have a hell of a time trying to find them." asked Will.

"We have no choice. We can't leave an unknown Chohish force hanging around our rear. We may need to come back through here in a hurry. So the question is, how are we going to smoke these babies out?" asked Zeke. "Let's go to the conference room, have something brought in to eat, and discuss our options. Isolde, ask Jax and Jamie to join us. Give them an update on the issue and ask them to bring along anyone they think may have a suggestion. Have Selena cover for you and make sure you put a note in Selena's record on catching this; I will cosign. Excellent job there."

It was only a few seconds later that Selena entered the bridge as she had already been on the way. No one saw the blush that came to Selena's face seeing everyone looking at her as she stood beside Isolde. As Isolde pinged Jamie, she leaned over to whisper into Selena's ear. "The captain is right, Selena; it was a great catch. That single action may save hundreds of lives."

Getting settled in the small conference room, the experience with the Chohish fighters had apparently drained the energy out of everyone present. Almost all slumped back in their seat or rested their forehead on the conference table.

It was quiet for a few moments before footfalls echoed from the hall. Lieutenant Commander Jax Andrews came in with a scowl on his face.

"Captain, reporting as ordered. You know we are working with Jamie's group to get all the damaged fighters repaired, right? They have many more fighters than normal and need more assistance than is available. So maybe you can ask for the correct number of fighter support personnel next trip?"

"Jax, my friend, I knew you and your group would be bored playing with all the new toys by now and would like a new challenge. It looks like from your scowl, it's working; never seen you so happy," responded Zeke with laughter

"Don't give me that crap; what can I do…" where he stopped as several people entered the room bearing sandwiches and energy drinks of all types. "Damn, you should have told me that you would have food. I am starving; I haven't eaten anything all day." Upon which Jax grabbed several sandwiches and a drink before moving to the end of the table where he put the food down before leaning against a wall while eating.

The next to enter was Caspian, followed by Isolde with Gunner at her side. The quiet laughter from Jeanne and the smiles around the group made Isolde turn quickly to see Gunner wiping lipstick off his lips. Isolde had been terrified for him when he was out fighting the Chohish and had to confirm to herself he was still alive. And a kiss sure went a long way in doing that.

Although it sure would have been nice if Gunner could share some of Isolde's embarrassment. He just stood there wiping his lips with a handkerchief streaked with red wearing a face looking puzzled by all the attention.

Almost everyone had grabbed something by the time Lieutenant Commander Jamie Chandler arrived. Walking in behind her was a man that few knew. He was of average height, with short brown hair, slim with what you would initially think were lazy eyes until they looked at you. Then it felt like those eyes pierced right through you.

Seeing who had come with Jamie, Zeke, who had sat down to eat, rose before making his way over to shake hands with the newcomer. "Everyone, I am not sure you have all met Lieutenant Commander Roy Dean. Roy and his staff are with our Bomber crews. They were part of the crew that brought the Lucky Strike back from the repair yards. And yes, Jax, they also brought along some Bomber support staff that now reports to Jamie."

"Jamie, Roy, grab something to eat and join us at the table. We have a puzzle we are trying to figure out. Not sure how much you know, but Isolde will give everyone an update before we proceed."

Everyone stood to shake Roy's hand as he passed by. All until he reached the admiral, who ignored the outstretched hand to pull the man in for a hug. "It is good to see you, my friend. My last word of you was that you were in the Perileos action. That was a rough one; glad to see you made it out. Spencer with you?"

"Been a while, Admiral; what's it been? Almost five years now, isn't it?" said Roy in a quiet voice. "The Perileos was bad, really bad. We lost a lot of good people there. Spencer is here. Still, my copilot, it wouldn't be the same without him. Spencer is like a brother that I never had. And I want to thank you, Sir, for all you did for the wife and kids. My wife said you checked up on them while I was away. Even helped them out a few times."

Seeing all the stares, the admiral started laughing. "Sorry everyone, me and Roy go way back. We were classmates at the Academy, where we became close friends. We were fortunate enough to be assigned the same carrier after graduation. I to a fighter group while Roy, a bomber squad. I cannot remember how often this crazy nut and his crew pulled our butts out of the fire. A few years later, I moved on, but Roy stayed on even though they had offered him a captaincy. You couldn't have gotten a better person for the job."

"I do not have the desire to be a captain, Admiral; I just want to fly with my crewmates. Fly my bomber with Lance. Besides, I hate useless meetings, which seems to be the major activity of officers, not counting this meeting, of course." Roy said so quietly that most could not make out what he said, but all could see the glare he gave Jamie, who silenced him with a wave of her hand.

Now that everyone expected was present, the meeting got underway. First, Isolde summarized the issue with a halo display of the Nebula side by side with the image Selena found.

Next up was Jax, who described the detrimental effect staying in the nebula has on ships but mainly on how it tore up the engines. Staying in the nebula was not a long-term solution for the Chohish carriers. Still, they could probably survive for days there long enough as the RGN fleet could not wait for them to come out.

Ideas flowed freely, but practicality eliminated most.

Saturate the nebula with probes, but due to the properties of the nebula, data would be minimal. Another downside is how many probe units would be required. They would be short of probes in the future.

Fire missiles in with timed fuses, hoping to scare the carriers out. That was deemed impractical and quickly dropped as they could not afford to waste that many missiles for a near-zero result considering the nebula's size.

Send in the fighters to find the enemy carriers, followed by the warships. Again, the nebula would allow the Chohish to hide once more before the three warships arrived.

Other ideas were suggested and dropped as impractical. Silence reigned for a few moments before a silent cough came to their attention.

"Excuse me, Captain, I hate to interrupt, but I am guessing Jamie asked me here for a reason. May I make a suggestion?" asked Roy.

Most would have waited for an ok, but Roy continued without a pause. "Send in the bombers."

"Send in the Bombers? Why would it be any different than the fighters? Please elaborate." A puzzled Hawke asked while rubbing his arms.

"Fighters alone cannot do any real damage to a Carrier if the Chohish Carriers are anything like ours." Roy stopped to point to the image still on the screen, "Which the image displayed; suggests they are. Only many fighters, all attacking at once, would be required to take a ship of that size out. But a Bomber, that is what we do." Roy said it like everyone should have known that, which Zeke agreed with as he thought more about the weapons on a bomber.

"We have a dozen bombers on the Lucky Strike. With the new

launch systems, you can deploy the Bombers over a large area in a relatively short time. The bombers have a much better detection suite than a probe. They will be affected, but we should be able to find the carriers as we navigate the Nebula. Unlike a fighter, Bombers do have the firepower to hurt a Carrier," explained a calm Lieutenant like he was instructing the first-year class at the Academy.

"And if they run, we could be waiting for them outside the Nebula if, when, they appear with all available fighters deployed. You know, that could work." an excited Will exclaimed. "How much time do you need to have your crews ready, Lieutenant Commander?"

The smile on Jamie's face answered the question for Zeke before he even heard the verbal confirmation from Roy. "How much time does it take to take a crap? Both the Bombers and crews have been ready since we entered this damn system. But I would like my crew to take a dump before they head out. We have been sitting idly by near our Bombers for a while, and we may be out there awhile. And even though the suits handle body wastes pretty good, it sure sucks having to clean them upon return." a deadpanned Roy answered.

At first, it was just a chuckle from one or two present until the absurdity of the answer finally struck home. Then the room burst into full-throated laughter, significantly so since the expression on Roy's face never changed, not one iota.

BOMBERS AWAY

SITTING IN HIS seat, Roy contemplated why he had come on this mission. Looking at his copilot, Spencer, he knew his reason was no different than the rest of the Bomber crews stationed on the cruiser. Roy still remembered when they were all sitting in the bar, drinking and toasting their lost comrades from the Perileos action. When he told the Admiral it had been bad at Perileos, he did not tell him just how bad. They had lost over half of the crew, and many others had severe injuries that they would never fly again. They had started that campaign with the regular complement of a hundred bombers and finished with enough crew to man only two dozen ships.

Half of the survivors jumped on it when the call went out for Bomber crews for this mission. They, like most in this sector, had seen the atrocities perpetrated by the Chohish. The other half were not ready to enter into something that was probably more dangerous than what they had gone through at Perileos. But Roy and the rest wanted to help; that's why they enlisted in the Navy in the first place.

So here they were, flying into a Nebula looking for Chohish Carriers. A ship they had no idea what it looked like, except for a faint image of something significant. They did not know the offensive or defensive armaments. Not going in as a group, but individual ships spread apart further than he could ever imagine, let alone experience.

"Seems like I cannot follow one of my own rules. Never volunteer! That is a good way to get killed." And yet, here he was again. *"Somehow, my wife was not surprised I would volunteer for this assignment. When she saw the dead children on Niflhel, she knew that somehow, I would be getting involved. She knew my heart would not let this go unavenged. Even though she did not want me to go, that wonderful woman did not try to stop me. She knew someone had to go, which comes with being married to a Bomber pilot with a heart and a sense of duty. But that did not mean she and the children did not cry for days before I left."*

The Bomber moved into the nebula slowly because it would be like hitting a wall if he went in at full speed. They needed to work their acceleration up gradually, giving their shields time to start creating a plow to get through. It was risky, but he had ordered the pilots to redirect all force shields toward the front. Speed was essential.

As expected, their communications and sensors got worse the further they got in. The enormous clumps of dust and gas affected everything electronically. Slowly their speed increased.

Even though the ship AI kept the temperature regulated, they still did not stop either of the pilots from sweating profusely. Roy knew it was due to the constant stress, not any heating issue. It was a sound suggestion he made, but he also knew it was risky as hell. Just the thought of a lone bomber going against a Carrier was enough to scare any pilot, let alone in an environment like this. Roy could not remember ever hearing about a lone bomber attacking a warship the size of a carrier; *hell*, he knew he would have remembered *that*.

Now moving near half speed, all they were willing to risk, they made their way through the nebula. Communication between the Bombers was intermittent at best, not that they could assist each other; the distance between them was too far. But so far, the few times they were able to chat, no one reported any sign of the Carriers.

An hour passed, then another. Roy slowed down as they came up to a very dense dust cloud. This spot would be a perfect area where a Carrier could hide. But if he went in to check it out, he would be almost blind; he doubted that would be the same for the Carrier.

Turning to the side, he slowed even further. Then, turning once again, he faced the dense cloud directly. Looking at Spencer, there was no need to tell him what he would do. They had been partners for years; they knew each other's moves like it was their own. Without being told, Spencer armed the missiles snuggled in their cradles for proximity detonation.

"Hang on, my friend, we may be stirring up a hornet's nest," Rob said as he fired a brace of missiles into the densest part of the cloud.

Bracing themselves, they watched the tail of the missiles disappear in the dust. Then, expecting the rockets to take a few minutes before they detected any large object, both were surprised by the massive explosion just seconds after disappearing in the cloud.

Frantically, Roy sent another pair following the path of the others. Meanwhile, Spencer turned the ship around to head them away from the blasts. Unfortunately, they had not gone far when another explosion lit up the area, followed by a massive object approaching them.

"Send out the signal; they are all here. It looks like the nebula is affecting the Chohish defensive systems. They cannot lock onto the missiles." said a frantic Roy as they watched several large shapes head around the first carrier that was leaking flame and debris from the front and side. "So much for going slow."

The bomber raced away while alarms shrilled loudly due to the dust impacting the hull as the dust overwhelmed the shields.

Suddenly, the Bomber shook violently as the damaged Carrier exploded violently. "What the hell?" yelled Spencer.

"Gas from the Nebula," Roy yelled while taking over flight control. "That is what is going to happen to us if we take a hit," Rob said while he took evasive maneuvers. Not having time to take his hands off the jerking steering stick, he yelled, "Fire some more missiles, dammit!"

Two more Carriers came lumbering toward them. The image on the screens showed several vast dust clouds being pushed rapidly toward them. Roy, straining to keep the Bomber flying straight, was glad he had taken a dump before he left, although he doubted anything could come out as his sphincter was closed tight in fear.

Spencer fired another pair and another until there were no more missiles to fire.

The Carriers were too large to miss, even with the missile guidance being affected by the nebula. Hit after hit rolled behind the bomber as the Carriers kept coming at them. Anyone watching would have seen a dense cloud of dust with flames spewing out between the dust particles. Suddenly, one started slewing sideways while slowing down. Surprisingly, against everything the Chohish had done before, the other Carrier followed suit to stay even with it.

Both Carriers were still moving but at a much slower speed. When just as Roy thought they would get away, both turned back, following the Bomber. Roy knew they could not outrun the carrier even at the reduced rate.

"They know they need to get rid of us, or their positions will be known, although I do not know how our people could have already missed the explosions and fire." Spencer theorized.

The Bomber flew on, but they both knew they were flying too fast. The warning lights looked like a Christmas tree. But the ones that concerned Roy the most were the engine and hull integrity lights. Both indicated imminent failure.

"Come on, baby, just a little more..." Roy said as he felt the ship shred some armor. More and more pieces followed. He knew his time was over. The Carriers may not have any weapons available, but they would run right over them. There wouldn't be enough pieces large enough left to identify what it had been.

With a loud whine, then bang, the engines shut down. Knowing there were only a few minutes left before their forward momentum died, Roy glanced at Spencer, who shrugged helplessly. The situation for them looked hopeless. Bombers pilots were not known to have a long shelf life. Roy was glad he had finally finished the long-overdue letter for his wife and children before coming on this trip. He knew the admiral would see it was delivered if he did not come back.

They watched helplessly as the dust cloud barreled down on them as the bomber slowed.

Suddenly, something huge came flying between them and the Carriers. And it was spitting out missiles by the dozens. The Carriers swung wide, trying to hide in the dust, but the new ship followed with no let-up.

Sections of the Carriers fell away in large chunks, but the Carriers flew on, dogged by the newcomer. One of the Carriers had a large explosion before slowing down and stopping altogether. Surprisingly, the other Carrier slewed to the side, trying to protect the now motionless, damaged Carrier.

It was not to be. The Bomber AI could not understand the garbled transmission that came through the speakers; nevertheless, Roy would recognize Isolde's voice anywhere. How the hell did the Lucky Strike get here? Regardless, the explosions that rocked the

Bomber notified them that the Carriers were going nowhere. Then again, at the moment, neither were they.

Drifting would not usually overly concern him, except the flashing red lights indicated more systems were shutting down. If the shields went down, it would not take long before the larger dust particles penetrated the hull. Their suits would not be a hindrance except to contain the blood leaking from holed dead bodies.

Typically, they could reroute power from one unneeded system to another to get around a power failure in a particular system. In this case, the central power core fed all the systems. There was nothing they could do except hope that someone came to rescue them.

The current situation reminded him of another when he was a young teenager. He had been with his grandfather restoring an antique car that was hundreds of years old. A hobby his grandfather loved to do with his grandchildren. They were both working on a rusted bolt when a wrench slipped from his grandfather's hand to fall and landed on Roy's foot. As Roy screamed in pain, he straightened up only to smack his head against the hood. Meanwhile, his grandfather, now off balance, slipped on some oil where he fell against the car. The car fell off the jacks, then slid to smack against the wall.

After they spent a good bit of time putting it all back in place, his grandfather tried once more to loosen the bolt, only for the bolt to break off. Roy still can remember how his grandfather looked at him in amusement after Roy said the car was jinxed.

"No, it is just Murphy's Law. Anything that can go wrong will go wrong." his grandfather stated. But as bad as the day had been going, it ended up being a great day. They got the bolt out and replaced it, and his girlfriend showed up just as they finished replacing it. She saw bleeding from the bump on his head where she left to get some ice from his grandmother without saying a word. When his girlfriend returned, she hung on his shoulder, holding the ice

against his head. He described all the work they had completed and what was still pending. Then she asked if she could help, and all three spent the next several hours working, sweating, swearing but loving every minute of it.

His grandfather later told him that things happen. When they happen all at once, people blame it all on Murphy's Law. But he also said that you should not let it discourage you as it may also be why something extraordinary happens. He said this part smiling as my girlfriend was hanging on my arm, examining my bruised head with her fingers. We married two years later.

The change of the alarm tone jerked Roy out of his daydreams. The warning tone change was the final warning before the power shut off. The failure came quickly after the notice; he wondered why they even bothered setting the alarm. But he knew whose fault it was; it had to be Murphy's Law.

Blind, no power, drifting, what else could go wrong. Roy quickly found out. A speck of dust blasted right through the hull on one side and out the other. On the way, it passed through Roy's leg and left a pair of holes in his suit in its wake.

Hobbling to one of the storage containers to grab repair patches, he was startled to see a shuttle through one of the portholes. He stared in amazement as he saw another pass by to take up a position near the ship's rear. *"What the hell are they doing?"* thought Roy.

Limping back to his seat, he saw Spencer looking out another porthole where a third shuttle was visible. The whole thing was getting stranger and stranger. The noise from the front of the bomber indicated they were connecting a tow cable. In this soup, a tractor beam would be unreliable.

With his mind so foggy, it took a bit, but he figured out why all the shuttles. I wonder if Lance figured it out? He sure has been quiet. The shuttles are using their shields to protect the Bomber. *"Smart, genius. Wonder who thought of that?"* wondered Rob. But he had no time to think about that as he could feel the blood leaking down the suit's pant leg. *"Yep, it has to be Murphy's Law,"* was Roy's final thought before he passed out.

"Ow... damn... where am I?" Roy thought hazily. He felt so tired. His leg throbbed and hurt like hell, so he knew he was alive. The light was so bright; it came right through his closed eyes. *"Well, I know I am not at the pearly gates; I hurt too friggin much."* Roy tried hard to open his eyes, but they felt so heavy that he failed.

He wiggled his hands, which told him he was lying on sheets. Again, he tried one more time to open his eyes. They opened just enough to see he was lying in a medical pod. He let his head fall to the side and saw he was not alone. There were dozens of others, most occupied.

"Well, look who finally woke up; about time."

Squinting, Roy saw Dr. Javier Preruet standing next to his pod while entering something into a hand-held device.

"You had us scared there for a moment, Lieutenant. Another five minutes and the captain would have to write your wife and children a long, sad letter." Doc said as he injected something into his leg.

"What? What happened? How did I get here? Spencer? How is Spencer?" he asked weakly.

"Why they beamed you across, of course. The aliens got the transporter working just in time," answered Doc smartly.

Comprehension was long in coming. Roy's head was so foggy. *"Transporter? Aliens? Huh? What the hell is he talking about?"*

"They pulled your Bomber back into the bay, where they pulled you and Spencer out. You had very little blood left. That piece of rock nipped an artery. Your Bomber will be stripped for parts as it is now officially a piece of junk." Doc responded.

"How did Lucky Strike know where we were? Did we get all

the Carriers? Who thought of using the shuttle's shields? Who....?"
Roy rattled weakly.

Holding his hand up to pause all the questions, Doc replied. "Whoa there, my friend, you are asking questions I cannot answer. It would help if you held those until after you get some rest. I do not think you paid attention to me earlier; you were just mere minutes from death. And if your cluttered mind cannot remember where you are, you are in my medical bay. Where I have undisputed jurisdiction—got that? I will let Jamie know you are awake. Maybe, and that depends on you implicitly following my instructions, I will have her stop by when she gets a free moment where you can ask her all the questions you want."

About to answer, Roy could see by Doc's expression that arguing would be useless. Besides, he had no energy to put up a fight. Sighing deeply, he relented what his body was telling him and allowed himself to sleep.

He would have seen Doc look down at him in sorrow if he had stayed awake. *"I could not tell him that Spencer did not make it. A group of rock dust, no larger than a grain of sand, went through him in dozens of places before the Shuttles could fully envelop the Bomber with their shields. I do not envy Jamie on this one. When Spencer got it, I heard they were seconds away from completing the envelope."*

GOODBYE

THE MOOD ON the Bridge was subdued by the feeling of loss at the death of Lieutenant Spencer Hamilton. To lose Lance by just seconds was hard to take. The only comfort they could take was they were able to save Lieutenant Commander Roy Dean. And that had been a miracle to get him back in time.

Spencer was not the only one lost; it was just how close they missed saving him. Per the shuttles AI, it was just a few seconds. The nebula caused the shield envelope to fluctuate just before it solidified around the Bomber. That fluctuation was when the dust ripped through the Bomber and killed Spencer.

The other Bombers came out of the nebula without issue except for some heavy pitting from the dust. Not detecting any other Chohish ships in the nebula led them to hope the three Carriers were the only ones present.

The small fleet headed again toward the slipstream they hoped would lead them to the Chohish home systems. It would take them at least twenty-some hours to reach the slipstream as the fight in the nebula had taken them further away.

The three ships headed onward with no fighter escort. Zeke had the system flooded with plenty of probes, so he believed they should get plenty of warning if any danger presented itself. The pilots desperately needed some rest if they were going to maintain their effectiveness, so they were grounded until required.

Then there were the fighters themselves. Most needed repairs, some so damaged they would have to be replaced. Replacement fighters were available in crates. However, it took many hours to unpack, reassemble and run the necessary tests before they put a pilot in one.

With Will on the Bridge, Zeke decided he had time to visit the sick bay. Walking out, he was surprised that both Jeanne and Nkosana joined him. They were somber as they entered the lift, thinking of where they were going and why.

Exiting the lift, they presently entered the medical bay. The number of injured surprised them even though they knew how rough it had been. The numbers they expected did not correlate with the number they now saw. It was always like this. Seeing all the injured brought the numbers to life.

Each of the three managed it differently. Where Nkosana would talk to the wounded about how proud the RGN was of each individual, Zeke would ask how they were or what they needed.

Both wished they had the skill or compassion to do it as Jeanne did. Jeanne would swirl in a dance around the patients, with laughter effortlessly rolling off her lips while stopping by one here or there to ask about their family with compassion. Where Jeanne went, there were smiles and laughter left behind.

All until the three met up with Roy. Even though Roy had blood transfusions, he still looked pale and ghoulish-looking. But Zeke did not think that blood loss was the only reason. The vacant look in Roy's eyes spoke of personal loss.

Even as Zeke stood beside the pod, Roy never spoke but nodded.

"Hi Roy, how are you doing?" asked Zeke.

"I am doing better. But I cannot get anyone around here to

update me on Spencer. When that happens, it becomes obvious; that he did not make it. He didn't, did he?" responded Roy with sorrow.

Keeping his eye contact steady, Zeke answered. "No, Roy, I am sorry to say he did not. The shields on the shuttles were negatively affected by the nebula. It fluctuated before fully deploying around the Bomber. Multiple dust particles got through."

They watched as Roy closed his eyes and shuddered. "Sorry, Captain, Spencer and I had been through a lot. We always thought we would go together in one quick blast. Best copilot you could ever have."

"Nothing to be ashamed of, Roy. Most here have it, survivor's guilt. You also have to think of what you two accomplished. You two took on three carriers, unheard up for a single Bomber, and obliterated one while seriously damaging another. We will never know how many personnel you two saved. Spencer and yourself will go down in the military history books."

That did bring a small smile to Roy's face. "Spencer always joked about making the military journals. We would go down as the Bomber crew who had the stinky bombs. Spencer had intestine damage from an earlier engagement. Made the scrubbers work overtime, if you know what I mean. He would like to know he made the journals for something else."

"Captain, maybe you can help with something puzzling me. How did you know where we were? How did you get there so fast? And who had the brilliant idea of using the shuttle's shields?"

Sitting on the lip of the medical pod, Zeke regarded Ropy before he answered. "You can thank

Lieutenant Commander Andrews, you may know him as Jax for finding you. Knowing you would go into the Nebula, the Commander installed a drone transponder for all the bombers and an extender. They boosted the bomber's transponder's power to allow the signals to get through the Nebula. Not perfectly, intermittently still, but enough to give us an idea of where you all were. I thought the Chohish would head to the heaviest dust clouds, so I positioned the Lucky Strike inside the nebula as close to the densest one as we could detect. So we left the destroyers with all the fighters in case they came out elsewhere. Once your transponder showed you were slowing down, we headed for your position at the best possible speed."

"Damn, that was some good planning. And the shuttles?"

"I think you met Lieutenant Morison? If you haven't, you should stop by and see him when you get out of here. You two are much alike. Once he saw your transponder start fading out, Gunner realized you were losing power. He has had some experience being in a nebula while flying a fighter. So anyway, he got with Lieutenant Commander Chandler, who deployed all available shuttles to find you so they could extend their shields to encompass your bomber."

"One more question, Captain; this one is for me. I will understand if you do not want to answer." Roy asked this as he looked directly at the Admiral. "Is it normal for staff to do these things without going through you first? I ask, sir, as most ships I have been on have a stick-in-the-mud officer that only goes by the book. Excuse me, Admiral, but that be the damn truth," even though he showed no signs that he gave a crap what the Admiral thought.

"To answer your question, Lieutenant, I expect this of them. You know, as well as I do, that parameters change on the fly once you engage. They are experts in their fields; I trust their decisions. They took the necessary actions at the time, as they did in your case; not all decisions can wait for my approval. Make sense?"

"Yes, it does. And one, I am glad to hear. It has been a while since I reported to a commander that trusted their officers. If it is ok with you, I may stick around for a bit." a sad Roy asked.

Smiling, Zeke patted Roy on the shoulder as he turned to look at the Admiral and Jeanne. "Works for me; we can use your help. Besides, it's not like we can drop you off anywhere right now. Unless, of course, we find another Chohish station. We can drop you off there if you want."

That brought a smile to Roy. "You know, you sound a bit like Spencer. He would say something smartass like that to me all the time."

"Get well, Lieutenant; we need people like you. You will fit in nicely with this crew. I would stick around, but the faster we find out where the Chohish comes from, the sooner we can go home. Until later, Lieutenant." with that, all three walked away.

As they walked out of the medical bay, with Jeanne and Zeke's arms wrapped around each other, Roy saw the rest of the injured smile and wave as they walked by. "*You know, at first, I thought what I heard about this Captain was the same old crap I hear every time I get reassigned to a new ship, only to find out it was hype all over again. I know what the news reported, but everyone knows how those articles get manipulated. But the injured do not hide their feelings; they have suffered enough without putting up with incompetent officers. You left too early, Spencer; I think you would have liked it here. Goodbye, my friend.*" Roy laid back on the bed to dream of the past when he had his friend by his side.

SURPRISE

THE HOURS WENT by with no further incidents. Shifts changed, and repairs progressed. Crews rested while others worked frantically, and all the while, the three ships moved closer to the slipstream.

The ship shuddered as fighters repeatedly launched before the shields went up. Walking onto the Bridge, Zeke and Jeanne took their seats in silence. Nodding to Nkosana and the ever-present Marines, they watched as a group of fighters took point with another smaller group following.

While waiting, Zeke conferred with Nkosana on the plans for entering the next system. "We are going to send in two sets of probes. Hopefully, the first set will get a quick scan and trigger any Chohish hiding to power up and start moving when the probes leave. The second set is to see what the first triggered if anything. Unless, of course, the first set of probes found something."

"Glad you decided to hang with us here, Jeanne. Why the change?" asked Will.

"I have been getting pestered by the Fox crew to knock it off. Finally, my sis gave me an earful. Said I scared the crap out of her the last time, and if I did not do it voluntarily, she would do something about it. That will teach you, Will, about having too many of your family and friends on your ship."

That was all she got out when they were interrupted by the sound of marching. Jeanne looked at Michale to see if the Marine knew what was happening. More Marines? Upon seeing no expression change other than a slight smile, she knew he knew what was happening but would not spill the beans.

She groaned when she saw who entered the Bridge leading a four-person squad of Irracan Marines, all in full Marine armor and armed.

Sergeant Jan de Bouff marched up to Jeanne's chair, directing all four Irracan Marines to circle her chair. Once all were in position, shoe magnetics sounded loud in the sudden quiet.

"I was reminded, in no uncertain terms, mind you, that I have been lax in my duties, Captain de Clisson. Per orders from Commander Anne Dieu-Le-Veut, I am to ensure you do not get in a fighter nor go anywhere without an Irracan Marine escort. No offense Corporal Lance."

"Understand, Sir, no offense taken. But I have not been relieved of my duties either, so I will also be part of the protection detail." a calm Corporal responded. Jeanne would swear he was close to laughter.

"Jan, I outrank my sister. This stupid order is rescinded effective immediately." a flustered Jeanne responded with outrage. It would have sounded better if not for the outright laughter from Hawke, who got a severe stare from Jeanne.

"The orders come from your uncle relayed through your brothers, Dante, Stewart, and Javier before we left. They were given to Commander Dieu-Le-Veut to be executed at her discretion when she, and she alone, felt it was necessary. It seems your uncle knows your prerogative to throw yourself in danger. No offense, Captain, but the orders stand."

When Zeke grabbed her arm, Jeanne was about to jump out of her seat to get in Jan's face. "We do not have time for this, Jeanne; we are just minutes away from the slipstream."

"Damn you, Jan; I know you timed this, so I could not fight it. Remember this when you find Dragon ants in your bed," Jeanne stated.

"Thanks for the warning, Captain; I will inform Major Richards. Although I know I would not want to piss her off, she's not very big into jokes, but it's your choice." Jan said with a massive grin on his face. The four Irracan Marines shrugged when Jeanne looked at them.

"Enough, all of you. We are here," ordered Zeke sternly.

"First series of probes launched, Captain," Caspian announced. Probes shot in front of the fleet, where they spread out into a line far apart from each other.

Everyone watched as the probes moved toward and then entered the slipstream. They continued toward the slipstream. Minutes passed.

"Second set of probes is ready to be deployed," announced Caspian.

Minutes ticked by before the first set of probes returned.

The Bridge was quiet except for Isolde and Selena. They were frantically reading the data from the first set of probes.

"Captain, there are four destroyer-sized ships and dozens of fighters about fifteen minutes from our planned entry point," Selena reported nervously.

As they moved onward, Isolde hurriedly added. "Captain, further back, dozens of ships are not in our database. They look a bit smaller than one of our frigates. They are moving in a coordinated manner that is in the process of turning around. It looks like they saw our probes. They are moving slower than the Chohish ship's normal max speed."

"Continue, enter the slipstream as planned. Have the Bombers deploy once in the system, but hold in position behind us," ordered Zeke. "Isolde, send us the details on these new ships. Jeanne, if you would. Caspian, hold the second set of probes."

"Meghan, Lance, let the Lucky Strike take the lead. You two hang back a little and come at them from the sides. I cannot stress enough. Stay away from them. I believe they are desperate until they can bring up additional forces. Be careful of ramming. Lieutenant Morison, concentrate on the fighters coming at us. Lieutenant Barbarossa, once through that group, your fighters are on ship protection. Do not let any of those fighters through."

"All probes recovered," uttered Caspian.

Then the fighters entered the slipstream, followed by the rest of the fleet, following less than a minute behind.

The first fighter came out of the slipstream with Gunner at the helm. Dizziness occupied him for a few seconds before he could check his scans. The AI would have alerted him if he was in immediate danger. A quick scan saw no enemy in the immediate area but numerous blips moving toward him. What was different from prior engagements was that half of the fighters had returned to screen the destroyers, which had grouped into a four-point diamond.

As other fighters came through, Gunner instructed them to pair up in groups of eight. "Group A through Group F, create a line two deep. The second line targets any that may try and force their way through without scrimmaging. Groups G and H are to stay behind the other groups and catch any that may get through but keep your distance from Groups A through F. We outnumber them three to one. Too many RGN fighters in one area can work for the enemy."

The lead group of the Chohish fighters merged into one compact group. Gunner noticed they changed direction to match Fox's new position.

He knew they should have seen the change going to the

designated channel for his fighters, but no harm in stating the obvious. "I am sure you saw the same thing I did. They are going after the Fox. Let's show them that we have other ideas." with that, Gunner pushed his fighter in a new direction.

It was not long before they were in missile range. Many of Gunners' prior captains argued with him constantly about leading his team from the front but staying back was not his style. Instead, he was able to segment out all the icons at the same time as engaging with enemy fighters. Somehow being out front sharpened his focus while engaged, enabling him to see the overall picture more clearly. Only Captain Kinsley seemed to understand and never asked him to change.

Gunner headed toward the lead fighter triggering a pair of fire-and-forget missiles. He watched as his missiles passed by several rockets fired by his opponent.

Going into a sharp turn, he released chaff and EMC. One missile flew off after the electronic chaff, but the second stuck to his tail. Hitting the afterburner, he went into a tight spiral releasing additional chaff. That did the trick.

Coming out of the spiral, he checked his scanners to see that the fighter who fired them was no longer registering. His missiles must have destroyed it. But without stopping to check, he made a beeline for another pair just off to the side.

Barreling toward a pair, he fired his plasma lasers on both sides of his cockpit. Both the fighters split into separate directions. One came at him directly; the other swung to the side. He went into a loose spiral after the one heading straight toward him, so he never presented a steady target. He also saw that none of the enemy fighters had yet made it through to Group G or H.

Keeping a side-eye on the icon for the second Chohish fighter, he punched his afterburners to bring his fighter over the top of the Chohish fighter. Jerking on his control stick, he swung around in a wild whipping motion to face the rear of the enemy fighter. Fighting back the blackness that threatened to overtake him, he, now traveling backward, held his plasma triggers down. He tracked the plasma bolts through the back of the fighter. It took several hits before it got through the shields. Nonetheless, they finally did, the fighter exploding with no pilot ejection.

Not forgetting the second fighter, Gunner saw it was heading toward him. Turning in a full half-circle, he again punched his afterburners to regain his speed. The inertia dampers whined as they tried to compensate for the sudden changes, but the extreme pressure on his chest let him know there was a limit. Holding his breath until the tension eased, he fired another fire-and-forget missile. Lining up his fighter, he fired his plasma guns.

The Chohish fighter, trying to evade the plasma shots, ran right into the missile's path, which exploded once in proximity. The shields held, but the Chohish pilot, rocked by the blast, could not react fast enough to a second RGN fighter as it swooped in to blast through the shields making slag out of both the fighter and pilot.

"I was afraid you had fallen asleep, Librada. I know you had a golden birthday last week," teased Gunner.

"I was just overwhelmed watching the great Gunner Morison do his thing. Then I remembered all the paperwork I would have to fill out if I let you get blown away." teased back Lieutenant Librada Hindman

Checking his scanners, he saw no more Chohish icons in the immediate area. The only Chohish fighters left were grouped around the Destroyers. Checking his group, he saw two RGN fighter icons missing, but he saw two ejection pod icons on the side monitor. They would need combat search and rescue, better known as CSAR, out quickly before leaving too far from the field of action.

But first, the mission comes before any other request. "Captain, your orders?"

"Lieutenant Morrison, regroup your fighters behind Lieutenant Barbarossa. After dealing with the fighters, Lieutenant Barbarossa will join the main fleet in attacking the four destroyers. Captain de Clisson believes the fleeing ships resemble our tugboats based on the power readings. We cannot detect any offensive or defensive signatures except for half a dozen ships that seem to be a protective screen. These last are slightly larger than a fighter. Jeanne believes that this group was on their way to get that station we took out. Once we engage, have your group take out those ships. I do not want any getting away to give additional warning of our presence. Captain out."

Knowing the Captain would not expect an answer, he went to his com to check in with his group leaders. "Status check."

"Carolyn and Santiago had to eject. Carolyn is ok, but Santiago is not responding. His pod is registering that he is seriously wounded. Drugs are being administered, and the suit is compressing the wound area, but he is still slowly losing blood pressure. I need a dust-off for him ASAP. Several ships in all the groups have minor damage. However, they are still operable." responded Ramiro Fletcher, lead pilot of Group B.

"Get with the Fox about dispatching CSAR; they are closest to us. Lieutenant Barbarossa can escort them back after they take care of the fighters around the destroyers. Leave several fighters to watch over the pods. The rest, well, we have other fish to fry."

Glad to be given another task, Gunner wished he could explain his passion for flying to Isolde. The thrill that flows through his entire body as he felt the pressure when he made sharp turns. How alive he felt when facing off against another fighter. Isolde wished Gunner would step away from being a fighter pilot. Still, he could not imagine anything else that would bring the feeling of being so alive, except, of course, when he was with her.

As he and his fighters swung around behind Lieutenant

Barbarossa's group, he watched as the Lucky Strike and the rest of the task force headed toward the Chohish. The Fox and Jackal swing wide while the Lucky Strike leads straight in.

It was rare that Gunner got to sit and watch a battle unfold. He had flown with Lieutenant Hayreddin Barbarossa before and knew he was good. And the Lieutenant confirmed that once more. Hayreddin positioned himself in the front and middle of the fighter groups. He watched as the fighters broke off in pairs and went after the Chohish together.

He had considered that tactic since he outnumbered the Chohish, but he had too many new pilots who had not flown with their partners as a team. Individually, they were good. But working together in pairs required a lot of training until you knew what the other would do without thought. Even though each pilot teamed up with a wingman, they did not have the experience of working together to work as one, unlike Librada and himself. Librada has been his wingmate for many years. And Librada was just as good as he was. But someday, between Librada and himself, they would make it happen for the rest of the new pilots.

Hayreddin's fighters were all Irracans and had been flying together for years. They were good, very good. And Jeanne was the best of the lot. But he knew one individual that was better than himself or Librada, the best he had ever seen in combat. And he saw an awful lot of pilots in action during his career.

Although Zeke did not fly a fighter anymore, you had to have seen him in action when he was a fighter pilot to realize just how good he was. And Gunner should know; he was never Zeke's wingman as much as he would like to have been but flew in his fighter group for years. Zeke and his wingman at the time, Lieutenant Vicky Wright, flew as if they shared the same mind. It was like watching a pair of fighters weave a dance, a very deadly dance, mind you, but still, something beautiful to watch.

Most of Hayreddin's fighters were in front of the Lucky Strike, with much smaller groups around the RGN destroyers. But now, Hayreddin and his pilots showed Gunner what he hoped he could make one day out of his group.

They flew in pairs in a tight spiral around the Cruiser. When the Lucky Strike started firing anti-ship missiles on the enemy Destroyers, the fighters fired their afterburners to trail behind the rockets.

While the Chohish fighters concentrated on taking out the missiles, the Irracans focused on taking out the Chohish fighters. In minutes, it was apparent who would come out on top.

The Irracan fighters twirled like they were caught in a tornado and fired their plasma guns in tandem, forcing the Chohish, in their effort to avoid one, to run into the other. When a Chohish fighter fired their missile, one of the Irracan pair would lead the missile off while the other took on the Chohish fighter in close combat. And there, the skill of Irracan pilots showed dramatically.

It was not long before Gunner saw that Chohish fighters were losing the battle; they could not compete against the Irracans. Gunner noticed that the Irracans had not used any of their missiles, and he smiled as he knew why they were saving them. Now, though, it was time for the Capital ships.

A Destroyer matched up against a Cruiser, one on one, would be a long shot at best. But four Destroyers against a lone Cruiser was a different game entirely. But the Lucky Strike was not alone, which soon became very evident.

The four Chohish Destroyers came at the Lucky Strike head-on. The Lucky Strike, though, did not play their game. Instead, it did a quick port turn while constantly firing its much longer-range missiles. Between the four destroyers, they made short work of these missiles. But the additional rockets from the two RGN Destroyers paralleling them were more than they could handle.

Shortly, one missile got through to one of the Chohish

Destroyers. Gases started venting from the Chohish Destroyer, but it was not out of action. Instead, it continued onward, trying to catch the Lucky Strike.

It was then the Irracan fighters showed why they had saved their missiles. They all came barreling toward that one Destroyer, where every fighter fired a missile to coincide with the rockets from the Cruiser and Destroyers. Obviously, there was coordination between the RGN Capital ships and the fighters. All the ships had changed their targeting to the one Chohish Destroyer, so all the missiles hit simultaneously.

The Chohish Destroyer erupted in explosions, again and again. It was left a drifting wreck that Gunner doubted had any survivors. Gunner and his groups went to the side to bypass the primary fight to head off the new ships. As he passed, he saw that without the fourth Destroyer, the protective missile envelope for the Chohish destroyers degraded.

The Chohish should have tried to disengage and retreat, although Gunner did not think that would have saved them even though they did not take that action. Not when a new factor joined the equation, the RGN bombers.

They had been sitting by patiently waiting for their turn. Now the Bombers entered the scene and fired at one designated Chohish Destroyer in coordination with the Capital ships. Again, explosions rocked the Chohish Destroyer before it exploded from an overloaded reactor.

The two remaining Destroyers finally broke off chasing the Lucky Strike. They had not been able to gain any ground on the Cruiser with its new engines, so they swung toward one of the Destroyers. But Gunner knew that was going to be a futile gesture. They were now vastly outgunned by the two RGN Destroyers and Cruiser, let alone the RGN fighters and bombers, which still had missiles available. None of the ships would get within energy nor ramming range.

As he got closer to the group he was chasing, he saw the half dozen ships that the Lucky Strike identified as having weapons, separate from the other vessels.

"Beulah and Bertha, your turn now. Let's keep this to a missile duel if possible, as we have no detail on these new ships' toughness. Instead, take your two groups in, but be careful. Any fighters in Groups A through F still have missiles left; stand by, and be ready to add their rockets to the mix."

Beulah and Bertha, known affectionately as the B & B duo, were part of a fighter group that had come out with Rear Admiral Nkosana Okeke. From the short time they had flown with him, he could tell they had experience with no small amount of skill. That is why Gunner had left them with their original group, covering their rears when they met the Chohish fighters when they entered the system. Now he could see if they performed up to his expectations.

He was not disappointed. Beulah had her group swoop to port while Bertha took her group to starboard. The half dozen Chohish ships headed straight toward Gunner and the other fighters who had slowed to watch. Beulah and Bertha had their groups hit their afterburners toward the enemy. They each released one missile, then another, before turning sharply away.

What came as a surprise was the lack of adequate shielding on the Chohish ships. Being half a dozen times larger than a Chohish fighter, he had expected better protection from these new ships. No chaff, ECM missiles, with very minimal shielding. Half were flaming wreckage before the second missile even hit. But all were gutted and drifting after the second missile. What shocked him the most, though, were all the bodies tumbling out of the wreckage—many more than what was needed to run the ship.

Concentrating now on the ships in the far distance, he was

puzzled when he saw the vessels start slowing down. They did not change direction, just slowly come to a halt to hang motionless in space. So what the heck was going on?

"Not sure what we got here, people, no idea what the hell is going on. I am going to get closer. Split up, surround, and destroy any that start moving again. Gunner out."

Flying cautiously, Gunner kept his foot on the pedal for his afterburners. Before he reached maximum missile range, he was surprised to hear a noise coming in through his speakers. At first, it was overridden by static, but enough came through to let him know someone was trying to communicate with him.

"Lieutenant Gunner Morison here, please repeat...."

Zeke stood up from his command chair so he could stretch to relieve the cramps he was feeling in his back. He needed to get his back looked at sometime soon. It was bothering him too often lately. Without glancing around, he could feel the Admiral's and Jeanne's glare. The battle with the Destroyers and the fighters went much better than he could have ever hoped. But now, he was concerned as he saw Gunner's fighters sitting motionless surrounding the odd-looking Chohish ships.

Walking to Isolde's workstation, Zeke leaned in to ask her a question when a signal came in from Gunner's fighter.

"It's a video message for you, Captain." a surprised Isolde said as she looked at him with wide, open eyes.

"Put it up on the main screen Isolde." directed Zeke.

"Video on the main screen, sir."

The video showed the inside of a fighter with a pilot in an RGN flight suit. It was obvious who was on as you could see his nametag on his helmet and suit. It also helped that the helmet's visor was set to opaque where Gunner's face was visible. The expression on his face was unreadable, but that changed when the video connection cleared up. Zeke would swear Gunner was about to laugh.

Without warning, another image popped up next to Gunner's, this one of a broad squarish grey-skinned face covered in wrinkles. Thin brown hair hung down over the forehead just above the eyes whose lenses protruded outward. Underneath the eyes were three holes that fluttered. Now, all on the bridge had seen aliens before and were not shocked by what they saw. What did surprise everyone, though, was the image had a mouth similar to a human's, which was currently open in a huge grin."

"Lieutenant Morrison here, sir. I asked for a video feed to introduce Uv'ei of the Kolqux to you. I did not think an audio report would do it justice."

NEW ALLIES

THE SHIP WAS abuzz as the captain walked through the hallway toward one of the small fighter bays. Entering, Zeke was amazed at how small it was in comparison to the old bay. This new bay could hold a few fighters or shuttles but was not even close to the enormous size of the original. Then again, the earlier design only supported a fraction of the current ship's capacity for fighters, let alone having bombers.

Walking further into the bay, he saw several damaged ships repositioning on the rail system to send it deeper into the ship where the new larger bays resided. He was pleased with how well the new setup worked. Normally such a new system would encounter several significant issues that required being sent back to the shipyard. But so far, they had only identified minor ones that Jax and Jamie's engineering crews were able to resolve.

But what he saw waiting for him amazed him even more—floored him. Even though they had found evidence to support a new race, meeting one so soon after the Chohish was unexpected. He knew without uncertainty that the next few moments could affect how the whole war went, so he needed to pull himself together.

Gathering himself together as he walked, though, was a bit

difficult, as the noise from the metal soles of seven marines was so intrusive into his thoughts. But most of all, the excited chatter from Jeanne, Hawk, and Jan was even worse. It took all he could to not yell at them to shut up, but he did not think Nkosana, who was quiet as a mouse, would appreciate an officer losing his cool.

In the distance, he could see Gunner standing next to Jamie and an armored-up Khaleesi. They were not alone. Another half dozen armored marines were standing around the bay, but what was occupying his attention was the pair of miniature figures standing between Gunner and Khaleesi.

LS1 had informed him that the Kolqux ships were sitting idle on his way here. They were in a powered-down state reasonably far from the RGN ships except for the one that sat inside this bay. It was a blockish-looking ship with no distinctive features. One exception is the rear of the vessel.

What he saw on the rear of that ship was something he was very familiar with. The end of the vessel had a substantial solid eyelet made out of metal. RGN tugboats had the same feature. Tugboats would use tractor beams on most occasions. Still, adding a towing cable for backup might be necessary, as he had recently witnessed when they pulled the powerless wrecked Lucky Strike to the repair yard.

Getting closer, he could hear the newcomers speaking nonstop. Both were similar outfits. Their clothes were a loosely buttoned shirt over large platoon pants held up by a rope tie. Looking at Gunner and Jamie, he could see they were trying to say something but were constantly interrupted.

Walking up to stand next to Gunner, it was a few seconds before Gunner could interrupt the two strangers long enough to introduce Zeke.

"Please... one sec... excuse me... please... excuse me... let me introduce Captain Zeke Kinsley. He is the captain of this ship and in charge of this operation."

Only the seriousness of the situation kept Zeke from cracking a smile seeing the frustration on Gunner's face mirrored on Jamie's. Zeke had trouble keeping a straight face when he looked over through Khaleesi's opaque faceplate, where he saw her eyes roll when she saw him.

No sooner than Gunner introduced Zeke, the two turned to him and started barraging him with unending chatter. Luckily LS1 could interpret what they were saying to him through the ear insert he put in before coming to the bay.

"Are you the captain? Good to meet you. We are Uv'ek and Uv'ei. We are brothers. It is nice to meet you. Are you at war with the Chohish? Will you win? We are excited to see you. We hope you can help our people. We want your help. Please…" and on and on with no break.

Raising his hands in what he hoped was the universal sign for '*wait*,' he saw both of the Kolqux shrink back in terror. The pair of Kolqux started chattering at each other excitedly nonstop. He understood what had happened. "No, no, no offense. That is our universal peace sign."

The two Kolqux looked at each other again before they panicked and started chattering all over again. It was Jeanne that resolved the matter. She calmly walked up to the pair putting her hand on each of their arms, smiled at them warmly, and started moving them to the hallway. Zeke could see and hear the pair finally relax while keeping an eye on his guests, but they never stopped talking to each other rapidly.

The glance backward with her tongue out had Zeke shaking his head in resignation. The entire group headed after Jeanne, led by a dozen Marines, including Khalessi.

In short order, they were in a conference room where everyone, excluding the Marines standing at attention, was seated. Refreshments were still on the way. They had to wait on the Kolqux to be scanned thoroughly, discreetly, to see what their metabolism analysis indicated they were safe to drink and eat.

The Kolqux had not stopped talking the entire time since they left the bay. Jeanne, who sat between the two Kolqux, showed no indication she was tired of the chatter, which was just a repeating of the same thing over and over again.

It was when the drink and food came that the Kolqux stopped talking. Coffee, tea, water, multiple types of fruit juices, several appetizer plates of cheese and meat, and one massive platter of tiny sandwiches.

Both looked at the drinks and food, enthralled but concerned. They glanced at each other before looking back where they continued their jabber, but now, to each other.

"Brother Uv'ek, what is that? Is that something to eat? I haven't had to eat anything in a very long time. The Chohish would not let us bring any food onboard. The Chohish told us it would give us an incentive for getting that damn depot back to Sobolara quicker. Do you think they have something we can drink? That barely gave us enough liquid to stay alive."

"Brother Uv'ei, I sure hope so. It looks much better than the horrible paste they feed us. You try it; you are the oldest brother, so test it. We have other brothers in case you die. Try the drinks first."

This chatter continued for a moment or two before Jeanne did her thing again. Grabbing a piece of cheese, Jeanne slowly ate it while gesturing to the pair of Kolqux. "Per our ship doctor's scan, your metabolism can handle anything here."

The Kolqux looked at each other before diving into the drink and food, and from how they tore into the food, they were hungry.

Gesturing to one of the servers, who had hung around, Zeke pointed to the trays and drinks, where he quietly signaled for two more of the same. The server laughed after seeing how the Kolqux devoured the food before leaving.

After the Kolqux had devoured most of the food, it was quite a few moments later that they finally sighed and sat back. Only then does Uv'ei takes a moment to look closely at the Marines. Then, satisfied, he scanned the room, turning his whole body when he looked directly at Rear-Admiral Okeke. Uv'ei had recognized the respectful deference given to the Admiral. He changed his position to face Zeke when the admiral had no reaction.

Any resemblance to the chattering fool disappeared when he spoke. His posture changed from relaxed to attentive and alert in a surprisingly warm, soft voice.

"I am Uv'ei, chief of my clan, and speaker for all Kolqux's on Sobolara. From my observations, you have several chieftains here, but you command all, including one that is normally over you. Why, is no consequence to me. What matters, though, is what you plan to do with us. More importantly, what do you want from us, since you did not kill us out of hand."

If Uv'ei expected a reaction from Zeke, he did not show it when Zeke calmly chuckled before responding. "I am glad you finally stopped all that pretense; the whole thing was old. You were observing us, paying close attention to our actions and words. And that meant you must also have some method of understanding our language. Something embedded? That would make sense so you could understand the Chohish."

"Regardless, I am Captain Zeke Kinsley of the Royal Galactic Navy, in charge of this group. We were assigned to look for the Chohish home planet. To the right of me is Rear Admiral Nkosana Okeke, also of the RGN. To my left is Captain Jeanne de Clisson of the Irracan Navy, whom you have already met."

"I will let the rest introduce themselves to you later, but right now, I want you to meet Hawke. He is the individual next to Captain de Clisson, a representative of our ally, the Soraths. Hawke is also this ships Science Officer while being my close personal friend."

With that, Hawke rose and partially fluffed his wings. Speaking in a firm voice tinged heavily with anger, Hawke bent over the table to look directly at Uv'ei.

"My race was attacked and nearly exterminated by the Chohish. Like the rest you see here, we just came from several planets of humans that the Chohish attacked, killing hundreds of thousands without mercy. Children were tortured for no reason that we can determine. If you are with them, you will never be a friend of the Soraths, nor the humans, as we plan to destroy the Chohish and all their allies. You indicated that the Kolqux want to be free of the Sorath influence. If so, then we can become friends, maybe, in time. Which will it be?"

Uv'ei did not respond immediately but looked at Hawke without blinking for an extended period. When he spoke, it was with even more anger than Hawke's.

"We watched as you destroyed the small Chohish fleet with ease. Per Chohish orders, we were to self-detonate before allowing our ships to be captured. We didn't. If the Chohish found out that we disobeyed them, our entire family would be tortured before being killed. My brother and I risked our all, hoping, finally, after almost close to three thousand years, maybe, just maybe, someday we could be free of these monsters. To end the extreme suffering and humiliation of being under their rule."

Standing so swiftly that all the marines reacted by leveling their weapons on the pair of Kolqux, Uv'ei turned to jerk his loose shirt up to his shoulders. Gasps of startlement sounded around the room. Even Hawke was taken aback at the sight of so many scars.

Turning back to face Hawke, Uv'ei came close to yelling when he finished. "This is what Kolqux's deal with every day. We get whipped, beat for the slightest infraction, killed out of hand, sometimes for no reason other than to satisfy their need for cruelty. We live in fear daily, if not for ourselves but for our loved ones. Do we want to be free of the Chohish influence? We want them dead, all of them. We have dreamed of it every moment, of every hour, for our entire lives. I had a dozen brothers and sisters, but only five remain. None died naturally."

He was leaning his body over the table so his face was inches from Hawkes. With spittle flying from his mouth with intensity so strong that no one there had any doubts, Uv'ei meant every word. "We have waited thousands of years for help, for the slightest chance to end this hell. You cannot hate them any more than we do. Even if it might mean the end of the Kolqux, we will grasp at any chance to be free once more."

Silence hung heavy in the air as everyone waited on Hawke to see how he would respond.

Slowly, Hawke smiled, spreading his wings which pushed against the people sitting next to him. No one minded; it was Hawke. "I am starting to like you already, Uv'ei; let's go hunting."

"First, though, we need to understand what we're facing," commented Jeanne.

"Exactly!" concurred Zeke. "Uv'ei, what can you tell us of the Chohish fighting capabilities?"

Rubbing his chin, Uv'ei stopped to look around the room before coming back to look at Zeke. "If you have fought them, you know they are fearless. Whatever hell planet they come from, it must be pure hellish to breed creatures like this. We were a peace-loving race and had no real defenses when they attacked us ruthlessly. Even though we did not put up much of a fight, they killed indiscriminately. We lost over half our populations on all our planets. Since then, we have been nothing more than their labor force in this part of the galaxy."

Sighing, Uv'ei lowered his head, where he discreetly wiped his eyes, before he plopped back down in his seat. "My people populated four planets in three adjoining systems at the time of the invasion, but now we are on seven planets in the same systems. At a great cost of life, the Chohish forced Kolqux to terraform or live on planets we would have never considered so that they could supply a labor force to build their war machine. We are not the only conquered race but have not met any others. We only know because we have to work on ships produced by another race which requires us to learn their language."

Leaning toward his brother, Uv'ek, whose breathing flaps underneath his eyes were fluctuating widely, whispered heatedly into his ear. They did not know LS1 was relaying the translated conversation to all the others. The ship's AI could hear a fly walking on a wall, let alone a whispered conversation.

"What are you doing, Uv'ei? Dare we talk to them? Are you thinking of helping them? The Chohish would kill us painfully, and not just us, but all our families. You cannot be thinking of that, could you? They are only three ships." pleaded Uv'ek.

It was evident that Uv'ei was disappointed in his brother. Looking at him sadly, he replied softly enough that he was sure the humans would not hear it. "Think on it clearly, brother. Try to get past the fear the Chohish has put over you, all of us. These ships are only scouts. They had to have come past the station. You know the formidable defenses that station had. They are not weak. Look how they took out the Chohish ships. Can you imagine the possibilities? Is it not worth the risk to free our people? To be able to go out and stare at the sky in wonder and not be scared? To hold my kids close and my wife even closer?"

Listening to the Kolqux, he whispered through his communicator to Isolde. "Can you create a video loop of the battle we just had with the station, the fighters, and the carriers? Let's show them more of what we can do. Take it as far back as you can go."

The two Kolqux continued to chat for a few moments before a video started playing on the half dozen large screens around the room. Even the RGN members and Hawke were enthralled watching it. Being part of the battle was one thing; seeing it from a camera view from multiple cameras was different.

The Kolqux did not miss the power of the RGN displayed in the video. The skill of individual fighter pilots, single and paired pilots, whole groups working together, and the bravery they showed against overwhelming odds. And that bravery and skill were mirrored in the destroyers and cruiser personnel. How they faced certain destruction but never gave up. Surprisingly, it also showed the apprehension and the fear many had felt during the long desperate battle with the fighters and how everyone worked together during desperate times.

It was a moving video that lasted close to five full minutes, even though fast-paced. Most of all, it showed how the crew members of this small fleet cared for each other. The compadre, the laughter, the bravery, the concern for those injured, but most of all, the sadness they felt upon the loss of their comrades.

The amazement and wonder in the Kolqux eyes as they stared intently at the screens gave hope to Zeke that this would push them in the right direction.

But just when Zeke was ready to resume the meeting, the video started up again after a short pause. This one started with images of the death and destruction on both Niflhel and Nocuous, continuing with the land battles. It showed the people of Niflhel deep in their bunkers. Then it moved on to the desperate but bold fighting in space. Pictures of the Lucky Strike when it was just a wrecked hulk with a Captain barely alive standing alone on its bridge that was in flames and smoke. That same Captain lay in a medical station, only seen again as he stepped back onto the rebuilt cruiser with his crew. Again, another violent battle, but now with many different types of ships with multiple races involved. It even included the conversation held between Zeke and Admiral Timeti.

"We knew we would take casualties to complete the surprise; it was acceptable. Captain, understand this; we would have sacrificed all the ships and lives they hold if that is what it would take to eradicate this force. All on those ships are volunteers and knew the risks. This war has only started, and my people will make sure the Chohish never get a chance to repeat what they did before. We will be taking the war to them this time around."

The video finished with Admiral Timeti and Hawke humming their strange soft tune with the comment from Zeke overlaid. "Every Sorath family has a unique song that they hum when one or more are going into harm's way, and the odds are; they will not return. The closest we humans come to this is a funeral dirge. Admiral Timeti is saying goodbye to his nephew. I imagine neither expects to return home."

Both of the Kolqux looked at Hawke with glances that could only be called admiration. But that was nothing compared to when they both turned to look at Zeke. It was the same look Zeke's younger brother gave him at his graduation from the Academy, adoration.

It was Uv'ei that broke the silence with awe in his voice. "This ship was that flaming wreck with you standing alone on the bridge, wasn't it?" Looking at the people present, Uv'ei whispered, "and you were all there too, no?"

Without waiting for a reply, Uv'ei turned to his brother. "This may be the only chance for our people to break free of this horrible cycle we have to live. You say our families may be punished, killed even. But that is true without even doing anything wrong. And now, with the Chohish having pulled most of their forces away, is the best time to take our gamble. We have prepared for this for thousands of years. Millions, billions, have died to get us ready for this day. Even if we die, brother, I would rather that than not even try."

Glancing once more at the video where it had paused with Admiral Timeti and Hawke's heads touching, Uv'ek sighed. He then rose to his feet with his hand on his brothers' shoulders. "All my life, I have tried to keep our family alive. Yet, I failed many times. Our brothers, sisters, mother, father, and children died for no reason. I felt guilty to be alive as I could not protect them. If we are going to die, brother, let's take some of the monsters with us."

With that, both brothers stood to hug each other tightly. Straightening, both of the Kolqux turned to face Zeke.

"We will help where we can; what do you want us to do?" they said in unison.

"It all depends on what we face. We have a large fleet following us, but they are waiting to hear from multiple scouts similar in size to know where to go and what they face. They are at least several weeks, if not months, away from departing our forward base. What are we up against? In what direction?" responded a somber Zeke.

Again, both Kolqux looked at each other before they turned around to respond excitedly. "You cannot wait that long. The Chohish will send another fleet; if we are going to act, we need to do it now."

"Not sure what else we can do? As you stated, we are just a scouting force," replied Zeke while gripping his hands on the table.

"The Chohish stripped the planets and space stations to support the large fleet that left just over several weeks ago. From what you showed us, your fleet destroyed that fleet. It will take time for the Chohish to replace that many personnel and ships. If you can take control of the space stations..." an anxious pair of Kolqux said as one.

"How many space stations are there? And if the Chohish return, we are not enough to stop them." Admiral Okeke calmly said, but with a hint of exasperation in his voice. "I cannot think of a situation that would work. Our scouting fleet is not large enough to do what you ask."

The Kolqux looked at the Admiral in despair, and they both slumped down in their seats and put their heads down in their hands.

"Uv'ei, you did not answer the Admiral's question. How many space stations are there?" asked Zeke calmly, who raised a hand when the Admiral turned to him, ready to say something. "Admiral, you did say you were a bit crazy, which was one of the reasons we agreed to let you join us."

The laughter coming from Hawke made everyone turn to look at him. "You did say that Admiral, didn't you? Wishing you could take that back now?" Turning to look at Zeke with an intensity none could ignore. "Let's go hunting, my friend; we did not come on this trip to be meek—time to be bold and daring. Doubt me? Look around this room; they agree with me."

The Kolqux, hearing the interchange, raised their heads in hope. Looking around the room, they could see that all were smiling while shaking their heads in agreement. It was the video conference call that raised their hopes even higher.

"We still have payback due us, Captain, so count us in if you think we can do this. My lads and ladies are itching for a fight." drawled Meghan, surrounded by the Irracan bridge crew on the Fox.

"You can remove any thought of sending the Jackal back home, Zeke; we have communication modules with us this time that can do that job just as well. You need every ship for whatever your devious mind is chewing on." Lance proclaimed. The screen showed he was also surrounded by his crew, nodding their confirmation of what he said.

Buoyed by what he heard, Uv'ei feared that if he delayed

responding, someone else might say something against helping them. So he blurted out the information requested without pause. "There are three stations split between the planets at our main home system and two at each of the other systems. Each system has multiple shipbuilding facilities, but all are operated mainly by Kolqux."

Uv'ek stood up, where he continued as Uv'ei paused. "The Chohish have guards posted, but they are very limited in number. Only the space stations are armed, very well-armed. These stations are humongous and armed to the teeth. That is how they control us. They would bombard us to oblivion if we tried to fight them. We never found a way to neutralize the stations."

"Chohish ground troops are located in all our main cities. Spaceports have a heavy Chohish presence where they control all the shuttles for the workers to and from the shipbuilding facilities. Many garrisons left with the large fleet that your fleet destroyed. More was placed on the transfer ships your fighters took out; they were heading to strengthen the station you took out just before meeting us."

"Would those ships be the ones we took out before you signaled us?" asked Gunner. Seeing Uv'ei smile, Gunner smiled himself before continuing. "That would explain all the bodies. There were many more than a ship that size would normally hold."

"As I said, they were going to bolster the defense forces at the depot. They were warned that you were heading in this direction." Uv'ek confirmed Gunner's statement.

"If you could gain control of the space stations, we have a chance." a now excited Uv'ei stated as he gathered that there was a chance.

"What about the forces left on the planets? We definitely could do nothing about those," asked Zeke.

The Kolqux then surprised all by grinning. Everyone thought

the Kolqux would look depressed when Zeke said that was not something he could assist with.

"You leave those Chohish to us. We Kolqux have been preparing for this longer than my new friend." Uv'ei said while looking at Hawke. "It is the stations and their fleets that keep the Chohish in power. For the first time in all these years, their fleets are no longer circling our planet. If the stations can be neutralized, we will have a chance. A desperate chance, but still a chance. And that is all we ask of you. We will also take care of the Chohish on the shipbuilding facilities."

Uv'ek explained. "They removed most of the ground troops along with their air power. What forces are left, we believe we can manage."

"Uv'ei, this is very important; where are your tugboats stationed normally? At the shipbuilding facilities? Is it unusual for the tugboats to go to the station? And how many Chohish are stationed on the space stations?" asked Zeke. "First though, where are the finished warships docked? At the shipyards?"

"No, all completed ships are usually docked at the space stations. None are there now; they all went with the fleet. If not in use, ships, especially specialty ships like ours, are stationed a distance from the stations and powered down until needed. A small group of my people is assigned to reposition any of the ships that start to drift. As to the number of Chohish, we are not given access without escort to the main sections of the stations, so there may be more than I have seen. I would make an educated guess of around five to six hundred per station. And that is based only on what a cousin saw when he had to make an emergency repair several days ago. There are usually many thousands, but most of those stationed there left with the fleet. Why?"

"Do you know how they are armed? Armor?" Zeke continued without answering Uv'ei's question.

"Sidearms, never seen anything larger. I am sure they have something bigger but have never seen any. Oh, and most have some type of sword. Never seen any armor; I doubt they believe they would need it against a Kolqux, small as we. Why, what are you thinking?" Uv'ei replied.

A signal came to Isolde from LS1 to turn on the monitors. An image popped up on three of the monitors. Each monitor showed a different space station with measurements and locations listed on the side of the picture.

Raising an inquiring finger at the images, Zeke looked at Isolde, who negatively shook her head while mouthing "LS1".

"Yes, yes, those are the stations. You must have pulled that from the logs on our ship." an excited Uv'ek exclaimed. Zeke felt that Uv'ek was now fully committed since the video feedback.

Walking to the primary monitor, Zeke looked at it closely. Then he walked to each of the other monitors to examine the information displayed in fine detail.

"These stations are huge, a good deal bigger than one of ours. Then again, the Chohish are much bigger too," stated Zeke.

"That is true, but that is not all why they are so much larger. The armaments take up the majority of the station. That is to ensure we never rebel. They showed us early on how effective they are by destroying several large cities with all inhabitants." explained Uv'ei.

"The question then is, how to subdue the stations before they can fire on the planets. That will take some planning. You do realize the risk would be enormous, don't you?" Jeanne asked the Kolqux brothers.

Again, where she expected the brothers to show some sign of despair, they instead smiled. "If we can get close to the stations, we may be able to shut down the station's main power remotely. The shipbuilding facilities are close, so they should not suspect our ships. Not sure for how long, as they should be able to trace it back to the hardware override planted on all the stations many years ago during a maintenance upgrade. Hopefully, it is functional; my ancestors built it, knowing it may be many centuries before we got an opportunity. We could not chance using it before due to the fleets that always circled our worlds. But now with the fleets gone…. if we can subdue the Chohish before they find it…" a very excited Uv'ei stated.

It would have been comical watching the Kolqux if the situation was not so serious. They were now bouncing up and down in excitement, with their nostril holes fluttering in and out.

And it was Jeanne who noticed the change in Nkosana. Where he had a concerned expression before, she now saw the beginning of a smile emerge.

"Why Admiral, I believe you are coming around," she announced to the room.

"Details, Jeanne, missing details was the cause of my hesitancy. And even though Hawke may question my being a bit crazy, my wife does not doubt it. She always said that is one of the reasons she loves me so much. Besides, from the look on your partner's face, I think he has come up with the beginnings of a plan. Am I right there, Captain?"

Swirling to look at Zeke, Jeanne knew instantly that the Admiral was right. The crooked smile was a dead giveaway when matched with the lowered eyelids. It was almost like he was living what he was planning in real-time inside his head.

"Yes, I believe we may have a way to make this happen. Time is the main enemy as we must get all this done before any enemy fleet arrives. We also need to notify our people asap of our plans and hope they can get here in time to back us up if another large fleet does arrive. Since we have all the main parties here, there is no time like the present to flush out my ideas and get something that may work." Zeke replied. "Now, here is what I was thinking…."

SLIPSTREAM

STANDING WAS NEVER an issue for Khaleesi; she preferred that over sitting most of the time. But that was when she was standing straight up, not hunched over in a compartment that was only six feet high, while wearing the new armor that made her height closer to eight feet. And that was without her helmet on.

The new armor had some significant updates that she approved of. But the old set allowed the user to lock the armor at any angle. However, the new armor limited that feature to allow for improved armor thickness. Well, she had been through worse. If standing in an uncomfortable position in this crappy tugboat got her to her destination undetected, so be it.

But there was one thing she could do. Standing on one leg, she kicked backward forcefully into the leg of the marine behind her. The marine behind her, caught by surprise, lurched sideways, stumbling into another marine.

"What the hell Major, what was that for?" he yelled.

"Your consistent tapping on the ceiling with your fingers. Were you not instructed to keep quiet? We do not know when the Chohish will contact our pilot."

"You could have just said something."

"More fun this way, and the lesson will stick with you. Now shut the hell up," ordered Khaleesi. The marine was one of the new ones who did not have a lot of experience. She wanted to ensure he survived long enough to know what to do on his own.

Another half dozen marines and several dozen army personnel from Niflhel stuffed in here with her. They were so tight in the storage area that they could not wear their helmets. Their helmets were under wraps in the pilot's room, hopefully not visible when the call came in. However, that was the only available space as neither the marines nor the army would give up their weapons. Most of the tugboat's free space consisted of engines.

Three tugboats were heading to each space station hanging over the three planets in the Kolqux home system. Uv'ei and Uv'ek were piloting this tugboat and would be the individual the Chohish contacted since he spoke for all Kolqux.

Each Kolqux planet had one space station used to control the Kolqux, along with multiple shipbuilding facilities. The number of facilities varied, with the majority in the home system.

While they waited to reach the station, Khaleesi thought back to the planning session. It was a heated session at times. The final plan called for the three RGN ships to separate. The Lucky Strike would be going to the home system, the Furalla Eaara Star System, with its three Kolqux populated planets. Not only because this system had three space stations, but because the one that circled Sobolara was twice the size of the other stations.

Hence, she was part of the force headed toward that station with double the number of marines sent to the other locations. Three marines and dozens of army personnel were in the other two tugboats. All the army personnel was the best among the thousands she and her officers had trained this past half-year. Hopefully, it will be enough.

The destroyers would split up to go to the other Kolqux

populated systems, The Wartos Quadrant and the Oxtaria Pulsar System. Each of these had a pair of Kolqux inhabited planets; hence, both systems also operated two space stations by Chohish. They would follow the same deployment as being done here. They had delayed executing the attack in this system until all the forces were in place to make the attacks simultaneously.

But what happened in those other systems is not something she could control. She had placed a pair of her officers to take charge in each scenario. They were more than competent, in her opinion, and had her complete trust in doing a great job.

Besides, she had more than enough on her plate. The ship was starting to slow down before docking. For good measure, whispering into her handset, she gave one last set of orders before they would disembark.

"Ok, ladies and gentlemen, showtime is upon us. I expect we will hear the Chohish contact the tugboat anytime now. When it does, we need absolute quiet—no talking or movement. You know what we have to do when we get there. The Marines will lead, with the army personnel following. Follow the plan. Marines are the shock troops; the army is the follow-up support. You are armed; you have the will, the skill, and one more thing. Every one of you has a reason to be here. You have seen what the Chohish are capable of; most have lost a loved one because of the Chohish. Now, let's make them pay! Khaleesi out."

Within minutes, Khaleesi heard Uv'ei on the ship's communication panel. She could not determine what was said, but it did not last long. Once it ended, Uv'ei spoke into the ship's intercom.

"We have been granted clearance. The Chohish are somehow aware of the loss of their destroyers. They are upset that we did not try to ram your ships even though we told them we were following orders to return here to warn the Chohish. Oddly, they have instructed us to dock at bay number six at the station itself. The other two ships will be docking on bays five and seven."

"Major, stay in the ship until I signal you that I have shut down the power. We did install two overrides just in case. One is a physical switch located behind the bay. Once I switch on the first override, I will try to reach the second one to delay bringing the power back on. But time is limited no matter what."

Uv'ei said time was limited. But how much was that? Minutes? Hours? No one knew. This fact weighed heavily on her mind on what could happen if the station power did not shut down or restarted before they took over the bridge. That factor made Khaleesi put together what she believed was their best plan of attack. Even though there were a lot of risks, she would not usually accept them. Thankfully she had blueprints for all the stations. Otherwise, it would have been impossible to put together any plan.

The hard jerk and bang of metal on metal indicated they were arriving in bay six. The sound of metal grinding sounded loud in the storage tank as they slid to a halt. These ships did not have modern landing gear.

The silence fragmented when the cockpit door opened, with Uv'ek peering in with a finger pressed against his mouth. Uv'ek stepped back inside the cockpit, leaving the door open so Khaleesi could hear a conversation between Uv'ei and what sounded like a Chohish individual through the entrance to the cockpit.

Pulling her sidearm, she slid her index finger down to switch the safety off. The plasma rifle connected to her back clicked as the suit armor AI turned on the unit, arming the gun. The Ai in her suit knew it was time for business when she pulled her sidearm.

An odd sound flooded the area as all the AIs followed suit. Smiling, Khaleesi wondered what the army personnel from the Pandora system thought upon hearing their weapons armed without their input. Even though she mentioned during boarding that this would happen, she doubted anyone had paid close attention to it. Training for the army personnel never got the time to teach this; too many other things to learn to stay alive.

The conversation faded as if the participants were moving away from the tugboat. Still, she waited quietly. Uv'ek, during the meetings on the Lucky Strike, said the space stations had an AI unit, although it was primitive compared to the ones the RGN had. The AI would raise the alarm if it sensed armed personnel coming out of the tugboat, so they had to wait for the power to go down before they could leave.

It was another seven minutes before the lights in the bay flickered, then shut off, before the emergency lights came on. Khaleesi, though, had started moving as soon as the lights flickered. It was only a few seconds later that the emergency lights went out. Squeezing through the hatch, she grabbed the helmet Uv'ek passed to her before she walked out the pilot's door to the cavernous bay.

Calmly, she connected her helmet while waiting for the rest of her marines. The helmet's night vision brought out the bay in great detail. Five more marines were beside her only seconds later, armed and ready to move out. The last would stick with the army personnel if they needed heavier firepower and guide them where they were to go. Khaleesi and her crew had one goal, to take control of the bridge. Meanwhile, Uv'ek dropped the sidewall of the tugboat used to load the tugboat allowing the army personnel accessible egress.

With Uv'ek trailing, Khaleesi and her team made for the large opening framing Uv'ei standing over a prone Chohish soldier. Another soldier sprawled on the ground was visible further up the hall. In Uv'ei's hand was the small pistol that Khaleesi had given him. It was a needler that shot hundreds of lethal tipped needles per minute. It was an assassin's weapon. Deadly, quiet, and short-ranged while useless against armor, it was perfect for this situation.

Moving past Uv'ei, Khaleesi started a fast skipping using the magnetics on the soles of her boots. The skipping kept her feet close to the floor but allowed rapid movement down the hall. As she skipped, she sent several portable scanners flying down the passageway. She was just over halfway when she detected activity on the video feed from the scanners.

Knowing only Chohish personnel would be on the station made her job much more manageable. Smiling, she pulled a grenade and set it for wide dispersion. Throwing the grenade, Khalesse watched as two other grenades joined it. The grenades reached the end of the hall just as four Chohish came strolling around. They screamed in rage when they saw them and started in their direction, only to disappear in a ball of flame.

The marines didn't slow down but kept on skipping down the hall. Two marines at the rear moved up onto the side of the walls. Another pair continued up to hang from the ceiling. Six marines were in a solid group as they came to the end of the hall.

All six marines holstered their sidearm as their plasma rifles swung around toward the front, where the marines grabbed them smoothly in one quick motion. Scanners showed the arrival of over a dozen armed Chohish rushing through a junction at the end of the hallway.

With precision that must have taken many hours of practice, the Marines turned the corner as one. Their sudden arrival must have been a shock as the Chohish were not wearing any night gear. The marines must have looked like shadows appearing out of nowhere.

The Chohish never got a chance to bring their weapons to bear. The plasma firestorm rained down on the Chohish would have been frightening to watch, let alone experience. Still, to these hardened, experienced marines, it was something they had experienced many times. Sometimes on the wrong end. All the marines in this group, including Khaleesi, wore scars from those times.

Time was not on her side, so Khaleesi picked up her speed with the rest of the marines matching. The marine skipping now looked like they were running without moving their feet off the contact to the ground, wall, or ceiling. The suit AI was controlling the speed based on commands from Khaleesi.

The marine on the ceiling and walls dropped back, facing backward while still moving backward at the same pace. The marines were a blur as they raced toward the area defined as the control section. They came across groups of Chohish as they ran along, whom they eliminated with precision. The scanners, up to now, had not been detected and were giving them advanced warning of impending Chohish presence. Khaleesi, though knew this would not last.

Soon enough, time to use the flying scanners, but she had other tricks. From the soles of her boots, a pair of miniature scanners sped away the size of a small fingernail. Unfortunately, they did not have the clarity of the flying scanners. Still, she did not need that type of clarity when she knew that anyone or object she saw in front of her was an enemy combatant.

Destruction raged around them as more and more Chohish came at them. The three facing backward were also now heavily engaged. One thing was evident to Khaleesi: the Chohish soldiers she was fighting here were not near the caliber she fought in the Pandora star system. The Chohish here must have become complacent as they fought her marines like they had no actual fighting experience.

Until now, no Chohish had worn any armor, and their weapons were limited to underpowered lasers that their armor could tolerate.

With that in mind, Khaleesi decided to take a chance. "Della, I am going to lay heavy fire down the hall. I want you and Otis to take out the walls to our left. Keep burning through straight to their bridge. I would never do this normally, but I think it is worth the chance with this group."

"I agree with you, Major; these fighters are not very good. So let us first fire a few rounds of plasma down the hall to mask our intentions," Della replied. No sooner said than all three let loose a sustained burst of fire down the hallway.

Without delay, Della and Otis turned to open fire on the wall to their left. Their fire punched through the wall with ease. The marines continued firing as they used their armor to push through the weakened wall.

Seeing a pause in the attacking Chohish, Khaleesi had the two marines covering their rear join Della and Otis. "Jo, how long before you get here with the army support?"

"We are just a few seconds away. I have been clearing up some Chohish trying to get around us. We have lost a few army personnel, but they are holding up pretty well considering it is their first action."

The fire coming from the rear slackened until it stopped altogether. Khaleesi saw Jo skipping around a corner with several army personnel behind. Pointing to the opening made by Della and Otis, Khaleesi and three marines jumped through.

The four marines continued through the next wall as Della and Otis had not stopped but continued passing through the walls. The wall destruction went on for a while as the station was gigantic.

It soon became evident that Della and Otis were encountering Chohish as they blasted their way through the walls. The four marines came across bodies here and there as they went. Not all were soldiers, as most were the more petite type identified as engineers. That made sense as they would be critical in keeping a size station running effectively.

As she went on, Khaleesi noticed that Chohish must have been taken entirely by surprise. The soldiers she did come across were wearing no armor, nor was there a weapon evident in most cases. Some were, but most looked to not have had the time to arm themselves. That also indicated that whoever was in charge did not have much, if any, experience. She would never send unarmed soldiers to attack someone armored with a modern weapon. Then again, maybe the Chohish was still blind and thought it was the Kolqux attacking. Regardless, it was either arrogance or stupidity not to arm the soldiers before sending them out.

There were making good time to the bridge, but Khaleesi knew time was running out. Almost as soon as she thought it, the lights flickered back on. The lights were quickly followed by heavy machinery starting back up.

"Della, the bridge is three more hallways away. Stop there so we can join you and enter together. Jo, I need your group to join us on the bridge as quickly as possible. Speed is of the essence here, people." With that, Khaleesi and her group jumped through another destroyed wall.

As she joined Della and Otis, she felt the station jerk repeatedly. "Crap, they are firing on the planet. Looking at the marines, she pointed to the wall in front of them. All let loose a coordinated plasma fire on the wall, which disappeared in a wall of smoke. All the marines jumped through, firing as they went.

Standing on the bridge surrounded by armed soldiers was the Sovereign she expected to find. As she swung her rifle around, something slammed into her, sending her flying across the room. Extreme pain in her legs, chest, and arms let her know she was injured. Her consciousness flickered in and out before everything went black.

RECOVERY

"WELL, HELLO, YOUNG lady, glad you could rejoin us. Hmmm, I have been saying that much too often lately. How are you feeling?" a voice came through the haze and pain as she started to wake up.

Barely awake, her mind was swimming in a thick soup; Khaleesi could scarcely make out Doc through her squinted eyes standing over her. "What the hell? Where am I?"

Tapping on the control pad on the medical pod, he replied while still reading the results of his query.

"You are in the medical bay; otherwise, why would I be here? It is not a dream, or is it?" Doc said, tinged with humor in his voice.

Pushing her hands down to lift herself out of the pod, she only got raised several inches before a large shadow shoved her down. Unfortunately, that did not take much effort on the shadow's part, as she had no strength to fight back. The shadow slowly resolved into the image of Jan.

"And just where do you think you are going?" Doc said sternly. "You are lucky to be alive Major. You will stay in that pod until the nanos have time to repair your legs. Unless you do not want them, that is. If so, you can crawl out of that pod whenever you feel up to it."

Which she would have tried regardless if only she had the strength. Sinking, she looked up to see a very concerned Jan hovering over her. "Ok, Doc, you win. I doubt the big lug standing by you will let me up anyway. Can someone give me an updated status? How are my marines? Army?"

Surprised at the laughter coming from Doc, she was about to ask what was so funny when she figured it out by his comment.

"I told you, asking about her people would be her first words." a smug-looking Doc said without stopping entering commands into the pod's controls. "I have known her for years, always the same, never changed. Status of her people, before herself, even if near death. Tough as nails with a giant heart."

"Well, I am out of here; I have a lot of patients to care for. I will see you later, Major, Jan." with that, Doc made his way to another occupied pod.

Leaning on the edge of the pod, so he was leaning over Khaleesi, Jan looked at her closely before responding. "You have been out for almost forty-some hours. The captain just left; he would have been able to give you a better update than I can. Then again, he probably did not have time as he wanted to visit as many of the injured here as possible. The captain just left for the bridge. Cap must be exhausted; he has not taken a break since this started. Doc refuses to give him any more stim shots."

Sighing, Jan swiped her hair toward the back of her head, what little he could reach. "I can tell you the basics, though. Everything went as planned up to a point. The second switch that Uv'ei was counting on to give you some additional time to reach the bridge failed. It looks like age got to it. The unit had been installed secretly, so it was hard to check up on over the years."

Seeing the despair on his face, Khaleesi knew something terrible had happened. There was only one thing that could mean. "The Chohish fired on the planet, didn't they? How bad?"

"The Lucky Strike had deployed all the fighters and bombers around the station. The captain hoped they would be to stop anything fired toward the planet from all three stations. Between the Lucky Strike and the fighters, they stopped a lot of missiles. The bombers were pretty much useless for this. Even though they tried, they got all except for two missiles. The missiles took out two cities in Sobolara. They were two smaller cities, but nearly two million Kolqux perished with hundreds of thousands injured."

Whatever else he was saying was lost in the sadness that overwhelmed her. Two million? How many children were part of that mix? If only she could have reached the bridge faster. She knew it was not her fault; the Chohish were to blame. But it did not help. She felt like the weight was going to crush her, but she did not care at the moment if it did. Tears would not come; she would not allow that; she was a Marine Commander. But it did not mean she didn't have feelings; right now, she felt like crawling inside her private shell and never coming out.

"I know it is hard to accept, my dear, but you are not responsible. You did the best anyone could have hoped. You saved millions by going through the walls and cutting down on time to get to the bridge drastically. Uv'ei and Uv'ek wanted to be here, but they were on the planet helping get a government setup. But they did tell the captain to thank you; without you and the rest risking your lives to help them, many more would have died. And it was an acceptable loss to them. It is hard to believe, but they knew that loss of life would be high, in the best case."

Then, Khaleesi realized that tears were running down Jan's cheeks. "You have to understand; life was horrible for them for over three thousand years. Three thousand years. Whipped, beat, killed, all for no reason with no recourse but to accept it. Can you even imagine living under those conditions? For three thousand years?"

Sitting up straight, so he could wipe the tears off his face with the sleeve of his shirt, Jan continued. "The Kolqux lost another hundred thousand fighting the Chohish on the three planets and the shipbuilding facilities in this system. It seems they had some homemade weapons that were pretty effective. But their numbers won the day; the Chohish were not going down without a fight. The Kolqux threw themselves at the Chohish, tearing them apart when they got their hands on them. Khaleesi, you should see some of the videos. You would have been cheering them on as they flung themselves at the Chohish without concern for their safety."

Jan leaned over until his face was just inches away from hers. "You may feel bad about what happened, but the Kolqux think of you as a hero. Uv'ei saw the videos from your armor and the rest of the group. The captain allowed him to make them available to all the Kolqux. They watched the battle in the station, not just yours, but from everyone on all three stations. The Kolqux believe you all are heroes that brought them their freedom."

The pain in Jan's eyes when he said 'heroes' made her ask her original question again quietly as she knew she did not want to hear the answer. "How are my marines? Army?"

She watched as Jan closed his eyes before he lowered his head. Whispering so quietly, she could barely hear, but what she heard was louder than a bomb going off in her ear.

"The Chohish knew you were coming. Della and Otis were both killed. They died in the same bomb blast that almost killed you. Jo, thankfully, was a few seconds behind you. He and the rest of the marines and army subdued the Chohish on the bridge. Still, we lost over twenty army personnel to get control of that station. The Chohish lost over five hundred. Our forces captured the other two Chohish stations before getting the power back up. We lost another pair of marines, and again, over several dozen of the army was lost."

"There is one good thing, though. Jo was able to capture the Sovereign that was on the bridge alive. We believe he was in overall command of all the Kolqux planets. If we can get him back home, we may get some useful information out of him. Doc has him in stasis, locked in the brig. Plenty of Chohish was captured alive on the stations, but we gave these to the Kolqux. We do not have any space for prisoners. It seems the Kolqux don't either; they hung them all from the nearest buildings, with all the other ones they killed on the planet."

Jan looked at Khaleesi closely as he knew how close she was to her marines. Death was common in their profession, but it was still hard when you lost one. Being a marine meant you lived, slept, trained, fought, bled, and died together. Rarely did they ever fight alone. They were as close, if not closer, as the brothers and sisters they grew up alongside. But when you led them to their death, it was even more painful.

What he saw was what he expected, determination. He watched as the sorrow was put in that corner of your mind, hidden away so no one could see it, only to be released when in private. Jan knew because he had his special place where he hid the painful memories of the lost friends he commanded.

Seeing the change come over her, Jan decided she needed something positive to brighten her spirits even more.

"We haven't heard from the other systems yet, but Zeke thinks that is good news. He expects to hear from them in the next several hours. We are still cataloging everything on the stations; it will take a while, even with the Kolqux assistance. The stations contain all types of equipment the Kolqux can use. The Kolqux are reviewing all the defensive and offensive capabilities in case the Chohish return before our fleet arrives. It is impressive; we would never have been able to take these stations on our own."

Leaning in to kiss Khaleesi, Jan stroked her cheek. "But what I need now is for you to get back on your feet. We are not out of this mess yet. You must get some rest and let your body heal. We need you."

The look Khaleesi gave Jan made his heart beat fast. The smile she gave him before she fell asleep from the medical pod's injection gave him hope she would recover quickly. If the captain was right, the worst was yet to come; they would need her.

Making his way out of medical, he thought of what he saw happening on the planet. It was like chaos run amok. Kolqux by the billions were streaming all over the surface. Thousands have already arrived at all three stations, much more than needed to run the station. Many thousands more. Why so many? He had no idea what they were planning. But one thing did stand out. Jubilation!

Even with all the death that had occurred, the jubilation was contagious. The songs, the dancing, and the laughter could be seen and heard all over the planets. The images of the Kolqux adults holding children over their heads while twirling in laughter and dance were everywhere. To watch this was to be humbled, knowing you had a significant part in making this happen.

Time for reflection would have to wait. He needed to get back on the bridge; he had a feeling that things were about to get interesting, very interesting. If he had been on the bridge at that moment, Jan would have had suspicions confirmed.

PREPARATION

THE BRIDGE WAS a flurry of activity. Uv'ei and Uv'ek had returned where they were standing by Zeke's command chair in a heated discussion with Zeke, Jeanne, Will, Hawke, Isolde, and Nkosana.

"As I told you, Uv'ei, the Lucky Strike cannot take on a large Chohish fleet by itself. Our probes have picked up Chohish warships. They are transitioning through the remote slipstream as we speak. They have not progressed farther into the system nor made any attempt at communication that I am aware of. They must be aware they are no longer in control of the space stations." Zeke explained.

"We can confirm that. We should have told you immediately, but the Chohish tried to signal the station upon arrival but did not know the response codes requested. Nor could we produce the Sovereign. They let us know what they were going to do to us." answered a distraught Uv'ei.

Uv'ek, standing next to his brother, was even more agitated. He kept fidgeting with his suit of armor. Although Zeke doubted it would be very effective against any modern weapons, it was old and worn in places but still looked serviceable.

"Captain, we understand that one ship cannot stop a Chohish fleet, but that is not what we need. We have no experience with war. We do not have anyone who could direct us in fighting the Chohish. That is what we need from you. We need you to guide us, direct us, tell us how to fight." Uv'ei pleaded.

"Fight with what?" an exasperated Zeke replied. "We hoped the RGN fleet would arrive before the Chohish counter-attacked, but we have not heard anything from the RGN. And now.... Isolde, how many Chohish warships are now present?"

"Captain, there are a half dozen battleships, a dozen cruisers, three dozen destroyers. And unless I am mistaken, half a dozen carriers, huge carriers, unless they are freighters. No additional ships have arrived in the past hour. The Chohish fleet has positioned itself about two hours from the slipstream. They are just over fifteen hours from our location." reported Isolde.

"Thanks, Isolde; keep me updated on any changes." Standing, Zeke, followed by the rest of the group, moved over to the 3D simulation table that showed the system with everything identified in the system.

"Uv'ei, without additional forces, there is nothing I can suggest that will have much impact on a force that size. They can stand off and fire on the stations at will. Even though you have identified that the stations can move, you know as well as I that it is only for repositioning, not for fighting a space battle."

Putting his hand on Uv'ei's shoulder, Zeke swept his hand out to indicate the personnel on the bridge. "Uv'ei, we have come to like the Kolqux, and we wish we could do more. You know the dangers we put ourselves in for the Kolqux. Then, there was a chance of success, small, but a chance nevertheless."

Still looking at the crew, who paused for a moment to look at Uv'ei, he went on. "Part of their reason for coming on this ship is they trusted their commanders to look out for their welfare—especially with their lives. I will not betray that trust. You cannot ask me to throw away their lives for nothing, no gain. One cruiser cannot stand alone against a force that large with any hope of survival."

Then to the bewilderment of all, the two Kolqux looked at each other before they laughed. Both turned to Zeke, where Uv'ek broke the spell that the laughter brought on by uttering. "You did not hear my brother earlier. He said we needed a leader. Who said you would be alone? We have been waiting thousands of years for this day. We knew we would have to fight a Chohish fleet if we could ever take over the stations. But we have only fought one major war, three thousand years ago, and we all know how that went."

Then the laughter stopped suddenly. Both turned to Zeke with no humor in their expressions. What Zeke saw was hatred, pure undulated hate. "Lead us!"

"Again, I ask, with wh…." Zeke started to ask when he was interrupted by Caspian explaining. "Holy shit!"

Believing they were under attack, everyone in the group started to scatter until they all heard both Kolqux start laughing once more.

Zeke realized something else was happening. Having jumped back into his command chair, Zeke asked Caspian what the 'holy shit' meant.

"Sorry, sir, it caught me by surprise. Fighters, hundreds of them, are coming out of the stations. And there are more coming from the planets, thousands more." Turning to look at Zeke with eyes as wide open in amazement. "Captain, the sensors are now reporting Chohish battleships, cruisers, and destroyers coming from the shipbuilding facilities."

"Bring it up on the screen Ensign Raske, up on the screen," ordered Zeke. Without taking his eyes off the displayed images, "Uv'ei, I hope these are not Chohish…."

"Relax, Captain; they are flying under Kolqux's control. Few, if any, though, of the larger ships are completed. Although I believe one battleship may be close. But we figure anything is better than nothing." The prior said flatly, but then Uv'ei's tone to menacing. "But all the fighters are ready and armed. We just need someone to tell us how to fight."

As soon as Uv'ei finished speaking, Nkosana caught everyone's attention. "Oh well, it looks like we are going to stick around. There goes that look again."

"If you ladies and gentlemen would join me in the conference room. Isolde, please join. Ensign Bonilla, the com is yours." a crooked smiling Zeke ordered.

They all gathered on the bridge three hours later, except Jan and Hawke, who had left to check on their fighters. Jan agreed to the necessity of Jeanne leading a fighter group as part of the plan worked out, but only if he and the security squad could tail along with her. Seeing as everyone knew all Irracans were expert fighter pilots, no one argued the point. Jeanne would be joining them later.

Gesturing to the two Kolqux, Zeke asked, "Uv'ei and Uv'ek, can you join me for a moment?" He led them to a corner on the bridge where they could talk privately. Puzzled glances went around the bridge, regardless of rank, on what they could be discussing. At times, it became heated; Zeke spoke while the two Kolqux stood with heads downs listening intently, speaking rarely. It went on for a good twenty minutes before they finally broke up, with Uv'ei and Uv'ek running out of the bridge with barely a glance at anyone on the bridge. But the glance they did give showed two sorrowful faces lined with determination.

Zeke had not moved from the corner with his back facing them, so Jeanne started toward him, concerned. She stopped when he raised his right hand, signaling no. Jeanne halted temporarily but continued when Zeke groaned. She raced over while signaling the others to stay where they were.

Reaching Zeke, Jeanne kneeled in front of him, where they held a quiet conversation. The moan of anguish from Jeanne before she covered her mouth to contain whatever grief she was feeling alarmed everyone even more.

Both rose together where Jeanne and Zeke hugged, after which Zeke raised his head to stare at the ceiling while whispering something only Jeanne could hear. The silent hugging went on for quite a few moments as Jeanne looked on with sorrow unmistakably visible in her eyes.

Turning slowly to face the crew, Zeke sauntered to sit and lean back on his command chair, where he asked that all officers call their backups up on the bridge as they needed to rest. The coming hours or days would be tiring for all.

"Commander Farren, if you would, please take command while I get some rest. I will relieve you in eight hours. Let me know immediately if the Chohish makes any moves." With Jeanne still by his side, Zeke started to leave before stopping to ask Isolde to have Jax meet him in his suite.

The bridge was silent as they watched the pair leave, only to break out in a muted chatter on what had happened. Something happened during that discussion with the Kolqux that had deeply upset the captain. What, no one had a clue.

Nkosana, standing next to Will, asked him as quietly as he could. "Commander, you know the captain pretty well. Any idea on what could cause what we saw?"

Without looking at Nkosana as he was still staring at where the captain had left the bridge, he shrugged while answering. "I have been with the captain for years. We have been through some hairy times together. One thing you could always count on was the captain remaining solid as granite, never flappable. The only time I ever saw him flinch was when we witnessed the atrocities committed on Niflhel. I cannot imagine what the captain discussed with the Kolqux to cause such a reaction."

He was turning to give Nkosana his full attention. "But whatever it was, God help us because it must have been horrific. And I doubt it was something in the past." With that, Will, out of character, patted Nkosana on the shoulder. Afterward, he went to sit in the command chair, directing the arriving backup crews where he wanted them.

Nkosana, moving to sit in the chair assigned to him, watched as images floated on the side screens showing the Kolqux warships making their way back to the station or the factories. That is, he thought, if you could call them warships. Many had no actual fighting capabilities, just an armored shell with an engine. Others had shields only, others had missiles, but few had a full complement of equipment. Per the plan discussed, they were to try to add, fix, or complete any system they could while waiting for the Chohish to make their move. Shields being their top priority, point defense second, and anti-ship missiles being the third. Hope to get the ship close enough to fire all missiles, detract fire from the fighters, then run like hell.

The bridge settled down where they went about duties. Only five hours had passed before the two captains showed up again. Zeke seemed to have recovered from whatever he had discussed with the Kolqux. But, of course, that could be because Jeanne had her left arm wrapped tightly in his right arm.

Walking to stand next to Will, Zeke told him to sit when he started rising out of the command chair. "Any movement from the Chohish?" although he knew that would be a no as Will would have notified him already. But no harm in confirming.

Getting the negative confirmation from Will, he pointed to behind the chair. "I came to talk with Corporal Dennison here, along with you. I need your opinions on who best to take over the Majors duties until she recovers."

Startled, Will had forgotten about Shon, who was now standing behind him once more. The last time he saw the corporal was when he and Michale followed the Captain and Jeanne out of the bridge. How can he creep with all that equipment?

The deep voice of Shon, who sounded amused, could be heard by all even though it was not loud. "I am not sure the Major can or would care to be replaced by you so easily, sir; no disrespect intended."

"Well, no disrespect to the Major, but I need to send over marines and army personnel to protect the stations from any Chohish boarding attempts. Who do y...?" When he was interrupted, once more, by the sound of heavy marching getting closer.

"What the hell now?" a frustrated Jeanne exclaimed.

Major Richards came marching into the bridge in full marine armor with her helmet cradled in the crook of her right arm, followed by two other marines.

"Damn it, Major, what are you doing here? You should still be in the infirmary. Has Doc officially released you yet? I did not get any notification on that." exclaimed Zeke.

Snarling, the Major pointed her left index finger at Zeke. "Like you have any right to ask me that after what you did in the Pandora System. Besides, Doc did release me; he just doesn't know it yet."

"A friend of ours," Khaleesi said, pointing toward the ceiling, "told me about your concern for the stations. Leave that to me; that is my job. It is what marine majors do, not ship captains. I will leave you a small contingent of marines and army personnel for this ship, but I will take the vast majority over to the three stations. You concentrate on your job; I will take care of protecting the stations. Count on it."

Turning, she took several steps before stopping to look over her shoulder. "I need you to notify Lieutenant Commander Chandler that I am authorized to take any equipment, armaments, or personnel I may request. And I mean anything, no questions asked, she is to fill out my requests." Then, without waiting for Zeke to confirm, the Major turned and walked out with the two marines that came in with her. Shon and Michale soon followed Khalessi without saying a word. There were no spare marines to guard the captains. They would have to protect themselves in this desperate gamble of Zeke's.

"Whew... it's good to have Khalessi back with us. I wonder what she needs that the Lieutenant Commander would balk at?" Zeke paused as he received a ping from Doc. Chuckling, he told the group around him about his ping. "I guess that is Doc telling me he is missing one Major. Will, can you let the Lieutenant Commander know that she is to honor all the Major's requests, no questions asked. That includes any assistance she may request. No need to confirm with us."

Smiling, he hugged Jeanne before swinging her around in a circle. With Jeanne laughing, the crew could hear him asking her how it felt to be free of marines watching everything they did, well, mostly everything.

There was one exception. Lance Corporal Marianne Chavez still stood behind Nkosana. She responded when Nkosana questioned why she was not joining the others. "Following orders."

Dropping Jeanne back on her feet, Zeke notified Will to get some rest. Eyeballing Nkosana, he suggested that he should also get some rest. They would need him refreshed for his part of the plan.

Will said he would stop by to talk with Jamie before catching a nap. He wanted to personally see how things were going in the bay with the new setup. Both paused before leaving, hoping Zeke would explain what happened earlier. Not seeing any indication that Zeke would speak on it, Will asked Zeke what occurred with

Attack Chohish War

the Kolqux. Seeing Zeke shake his head no, they knew he would not divulge what he had discussed with the Kolqux.

Nkosana almost reneged on his promise not to interfere; he was about to order the captain to answer but decided against it. Nkosana had made a promise that he had every intention to keep. Now was not the time to break it.

The ship was not idle during this time; it was preparing for the upcoming conflict. With Nkosana and marine Chavez trailing along, Will made his way to talk with Jamie. He saw the crew working frantically on many different projects.

A team of technicians installed temporary bracing for the walls; heavy weapons were placed strategically around the ship. Even more, were placing manual fire suppression canisters to support the automation, and so on.

As Nkosana walked with Will, he was glad to see the ship make preparations. It was no different than what ships under his command did, but he was still pleased to see it. Spoke volumes of the ship's men and women along with their officers. He wished all ships were this competent, but unfortunately, some had no respect for their command structure. Hence those ships paid a heavy price when called to fight. Thankfully, they were few in the RGN.

Reaching one of the fighter bays, the two officers stepped through a hatch into a buzz of activity. It took Nkosana a moment to adjust to the much smaller size, and he could not see any possible opening to allow ships to leave the warship. Fighters lined up along two sides of the wall, with shuttles against one of the other two walls. All were sitting on a track. What amazed him was thinking there were half a dozen of these bays spread around the ship. Just unique, so different from his old ways of thinking. But one constant remained, the heavy smell of lubricants and fuel.

It did not take long to find Jamie arguing with one of her crew.

"What the hell did the Major request? No frigging way. Don't do anything until I check in with the captain. You got that?" Seeing the two officers approaching. Jamie waited until Will was next to her before asking. "Since you are here, you must have an idea of what that crazy Major is requesting from me. True?"

Stifling a smile, Will replied with as much calm as he could muster. "I have no idea. But I was instructed by the captain that the major is authorized to request any supplies or support she requires. No questions asked; just honor her request and supply it. The major has the impossible task of securing all three stations. You know she does not have enough personnel to support that task adequately. But the major must have some plan in mind."

Slightly surprised when Jamie started laughing, Nkosana was even more surprised when he heard the Commander comment. "Well, I'll be damned. The Major asked the captain first this time. Usually, she takes what she wants and then asks."

"What did she request, if you do not mind me asking?" asked Nkosana.

"I think I better not tell you; you might not like what you hear. I will leave that up to the major to inform you." With that, Jamie asked if they needed her for anything else. She had a lot of work ahead of her to honor the Major's request. Not counting prepping all the fighters and bombers.

Confirming that was all, Jamie slowly walked away, still chuckling while shaking her head. They could hear her muttering, "*ha… she went to the cap first… she knew I would deny that request. What marine in their right mind would request what she wanted? Ha-ha…. I sure wish I knew what she is planning….*"

They saw marines walking down the hall toward them as they left the bay. None were in armor, which surprised them both. Hugging the wall, with his palms spread behind him to give him balance as the marines passed by, Nkosana glanced over at Will with raised eyebrows.

Shrugging his shoulders to indicate he had no idea, both were surprised as a ship, fighter, or shuttle, they could not tell exactly, was ejected from the bay. The noise was surprising, not as loud as they expected. But they could feel the deep vibrations in their feet as the ship went down the rails.

The marines saluted as they filed by but did not wait for a return salute, although it is usually required. They had no time for silly procedures when about to go into combat. They were long past when the admiral got his hand off the wall and returned the salute. Will never even attempted while they were present except to salute the backs of the marines as they entered the bay.

Walking next to the Commander as they walked toward their quarters to get some much-needed rest, Nkosana asked Will what he thought of the crew.

Surprised at the question, Will almost missed his step. He took a few moments before he responded.

"The crew? They are the best I have ever had the pleasure to serve with, sir. I have been on a half dozen ships or more, and I liked all the crews. They were all dedicated, brave, and talented. But this crew, well, how can I put this correctly?"

They paused to lean against the wall to allow a running technician past. "They always seem to rise to another level when needed. You've seen the fighter pilots fight, best of the best. Bomber crews need no explanation. Isolde with the video for the Kolqux. Selena with the carrier image. I could go on and on. They offer opinions, insights, recommendations, and take extraordinary risks."

Smiling, he rubbed his arms as he related. "I still remember the first action I was in with this crew. The battle raged fiercely, with damage in multiple areas, resources strained, and we had taken a missile hit to the front starboard hull. An uncontrolled fire raging in the area that we could not smother as multiple hatches could not be closed."

Pausing again to allow more marines past, Will continued once they marched. "I went to check it out. I reached the area just in time to assist as four individuals placed a wedge of emergency hull replacement panel on a hole large enough to swallow a large person. The air escaping, the intense heat and smoke, on top of the area still being sprayed down by the auto fire retardant sprinklers, made it almost impossible to work. Luckily, I had put on a fire suit; it was brutal there."

Here the Commander stopped while he scratched a nonexistent itch. "Once the panel was in place, the fire retardant stopped spraying; the fire was out. I didn't have a chance to look closely at the four individuals through the smoke earlier; I was shocked at what I now saw. Only one had put on his protective gear. Their eyes were nearly swollen shut; their hands and arms severely burned."

Sighing, he leaned against the wall before he finished. "They had placed the panel by feel alone on a wall heated by flames while breathing smoke and retardant. And who were the four? You would think all should be engineers, right? One was an engineer, wearing protective gear that was hanging in shreds. The others? How about a chef, a marine, and finally, the last was a nurse that must not have weighed more than a hundred and ten pounds dripping wet? They had propped themselves upon the opposite wall, holding each other's burnt hands, waiting for the medical attention I told them I had called. That is an example of what I see consistently from this crew. I am honored to be a part of this brave team."

Continuing, the two officers passed crew members going about their tasks. Reaching the elevator, Will stopped to say goodbye to Nkosana as he had another job to do before heading to his room. Waving away the Admiral's offer to assist, Will continued down the hall.

That worked for Nkosana as he had a lot of studying before

feeling comfortable doing what Zeke had asked him to do. But he needed some rest first. He learned best when not so tired.

About seven hours later, Will and Nkosana returned to the bridge. Notification had gone out; the Chohish had started deploying fighters and shuttles.

The Lucky Strike and the Kolqux fighters had moved closer to the Chohish as they did not want the battle near the stations. More Kolqux fighters kept arriving to bolster the forces already deployed.

"Lieutenant Bonilla, you and Rear Admiral Okeke, please adjourn to the backup bridge. Lieutenant Iverson, you are now managing communications and sensors. Ensign Caspian Raske, you are in charge of all weapons and defensive armament.

"Commander Farren, the ship is yours. I will join Lieutenant Morison, where we will deploy as planned." Zeke said as he went ramrod stiff and saluted. "To all on the Lucky Strike, it has been my honor to serve with you. Let me share with you one of my favorite quotes from ancient history. *'Courage is not having the strength to go on; it is going on when you don't have the strength.'* Remember that when the going gets tough. Until later, my friends, happy hunting."

With that, Zeke walked off the bridge to a sound of cheers. As he made his way to his assigned fighter, he passed technicians, medical personnel, marines, and many others. All stopped to stand at attention and give him a stiff salute. He did not have time to return them, so he gave them a nod. He received a smile in return. Those smiles meant more to him than any salute.

Walking with Selena, Nkosana thought about what he had been tasked with. While Commander Farren was managing the ship's direct fighting, he would be watching the deployment of the Chohish. Using that info and relaying the information to the RGN and Irracan pilot groupings as the battle commenced. They would follow his recommendations where needed most. For the last few hours, he studied all the information available on Chohish ships and tactics. It was more of a refresher as he had reviewed all this before coming on this voyage, but he did not want to make a bad call on something he forgot or missed.

Entering the small fighter bay, Zeke still could not believe the changes as he jogged to a fighter where a technician was waving.

"Hi Captain, let me help you with your suit while we run through the final diagnostics on your fighter. Lieutenant Morison has already left." The crew member held the flight suit up while Zeke stepped in and watched as it started sealing itself. He added, "Cap, all the crewmembers here wanted me to thank you for being our Captain. We are proud to have served under you no matter what happens."

"Not under me, my friend, served with me. And I am honored to serve with you and them. A captain is not above anyone; he is just another crew member with a different job. But he is only as good as his crew, and I have the best, the very best. Please let them know I said that."

With that, Zeke's suit finished sealing, at which point he took the helmet the attendant handed him. Zeke looked around before climbing into his fighter to see the hustle and bustle around him. He could not imagine being anywhere else but on the Lucky Strike. In his heart, he knew this was where he belonged.

Sitting in his fighter, he put his helmet on, listening to it as it sealed tight. Then he watched the green light flicker on his view plate, indicating a proper seal before disappearing. It would only show again if the seal failed with a red flashing light in the lower left-hand corner.

The engines started once the fighter's AI verified that his helmet signaled green. Then, massaging the joystick, Zeke toggled it back and forth to get familiar with how tight it was. He felt the fighter push off and climb onto the rail that would shoot him out to space.

It was not his first time going out in this fashion, but it still took his breath away with the speed and pressure he felt until the fighter could build up its inertia damper. He was flung out of the cruiser at such a speed that it had shocked him the first time out. It was harder on his body than a normal liftoff, but the advantages of such a fast ejection made it all worthwhile.

Arriving outside, he flew around the Lucky Strike to get in position to settle on the pad situated on the outside Lucky Strike. Engineers had one final hookup to make before he would be ready. Zeke could see another half dozen fighters getting set up as he sat waiting for the engineers to complete their work.

Less than a dozen minutes later, one engineer stepped away from the fighter with his back to him. The technician raised both hands straight up before dropping them quickly into a straight line forward. Even though the AI had already signaled he was ready for takeoff, the Navy insisted on maintaining manual confirmation procedures. Who knew when damage would make it necessary to communicate that way.

Taking off again, he swept toward the front of the cruiser, where several dozen fighters joined him. The same thing had already happened to Jeanne, Gunner, and Hawke. They idled in front of the cruiser behind thousands of Kolqux fighters.

Pushing his throttle to swing his fighter back and forth, Zeke could feel the weight of something he hoped unsettled the Chohish. The new fighters he was sitting in had a connection under their belly. The hookup connected with a pair of missiles customarily used in a bomber.

Pilots always complained that they lacked heavier missiles when fighting warships. Since they had already put bombers in the new specs, they added this to the wish list. The pilots were ecstatic when the new fighters came back updated as they requested.

This new connection allowed a pair of these missiles in addition to their usual complement of fighter missiles. Zeke was hoping the number of Kolqux fighters would cause enough concern to the Chohish that they would send the warships in at the same time as the fighters.

The RGN fighters needed to expel the oversized missiles before dog fighting or returning to the ship. Due to location and size, they needed to be secured from outside the warship, hence the just completed pitstop. The missiles covered all the required connections for the new rail system. Thankfully, the Chohish gave them the time to equip all the RGN and Irracan fighters.

Leading the group, he flew toward the location assigned to his group. It did not take long as they would be far behind the Kolqux. Instead, he brought the fighter to a standstill where he could look out to see what he hoped would be enough to stop the Chohish.

Over forty groups of around one hundred Chohish fighters were in front of him, piloted fortunately by Kolqux. "I guess I should say Kolqux fighters now," thought Zeke. Although there were thousands of fighters and pilots, most of the Kolqux pilot's only training was through game simulators modeled after the fighters. The only exception was the few that had flown shuttles and tugboats.

Hence the RGN and Irracan placement would add the backbone where needed. Break up any Chohish fighter breakthroughs against the Kolqux novices. Once the warships entered the picture, he had genuine concerns, as he had significant doubts that any of his plans would work as he hoped.

Every military leader, good ones anyway, knew the centuries-old quote from the German military strategist Helmuth von Moltke. "*No battle plan survives contact with the Enemy.*" How well he knew that. His only hope was that enough of his current plan would suffice to scrap the necessity to execute the emergency backup plans he agreed to with the Kolqux. Those plans weighed heavily on his mind where. He wished he could come up with anything other than having to order their execution.

Attack Chohish War

The Kolqux fighters were an odd mixture. Designs were similar, but Zeke knew what the difference was. He had seen the newer fighters in the station's enormous cavernous bay. The older ones were from the planet. They were easy to identify due to their blockier structures while a bit slower than their counterparts.

Checking out all the green icons, he remembered his complete surprise when Uv'ek told him how they mothballed all the old fighters the Chohish thought were junk. Year after year, the Kolqux repaired and maintained them just for an occasion like this. Hence the game they created to simulate a fighter. And in those thousands of years, the Chohish never knew; why would they? The Chohish held the Kolqux in contempt. What if the Kolqux did have some old fighters? If they revolted, the Chohish would bombard the planet. And up to now, they had been right.

And more was still coming from the planet. Not in a mad rush, but a steady stream as the fighters were uncovered and prepped for flight. From what Uv'ek said, they were many more thousands on the three planets, many, many thousands. Time was that the Kolqux needed to get them all ready. Many had hidden in plain view hanging from rafters in the large warehouses. The Chohish probably thought they were useless museum pieces. That last was all conjecture as the Chohish never talked to the Kolqux except to belittle or demand something.

Behind the cruiser was an odd assortment of Kolqux warships that were the last resort. Not all the Kolqux warships were available, as many were at the space stations or shipyards getting prepped. Shuttles between the Lucky Strike and the three stations were ongoing nonstop. Behind the Kolqux warships deployed was a growing line of Kolqux fighters still arriving.

The Chohish had not made any moves toward them yet, which was ok with him, as he wanted the Kolqux to have all the time they could get to familiarize themselves with their fighters. Playing a game was one thing; flying a fighter in actual combat was another. Zeke was willing to give the Chohish all the time they wanted.

That thought bore fruit when he watched two Kolqux fighter icons run onto each other, where they broke apart with no sign of pod ejection that he doubted any of these fighters had. The crash was barely a dozen miles ahead of his fighter. Sadly, he expected more deaths like this to occur before the battle even started. Then, the Kolqux would die more numerously against a much more experienced foe, the Chohish.

THE BATTLE BEGINS

TIME PASSING WHILE waiting for the action to start has to be the most challenging issue for a pilot in a fighter. The Kolqux were not skilled enough to attack the Chohish; there would be little gain. Their only hope was to meet the Chohish defensively, where Zeke hoped that the plan they had devised would be enough to drive the Chohish from the system.

The RGN and Irracan pilots were sitting motionless, waiting for the enemy to make their move to save fuel. All pilots, including the Kolqux, had brought provisions to stay in position for an extended period. The flight suits, even the oversized Chohish suits that the Kolqux wore, could handle body waste for several days.

The Kolqux pilots had finally settled down after getting a feel for flying. It was getting close to the time to see how much they had learned. Nkosana, per Zeke's request, was coordinating with Uv'ei to have the Kolqux fly back in selected groups to refuel. Most had burned up more than half their fuel learning how to maneuver their vessels.

It had been a surprise to see the Major back in action. As much respect Zeke had for Khalessi's officers, Khalessi made her marines so deadly through her planning and leadership. It was not just his opinion; her officers have made that clear to him several times. Although defending the three stations may be more than she can handle. But that is not something he could worry about; he would be lucky to survive the next several hours.

If only the Chohish would give him enough time to finish putting together the surprise he hoped would tip the scales in their favor. Every moment they sat there, the better. Jamie could not assure him she could meet his timeline. Seeing her standing there with her engineers, who looked at him like he was crazy after letting them know what he required, was something to see. Jamie, though, never said they could not do it.

Hours later, he got notification from Nkosana that the bombers were about to deploy. That gave him some hope Jamie was able to do what he wanted. As the first bombers flew from the cruiser, the Chohish made their move. It was almost as if the bombers appearing triggered the action, although Zeke knew that it was just a coincidence. He had doubts that the Chohish could identify individual ships of that size so far away without having probes deployed. Although, it could have been because they were coming from the cruiser that triggered the Chohish, although shuttles had been coming and going non-stop.

It would be hours before the Chohish reached the missile range, allowing enough time for the Kolqux to complete refueling and get back in position. Meanwhile, Isolde sent him details on how the Chohish were deploying. His hope that the warships would mix with the Chohish fighters did not pan out; their warships were moving but staying a reasonable distance behind.

"Uv'ei, you on? It looks like the Chohish needs encouragement to join the fighters. Please pass on to your fighters that they need to go to plan B. They are to wait on Rear Admiral Okeke to give the order to move into the positions we discussed and reviewed. Make sure no one gets trigger fingers. No one, and I repeat, no one, is to fire until they get the order from the Admiral. I cannot stress that enough."

"I am on Captain. I will let the group commanders know. They will make sure everyone waits on the Admiral. We have been waiting a long time for this; no one wants to ruin it now."

"Rear Admiral Okeke, I know I do not have to say this, but I will anyway. You are key to the whole plan. You are to coordinate the Kolqux. With all the probes we placed in the system, you should have a clear view of the battlefield and be able to call the shots. I do not understand why they have not removed them, but it may relate to why they do not deploy probes. Commander Farren and Lieutenant Iverson will run the ship from the backup bridge. With that in mind, keep the ship out of the action unless necessary. Zeke out."

There was no response, none needed. Zeke and Nkosana had reviewed what to expect a dozen times before Zeke left the cruiser. Nkosana knew what he needed to do; he had been commanding large fleets for many years. Only this time, he would be mainly commanding Kolqux forces, who were untrained without any battle experience. It opened up all kinds of possibilities, none being perfect.

Again, time slowly passed, with tension rising as the Chohish crept closer. Even though they moved with incredible speed crossing large distances every minute, it showed as barely moving on their scanners. It was hard to tell someone who has never been in space just how large it is.

It was another three hours before Zeke figured Nkosana would start making his moves. Being on the waiting side while others made the call was humbling. Zeke could feel his impatience getting the best of him, but it was now out of his hands.

Shifting in his seat for the thousandth time, Zeke closely watched the Chohish fighters as they got closer. Behind them, the

Chohish warships kept a healthy distance between them. "*Well, let's see if we can't change their minds.*" thought Zeke.

Suddenly, one group of Kolqux fighters started moving. All had been sitting motionless, waiting on the Chohish to get closer. Now though, one, then two, started moving to merge into another group. Soon a good half of the fighters were slowly moving.

Zeke knew his AI could never display all the fighters individually. So he had his ship's AI show the groups of Kolqux fighters as one individual icon. Zeke saw one group after another merge until it finally resolved into ten groups. He had been reluctant to group the Kolqux fighters so close to each other, but this was necessary to execute the next stage of his plan B.

"Uv'ei, the next part of the plan is the trickiest. Let the pilots settle their nerves for a moment before executing the next stage. Remember, fire, turn slowly, minimal thrust acceleration until at full thrust forward. There is to be no special flying, no playing with the controls. They are to wait on the Admiral's command. The Admiral will tell them when to stop and turn around. Again, the Admiral will direct them on what to do. Make sure they understand that. I do not want to lose fighters because they are over-anxious." ordered Zeke.

"Captain, they are aware. They know they do not have the skill to match the Chohish. They will follow the Admiral's orders to the letter. They have lived their whole lives hoping against hope to be in this position. They are not going to screw it up now." Uv'ei responded.

"Oh, Captain, one more thing. Khaleesi said all her preparations were now in place. Told me to tell you that if you see any shuttles that look like they carry boarding parties, ignore them; let them come on. So please do not waste any resources on them. Any fighters that are escorting them, the station will take them out.

Khaleesi said she would handle the boarding parties. Said something about you do your job and let her do hers."

Just as he thought Uv'ei was going to sign off. He heard a click taking him to a private link before a soft voice barely audible continued. "Captain, just one more thing, Khaleesi is one scary person. Her marines are not much better. I had to replace many of my staff as they were experiencing breakdowns from being near them for an extended time. I sure hope all the stuff she and her marines made us do, works as expected. I sure do not want to face her wrath if they fail." at which the communications died.

Knowing Khaleesi, he could not disagree. She was direct and to the point when prepping for a battle. Sloppiness, laziness, or inattention were quick ways to get on her wrong side. Even Jeanne, who relished playful feuds, stayed away from feuding with Khaleesi. No one wanted to get on Khaleesi's bad side. It never ended well.

Sitting there, he wondered when Nkosana would pull the trigger. The Chohish fighters' icons looked close enough for this part of the plan. Unfortunately, Zeke did not have all the sensor data that Nkosana had. He had no desire to bother the Admiral when he knew it was just his nerves causing the issues.

Fifteen minutes later, eight thousand missiles blasted away from the Kolqux fighters without warning. Followed by another eight thousand half a minute later. Zeke watched as the Kolqux icons slowly turned and headed out, picking up speed.

The Chohish responded with several thousand of their own, followed by the same with barely a pause; Zeke smiled as this part of his plan had worked anyway.

"Ensign Bonilla, this is Captain Kinsley; please keep me updated on the progress of the Chohish missiles. The data I need are speed and distance. Do they match our prior estimates? Zeke out."

"Captain, speed is matching what we expected. I will send the distance once available. Selena out."

Now, if only everything worked as he planned. The Chohish fighters were heading toward the missiles fired at them while the Kolqux fighters were moving away from the missiles fired at them.

Minutes passed until the icons that represented the RGN missiles reached the Chohish. But his display could not display them individually, so he could not tell how effective the barrage had been.

While waiting for information to arrive, he saw the Kolqux had slowed down to a stop. Then he watched as the groups moved as one to the right. While watching this, Caspian reached out to him.

"Captain, Ensign Bonilla is working on something for the Admiral, so unable to gather the information you requested. The missiles from the Chohish have stopped thrusting. They are displaying the same attributes as the missiles we are familiar with, same speed, same range."

"Ensign Raske, status on damage to the Chohish fighters?"

"Getting final tallies now. The Chohish took about a twenty-three percent loss while the Kolqux lost just under a hundred. The Kolqux losses were due to their pilots not getting out of the way of each other. Otherwise, the Chohish missiles shot right past them without fuel."

While discussing with Caspian, the Kolqux launched another salvo, paused for a few seconds, then fired another. Again, they followed the same procedure before turning and flying away from the Chohish.

Keeping an eye on the Chohish, his fighter AI notified him that the Chohish fighters were slowing down. It was confirmed when Caspian sent him the same information seconds later. It would not help the Chohish avoid the missiles fired by the Kolqux, but they looked to be waiting on the destroyers to join them.

"*Alright, they realized they had to get some defensive fire involved to minimize their losses.*" Zeke thought as he pounded his two fists together.

"Ok, ladies and gentlemen, we wait on the Kolqux to get to the prearranged location where we will mix in near the back. Our targets are the destroyers. The Kolqux will lead the way and cover our approach."

He knew the Kolqux would take massive casualties to cover their approach, but it was not the Chohish fighters that concerned him. It was the battleships and cruisers. They could rain down destruction on the planets without retaking the stations. Those were what he had to stop, and he could not do that without taking out their protective screen of destroyers.

This stage of the planning was the heated discussion he had with Uv'ei. Uv'ei insisted Zeke's battle plans were to ignore Kolquc losses. The Kolqux either won or risked elimination as a species. Every Kolqux in the fighters, warships, and stations knew that. They knew they were expendable. That did not make it any easier on Zeke, though; he knew today would probably haunt his dreams for the rest of his life.

The distance was too great to see when the Kolqux missiles arrived, but he could envision what happened. Unfortunately, the loss of missiles was much more significant now that the destroyers were involved.

The ping from Selena interrupted his thoughts. "Captain, the ship's AI calculates that the Chohish lost another quarter of their real fighters. They would have lost a lot more if not for the destroyers, as there are not as many fighters to target after the first missile barrage.

However, what surprised him was how well the Kolqux fighters were flying. They had reached the location where they were to stop and turn. They did this with no pause, even though this turn was more complicated as they had to fly to a position away from the path of the original and second set of Chohish missiles. They were soon all in place in front of him. Broken out into their initial grouping, as he had positioned the RGN fighters at the final location before they would merge to allow the Kolqux a visual of where to go on their screens.

Shifting one more time to get comfortable, he took a moment to settle his thoughts. The next few hours would require him to stay vigilant for his safety and overall battle. He was on the front line, not just to fly a fighter or lead a group of fighters. But because he needed to be up close to identify any unexpected changes.

Being at the back of the battle meant details came in slower, which may indicate a lost battle as the response may be too late. Nkosana, Jeanne, and Will understood that, which is why they agreed to him leave the Lucky Strike.

The Lucky Strike had a different task this time around. They needed to coordinate the Kolqux and be the final defensive major asset to contest access to the planets. That might be stopping missiles from destroying cities or attacking a warship. They would be busy enough surviving, let alone worrying about a battle that would be millions of miles away.

As Khaleesi would say, that was his job. Zeke had confidence in Will to protect the ship and do what was needed to protect the planets. Zeke had been in campaigns under the Admiral, so he was confident in Nkosana's ability to manage the deployment of the Kolqux.

Those two aspects of the coming battle have been removed from his control. Now he could dedicate his time to what they needed to do. Remove the Chohish warships from the equation.

Well, his time for reflection was over; it was time to take the battle to the Chohish.

The Kolqux fighter groups started moving toward the Chohish as one, with the RGN fighters merging into the back of different groups. Speed was picking up slowly, with the Kolqux warships idling behind the final line of late arrival Kolqux fighters grouping behind them.

Chohish and Kolqux fighters fired another set of missiles as their distance closed. Zeke knew the Kolqux would pay a much heavier price than the Chohish, and his assumption was soon a reality. The updates he was getting from the Lucky Strike reported heavy Kolqux losses. The Chohish also took severe losses but not near the same degree.

Being at the group's rear, he was required to avoid a lone missile only once, which he accomplished with chaff and ECM only. He was thankful for that as he doubted he could have avoided it otherwise with the heavy missiles attached.

Then the alert he was waiting for came; he was now in range of one of the Chohish destroyers. Two other RGN pilots were synced in with his AI so all three would fire their missiles and arrive at the destroyer simultaneously. First, they would fire a pair of standard missiles, followed closely by the huge bomber missiles.

The distance between the two opposing groups shortened. It would not be long before they met. Without notice, the AIs took control and fired off the first set. The fighter shook more than he was used to when firing a missile, but he was shocked when the larger missiles fired.

Fighters were lighter framed for a reason, to allow for rapid change of direction. The sudden release of the heavier missile weight caused the fighter to change direction faster than the ship's AI could handle.

It took a few seconds for him to get control again. And none too soon. Ahead of him were a pair of Chohish fighters coming straight at him as they recognized his ship as being different from the rest.

Determining their trajectory, Zeke went into a tight spin aiming his lasers on one of the fighters. Then, as the first fighter burned, he went into a wide loop, chasing the second fighter. That fighter lasted no longer than the first.

Flying around the debris, he quickly surveyed the fighting around him. He grimaced at the number of Kolqux fighters his AI reported no longer reporting. But he also received some excellent news from Lucky Strike simultaneously.

LS1 reported that the Chohish fighters had difficulty identifying which fighters were piloted by Chohish or Kolqux. There was a delay from the Chohish firing on another fighter sending out the same transponder as their own. They had to wait until being fired upon before returning fire.

That was the deception that Zeke needed Jamie's support. So leave the Chohish transponders but add one that the RGN could recognize.

Most of the Kolqux fighters were an older version with an old transponder. Jamie had to figure out how to change the existing transponder to broadcast two different signals. She must have gotten with Uv'ek, who had said he could assist when Zeke told him what he planned.

Now he wanted to watch what happened to the destroyers. Zeke directed his fighter toward the rear, away from the front. The pair of fighters he had fired in conjunction with now acting as a protective escort.

A destroyer way off to port grabbed his attention first. It exploded in a massive ball of flame, matched shortly afterward by another large explosion. It was not the last.

Finally, the explosions stopped altogether. Zeke then received an emergency ping from Caspian, accepting the connection. He heard Caspian's report.

"Captain, as requested, LS1 kept track of the Chohish destroyers with a report to be put together for you asap. Only four of the three dozen that started the action are still moving on their own.

Six are motionless, three of which are still showing offensive capabilities. The Admiral reported having the Kolqux concentrate on taking them out. Caspian out."

Disconnecting from the call, he notified his escort they could join the fight, leaving because a fighter marked in red and black arrived.

"Hello, my love, ready for some fun?" asked Jeanne over a private link.

"Thought you would never ask," responded Zeke as he engaged his thrusters to the maximum.

Heading into the areas where the Kolqux had the most problems, Jeanne's fighter rode next to him on his starboard. Seeing a group of six Chohish fighters tearing into the Kolqux, they fired their afterburners to tail behind the group.

Firing one missile, Zeke went after another Chohish fighter with his lasers. The Chohish must have received the alert he was on his tail as it swerved sharply to port. Still firing his afterburners, Zeke shouted "*yahoo*" while tensing all his muscles; simultaneously, the seat inflated to put pressure on his thighs to keep from blacking out.

The Chohish twisted again sharply to starboard, but it did not do him any good; Zeke took him out anyway. Heading back to the action, he saw that the group he had been following had been reduced by another two. "*Looks like Jeanne has been busy too.*"

The two fighters left in the group they had been chasing took off in another direction, followed by a group of Kolqux fighters. Zeke shut down his afterburners as he went in search of others, with Jeanne sliding onto his port side.

REINFORCEMENTS

THE FIGHTER DUEL went on for another hour before the remnants of the Chohish fighters retreated.

Seeing the retreat, Zeke ordered the RGN fighters to regroup back at their original starting point. Nkosana ordered the same for Kolqux fighters.

Zeke's fighter AI indicator showed that he had lost thirteen RGN fighters. The AI could not identify an ejection pod signal from seven of them. Hopefully, the pods were malfunctioning, though he had his doubts.

As they pulled back, he checked on how the Kolqux had fared. Close to thirty percent had perished. They had no pods to eject with, so any fighter failure meant death within minutes. Their suits had nothing to counter the cold of space.

As sad as he was at the loss of so many Kolqux, he had expected worse. The remaining number would allow him to put the next stage of his plan into play. What surprised him most was the Chohish cruiser and battleships not joining the battle. The carriers were nowhere around, but he had not expected them to stay. It changed his plans a bit, but nothing major.

One thing he was sorry about the delay meant that Jeanne went back to her group. They had agreed she would lead her group in but once engaged, they did not need her assistance and could join him again where they could fight as a pair.

The RGN pilots were still returning when he pinged Jamie, seeing the Chohish warships still had not moved.

Upon her return ping, he connected to the sound of the loud banging of metal on metal. "Lieutenant Commander, everything Ok?"

"Sorry, Captain, let me get out of the immediate area." Zeke could hear her walking as she was wearing her magnetic boots.

"Ok, now we should be able to hear each other. Since the Marines are short-staffed, they are fortifying the hallways by building extra barricades with booby traps. Most marines and army personnel have gone to the stations with the Major." Zeke stopped talking briefly as he could hear her responding to someone.

"Damn chefs, who did they think the marines were going to requisition for guard duty? Anyway, what did you need, Captain?"

"The Chohish battleships and cruisers did not join the action as I expected. Giving us an opportunity I would like to take advantage of if possible. Most of the fighters need replenishment. I know you sent many of your people to the stations to help out there. Do you have the staff available if I send them back?"

"Yes, that should not be a problem. Most of my staff have returned. The major did not need the technician's assistance anymore. The Kolqux can finish whatever else she may require; all in all, the Kolqux are pretty good engineers. But I have no more of the Bomber missiles if that is what you hoped. Just the normal fighter missile compliment."

"Damn, I was hoping we could get one more shot with the larger missiles. Oh well, the regular missiles with do. Skip the fueling unless it's doable within the same timeframe. I do not think we will have that much time, and I would like to get as many loaded up as possible."

"Send them on, Captain; we will be waiting on them. The chefs will just have to work a little harder. Jamie out."

With no delay, Zeke contacted the other RGN group leaders to arrange a schedule to get the fighters rearmed. Nkosana, who had been monitoring the conversation between Zeke and Jamie, let both know that he would have Uv'ei start doing the same for the Kolqux fighters.

Satisfied that everything was moving nicely, Zeke had Selena send him the latest system layout for personal review. *"Why did the battleships and cruisers not join the attack? What are you waiting on?"* he wondered, looking at the Chohish warships sitting idle.

"Jeanne, Zeke here. I am concerned about why the battleships and cruisers are not making any move to attack. I believe they are waiting on reinforcements. We cannot allow that to happen."

"Hi Zeke, I was thinking the same thing. Going on the offensive will cause horrendous casualties, but if we wait, I am afraid it will be magnitudes worse. It is doubtful we can take them out as it is."

"I will start a conference call as we need to get buy-in from everyone. We will have to change our plans."

Sending a conference ping out, Zeke relayed his concerns. Nkosana and Will concurred; they were also thinking the same thing. Uv'ei said the Kolqux would follow whatever Zeke ordered.

"Uv'ei, if we do this, many Kolqux will die. They do not have the skill, but we need them to deflect attention from us. Otherwise, the RGN pilots will not even get close. I am not even sure we can be successful. We can wait and hope the RGN fleet shows up or risk it all on an attack. Uv'ei, it is your call."

There was a muffled conversation from Uv'ei's link. "I relayed the question to the council. They unanimously said they do not know war; they have no idea what to do. They will abide by whatever you think is best. One thing they did tell me to tell you. Please do not hold back due to any concern about Kolqux losses, as I already told you. We are fighting to survive as a race."

With a heavy heart, Zeke knew what he would and had to do! But first, if given the time, he would resupply his fleet. The next stage would require all the firepower he could muster.

Several hours later, the Chohish still had not moved. All ships had been resupplied and repositioned back to their starting positions. Jamie was one of the first persons he requested when they assigned him to the Lucky Strike. You lived or died by what you fought with. What good was having the best pilots if they sat in a fighter with no fuel or weapons?

Nkosana, working with Uv'ei, combined the Kolquxfighters into new groups to full strength. New groups were created from the fighters still arriving from the planet.

One thing, though, did bother Zeke after getting a report from Nkosana, a large group of several hundred Kolqux fighters stayed near the Kolqux warships, with more joining frequently. Nkosana informed him that Uv'ei said they were older models that could not keep up with the other fighters, so Uv'ei would have them stay with the warships. That made sense, so he let it be.

The lull was a luxury that burned both ways. It allowed Zeke time to resupply and work out an attack plan. Yet, it also allowed whatever reinforcements the Chohish were waiting for, if he was correct in that thinking, to get closer.

They could not hold off any longer; it was time. "Admiral Okeke, we can no longer delay any longer, if you would."

Again, one group of Kolqux fighters started moving, another, and so on. What was different this time around was the Kolqux warships were moving. They were leaving a large gap behind the main fighter groups. The fighters holding back, now numbering close to a thousand with more still streaming from the planets, stayed close to the warships.

The RGN fighters followed in a straight line behind the Kolqux fighters. The RGN fighters would obviously be the main target after the last engagement.

But the RGN fighters had a different job this time around. Protect the bombers which were following just behind.

The Chohish did not move until the Kolqux reached their warship's missile range. It was now apparent that the Chohish were reluctant to move away from the vicinity of the slipstream. The only reason had to be they were waiting on reinforcements.

Both sides fired the missiles as they did before. The RGN pilots held off on firing theirs as they would need them later. The Kolqux fighters fired all their missiles in succession as they all were manual. Flying and firing were beyond their capability at this time.

This time around, the Kolqux paid a horrible price. The Kolqux tried to outmaneuver the missiles when warned that a missile was targeting them, but many failed. Over a thousand perished within minutes.

It was not all one-sided, though. The Chohish did not have anywhere near the number of fighters they had started with this time. They had a lot less. If Zeke got accurate reports, the Chohish were less than a hundred fighters.

Even with the reduced numbers, the Chohish fighters came on with the battleships and the cruisers following.

It was not long before the Chohish warships started firing nonstop. The damage they caused on the Kolqux was terrific. Yet, the Kolqux did shy away from the battle. They knew that was their primary function, distraction.

The RGN fighters entered the fray. Only a few Chohish fighters left; even though the Kolqux were not expert pilots, they had ganged up four to five for each Chohish fighter. But the ones that were left knew the RGN ships were the real danger. They made a straight run for them.

Zeke, accompanied by Jeanne, hit his afterburners to intercept a group of Chohish fighters. Half of the RGN fighters broke into pairs, where they swung in a tight circle to escort the bombers, and the other half paired up to chase after the remaining Chohish fighters.

The fight with the remaining Chohish fighters was anticlimactic as the Chohish seemed sluggish. No RGN fighters were even damaged, let alone destroyed. But now, the real danger was barreling down on them.

"Lieutenant Commander Dean, I believe it is your turn now. We will lead the way."

Turning toward the nearest cruiser, Zeke, with Jeanne as his partner again, angled toward the port side. Gunner and Librada joined the fight by going topside.

Lasers and missiles were heavy around the cruiser as the Chohish cruisers point defense came online. Weaving and jerking the fighter to throw off the lasers, Zeke and Jeanne raced down the cruiser's side, firing their missiles almost point-blank.

Damage from their combined fire was negligible, but it did accomplish one thing. First, it masked the bomber assigned to this cruiser. It fired its missiles in coordination with all four fighter pilots, so they hit just behind the smaller missiles.

The bomber missiles tore huge gashes out of the side of the cruiser. Flame and debris erupted outward. The two pairs had flown in a wide arc and now came racing back once more firing another pair of missiles.

These missiles entered the chasms of destruction and caused massive damage. The follow-up bomber missiles were the cruiser's death toll, though. They followed the fighter's missiles, where they tore the cruiser in half. Defensive fire from the cruiser stopped immediately as the split cruiser drifted away.

They did not waste any time checking on the cruiser's carcass. Instead, Zeke and the group sped off to join the attack on another cruiser. They saw one of four fighters attacking the cruiser explode as they came close. Then, joining the other three, they drew the fire away from the two bombers attacking.

It took several passes to get through the defenses. Surprisingly, it was the Kolqux who made it possible. A dozen Kolqux fighters attacked, drawing the majority of defensive fire and allowing the bombers almost uncontested fire zones. The Chohish cruiser was a drifting hulk but at the loss of eight of the Kolqux fighters.

"Captain Kinsley, Admiral Okeke here. There are only a pair of cruisers left. The bombers look to be taking care of those. The Chohish battleships have backed off; they may be attempting to leave. I am sending in the Kolqux warships. For your information, the Kolqux have taken heavy casualties, over twelve hundred lost."

"Admiral, we must stop those battleships at all costs," responded Jeanne. "If Zeke is correct, if they can join another force, we will not be able to stop them."

"I know Captain de Clisson, I know. I will be bringing in the Lucky Strike to assist. There is nothing more I can do back here. Admiral out."

Then the chase was on. All the fighters and Kolqux warships hastened after the Chohish battleships. None held back; this was all-or-nothing. All that is, except for the older Kolqux fighters gathering behind the Kolqux warships.

Within minutes, the Chohish battleships surrounded by Kolqux fighters ran. Kolqux after Kolqux died. Yet, some got through the protective envelope, paving the way for the RGN fighters and bombers.

Explosions rocked the battleships, with flame and debris

erupting from multiple locations. Nevertheless, the battleships continued. They were vast beasts of war and gave as good as they took. They did, that is, until the Kolqux warships entered the scene.

The Kolqux warships may not have the full complement of weapons or shields, but most had missiles. A lot of missiles. Again though, they were not immune to the fire from the battleships. Explosions rocked the Kolqux warships, with some exploding into fragments.

Unexpectedly, two of the Chohish battleships exploded violently. Dozens of Kolqux fighters perished, along with several RGN fighters. One other battleship stopped firing and drifted without power while the other three continued their race for the slipstream.

Sweat running into his eyes blinded him for a second. When Zeke regained his vision after shaking his head violently, he was surprised to see the Lucky Strike between the Chohish battleships and the slipstream.

"*How the hell did they get around them? Damn, good job, Will. Go get them,*" thought Zeke as he swung his fighter behind a Chohish fighter trying futilely to protect one of the surviving battleships. Firing his lasers, he made short work of the fighter.

The Lucky Strike's first salvo devasted an already damaged battleship. The battleship tried to turn to port to run around the cruiser, only to be met by several bombers. In less than a minute, only two Chohish battleships survived.

"*Warning, warning,* ships are transitioning through the slipstream. Three Chohish cruisers and eight destroyers are present, with more arriving," shouted Caspian through the headphones on all ships.

"*Damn, we were so close. We are spent, have no missiles, are low on fuel, and over half of the Kolqux fighters have been destroyed. The Kolqux warships cannot stand against a Chohish armada, no matter the size,*" reflected Zeke.

"Admiral, get the Lucky Strike out of there. We will have to regroup. We are not strong enough to take on a new force without resupply," ordered Zeke.

By this time, Zeke's instruments reported that three additional battleships, four cruisers, eight destroyers, and a pair of carriers had arrived. Zeke could hear the Admiral ordering the Kolqux to regroup near the stations. They would make their last stand there.

Then what he had always feared the Chohish would do occurred. The carriers unloaded dozens of shuttles and fighters, all headed away toward the stations.

There was no force to stop them. By the time his fighters could catch up, the battle for control of the stations would already be over. But, of course, that did not even address the new group of Chohish warships issue. So how would they take care of them?

What happened next took him by surprise. The old Kolqux fighters arrived unexpectedly on the scene. Their numbers were now close to several thousand. They flew as one gigantic wave toward this new Chohish force.

Puzzled, he was about to ask what was happening when he knew without having to ask. Swiftly, he pinged the Lucky Strike. "Admiral, ignore my last orders. Attack the last pair of Chohish battleships. We need to take them out before they can rejoin the new force. The Kolqux will keep the new force busy for a while."

Taking his fighter into another tight turn, he ignored the pain in his shoulders from the pounding of such quick turns; he headed back toward the action. The seat might have gel and other materials to cushion the impacts, but it was never enough.

"Admiral, I am leaving you here to manage the Kolqux. I will take half the RGN fighters to the station, Zeke out."

Over the next several hours, he watched what he had figured out as he flew after the Chohish shuttles and fighters. Uv'ei may profess not to know how to fight, but he was not ignorant. He knew that there was no going back for the Kolqux. If they lost this fight, the retribution from the Chohish would be severe. Millions, if not billions, would die.

The old fighters did not fight or evade; they flew straight to the new Chohish taskforce. Zeke doubted most had working lasers. The Kolqux fighters, bolstered by the Kolqux warships, were shot down by the hundreds. But that still left over a thousand. And these flew at full power into the sides, the top, the front, and the rear, of the Chohish warships, where they exploded in horrific explosions.

The size of the explosions let Zeke know that the ships were packed with bombs or some explosive material. Zeke watched a Kolqux cruiser, burning and limping along, run into a Chohish battleship. The cruiser buried itself into the battleship to partially reach the other side before rupturing and exploding.

This scene occurred all over the battlefield. It was only later when Zeke got a priority message from the Lucky Strike as it swung past a destroyed Chohish battleship, that Zeke realized the battle was surprisingly over. Destroyed Kolqux fighters and warships littered space alongside the Chohish.

As Zeke raced back to the stations, he was concerned that he and the pilots with him would run out of fuel. Jeanne had warned the pilots about not using their afterburners, but even then, he had doubts.

As he flew, he put in a call to Khaleesi.

The sound of heavy breathing did not mask the frustration he heard on the other line. "Captain, are you calling to inform me of the Chohish shuttles headed our way?"

"Yes, Major, I am heading there with several squads of fighters if our fuel holds out."

"Captain, appreciate the heads up. Can I get back to work on finishing the warm welcome my boys and girls are planning to give them?"

As he was about to reply, he heard Khalessi sigh before continuing. "Captain, up to now, we have been fighting on their turf. Now, they will be fighting on our turf, my turf. My marines are angry, really angry. They are tired of fighting with their hands tied behind their back. We will show these Chohish bastards what happens when Marines get pissed off and angry. They get mean, they get mean, killer mean. I will say this one more time, relax, we got this."

The disconnect let Zeke know Khaleesi was done talking. For a second there, he almost felt sorry for the Chohish. Then, he contacted the station over the main planet and requested Uv'ei, only to find out he was with Khaleesi.

At the central station, Khaleesi turned to Uv'ei. "I told you the captain would call. He is one of the best captains I have served with, but now it is our turn in this war. The fighters are yours. The rest are mine."

Putting her hands on his shoulders, she leaned down until her face was a bare inch away. "Uv'ei, remember this; when the time comes, get mean. Get real mean; remember what they have done to you and your people. Do not let the anger control you; you control the anger. Let it feed your body, your mind. Let the enemy see that you will never let anyone control you again. Understand?"

Uv'ei looked at this woman who had been close to death fighting for his people. A marine who should now be in a medical bay stood before him, ready to risk her life once again. She towered over him in her armor, but he felt no fear in her presence anymore.

When he first met Khaleesi, she scared him; she had such an overpowering presence. Being scared was a way of life for the Kolqux for as long as they could remember. But now, he was no longer scared of dying; he was afraid of failing this woman who had done so much for them and was going to risk it all again for them one more time.

"I will remember Major; I will make sure my people remember.

We will take care of the fighters. You can count on us." Uv'ei saluted, then smiled.

"Then I must go, my friend; I must get dressed for my date. Hate for my guests to feel insulted because I underdressed. I am going to wear something special for them," with which Khaleesi turned on her heel and walked toward the cavernous bay.

Smiling, Uv'ei remembered the giant nasty-looking machines that had come walking off the marine shuttles. The machines had weapons evident all over the outside. The Kolqux had gathered to watch in amazement as they had never seen the like. They watched as these machines walked around the bay to end up behind the barricades the Kolqux had made under Khaleesi's direction. Then they gasped in astonishment when these machines opened up, and the marines stepped out. He knew what Khaleesi was going to get dressed in.

Returning to the command center, Uv'ei met his brother Uv'ek sitting in the vast command chair in the middle of the room. The chair dwarfed him, and his head was barely visible. At any other time, Uv'ei would have laughed. It looked so ludicrous.

"We ready, brother? The enslavers come for us in force."

"We are ready, brother. There is not much we have to do other than repair the damage. I have repair teams positioned around the station. We have replaced the station's AI with the one supplied by the humans. They told me it would be more effective and manage all the station's weapons independently. The Major said they had no personnel to spare to help us in this matter. We have no real experience that would be of any benefit to the AI. The tests the human engineers ran were very encouraging."

"Brother, I am going to leave you in charge. I will stay with the Marines if they allow it."

Startled, Uv'ek tried to rise from the chair, only to climb over the arm. Rushing to his brother, he grabbed Uv'ei's arms in panic.

"No, brother, you cannot. That will be certain death. You must let the humans do what they do without you in the way. They will not be able to protect you."

Wriggling out of his brother's grip, Uv'ei sat on his heels, resting on the floor. "I cannot sit here while the humans risk their lives for us. I know they were already fighting the Chohish, but they could have waited for their fleet to minimize the risk to themselves. Instead, they risked it all so we could be free. I must go and be there, brother."

Seeing the look on his brother's face, Uv'ek knew that Uv'ei had made up his mind. It was another punch in the gut. They had lost a brother several months ago because he unknowingly walked in front of a Chohish. Now, he knew the Chohish would take another away from him. When would this stop?

Gnashing his gums, he resisted the urge to yell at the brother who had risked everything many times for his family, for his people. He fought against wanting to scream out his frustrations. Instead, he knelt to hug his brother one last time. And, like always, his brother gave him some parting words. He did not know that they were the exact words that Khaleesi had told Uv'ei just moments ago.

As Uv'ei finished with, '*Let the enemy see that you will never let anyone control you again!*', Uv'ek felt it. The anger, the pain, the humiliation, everything he had suffered his whole life. Rage came to the forefront. But he did not let it control him; he guided it to where it belonged. And he saw the rage mirrored in Uv'ei's face.

"Ok, brother, I see; I feel what you are saying. You join the Marines; I will ensure we do what has to be done here. Go, and know I love you and will care for your family if anything happens."

Hugging each other tightly, Uv'ek stayed on the floor until he saw Uv'ei rise and run out. Standing, he looked around the command center. Every eye was on him. The rage he had felt earlier returned. Not at the Chohish, but himself, all in the room.

Climbing into the command seat, Uv'ek stood so all could see him. With sorrow mixed with pain, Uv'ei said. "My bother goes to fight with the Marines; more than likely, he will die. Is he any braver than us? Are we to sit here and wait for the humans to succeed or fail? Is that our future? Let others do what we are afraid to do? Did we not learn from what happened those thousands of years ago when we could not defend ourselves?"

The Kolqux then understood why they held Uv'ei and his brother, Uv'ek, in such high regard. "You may sit here and wait in fear; I will grab a weapon and join the human army personnel covering key locations around the station. I am tired of others fighting for us."

Jumping down from the chair, Uv'ek headed toward the exit. He had to pause due to the crush of others joining him. Uv'ek could see the fear in their expressions, but he also saw something that gave him heart. Anger and determination.

PAYBACK

RUNNING THROUGH THE hallways, Uv'ei could feel his heart pounding in fear. Knowing the Chohish were on their way made his two hearts flutter in panic. How could he, being so much smaller compared to the size of a Chohish, expect to fight them? They could crush him without even trying.

As he neared the bay, he slowed down. He did not know how to approach the Major. Would she throw him out? Would she laugh at him?

Entering the bay, he saw a flurry of activity. The vast machines called battleoids were clearing the bay of any obstruction. Item after item was picked up and thrown to the side, where they used to create large lanes. These lanes ran the entire length of the bay. Each route had an opening by the wall furthest away from the forcefield to allow movements between the lanes.

Seeing the Major symbol, he made his way over in trepidation and was in the process of picking up a spare landing gear when she saw him.

"Well, well, my friend. Now what could bring Uv'ei down here?" boomed the voice of Khaleesi out of the enormous machine.

Before he could answer, the battleoid opened up. Climbing

down the battleoids leg, Khaleesi kneeled in front of Uv'ei so they were eye to eye.

"I am guessing you did not come here to tell me something, so what else could it be?" Khaleesi said with amusement in her voice.

"I want to help. Uv'ek does not need me in the command center. But I do not know what I can do? Do you have anything?"

"Follow me," Khaleesi said. Standing, she walked toward one of the tiny structures that Khaleesi had the Kolqux build around the inner wall of the bay. Walking, more like jogging to keep up with her, Uv'ei noticed how different it looked from when they first entered the bay just a short while ago.

Next to the structure he was approaching was one of the large bulbous-shaped electronic devices that the engineers from the Lucky Strike had attached. Nearly a hundred units were positioned around the bay, all facing outwards.

The engineers were disinclined to tell anyone what they did. Said it would be evident in time. The laugher from the marines had caused consternation among the assisting Kolqux.

Leading Uv'ei behind the structure reminded Uv'ei of a wall that rose three times his height. It extended about three-quarters the length of a shuttle. Throughout the wall were slotted holes just over his head with a small platform under each near the floor. The structure had used slats available for repairing the skin on the station, so it was very thick. Laying on the floor, he could see multiple bundles stacked on each other.

Khaleesi picked one up, which she handed to Uv'ei. "This, my friend, is one of the suits the army personnel use when training. It will be a little big for you, but there are adjustments you can make, so it fits somewhat. It has armor and strength augmentation. You will need that augmentation to withstand the shock of firing a weapon. There are multiple helmets here; try a few out to see which one fits best. Sorry, you must wear your own footwear; we could do nothing for you there."

Khaleesi bent down again to pick up a pistol off the floor. "This is a plasma pistol. Anything larger would break your wrist even with the augmentation on that armor suit. Anything less powerful would have limited effect on a Chohish, especially if they are in armor, which I expect."

When handed the pistol, Uv'ei almost dropped it. It was a lot heavier than it looked. It took both of his hands to bring it up to face level. It was simple looking. There was a grip for the hands, a trigger for the fingers, and a pointed end that looked nasty. That pointy end had to be where it fired from.

A sudden realization came to him. "You had this ready for me. You knew I would ask for something. Why did you not just give it to me earlier?" asked a started Uv'ei.

"Because it is not something that someone should have to do. You had to decide on your own. Understand what it means if you do this. It is not for the timid Uv'ei. Killing anything is not a pleasant task. It will be dangerous, terrifying, gory, and exciting all at the same time. You may be hurt or maimed; there is a good chance you will likely die."

Holding the pistol, he could feel his arms trembling from the unaccustomed weight. He thought about what his wife and children would say. Then he thought about all the times he swore he would do anything to make the hell they lived in every day go away.

"I want, no, I need to do this. My people have suffered all their lives. They need to do this." Staring into the distance, he roared, "This must end now."

Smiling, Khaleesi patted his shoulder before she directed him to the end of the structure. "Get dressed, walk, then jog around the bay to get used to the armor weight and movement."

Pointing to the force field, Khalessi instructed Uv'ei. "Once you complete that, go there and fire a few shots so you understand what to expect with the recoil. Only do a few, as your muscles are not used to it and will get too exhausted to be of any use when the time comes. Then come back here, and I will tell you what you can do to help."

"Until then, I have more work to do." Upon which, Khaleesi jogged back to her battleoid, where it closed around her once more.

Once he put it on, the weight of the armor wasn't as bad as he feared. Instead, Uv'ei shook his body to get the armor settled around him before walking. *"A little awkward, somewhat heavy but not too bad, should be easy to get used to,"* he thought.

Finding a helmet from the dozen present did not take long as there were all close to the same size. What surprised Uv'ei was that it shook as he moved his head. He had expected it to fit more tightly.

Walking a quarter of the way around the bay had him rethinking his earlier assessment. Jogging the rest of the way around had him gasping, trying to catch his breath. *"I thought I was in shape, yet here I am, barely keeping my breakfast in; this is much heavier than I thought. The helmet is not something I will be able to wear; it shakes too much and blocks my vision."*

"Uv'ei, on the underside of your righthand wrist, you will see a covered button. Flip the cover, push the button, and repeat your jog around the bay. Do this before test firing your weapon," Khaleesi told him through the helmet. "Next time, you may want to look over your gear before you put it on. That is the power-on button. Training armor has no AI installed." Uv'ei could not miss the amusement that was in her tone.

Finding the button where indicated, he felt the unit powering up. The sucking sound when the helmet sealed with the armor almost made him panic until he found he could breathe with no problem. Tiny lights lit up in his helmet that he had no idea what they meant, so he just ignored them. He did notice immediately, though, that he no longer felt the weight of the armor.

Raising his hands in front of his face, he watched as the armor constricted to fit his fingers. He felt it doing the same around his ankles. The armor almost felt like an overlarge outfit that works in some sections but not others.

The tightening at the ankles puzzled him until he thought about it. He noticed connections on the leg bottoms when he put the suit on. "*It must seal the same way it does with the helmet but made it airtight as best it could at the ankles since it did not detect shoe contacts. I will have to ask Khaleesi if I survive this.*"

Picking up his pistol, he put it in the holster. The sudden jerk that pulled the gun a little deeper surprised him, but he realized it was magnetics holding it tight. Afraid he would not be able to get it back out, Uv'ei yanked on the handle. It pulled free with no effort. He realized the armor augmentation made it effortless. The gun now felt light as a feather.

Replacing the pistol, which must have looked like a rifle on his small frame compared to a marine, he took off jogging. Astonished by the ease, he quickened his pace to a run. He was close to shouting in joy when he heard a voice in his helmet. "Easy, my friend, easy. It would be best if you had more practice before going full out. It takes time. Now, do some firing as time is getting near. You need to rest before the Chohish arrives."

He asked as he moved to the open area before the force field. "Major, there were several more suits available. Are they for other Kolqux? Are there enough weapons?"

"Uv'ei, only if they are volunteers and understand the danger involved. Each barricade you built has two slots, some armor, and weapons. The army, scattered around the stations, has more, many more. And yes, there are enough plasma pistols. You would be surprised how many pistols are destroyed in marine training."

Pulling the pistol, Uv'ei gripped it tightly using both hands. Aiming toward the force field, he slowly, ever so slowly, pulled the trigger. Even with the suit's augmentation, the shock was so strong that it sent him flying back to land on his butt. His wrists, surprisingly, were sore but not overwhelmingly.

"Next time will be easier. The first one is always a surprise. When you do the next one, you will know what to expect and brace accordingly. It takes a lot of practice to be competent. Fire twice more and rest. I will be done in a few. I will join when I can."

Levering himself back up was more challenging than he thought. He was just not used to moving while wearing all this equipment. Bracing himself, Uv'ei raised the weapon one more time. Firing, his arms pulled back a little, but he kept his balance.

Firing one more time, he found this even easier. He did notice one thing, though, all the game training he did on positioning a weapon had paid off on one dividend at least; he was on target all three times.

Jogging back to the entrance to the bay, he pulled off his helmet before punching the communications button to reach the command center. "Uv'ek, are you there? "

"This is Yd'de; your bother, with most of the bridge crew, is currently headed to help the humans fight. I can patch you through the station intercom if you want."

"Thanks, Yd'de, that will work."

Impatience tore at him as he knew time was short, and he wanted to get with Khaleesi to see where she felt he could help. But it was only a few seconds before he heard the request for Uv'ek to call him.

The panel lit up and pinged seconds later. "Uv'ei, Yd'de said you called. What's the matter? Khaleesi throw you out?"

"No, bother, actually the opposite. The Major supplied me with some armor and a weapon. There are enough spares for several dozen, but they must be volunteers who understand the risks. That is her requirement."

In the background, Uv'ei could hear a conversation before Uv'ek came back online. "They told us the same thing here. They have a few of those armor units here too. I am heading off to another location to get one for myself. I will let others know to join you. You should see them in a few minutes."

"Brother, I do not know if we will live through the next several hours, but just in case. I want you to know how proud I am to have you as a brother. You have always been there for our families and me. They love and respect you as much as I do. Stay alive, brother, stay alive. I must go."

Disconnecting, Uv'ei rested his head against the wall. Was this the last time he would see his brother? Uv'ei could not remember a day when Uv'ek was not by his side?

Gathering himself, he headed to where he last saw Khaleesi. It was not hard to find her as she was headed toward him as he reentered the bay. He wondered why her battleoid was detailed differently than the rest, as that would mark her as someone special.

"If you are still going to go through with this, Uv'ei, follow me," Khaleesi said as she returned to where he had received his armor. Khaleesi stepped out of her battleoid to lead Uv'ei to one of the slots on the wall.

"This is what would help us the most. I expect the Chohish to put all their effort into gaining control of this station. It is the largest while also controlling the space over your home planet. They know if they can wrest this from your hands, they have a good chance of reclaiming dominance over your people. I do not think they believe you can put up much of a fight. I doubt they believe the humans are here in enough force to stop them."

The pause had Uv'ei staring up at Khaleesi. She seemed to tower over him even when she was out of the battleoid. What he heard, though, he knew was the truth. If the Chohish captured this station, they would regain control over the Kolqux.

"Before I let the Chohish take control of the station, we will have it self-destruct. The new programs you gave us allow that option. It will overload the reactors upon notification from any of the half dozen selected personnel stationed in the command center, myself or Uv'ek," responded Uv'ei.

"I know; I am the one that had that option added," replied Khaleesi.

Stunned, Uv'ei looked at Khaleesi in sudden comprehension. "You are willing to sacrifice all your lives to stop the Chohish? All this to protect us? Why?"

"Because your people have suffered enough. Someone must stop the Chohish; that is a good step in that direction." Smiling, she continued. "My marines know every day they stay alive is one more day than expected. Besides, I told the Captain, I got this."

"Here is what I need your help on," leading Uv'ei to one of the platforms.

Standing on the platform, he could see down one of the lanes created by the piling up of spare parts, junk, and old useless fighters.

"The fighting is going to get intense in here. I do not have the numbers that I would like to cover all the areas involved properly. We are stretched very thin. I need spotters to let me know the problem areas. If you or the others that show up see a Chohish getting behind one of my marines, let them know. We will have whoever shows up patched into the marine at that location."

Looking through the slot, he realized it was wide enough to enable firing his pistol through. As he thoroughly checked the area, he realized this had all been planned. The slots, and the platforms, were all made for Kolqux physiques. They were too small for humans, especially in their mechanical units.

He would have laughed at how well he had been played if the

situation was not so serious. Giving Khaleesi another look, he knew she had hoped the Kolqux would fight from the beginning but would not force them. No wonder her captain thought so highly of her.

"Uv'ei, remember to pass this on to everyone who joins us. When they hear '*down*' in their helmet, they are to drop to the floor and hug the ground for all their worth. They are not to get up until I, or if I cannot, one of my marines notifies you that you can get up. You will have only seconds to get on the ground; I cannot stress that enough."

"What is going to happen?" asked Uv'ei.

"*Payback*!" said Khaleesi, turning without another word and reentering her battleoid. Then, jogging away, she rejoined several of her marines, where they continued stacking parts to raise the height of the walls of that particular lane.

It was like a dream as Uv'ei met additional Kolqux who had come to fight. Several he knew, most he did not. But all he knew had some personal tragedy in their past: a wife, child, parent, or someone who had died because of the Chohish cruelty.

Instructing them on what to do, Uv'ei had them follow the same process he had observed, except for locating the power switch under the wrist. He was pleased to see they were serious, scared, but determined. He wished he could answer their questions on what would happen when they heard '*down,*' but all he could tell them was not to forget Khaleesi's instructions.

The expressions on their faces upon hearing this did cause him to laugh. Right now, at this moment in time, they were more scared of Khaleesi than they were of the Chohish. Chohish cruelty they knew; Khaleesi was an unknown. And she was here in the same bay with them. All the marines scared them, but Khaleesi most of all.

The Kolqux ran through the stages recommended by Khaleesi

and finished none too soon, as the warning went out that the Chohish would be in the area soon.

As the Kolqux ran to their assigned areas, Uv'ei hesitated to see what the marines would do. Each marine went to the wall where they yanked up a silvery fabric-looking sheet they pulled up over their heads to cover themselves. As the sheet covered them, the marines slowly disappeared from sight.

"Get out of sight, Uv'ei, no time to gawk," Khaleesi's voice came through his helmet. "Remember, what I need from you is to let me know if any Chohish gets behind me. And Uv'ei, when I yell '*down*,' you all get down, you hear me?"

"Yes, Major, I ensured all my people understood their roles. We will do what is needed." Getting behind the structure, he moved to stand on the platform.

He looked at the next platform and saw De'gu resting his plasma weapon in the slot. The pistol shook a little in his hands as De'gu nervously looked for any sign of the Chohish.

He was surprised that he was not nervous when he took out his pistol. Instead, he felt calm. He raised the pistol using both hands in front of his face. He had dreamed of confronting the murderers of his family and friends; unfortunately, he always died in his dreams as he was so small in comparison. But this time around, he would not be defenseless; this time around, he was armed.

"Get a grip De'gu; remember why you are here. The weapon you are holding can kill a Chohish. Think of your two infant daughters that these beasts killed because your children cried in fear as they walked by. Now you can get some revenge. Think of that."

De'gu nostrils fluttered as he closed his eyes while lowering the pistol. Tears leaking down his cheeks showed through the helmet, but Uv'ei could see De'gu slowly relax. The change was dramatic when De'gu finally raised his head and opened his eyes. De'gu rested the pistol back in the slot with no visible shaking. Glancing at Uv'ei, he nodded his head in thanks.

"It will be hard to get past the fear the Chohish held over us for all our lives. Even now, overpowering fear is holding us back. Hopefully, when my people see the humans fight and kill Chohish, they will overcome their fear and join in. Otherwise, what will become of us?" thought Uv'ei.

The sudden shaking of the station let Uv'ei know the battle had started. Flashes of missiles, lasers, and explosions were visible through the force field. The sight frightened him, yet it relieved him—no more waiting.

The violence escalated, grabbing his attention that he almost missed the first Chohish shuttle entering the bay; others soon followed it.

The backs of the shuttles dropped with a bang, followed by Chohish soldiers rushing out screaming while firing their lasers. This only continued briefly before they paused in confusion at the lack of resistance.

As more shuttles landed, more and more Chohish gathered. What they were waiting on, Uv'ei had no idea. Then again, he could say the same about the humans. How could they sit under their sheets with everything they must be hearing without moving?

What bothered Uv'ei the most was that he could only see what was happening in this particular lane. Was what he saw repeated in every lane?

A final shuttle arrived, where a large Chohish climbed out. Uv'ei now understood what the rest of the Chohish soldiers had been waiting on. The Chohish, whom the humans called a Sovereign, mixed in with the soldiers and pointed to the access hatch to the station while mouthing something he could not hear.

The arrival of that particular Chohish must have been what Khaleesi had been waiting on. Plasma fire and rockets shredded the sheets the battleoids had been hiding under. The impact was immediate since the distance was minimal.

The Sovereign did not have time to evade; he disappeared in fire and flame. Chohish went down by the score. But there were many more, and these responded in rage.

With screams that brought Uv'ei's fear back to the forefront, the Chohish charged the humans in their battleoids.

Expecting the humans to retreat, he was astonished when he saw them race toward the Chohish. The collision of the two forces was deafening.

What he saw next made him realize why the humans had been able to take the station away from the Chohish. Even though they had not been in these particular machines of destruction.

It was the ability to overcome their fear. Watching Khaleesi's unit, he followed her as she dived, twisted, jumped, and slid, all while delivering death using multiple methods. The weapon in her left hand never stopped firing while guns from her shoulders spat out death in a wide area. Her armored fist in her right, carrying a wicked large knife, smashed or cut the life of Chohish after Chohish.

What amazed him the most was even though Khaleesi looked to be amid the Chohish soldiers, no Chohish was behind her. The weapons on her shoulder targeted anyone trying to get past her.

Even though it was impressive, Uv'ei could see that there were just too many Chohish. They would overwhelm the humans.

Then he saw it, movement off to his left. A pair of Chohish were sneaking around to Khaleesi's rear.

"Khaleesi, they are two Chohish behind you." Upon getting no response, he yelled even louder into his helmet. "Do you hear me? Behind you?"

In a panic, upon only hearing silence, he leaned through the slot and aimed his pistol. "Please, oh please, do not let me miss."

Firing, his arm jerked back against the side of the slot. Pain ratcheted up his arm. Pulling his arm back, and just in time, a laser hit the spot where his hand had been resting.

Trying to get his pistol back up, he saw a lone Chohish come into view. Uv'ei could tell he would not get his gun up in time. Surprisingly, he was content as he had seen his one-shot had nailed one of two Chohish.

Just as he saw the Chohish grin before firing his weapon, he was blown backward by a plasma bolt. The scream from De'gu let him know where it had come from.

Putting his pistol back in the slot, he could see Khaleesi standing over another battleoid on the ground. If there was any doubt of the major's bravery, what he saw removed any doubt of it.

As blast after blast impacted her battleoid, with pieces blown off, she refused to go down. Uv'ei stood there in amazement as he watched her mechanical unit still give out death even though it had to be in its final stages.

He stepped off the platform and moved to the end of the structure, ready to dash out to help Khaleesi. He could not sit by idly while she died for his people. Pausing to get mentally prepared, he told himself. *"As she said, get mean, get killer mean."*

Just as he was about to rush out, he heard *"Down"* come loudly through his helmet.

Jumping behind the wall, Uv'ei dropped to hug the floor, his helmet clanging off De'gu's helmet as they crashed into each other. Later, he would watch the video of what happened, again and again, having a hard time believing anyone survived through the catechism that followed.

From all the bulbous-shaped electronic devices came a stream of destruction and horror, the like of which he had never experienced nor dreamed of. It blasted down the lanes blowing out through the force fields destroying anything or anyone in its way. It lasted less than a few seconds.

Getting to his feet, he realized his armor felt hot, sizzling hot. Walking out beyond the structure, he saw a scene of indescribable carnage through the heavy smoke. Smoke, fire, bodies, and destroyed machinery were everywhere.

Where the Chohish shuttles had been, nothing was left but smoking wrecks or gone altogether. Chohish bodies, what few were evident, were burned beyond recognition. The lanes created were now just a jumbled mess of melted slag.

But even with all that destruction, there were still some Chohish survivors. Many were injured, others walking around dazed. Into these survivors came the battleoids. Not many, all showing signs of heavy damage, but still functional.

Observing the battleoids, he thought about joining them until he realized he would only be in the way. They tore through the Chohish with deadly efficiency and, if he was not mistaken, anger. Several ripped the Chohish apart, which he doubted was a typical method. His only regret was that he wished he had a battleoid of his own to do the same.

Scanning the battleoids moving around, he could not find that particular marking on any of them. He panicked, afraid of what he would find. He ran screaming toward where he last saw Khaleesi. "Major, Major, where are you?"

A crackling broke the silence in his helmet, a soft, pained-filled voice barely audible filtered through the noise from the bay. "Behind you, Uv'ei."

Twirling, partially hidden by smoke, were two battleoids propped up against the wall. Both showed extreme damage. It was hard to identify the major symbols through all the burn marks.

Running until he reached Khaleesi, he scanned the battleoid looking for some access panel to open it.

"Let it be Uv'ei; the battleoid is all that is keeping me, us, alive. The medical team Doc assigned to the station should be here any minute. They will know what to do," gasped Khaleesi.

Kneeling, he leaned in until he was just inches away from the battleoids. "You risked everything for us. Why?" he whispered tearfully to a human he had come to care deeply about.

"Payback, Uv'ei, payback for both of us."

BATTLESHIP

THE BATTLE FOR the Sobolara station was over by the time Zeke arrived with the rest of the RGN fighters. At the same time, the Lucky Strike stayed near the slipstream to help hunt for survivors.

The Chohish had tried to enter through multiple locations on the station, but the bay had been their major thrust. The Chohish had concentrated all their forces on this one station, ignoring the others.

Reports were flowing in telling Zeke of the aftermath of the battle, both in space and on the station. It was with a heavy heart he heard the number of the casualties. The RGN had lost few while the Kolqux had lost thousands. The number of injured Kolqux was minimal in comparison as the Chohish equipment the Kolqux used did not have escape pods or medical treatment in case of injury.

The marines were lucky because they had not suffered many deaths. Still, most of the marines stationed on the Sobolara station experienced grievous wounds. More than half were in a medically induced coma while nano's worked to repair the damage. Major Khaleesi was one of the worst.

The army personnel had suffered numerous deaths at several

locations experiencing heavy fighting. The number would have been much higher if not for the last-minute bolstering by Kolqux.

As much as he wanted to land at the station, the landing bay was unusable. Repairs were underway, but it would take several days to make anything available.

His main concern, though at the moment, was fuel for the fighters. Most were near empty. Flying to one of the other stations would be impossible; it was beyond their available fuel range. So he had to order them all to go on standby until refueling would again be possible.

Uv'ek, who was back in the command center, said they were working on getting the refueling process set up in multiple locations outside the station's skin. The significant issue still being worked out was how to land and hold a fighter still while refueling on a place built to hinder any landings.

Fingering a tear in the fabric on his seat, Zeke reflected on the day's events when he was interrupted by an emergency alert from the Lucky Strike.

A stressed-sounding Isolde came through on the private link without waiting for an acknowledgment. He could not remember Isolde ever sounding so stressed.

"Captain Kinsley, this is Lieutenant Iverson. Men of war have just exited the slipstream from the Wartos Quadrant. We identify eight battleships, fifteen cruisers, twenty-one destroyers, and two carriers. All of the Chohish make."

"*Damn, that must mean the Fox did not make it. We are spread thin with little or no fuel nor missiles.*" But his thoughts were interrupted before he could reply.

"Update, Captain," Zeke noted that Isolde's voice had changed and now had a tone of relief. "The Fox just came through. Communication request for you from Captain Kennedy. Shall I pass her through? "

"Yes, Lieutenant, please put her through; stay on a private, secure channel. We don't know who may be listening in on us." responded a tense Zeke. The Fox in the middle of Chohish ships did not bode well.

Captain Kennedy's voice came across a few seconds later. "Zebra, Alpha, and of course Cocoa." His body finally relaxed in relief after Zeke heard the phrase. He was sure Isolde had heard it from Captain Kennedy before contacting him, but it was good to listen to it himself. They had decided on a silly phase before separating in case the Chohish had taken over any ship or person. Multiple phases had been devised so each one could give a status. Captured, tortured, and so on.

"Captain Kinsley, let me summarize it for now. I will send a full report later. The two stations in the Wartos Quadrant are now under Kolqux control. Minimal casualties on our end. Surprisingly few Chohish were encountered. We brought all the ships that are fully functional and armed."

"Excellent news Captain Kennedy. Please pass on my congratulations to your crew, incredible job. I wish it were the same here. It was pretty desperate here for a while. The Chohish bombed several cities on the home planet before we could suppress the Chohish on the Sobolara station. Millions of Kolqux perished."

Sudden static on the link indicated a broken connection for a few seconds before reconnected. Seeing the green link light, Zeke proceeded to give his report to Meghan.

"We were able to suppress the Chohish on the other two stations without bombardments. The Kolqux eliminated the Chohish presence on all three planets and all shipyards. The loss of life during that part of the campaign was very high. The Kolqux revenge against the Chohish was gruesome in many cases."

Taking a slow breath, Zeke rubbed his forehead before resuming. "Unfortunately, after all that, several Chohish fleets arrived to contest the system. We took heavy casualties but mostly in the fledgling Kolqux armed forces. It was touch and go for a while there. After eliminating the Chohish fleets, the RGN fighters raced back toward the planet just in case. They weren't, but now we are low on fuel. Lucky Strike is engaged in search and rescue near the slipstream, so unavailable to help us. Unfortunately, we cannot land to refuel due to battle damage at the Sobolara station. It would have been a huge task anyway due to equipment incompatibility."

"Oh, this tidbit you might find interesting. I had to ask for it to be repeated multiple times as I thought I heard it wrong when they first told me. Most of the damage incurred in the landing bays occurred when Major Richards set off over one hundred directional mines inside. Khaleesi fired the mines while she and her marines were still in the bay. And had our new ally's leader right there with her."

The last comment caused a silence before he heard a muted reply. "Holy shit, you have got to be kidding. Your marine major is one crazy lady. Are you sure she is not Irracan? Did she or any of the Marines survive? And Uv'ei?"

"The Major is in a medical pod along with over half of the marines that fought with her. The medical technician put them all in a coma so the nano's could do their work without pause. The rest of the Marines are injured in some fashion. Thankfully, none too seriously, as they ran out of medical pods."

"As for Uv'ei, he survived intact. Refuses to leave the Majors side. From what I hear, he keeps whispering '*payback*'".

"Captain Kinsley, any word from the Jackal?"

"No, nothing. The planets in the Oxtaria Pulsar System are much further from the slipstream than normal, so it is not surprising. We can only hope for the best. But since you are here, we could use your help to refuel the fighters. The Kolqux are working on

Attack Chohish War

putting together a process since we do not have the main bay available, but not sure they will get that done by the time you get here."

" That, we can do. We will head your way at the best speed. Until later, Captain, you take care. Captain Kennedy out."

What struck Zeke odd was that Meghan had not used the jargon he often heard from people on her planet. Instead, the last several days must have put a damper on that type of joviality.

One thing he did know, though, was he wanted out of this fighter. He was stiff and sore. He ached to get rid of the grit he felt on his teeth, but most of all, he wanted to take a long hot shower. He had been smelling his own sweat for hours now. No matter how hard the suit's air system tried to keep it clean, there was only so much it could do. There was no dignified way to put it; he stunk.

But while he had some idle time, he started thinking about what they should do to shore up their defenses until the RGN forces arrived. He had few doubts that another Chohish fleet was on its way. One thing bothered him. None of the battleships in the last two engagements had used their primary weapon. That was puzzling. Why not?

The first thing they needed to do was get clear of the slipstream. Zeke would have to contact Nkosana for an updated progress status and start moving all the remaining Kolqux warships back to be refueled and rearmed. That reminded him that he would have to get with Uv'ei and Jamie to see how their supply status was doing.

He also needed to know what happened in the Oxtaria Pulsar System. The usual choice would be to send the Fox, but if things had gone south, he would be sending the Fox into a bad situation. Losing the Fox would take away one of his best weapons.

For the next half hour, he worked through his project list. Finishing, he pinged Jeanne to review his thoughts on the Chohish weapon before adding Hawke, Nkosana, Will, Meghan, Gunner, and Jax into the call.

243

"Pass on to your groups; my congratulations on a job well done. But that is not the only reason I asked you to join me. Meghan, I am unsure if you have run into any battleships, but the ones we ran into here did not fire their main weapon. I doubt the issue is a failure on so many ships, so what could cause it? Jeanne and I have an idea, but we would like everyone's opinion to see if it matches ours."

"We did not meet any ships other than some local fighters. They were not very skilled; I expected better. They did not last long. Same for the soldiers on the stations; they were unskilled," responded Meghan.

"I noticed the same thing. I kept warning my fighter group about it. I was not surprised they did not employ it against the fighters, but when the Kolqux warships attacked..." piped in Hawke. "Gunner asked me about it later. We both thought it odd. Why not use your most potent weapon? We chalked it up to maybe the warships were older models that did not have that weapon installed."

"We agree; the reason could be that simple. With that in mind, Zeke and I compared all the images we had of Chohish battleships before this engagement. They match what we saw here. But Meghan, what about the battleships in your fleet? Do they have the weapon?" expressed Jeanne.

"No idea. I will have to get back to you on that," responded Meghan. "We did not encounter any Chohish crewed battleship, so we never saw that issue."

"We need to know for sure. That is why we need Jax and his engineers to check into it. Will, can you drop by the mostly intact battleship? The engineers will need a large security detail in case some Chohish survive. Meghan, can you have your engineers check your battleships?" asked Zeke.

"Will do. I think I will go over with Jax to take a look, as the Admiral can cover for me. I have not been on a Chohish ship yet and would like to look at one that the Chohish lived in," answered Will.

"Final item. What happened in the Oxtaria Pulsar System? I do not want to send the Lucky Strike or the Fox, as they are needed here. But we could send one of the Kolqux men at war. Admiral, if you could select an undamaged one, have it come to pick up Jeanne and me. Please ensure it is fast if we have to high-tail it out of there."

With nothing else anyone wanted to review, the group broke up. It wasn't until after Zeke got a ping from Uv'ei that something else came to mind.

"Captain Kinsley, you requested to speak to me?"

"Yes, Uv'ei, we wondered why the Chohish battleships did not use their primary weapon. Do they have different battleship models? Possibly older models where they did not install that weapon?"

"We have been building the same version you fought for as long as I can remember. The Chohish had us shut down all research; they feared we would develop a weapon against them. The Chohish made some improvements over the millenniums that they forced us to incorporate, but rarely, nothing important. But ships similar to what we built were constructed at locations that may not have had it."

"Thanks, that helps. Another question is, do the Chohish have some showers or cleaning systems we could use to clean off? Jeanne and I will hitch a ride on one of your ships to see what is happening in the Oxtaria Pulsar System. It would be nice to get some sweat and stink off us."

"Yes, they have a water system for bathing. I recommend having the Admiral get you a battleship. The Chohish individual you call Sovereign demanded cleanliness for all on his ship. I cannot say if that was true on the other men of war, so they may not have a functioning system."

"Uv'ei, your people fought very well. You should be very proud of them. I say this, but I hear the sadness in your voice. Are you ok? Is there anything I can help with?"

There was a delay before Uv'ei responded. "Yes, I am very proud of my people. The ones that died will never be forgotten."

"But that is not what is bothering you. Can you share what is bothering you with me? Or is it personal?" asked Zeke.

What came across to Zeke was a deeply troubled-sounding person. "Khaleesi. She is still in what your doctor calls a coma. He informed me that she was severely injured during the sortie to capture the station. He told me that she had not finished medical treatment, which compounded her injuries during the Chohish assault on the station. The Doctor gives her only a thirty-two percent chance of surviving even with your advanced medicine. I would be sad to see her die after all she did for my people."

"As would I, Uv'ei, as would I. I have come to admire and respect the Major and count her a close friend. There is one thing that may cheer you up a bit. The Major is a fighter; she doesn't know any other way. They have written her off several times, but she is still here. I expect she will be up and around when I get back."

"I hope so, Captain. If you have nothing else, I must run." There was a disconnect before Zeke could respond.

Then the waiting began again. It was not as bad as before as Zeke could run through some plans and ideas with Jeanne and some idle chat. Soon, she had him laughing, telling him of a joke she played on her sister when they were kids when the Kolqux battleship finally showed up.

Looking at it from the outside, he had significant reservations that it would last another five minutes. Let alone get them through a slipstream; it showed that much damage.

Flying through the shields on the landing bay, he saw that the interior matched the exterior. Finding a space devoid of debris that would allow him to land took several minutes. As he landed, he had concerns that there would not be anywhere for Jeanne to find a landing spot. Fortunately, Zeke saw space being cleared by what he guessed was a Chohish bulldozer pushing debris to the side.

As his canopy raised, a Kolqux pushed a rickety ladder against the fighter. Stepping on the ladder, it shook so much that he was afraid it was going to tip over. He finally reached the floor, where three smiling Kolqux greeted him. All showed some injury. One had his arm in a sling, another standing with a crutch, while the last had a bloody bandage around his head. Yet all were smiling.

"Captain Kinsley, we are honored to have you reside with us. We have made the…. how do you say…. the ex-commander of this ship's rooms made available for you," the Kolqux with the head bandage notified Zeke.

"Could you introduce me to everyone?" asked Zeke.

"I am Hu'de, the ship commander; with me are the ship's engineer manager Po'bs and pilot Ka'vc." the injuries made them rememberable for Zeke. The commander had a head wound; Po'bs was on the commander's left with the crutch, while Ka'vc was on the right side in the arm sling.

It was handy as Zeke could identify them all to Jeanne as she walked up. This simple act made all three smile in happiness that he could remember who each one was. That is what he told himself anyway. Then, of course, having Jeanne come up swirling that hat around in a circle while singing an old-time pirate song had nothing to do with the smiles.

Introductions concluded; the group headed out of the landing bay to make for the bridge. Zeke and Jeanne found the walk through the Chohish ship interesting. Everything was much more prominent. Hallways, hatches, rooms, and even the bolts holding it all together were oversized.

What was unusual was the stairways that were used instead

of elevators. These caused consternation with the Kolqux as their size forced them to crawl up the steps. But when Zeke and Jeanne copied their actions, even though they could have climbed the stairs, albeit with some difficulty, there was no mistaking the appreciation from the Kolqux.

It took more time than expected to get to the bridge. The three Kolqux were puffing with exhaustion by the time they arrived.

The bridge was garish in its luxury, which surprised the two humans. They did not see this on the destroyer bridge they had boarded to capture a Sovereign.

The contrast between the Kolqux and the bridge was sobering. The Kolqux wore threadbare and patched outfits while the command platform in the center of the bridge was covered in rare elements.

There were at least fifty Kolqux situated around the bridge. Several were standing on the hard seats the Chohish would usually sit. Others had jury-rigged a chair, an upside-down bucket, or a chair made from rubber foam.

The Kolqux offered Zeke the command platform, which he politely declined. Instead, he and Jeanne made their way to sit at two unused seats. Looking around, he was amazed at the number of workstations. Why so many?

His answer came after they got underway. Many functions automated on the Lucky Strike were manual here. When Zeke questioned Hu'de about the lack of automation, Hu'de shrugged. But Zeke was informed the new ships would be automated now that Kolqux would build warships to fit themselves. The smile let him know it was another feature they had held back from the Chohish.

Hu'de, once a tugboat pilot, knew the route they needed to take and the objective. Conversations went smoothly between him and Zeke while they discussed options while the warship headed toward the slipstream.

Unfortunately, it was apparent the mood on the bridge was not universal. The Kolqux would look around, then concentrate on their task before glancing around the room again. All the while, tension seemed to be building.

Recognizing the issue, Jeanne put her hat on her head and twirled to stand on the command platform. The tapping of her shoes on the metal surface grabbed everyone's attention. Dancing in a tight circle while clapping her fingers, she started singing a racy song that she hoped was correctly interpreted.

Jumping from the platform, Jeanne twirled around the room. Then, grabbing one of the Kolqux, she pulled him into her dance. At first, he looked around in panic until other Kolqux started to pick up the tapping tune with their fingers. Then slowly, he began to match her movements. Jeanne did not stop but grabbed another, then another, until half the room was twirling around the room.

The dancing continued for a long time until Zeke interrupted them, who swirled into Jeanne's arms and twirled her around the bridge, finishing back up on the platform with a flourish. The Kolqux burst into applause.

Still wrapped in Zeke's arms, she said, "That is how you get any group of people, any race, to relax. I do not know anyone who does not love music and dancing."

An hour later, Zeke was almost sorry about how much the Kolqux did relax. Jeanne was sitting on the edge of the master platform with her legs tucked under her, surrounded by Kolqux. The Kolqux, who was not busy, were massed around Jeanne, asking her questions.

What was her planet like? What did she do for fun? How many brothers and sisters did she have? What was the RGN? The Irracans? They heard there was another race with wings on her ship? Who were they? When did she first fly a fighter? On and on it went; it was never-ending. The majority of the time, multiple questions were being asked simultaneously. Every time Jeanne responded, one or more Kolqux would scream before laughing and clapping.

At first, one or two sat with Jeanne, then another, until the word spread around the ship. The bridge became jammed with Kolqux, thirsty for knowledge of other worlds, of different races, of a life without pain, without danger or being afraid. And Jeanne gave that to them for a short period of their lives.

While Jeanne entertained the Kolqux, Zeke, and Hu'de huddled, making plans. Zeke found Hu'de to be very intelligent and intuitive from the questions asked. Details on what the battleship was capable of did not leave Zeke confident if they encountered any Chohish warships. Hence it was agreed upon on any sign of Chohish, they would forgo any combat and flee back to the Furalla Eaara Star System.

Unable to take his stink any longer, Zeke asked Hu'de if he could lead himself and Jeanne somewhere they could freshen up.

Breaking Jeanne away looked near impossible until she notified the Kolqux that she would be happy to resume answering their questions when she returned. The excitement of having the two humans present did not diminish as they left. Laughter and loud chatter followed them as they walked through the hallway.

Hu'de brought them to a suite that dwarfed anything they had experienced. Even a commercial spaceliner had nothing as sumptuous and spacious as what Hu'de had taken them. The rooms were even more luxurious than the command platform on the bridge.

As lovely as it could be, it was too much for either of them. When asked for another smaller, less obnoxious room, Hu'de was initially afraid that he had insulted them. Turning to point at the room, they let him know this was not in their style, that they preferred things a bit simpler.

Taking them down the hall, he took them to another room a dozen times larger than they had on the Lucky Strike. Then, following them into the room, Hu'de explained how to use the shower.

Heading out, Hu'de asked if they were hungry. The Admiral had sent over some food packets when they decided to use this ship. No one knew if Kolqux food was agreeable to human digestion and now was not the time to experiment.

Upon their agreement to meet later, Hu'de departed, leaving the two alone.

Jeanne headed to the bathroom area, anxious to wash the filth off her. A significant circular depression in the ground accommodated both the shower and toilet. Stopping to press a button nearby, Jeanne watched water spray from the ceiling over a large area.

"Wow, they must have a large water filtration system to support the amount of water used if this is normal on the entire ship," commented Zeke.

There was nothing present to resemble soap, but they would do the best they could with just water and a lot of scrubbing with their hands.

The ever-curious Zeke walked around the room, trying all the knobs and devices in the room. "You go first; I want to explore," he offered while he pulled a cord hanging from the ceiling by the door.

"You called?" asked a voice out of nowhere.

"Oops, sorry about that; I pulled a cord to see what it would do," explained Zeke.

In the center of the room was a pile of pillows that Zeke assumed was a bed. He had no intention of using it as it might have some insects or microbes that could be dangerous to humans. They had already discussed sleeping in their fighters when the time came.

An hour later, they had cleaned up as best they could. Deciding to take a break before heading back to the bridge, Zeke and Jeanne sat on the floor, leaning into each other, exhausted.

Turning on the ground to face Zeke, Jeanne gazed into his eyes while telling him what it was like earlier on the bridge when the Kolqux mobbed her.

"They are hungry for any information, contact outside their immediate families. What I tell them is immaterial. The thrill of contact with a new race that will not harm them or their families. Seeing what life can be like for them, their families."

Before letting her finish, Zeke pulled her in close, combing some stray hair out of her eyes. "Zeke, my darling, what they have been through is horrendous. But being here now, one of the first humans they meet is awe-inspiring. Oh, how my father would have loved to be here. He had met a Sorath trader once and constantly spoke of his desire to visit one of their cities. Being here now would have been a dream come true for him. He would be in his element helping the Kolqux get started running their own lives."

Quiet reigned for the next several minutes while they basked in each other's company.

"Well, if they are going to run their own lives, we better ensure they get that opportunity. The war to free them is not over yet. But before we do that, I need to get something to eat; I am starving. How about you?"

Smiling, Jeanne leaned in to kiss Zeke passionately. After standing, she grabbed Zeke's hand, pulling him into a hug before both made their way out of the room.

Waiting for them outside, squatting on the floor, was Po'bs. His crutch was leaning on the wall next to him.

The nostrils on Po'bs face quivered as he took a huge sniff. "Well, you smell somewhat better. We did not want to insult you earlier, but we are very sensitive to smell. Hu'de asked me to wait to take you on a ship tour if desired. It will be another few hours before we reach the slipstream."

"We would like that. If you do not mind, weapons, shields,

and engines, in that order, " Zeke replied. "But could we start by grabbing something to eat as we toured your ship? We are starving."

As they toured the ship for the next several hours, they munched on an MRE meal. Zeke had no issue with his meal; he was used to them. But Jeanne made some nasty comments about hers as she suffered through hers. Prepackaged meals had made significant progress over the years, but the RGN Military always seemed to find the worst. From the expression given by Po'bs when they opened the meals, it was apparent the smell was not that appealing.

THE OXTARIA PULSAR SYSTEM

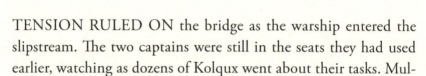

TENSION RULED ON the bridge as the warship entered the slipstream. The two captains were still in the seats they had used earlier, watching as dozens of Kolqux went about their tasks. Multiple Kolqux were sitting side by side in most locations as the crew had minimal experience.

Being the first trip through a slipstream for most Kolqux, it showed when completed. A dozen or more were retching while another half dozen collapsed.

Zeke and Jeanne were powerless to help except to assist a few Kolqux that had collapsed near them. Individuals that could not stand were assisted off the bridge while others arrived to take their place. Soon, the bridge was back to the entire staff again.

While moving away from the slipstream, Zeke realized that Hu'de might finally be able to answer a question that had bothered him.

"Hu'de, we have a question that has been bothering us for some time. We never found any external probes or devices to supply the Chohish with better data on a system. Like what their ship scanners do but on smaller units that can deploy like a missile. At the same time, star systems like yours would have larger, more permanent units. Why is that?"

Hu'de shrugged before responding. "The Chohish thought they were not worth the resources. What is your word for it? Lendy.... no.... lendolium.... is that correct? Your Admiral asked us about the abundance of that mineral. We have another name for it. The fuel used to power warships is scarce in this and neighboring systems. The Chohish supplied all the fuel used to power the warships. The Chohish have complained of major shortages for the last few decades."

"What do you use for power on the planets? The cities have power," queried Jeanne.

"Water generates most of the energy we need. We have many rivers and damns. We also have mountains where we convert the cold temperature into energy. Our spaceships were fusion-powered before the Chohish," responded Hu'de.

"Cold? How do you do that?" asked Zeke

"Contraction and expansion. Huge power units on wheels are rotated from a heated room into the frigid cold at the top of a mountain. There are many rooms around the mountain. The units never stop rotating. The contractions, tightening and expanding from the heat and cold, create more than enough energy to run the operation while supplying power for hundreds of thousands of homes," Hu'de disclosed.

"We almost had something like that until lendolium came along. Environmentally safe while producing extreme amounts of energy. We also used fusion power but could never get the same energy output as lendolium," apprised Zeke.

A clanging started that took Zeke and Jeanne by surprise.

"Ships have been detected. Dozens, many, many dozens, are headed our way. What do you want us to do?"

"Can they tell us the breakdown of ships? Oh hell, skip that; let me come over and see what you see." With that, Zeke sprinted out of his chair with Jeanne right behind him. They could hear Hu'de talking to whoever was on the other end behind them.

Running next to what he hoped was the scanning station, Zeke stopped to catch his breath. He realized one fatal flaw in coming to this system in a Kolqux warship. He had no idea where or who operated the scanning station; what he could see was that all the Kolqux looked ready to panic.

Thankfully, Jeanne did not have that issue. Having stopped behind Zeke at his abrupt halt, she went around him and walked over to a Kolqux staring at her with great big eyes staring at her full of fear.

"Hello Te'ln, what are you reading?" asked Jeanne.

Looking from Jeanne to Zeke and back again, Te'ln turned back to the screen before responding. After some keystrokes, the screen refreshed. Whereas before, it was showing small dots, now it was showing figures that meant nothing to either of the humans.

Te'ln informed them that thirty-two battleships, fifty-six cruisers, sixty-one destroyers, and seven carriers were headed their way.

The words explained to Zeke why the Kolqux was ready to panic. Hell, he had to tamp down his own dread.

Leaning down to look at the screen, Jeanne calmly asked. "How far away are they?"

"Less than an hour..." stuttered Te'ln.

"Any request to communications? They must know we are here, " Zeke said calmly, trying not to panic the Kolqux.

"Nothing, Captain. They have not attempted to contact us but have adjusted their course to intercept us," responded Hu'de, standing behind another workstation. "Orders?"

"I am surprised that they have not contacted us. When this force detected a Chohish warship, I would have assumed they would have attempted contact. And that must have been as soon as we entered the system if they are making adjustments already, "said a mystified Jeanne.

"*When did Hu'de get here? I need to be more aware of my surroundings,*" thought Zeke.

"This is your ship, Commander, although I have some suggestions if you are interested, " Zeke responded.

Surprisingly, Hu'de chuckled before he replied. "Less than a week ago, I was a shuttle pilot for ships between stations. That is the only reason I am commander. I have no experience commanding others in a time of war."

Walking over to Hu'de, Zeke put one hand on his shoulder before he swept his other hand around, pointing to all the Kolqux on the bridge. "See them? They, like you, are here to get their freedom from the Chohish. You do not want to fight for your freedom from the Chohish only to give it to another group. We are in a Kolqux ship; Kolqux built it, Kolqux crews it, and a Kolqux is in command. I am more than willing to make suggestions, but you have to make the final decision. Time for the Kolqux to take control of their own lives."

Hu'de stared at Zeke in stunned silence. He turned to study the faces on his crew before turning back to Zeke. "You are right; it is time we stood up for ourselves. But if I make the wrong decision, you may die from it."

Zeke shrugged. "Then we die. It may occur no matter what we do anyway. If we are allies, then we must be willing to share your dangers."

The expression on Hu'de was one of concern. "But I do not have the experience in this matter, please; I would appreciate your thoughts on what we should do."

There was no mistaking how Hu'de's posture changed. Where he had always stooped a little when in Zeke's and Jeanne's presence, he now stood straight. But the most telling something had changed in his voice. Now it was intense and commanding.

The rest of the Kolqux did not miss this and kept glancing between Hu'de and Zeke in wonderment before they also straightened.

"Think about it. We cannot run; there is nowhere to go. By the time we reversed course, we would fail. Going another direction would only delay being caught, if even that. Their destroyers alone could catch and eliminate us without really trying. With that in mind, we must consider what options are open to us." Zeke responded while walking around the bridge.

When he reached Jeanne, he stopped, looking only at her. "If you cannot go back, go around; what other option do you have, Hu'de?"

Caught by surprise, Hu'de stroked his chin while he thought about it. "If we can't go back, or run, then we only have one option. Go forward. But that is suicide."

"Once you know your options, you can focus your planning on those. You are correct; we can only go forward," advised Zeke, still looking at Jeanne.

"Think on this, Hu'de; what do they see and know?" interjected Jeanne looking only at Zeke.

"We are here because we are trying to find out the status of your ship, the Jackal, and our tugboats. If they were successful in their mission of subduing the pair of stations in this system," relayed Hu'de.

Now it was Hu'de's turn to walk around the bridge. "This force must be aware of said forces. But they do not know which side we are on."

"Excellent. The Chohish dare not fire on us as we may be carrying a Chohish we call a Sovereign. When contacted, you tell them that the Sovereign was injured in a desperate battle and is

Attack Chohish War

unavailable. Keep the video off. Say damaged if asked. The visible damage to the ship will lend truth to that lie. They will check. They will probably send some fighters to check us out. Hopefully, they will let you pass and head to the station," advised Zeke.

"They will know if you start powering up your shields or weapons. Keep them powered down. It's not like it would do you any good in the long run. More than likely, they will probably send an escort for you no matter what they finally decide—size unknown, but something strong enough to take this ship out. Which wouldn't be much with its current damage," added Jeanne.

"What if they want to board us? What then?" asked Hu'de.

"Make up some story about the landing bay being inoperable and contaminated due to battle damage. I doubt they want to delay long enough to board us. That would take too many hours." responded Zeke.

"Hu'de... uh, I mean Commander, there is an anomaly that I cannot determine," reported Te'ln, no more prolonged stuttering.

Waiting until she saw she had Hu'de's attention, along with the two humans, she continued. "I cannot fully penetrate a group of ships with our sensors. There is a cluster of six ships that I can only clearly identify five. The others shield the sixth. It is a ship size I cannot identify."

"And the anomaly?" asked Jeanne.

"From within those ships, I am getting a weird signal," a puzzled Te'ln reported.

"Can you send it through the speakers?" asked Zeke.

".--- .- -.-. -.- .- -.. .--- .- -.-. -.- .- -.. .--- .- -.-. -.- .- -.."

"Repeated over and over again," reported Te'ln.

"Keep it on the speakers, Te'ln. Something familiar about it. What the hell is it?" Zeke remarked as he started walking around the bridge, tapping his fingers into his palm in sync with the noise from the speaker.

"We are close to missile range, secure stations," ordered Hu'de. Chaotic activity occurred; it was apparent most did not know what they were supposed to do. Hu'de walked among his crew, calming their fears.

Jeanne watched as the Kolqux tightened the belts wrapped around their wastes, holding them onto their seats. She was aghast that they wore nothing to protect themselves from decompression or air loss. That was one thing Jeanne would get Uv'ei to start manufacturing once she met him next if she survived.

Jeanne felt self-conscious that Zeke and herself were in their flight suits. Their helmets were in their fighters, but their flight suits would deploy a soft head covering. They could pull that over their head if the suit's AI does not detect a helmet connection at the first sign of air loss or decompression.

"We are now in missile range. No communication request yet…" notified Te'ln.

Hu'de stared at Zeke, who continued tapping his fingers while walking around the bridge. Sitting near Jeanne, Hu'de asked her what was he doing?

"The noise is something familiar to him. The tapping is his method of strengthening his memory," answered Jeanne. "Ahh, I think he figured it out."

"How do you know?" asked Hu'de.

"See his crazy smile…?" answered Jeanne with a laugh.

Dashing to stand over Te'ln, Zeke jumped up to sit on the shelf beside her. "Damn, these things are too high. Ok, Te'ln, I need to send out something similar. I would do it myself, but I have no idea how. Can you do that?"

Getting a confirmation, he went on. "I want you to send the following exactly as I do. Let's practice it a couple of times first; then, we will send it out when you are comfortable repeating it."

Seeing the dismay on her face, Zeke spoke softly to lessen her concern. "Relax. Take a breath and relax. Now I just hope I remember it correctly."

Zeke then tapped it on the shelf with his fingers. ".-.. ..- -.-. -.- -.-.-- ... - .-. .. -.- ."

Waiting a few seconds, Zeke did it one more time. ".-.. ..- -.-. -.- -.-.-- ... - .-. .. -.- ."

"We are less than a minute before we are in energy range. We are getting readings; they are energizing their weapons," warned Hu'de.

Raising his left hand to pause Hu'de, Zeke stared at Te'ln. "Ok, Te'ln, watch my fingers. We are going to do what we call dots and dashes. Dashes are completed by holding down the key just a bit longer. We may not get it correct, but hopefully, enough will get through to be recognized."

"Now watch and listen… when I pause my finger on the desk, it is a dash. Here we go." Zeke made sure Te'ln was watching his fingers. ".-.. ..- -.-. -.- -.-.-- ... - .-. .. -.- ."

He waited a few seconds. ".-.. ..- -.-. -.- -.-.-- ... - .-. .. -.- ."

"Now you try tapping on the shelf, Te'ln," prompted Zeke.

Nervously, Te'ln tapped "...-..." before Zeke put his hand on hers. "Relax, take a breath, then try again. I will tap; you follow me, ok?"

Breathing in, Te'ln nodded and watched Zeke's hand closely. ".-.. ..- -.-. -.- -.-.-- ... - .-. .. -.- ."

At each tap, Te'ln matched Zeke's taps. ".-.. ..- -.-. -.- -.-.-- ... - .-. .. -.- ."

"Excellent, you did great. Once more…" requested Zeke.

".-.. ..- -.-. -.- -.-.-- ... - .-. .. -.- ." was done by both with less than a second difference between the two sets.

"You ready?" asked Zeke of Te'ln.

Every individual was quiet while both Zeke and Te'ln tapped. Zeke tapped it on the shelf, with Te'ln doing it on her keyboard.

Once done, Te'ln looked at Zeke with her great big eyes opened in panic.

Smiling, Zeke hugged Te'ln, "You did great, Te'ln, you did it perfectly. Now take what you just sent and send it in a loop."

All listened as the loop started non-stop. Every eye was on the workstation that was sending the message like that would help it, even though only one person knew what it meant.

Seeing Hu'de turn to look at him, Zeke shrugged. "Now we have to wait and see what happens. If not, we will not be here long enough to think about it."

Zeke, Jeanne, and Hu'de met by the command platform.

"Do you want to tell us what that was?" asked Jeanne.

"It could be nothing more than random pings, or it could be something Lance and I used to do when we flew together. We would get bored sitting there when in training, so we started tapping on the com channel. Used to drive our trainers crazy trying to figure out who was a jerk. Lance found a system called Morse code at one time to send comical messages back and forth."

"What did you send?" asked Hu'de.

"If I am correct, it has been many years since I used Morse code, so I am not sure I remember it properly. Anyway, I think the signal we were getting said '*Jackal*.' So I sent back '*Lucky Strike*.' We will see."

The ship continued forward, with the communication loop continuing to transmit.

Finally, a signal came through requesting a video connection. Following the agreed-upon plan, Te'ln explained why they could not do a video conference call and that the Sovereign was injured and unavailable.

It shocked Zeke when a familiar voice came across.

"Please tell Captain Kinsley that Captain Henry said to stop playing around and get on the damn video call. And if his sidekick, Captain de Clisson, is there with him, '*Ahoy ye matey.*'

The laughter erupting from Zeke and Jeanne startled the Kolqux, more so when Zeke and Jeanne high-fived, thinking they were hitting each other. It was only when they hugged did the tension relax just a bit.

"Hu'de, please have Te'ln initiate a video conference call with the ship that sent that last message," asked Zeke.

Appearing on the screen was a grinning Lance sitting in his command chair surrounded by a group of anxious Kolqux. "I am sure glad you remembered our playtime game, Captain; we were just moments away from taking steps that could have gone drastically wrong for you."

"Me too, my friend, me too. I almost didn't remember; I have not used Morse code since then. I was not sure I wasn't sending you a message to fire on us," laughed Zeke.

"I gather from you being here on a Kolqux ship with Jeanne everything went well back in the Furalla Eaara Star System, correct?" queried Lance.

"We were able to get control of the stations but at a horrible cost to the Kolqux people. We can talk more about that later. Right now, I need to get a status on how it went. Not sure who you have that you want to be on the call, so let us have a conference call in a half-hour?" asked Zeke.

It was odd to Zeke the smile that appeared on Lance's face while stating, "You may want to forgo the conference call and do it in person here. Some news requires being told in person to be believable."

Looking at Jeanne perplexed, she shrugged, showing she had no idea what was happening. Then, turning to Hu'de, he saw he was just as clueless. "Ok, Lance, we will board your ship in forty-five minutes. See you then."

"Hu'de, can you get a shuttle ready? Besides yourself, bring whomever you think should attend the meeting. So let's say we all meet in thirty minutes in the landing bay?"

Zeke and Jeanne moved to sit together on the shelf next to Te'ln, who looked at them with her large eyes opened wide in concern.

"Unless I am mistaken, Te'ln, Hu'de will ask you to join us. If he doesn't, we will, so you may want to take a few moments to freshen up." After which, both laughed when they saw her eyes widen in panic. Then still in a panic, she looked at Hu'de, who shook his head positively, which just about sent her over the edge.

Popping up onto her feet, Jeanne grabbed Te'ln by her hand and gently directed her to the exit. "Let's get ready, and you can tell me more about yourself."

"I have notified all who will join us for the meeting, Captain. I am sorry my daughter is such a burden for your mate. She was the only one who knew how to use that special equipment when this ship was ready to leave the dock," apologized Hu'de.

Slightly surprised, Zeke looked at Hu'de in a new light. "Daughter? Te'ln is your daughter?"

Nodding, Hu'de explained that most on the ship knew each other, with most having one or more relatives on board. Two of his engineers have a sibling, child, and grandparent working side by side. Families tended to work in the same field.

"Well, Hu'de, I am sure there are many more surprises the Kolqux have in store for me. But one thing you do not have to apologize for is your daughter. She has done very well, considering the situation. RGN technicians spend a year training at a minimum before being assigned a station on a warship. Te'ln had how much time? Besides, Jeanne would have wanted some time to get ready anyway."

Zeke and Hu'de walked off the bridge, making their way to the landing bay. Zeke was deferring washing up until he was on the Jackal. The accommodations here were not something he was comfortable using.

As he walked with Hu'de, he wondered if that would be one of the first things the Kolqux changed when they started building new ships, as they probably had some of the same issues. Then again, as he was sure the RGN would allow some technology transfer, the Kolqux would probably be building a new type of warship within a few years.

Now, though, he was worried about what was so crucial that Lance thought he needed to hear it in person.

THE ENDAENS

ENTERING THE CONFERENCE room on the Jackal, Zeke reflected more or less if he ever wanted to get on that shuttle again. The shuttle they had used was spartan in all its equipment. He would not have been surprised if it had fallen apart while on the way listening to the racket it made while in flight. It rattled even his nerves.

But, with his arm locked in Jeanne's, it was not something that seemed to bother Jeanne. She had sung the whole time like she was enjoying the ride. He must put visiting Jeanne's home planet Tortuga on his list of things to do. All the people he had met so far from that planet seemed to be thrill-seekers.

He was surprised that Lance had not met him in the landing bay but had sent his first officer, Lieutenant Commander Wilma Cross. The Lieutenant Commander was waiting for them as they exited the shuttle. The commander was small in stature, just over five feet, with close-cropped black with dark brown eyes.

As they stepped onto the deck, the commander saluted and, after getting a return salute, stepped forward with her hand stretched out for a handshake. "Captains, it is a pleasure. Unfortunately, I had been sidelined by personal issues while in the Pandora System.

I did not get the opportunity there to meet you two there. I hope we get a chance to talk more. Especially with Captain Kinsley after Captain Henry spoke of their shenanigans when on leave while serving in the same fighter squadron."

"I plead the fifth," Zeke stated while laughing at the startled expression on Jeanne's face.

"The captain would have come, but he is getting everything set up in the conference room. I think you will understand once you see what he has prepared," divulged Wilma. "If you follow me, we can get started."

It felt good to be back on an RGN warship. The Kolqux warship was not made for humans and had taken its toll; both were exhausted from little sleep.

When they entered the conference room, they were surprised by the numbers. The vast majority were Kolqux, with a few of Captain Henry's officers scattered around the room.

Standing in the center of the room was Captain Lance Henry. Lance was a tall, wiry man with short reddish-blonde hair and grey eyes. His height would not have been something that stood out in a typical setting, except now being surrounded by the much shorter Kolqux, where he now looked like a giant.

The noise was surprisingly quiet. Anytime Zeke had been in a meeting with the Kolqux before, they talked loudly nonstop. Was this change due to locality differences, or what had required Jeanne and himself to attend the meeting in person?

Upon seeing Zeke and Jeanne enter the room, Lance broke away from the group clamoring for his attention. Jeanne was slightly surprised to see Lance punch Zeke hard on his upper arm, only for Zeke to return the same hard punch. Both laughed before they hugged and pounded each other's back.

Seeing Jeanne's look, Zeke explained. "We used to spar together. I thought it would be easy the first time we boxed each other. A boxing ring was not unknown to me. He had the reach, but I had more muscle and weight. So I went straight at him with a right cross. I woke up on the floor fifteen seconds later. I found out too late that Lance floated through college on a boxing scholarship. He was an undefeated intercollegiate middleweight boxer for three years."

"Three years? Did you graduate early?" asked Jeanne.

"No, in the fourth year, my competition grew taller and had learned my style. They mopped the floor with me and removed all my big dreams of going into boxing," Lance explained. "I always wanted to travel, so after another nasty beat down, I signed up to roam the galaxy. No regrets, though; I belong here."

"There are a lot of Kolqux here; what is going on?" asked Zeke, looking around the room.

"It will all be explained to you. First, though, there are some special someone's you need to meet." With that, Lance returned to the middle of the room, dragging Zeke and Jeanne with him.

Nodding to Wilma standing by the door, Lance turned to his guests. "Please sit; you must be sitting before they arrive." Raising his hands, Lance clapped them to get the room's attention.

"It is time. Please settle down. Grab what seats you can; the four seats to my right are reserved for our guests; otherwise, please move against the wall to allow our guest's room to maneuver," directed Lance.

Nodding to Wilma, Lance continued to stand as Wilma led a group into the room that surprised Jeanne; turning to express her shock, she saw Zeke smiling.

"You knew?" whispered Jeanne in startlement.

"I had an idea something like this was possible," responded Zeke.

"How? When?" a startled Jeanne said as she watched several more special guests arrive, all wearing sidearms.

"The battleship we found. I had Isolde and Selena check

something out for me. They confirmed my suspicions," answered Zeke.

"What the hell was that?" asked Jeanne.

"No Chohish engineer bodies were found in the entire battleship. They did find an empty location in the landing bay where they thought a group of shuttles or fighters could have been parked. Who else could have architected that disaster?"

"I asked you all here to introduce you to the Endaens." Lance indicated to the individual next to him, "This is Vopengi Edoetti, leader of the Endaens; they are rebelling against the Chohish hierarchy."

An angry undercurrent started running through most of the Kolqux in the room after the announcement.

Keeping his voice low, Zeke whispered. "Jeanne, look at the Kolqux standing next to the Endaens. They were not surprised or concerned. I suspect that Lance has them there to stand guard."

"Not all of you know that the Endaens revolted a little over a month ago. Some Kolqux joined with the Endaens during the revolt. Both stations were cleared of all hostile Chohish, allowing my crew to enter the stations without further loss of life. Videos of that action are available to all."

"They are Chohish; they have tortured and killed my people for thousands of years. Kill them. They do not deserve any mercy," a Kolqux yelled with spittle flying out his mouth and nostrils.

Pushing up from his seat, Vopengi stood for a few seconds until the noise calmed down. "No Endaen ever tortured or hurt your people. Who among you can say that this occurred to someone they knew?"

The Kolqux that yelled before stood and pointed at the Endaen. "You helped the Chohish; we have seen it."

"And so did you. Did you not build Chohish weapons? Their warships? Grow their food? Make their clothes? Do the humans blame you for the untold numbers of dead on their worlds by the weapons you built for the Chohish? Why do you blame the Endaen who have lived under their thumb for longer than you?"

The Kolqux looked like he was going to yell at the Endaen again but stammered in confusion. "You?"

"Yes. Us Endaens grew up in the same world as the ones you know as the Chohish. We, like you, are smaller and weaker than the Chohish. Understand, though, we are not Chohish; we are Endaens. Early in our history, they hunted us for fun. That was until they figured out that keeping us alive as workers was better. Our history has always been living under their thumb. Do you think they cared about us? Do you think they did less to us than they did to you? That is our entire known history."

"Why now? If it as you say, why did you rebel now?" asked one of the Kolqux.

Pointing to Zeke and Jeanne, Vopengi went on to explain. "Because of the ones you call the Humans, the Chohish are scared of them. The first time we ever experienced them having fear. Until now, the Chohish have not run into any race that could stop them in their tracks so devastatingly. Smaller, softer beings who are now bringing the fight and fear to them. Although Captain Henry tells us of winged ones who were able to stop them many years ago."

"You knew, didn't you? You were on the ship that signaled the fleeing fleet. That, sooner or later, we had to travel through that system. You vented the battleship as a message to us?" asked Zeke loudly to get over all the side conversations.

Turning, Vopengi looked at both Zeke and Jeanne intensely before responding. "You are the two that scare the Chohish the most. You, they hunt for. Your two ships they search for. They want you dead."

Surprised, Zeke studied Vopengi. "Why? How would they know us?"

"Communications. The Chohish intercepted communications from your planets that spoke of your actions and images of you, your crew, and your ships. They passed this on to all Chohish. It would be a great honor for any Chohish who destroy you."

"If that is true, why would you risk everything now? There should be more Chohish in the area than normal. Something is not making sense here." Jeanne asked while she stared at Vopengi. "What are you not telling us?"

The smile on Vopengi's face let Zeke and Jeanne know she had guessed correctly. Vopengi had been hiding something from them.

"When word spread of their huge defeat, rebellion spread throughout the Chohish empire. The Chohish are extremely short of ships and soldiers. Fuel has always been in short supply, now even more," explained Vopengi. "You destroyed several of their combined reserve fleets and the main fleet for this sector. It will take many years to replace them. We wish to take our chance for freedom now; it may never occur again."

"I am still unsure how you think you can succeed now. Rebellions must have occurred before," queried Jeanne.

Vopengi pointed to a large display at the front of the conference room, showing icons of the Kolqux fleet as it continued heading toward the Furalla Eaara Star System.

"Endaens are responsible for thoroughly testing any new ships before they are approved. We reported to the Chohish commanding officer that we had identified a severe failure in a critical part that managed the fuel intake for the engines. As they explained to the Chohish, the entire shipment of that piece was defective. Historically, the Endaens do not check individual parts shipped from another manufacturer."

Speaking to the Endaen next to him, it was apparent something was funny. Vopengi waved his hands as if all understood the joke. "We crawled and pretended we were frightened silly when the commanding Chohish found out. That half-witted imbecile ranted and screamed at everyone. I enjoyed killing him. He cried like a baby when I slit his throat."

Both of the Endaens started laughing before Vopengi grew serious. "The Engineers and their families risked being skinned alive. But the Chohish had become reliant on us Endaens for so long they did not question the report. Ships built from multiple systems routinely come here for a final checkup before deployment."

Jeanne asked the obvious question. "Once you rebelled, there is no recourse for you. You have to fight the Chohish. How? With what?"

"Kolqux rebelled when we rebelled. We fought together. Many Endaens died fighting side by side with the Kolqux. The fleet you see here is fully built out and armed. We hope it will be large enough to hold off the Chohish while new ships built. Better ships, Endaen and Kolqux crewed."

What interested Zeke the most, though, was the news about the rebellions. Information was limited as it depended on one Endaen giving it to another. Info might be weeks, if not months, old.

What Zeke was able to determine was that war supplies were being drastically affected. Rebellion locations would be out of action for the foreseeable future regardless if the rebellion were successfully put down.

One item of interest that Vopengi brought up caught Zeke's and Jeanne's attention more than the rest. Vopengi had been describing that the Chohish had lost personnel they could not replace.

When asked why he said the rebellion, of course, he then explained that a few of the Chohish home worlds were part of the rebellion. Hearing this, Zeke and Jeanne asked for clarification.

Vopengi explained that it was because how a Chohish is raised has recently changed; he then explained.

A Chohish birthing was savage throughout the whole process.

Several times a year, the mother would eject a clutch of eggs that she attaches to her front chest with a secretion. Males compete in a battle frenzy for the right to fertilize the eggs. The death rates during this ritual are incredibly high. The Endaens believe that is due to a pheromone in the secretion. Once the eggs get fertilized, the males leave the mother, who raises the offspring until they are large enough for schooling.

Chohish male children outnumber females by a factor of ten. When Chohish males reach a certain weight and height, they enroll in a school where fighting is the primary curriculum. Many Chohish male offspring do not survive to adulthood, and females have no rights in Chohish society.

But due to a strain on finding enough Chohish males to supply the ever-growing war machine, this had changed several generations past. Now Chohish mothers are raising their children until near adulthood when an unexpected change occurred in the Chohish society over the years. The mothers demand greater control and independence, and their children support their demands.

Suddenly, Vopengi stopped explaining. The silence was deafening as everyone's attention was riveted on the Endaen. It was evident from the sly expression on his face that he had one final tidbit of information he was saving to the end.

"The mothers came to the one group that could help them, someone, that could get them weapons and ships. So they came to the Endaens."

"Holy crap!" whispered both Jeanne and Zeke at the same time.

DECEPTION

THE HOURS SINCE the revelation of the rebellion contained none of the initial excitement. The Kolqux went about their duties with constant glances at the two Endaens who sat with Zeke and Jeanne.

Zeke was still trying to process the jaw-dropping events and how, if possible, he could take advantage of any of them. He would have Nkosana or Will send updates back to the fleet as soon as they passed back through the slipstream. It had been over a day since they entered this system, and any further delay could have a significant impact. This information had to get back while it was still relevant.

Jeanne, Zeke, and Vopengi had returned to the Kolqux battleship as they wanted to show the Kolqux they were in this together.

Turning as Jeanne sneezed again, he would have laughed, except he could see the anguish she was going through. Her eyes were red, her throat sore, her voice hoarse sounding, and her face blotchy with red bumps.

The doctor on the Jackal had verified she was allergic to compounds present in the air on the Kolqux ship. Even though Jeanne now had drugs to combat the allergy, it would take time to work its way through her system. Jeanne stared at Zeke with fire in her red eyes when he suggested she stay on the Jackal. But, of course, it had nothing to do with him showing no signs of being affected. The glare worsened when he told her the Kolqux smell was hard to take.

"Prepare for passage through to the Furalla Eaara Star System," ordered Hu'de. The tone and timbre of his voice spoke of a different Kolqux than he had been just a day before. It was commanding and sure.

The difference between the ship's first time going through the slipstream and this one was dramatic. This time, the crew went about their duties with confidence and pride. Instead of frowns and hesitancy before transition, there was chatter and laughter while working their consoles efficiently. The control stations worked happily in tandem.

Unfortunately, the Kolqux were still heavily affected when transitioning. But Hu'de anticipating that, had extra crew standing by. What surprised Zeke the most was that the Endaen was not affected. He was smiling before, during, and after the transition.

They had no sooner entered than there was a communications request from a fighter standing off a reasonable distance away. Another dozen fighters were sitting idly nearby.

"Hawke for Captain Kinsley, Hawke for Captain Kinsley."

Seeing Hu'de look at him questioningly, Zeke pointed to the ceiling, signaling he wanted it over the loudspeakers.

"Since when do you call your friend other than by his proper name?" responded Zeke.

"Welcome back, Zeke. I had to verify that you were still free and onboard. Sorry, I forgot the order of the code phrases. A Chohish or AI would not know I never call you Captain unless in battle. You sure are returning with a large force. Ahhh. Now I see the Jackal. They must have their transponder turned off," a laughing Hawke replied.

"We have a critical situation you must be aware of, sir. The admiral sent us hoping our signatures are small enough not to be detected."

"What is it, Hawke?" a now worried Zeke responded. Hawke never missed an opportunity to hold a meaningless chat; he always thought it drove whoever else was on the call nuts.

"A large Chohish force transitioned through just after you left. The Admiral sent us here to wait on any returning force from this slipstream, so he knew what he would be facing. He will be glad to know you survived."

Unstrapping and running over to the communications station, Zeke bent over the technician. "Hawke, how many Chohish ships and where are they?"

"Close to two hundred and fifty warships of different makes and sizes. They are situated near the slipstream," replied Hawke. "The Admiral believes they are waiting on another force to arrive."

"Damn" exclaimed Zeke. "And where is the Lucky Strike?"

"Behind the station over the main planet. The admiral placed it there before their arrival, hiding our signature, just in case of unexpected visitors. Same with the Fox. The Kolqux operated ships arrayed around the station in a protective half-circle. Their men of war are badly damaged; they would be of little use against this force. You could not have come at a better time, Zeke. The Kolqux are panicking."

Turning toward Jeanne, Zeke could not miss that every eye on the bridge was looking at him. "Well, there is no way we can attack them head-on. I agree with the admiral that the Chohish must be waiting on another force; otherwise, they would have attacked."

"Hawke, does the admiral have any plans on defending the planets?" asked Jeanne.

"Just delay tactics. Load the fighters with bombs and use them as missiles. Same with the warships. Hopefully, enough damage will cause them to pull back long enough for the RGN to arrive," replied Hawke. "They started loading the fighters and warships as soon as the Chohish fleet showed up."

"Any word on the RGN fleet?" asked Zeke.

"None at all. The admiral sent a pair of modified shuttles back through the slipstream to see if they could hurry them along," reported Hawke.

"Shuttles? Unless the RGN is in the system next door, they are sending the shuttles on a one-way trip," an alarmed Jeanne stated.

"That was the modification. The admiral had Jax take some spare lendolium tanks from storage and put them inside the shuttle. I doubt anyone but Jax and his crew could have connected them to the main shuttle tanks in just a few hours. They left over eighteen hours ago. It should be enough to check out the other system and get back here," reported Hawke.

"You stated they had already started loading the fighters and warships with bombs. Do you know how many?" asked Zeke.

"Uh oh, Hawke, he has that crazy smile again. I am not sure we will like what he has planned, " Jeanne warned. "That smile is more crooked than normal."

"I need a conference call with Vopengi, Lance, Hawke, Nkosana, Will, Isolde, Jax, Jamie, and Meghan. Hu'de, you and your daughter, of course, will need to be present along with whoever is in charge of this Kolqux fleet. I forgot to ask after meeting the Endaens. We need to flush this plan out quickly as it will need a lot of work to have any chance of success. And we must do this before any more Chohish ships arrive, " Zeke ordered.

The communications officer on the Jackal, Lieutenant Tuan Tanner, was tasked with getting a secure conference setup between all parties. Tuan would use RGN communications as they had concerns about the Kolqux communications.

"Hopefully, the Chohish fleet gives us the time to put this all together," Zeke stated upon a questioning look from Jeanne.

Once connected, he said this is what we are going to do. They listened in silence until he finished. Then the shouting started.

It was annoying that Zeke would not give Jeanne any hint of what he planned before the meeting. Then again, after they all heard what he intended, she was somewhat glad he didn't. She wasn't sure she would have been unable to hold her laughter.

Several hours later, the fleet, heading toward the station over the main planet, spread out in an attack formation, Chohish fashion. Cruisers were in front, with the destroyers screening the battleships. The Chohish warships had slowed down, so they were moving at less than a quarter speed which meant they would not arrive until the next day.

Strapped in on the Kolqux bridge with a homemade seatbelt, Jeanne checked to ensure the strap was tight. *"And they say Irracans are crazy! I wonder if Zeke's daring is common among the people where he grew up? His plan is so insane that Mason voiced his opinion that Zeke be made an honorary Irracan. And that was supported by all on Fox. And surprise, surprise. My sister says to hurry up and marry him before another Irracan steals him away."*

A group of the Kolqux warships left the station's protection over the main planet, where they headed toward the fleet heading toward them.

Suddenly, the communications lit up with an image of a Chohish sovereign in luxurious robes standing by an oversized gilded command chair in the middle of a Chohish battleship bridge. In the Chohish language, a system-wide broadcast went out. The language was broken down first to the Kolqux language and then to RGN by the ship's AI.

"All Kolqux, hear me. I am Thizae, commander of the Oxtaria Pulsar System. Your rebellion in my system failed dramatically. Many

Kolqux died in their attempt. Now I am here to show you the might of the Chohish. How dare you rebel against the mighty Chohish who has been so kind to you. I demand your immediate surrender. Refuse, and I will destroy your pathetic fleet; next will be the station, then I will bomb your cities. Your people will see how easily I wipe away your defenses. Then it will be too late; they will be next. You have twenty-four hours to make your decision."

The message ended with an image of the Chohish Sovereign laughing into the camera before sitting in the command chair.

The Kolqux fleet continued heading toward the system's main planet and station. On the bridge of a Kolqux battleship, tension reigned. The Kolqux kept glancing at Zeke and Jeanne with apprehension.

"They are nervous, Zeke. And they have every reason to be concerned. Simply crazy, you know, this could go wrong quickly, " Jeanne whispered. "Will the Chohish track that message back to LS1 on the Lucky Strike?"

Zeke responded to Jeanne by ensuring he showed confidence while he replied even more quietly. "I don't think so. If they had system probes, yes, I believe they would have. We are very limited in our options. If the Kolqux loses this fight, they will suffer an untold number of deaths in retaliation. Our combined forces may or may not be able to handle the current Chohish fleet in the system, but we need to make an effort. They will remember who stood with them. They would never trust us or be our allies in the future if we left them when they needed us the most."

Yawning, he covered his mouth as he finished. "Who knows how large the Chohish fleet that is coming? We must deal with the present fleet before they combine. Once combined, it could tip the balance beyond anything we can hope to deal with. Hell, the one coming may be magnitudes larger, and this is all in vain."

Laughing, Jeanne shook her head, so her hair flipped over her right shoulder. "Even if we defeat the fleet we know of, I doubt we will have enough ships or fighters left to deal with another Chohish fleet of any decent size."

"This is why I sent the Jackal off to see where the RGN fleet is and speed them up. Lance did say he was the fastest ship."

The small Kolqux fleet heading toward them hailed them. *"I am pilot Ol'ce. We are not part of the revolt. We understand our place and wish to join your forces against the rebellion."*

The response in Chohish did not indicate who was on the other end.

"You must go to coordinates sent to you at your best speed. Once there, you are to power down all systems. Your ships will be boarded and confiscated. Any deviance will result in immediate destruction."

The small Kolqux fleet speed increased except for a few smaller units trailing behind.

Meanwhile, another Chohish scrambled communications came into Zeke and Jeanne's battleship.

"Sovereign Thizae, this is Sovereign Ukan, commander of the task force at the slipstream. I am in command of all forces in this system by order of the Supreme Council. So you are to place your forces under my command. We will wait here for additional forces that will be here within the next week or two. Once we combine all fleets, we will retake this system before proceeding to the human planets. This is not a request but an order."

"Sovereign Ukan, I Sovereign Ukan, hear and will obey. Before joining your fleet, I will take charge of the Kolqux fleet heading toward us."

The next dozen hours passed in near silence.

Walking over to Zeke and Jeanne, Hu'de wondered why they had only gone to relieve themselves and wash up—never leaving to get some sleep or something to eat. Both dozed in each other's arms strapped to their seats.

Zeke smiled, seeing the curious look on Hu'de's face through half-closed eyelids. "Situation is fluid. Best not to be away in case you need us. Food would make us tired." Laughing, he continued. "Next time, though, we must ensure we bring a lot of coffee."

Just as Hu'de was going to respond, Te'ln interrupted. "Dad, the ships we have been waiting on have reached their destination. They are starting to power down."

Turning to his daughter, Hu'de told her to notify the Kolqux and Endaens in the other ships to start sending their shuttles.

"Captain Kinsley, are you sure this is going to work?"

"I hope so. Welcome to command, Hu'de; most of the time, you are on the short end of the stick. We cannot go head-to-head with this force; we do not have the numbers or experience. Remember what we discussed earlier. Sitting and waiting for their reinforcements, which they confirmed are coming, is not something you want to allow to join this group."

Zeke pointed to the display of the ship icons sitting powered down. "Those ships have what we need to have any chance of success," answered Zeke with a yawn.

The looks from Hu'de and the rest of the Kolqux almost made Zeke laugh. Even though they knew the plan, he knew they thought he was crazy and they would all die.

It was another hour before the shuttles arrived and entered the powerless ships.

"*Sovereign Thizae, this is Hukat, leader of the boarding party; we have taken control of all ships. The Kolqux surrendered without a fight and were locked down. We are in the process of powering up. We will join the fleet within the hour.*"

Presently, both groups of ships were heading toward each other. As they neared, both groups slowed down and merged into one fleet. Some of the smaller vessels flew right into the battleships and cruisers.

One battleship had an odd assortment of personnel in the landing bay when a shuttle came to rest just a dozen feet from them.

Hu'de, Po'bs, Zeke, Jeanne, and Vopengi greeted Mason as he walked down the back exit ramp, even as it was still lowering.

He smiled before stepping aside to allow Lieutenant Commander Jax Andrews, Engineers Shannon Willis, and Ronald Estrada to pass by and exit the ship.

Mason followed them, with over a dozen RGN marines in powered armor following him. As the Marines marched off, they had to bend down as they exited to allow the large plasma rifle connected to their back the necessary clearance. All wore modular belts across their chest and around their waist. They held grenades, power reloads for the rifles, and the pair of plasma pistols each carried in holsters hung on their hips. A separate belt had surveillance drones and an assortment of other gear.

The last two marines were familiar to Zeke and Jeanne. They were glad to see them, especially since they saw that Shon and Michale each carried one of the two things they had both asked for, coffee and cocoa.

Seeing the scowl on Jax's face as he looked around, Zeke rushed to head him off before saying something their new allies could misinterpret.

"Jax, good to see you. I know, I know, the Lucky Strike is where you and your engineers should be. But we need your help. No one el…" but he never got the chance to finish the sentence.

"Cap, we get it. The Admiral went over it multiple times. We brought all the lendolium we could. So I got with the Kolqux engineers before coming to see if their ships can use our processed fuel."

"I only need it to work on the battleships, Jax, and only for one thing."

Zeke's look at Jax revealed that Jax was quite aware of what was needed.

"It will work, Captain. It will require some work, but we will get it done. You will only get one shot out of them, two if you're lucky. So we brought the needed parts based on the number you provided. I hope you got someone that can do all the work."

That was when Vopengi stepped forward, which caused Jax and his engineers to jump back in alarm.

"Whoa... Jax, this is Vopengi Edoetti, an Endaen; he and his fellows are with us. Long story, tell you later. Vopengi and his crew are the engineers you will be working with."

"Damn, Captain, what the hell did you get us mixed up in?" Then, seeing the outstretched hand of Vopengi, Jax hesitantly gripped it to shake their forearms. Then, pulling Hu'de and Po'bs over by their arms, Zeke made the introductions.

Laughter from Jeanne caused Jax and Vopengi to glare at her, who only laughed louder, but the laughter ended when Jeanne ran to Masson to hug him tight.

"Missed you, me bro; how is my sis doing?"

Mason replied by giving Jeanne a hard noogie on her head with his knuckles. "Your sis said to give you this for all the worry you are giving her. But she sent something along to help her with that."

Rubbing her head where Mason had rubbed it raw, Jeanne asked. "And what would that be?"

Swirling while swinging his arm out, he pointed to the back of the shuttle. Standing there was Sergeant Jan de Bouff in full body armor, holding his helmet in his left hand. The smile on his face brought a groan to Jeanne, and upon seeing the four other Irracan marines standing behind him, she sighed in resignation.

Tapping his wrist, Zeke reminded everyone that they had a lot of work to do in a short amount of time.

Telling Mason to walk with him and Jeanne, with their shadows Shon and Michale following, Zeke headed back to the bridge.

As they were walking out of the landing bay, several RGN

fighters flew in and landed. The deep-throated roar of a bomber caused all to put their hands over their ears. Zeke commented loudly, watching the bomber land, "Now let's see if we can pull off this subterfuge to our advantage."

Hearing Zeke, Mason voiced his concerns. "You know the bombers will only have half a dozen missiles each, right? And that is only because the Fox and Jackal were carrying a few. The Lucky Strike was full out."

"We are short of everything, Mason; we have to make do with what we have," responded Zeke as he stepped over the lip of the hatch out of the landing bay. "Besides, telling Roy to sit out in a battle we all may not survive is not something I think the Admiral could do."

The Kolqux fleet headed toward the slipstream. It would take just over sixteen hours before they arrived in the vicinity of the Chohish fleet.

Meanwhile, inside all the ships, the activity was hectic. Jax and his crew were covered in oil, grease, and fuel. Vopengi and Po'bs even more so while passing the instructions on what to do to all the battleships.

The main issue was getting to the locations to replace parts. One part required pulling hull and armor plating off the tip of the ship to get access to it. Others required the tiniest engineers to squirm over pipes and tunnels that were usually only ever accessed when the warship was in a repair yard.

Reports to the bridge where Hu'de, Zeke, and Jeanne resided were nonstop. Zeke and Jeanne let Hu'de review them first and only stepped in when requested, which was often in the beginning, but as time went on, less and less.

Meanwhile, Mason had returned to the hanger deck to check on his fighter that had just flown in.

Once more, the crew saw their captain, Hu'de, step up to the task. Orders went out, not just for the team on the bridge but for the whole ship.

The confidence he was displaying was contagious. Frowns became smiles; doubt became confidence. And none too soon.

"*This is Sovereign Thizae. We will not have another massive part failure like we had recently. These ships will be tested and retested until I am satisfied. You will not rest until I give permission. I will not be embarrassed again. Any ship that encounters a system failure while in combat, its engineers will be spaced. I expect ships to start testing their systems immediately. All repairs are to be completed by the time this fleet reports to Sovereign Ukan.*"

"Ok, Hu'de, it is time to start our little game. Ready for some fun?" asked Zeke.

Confirming what Zeke expected, Hu'de stood straight on the command chair, so he stood with a commanding air; he gave orders with a strong voice full of confidence.

"General Quarters. All hands man your battle stations. At'se, bring up our shields. Ie'wa, arm the weapons. Po'bs, take us to full battle speed."

The ship shook as the speed increased, and sparks flew out of several panels when the shield and weapons came online.

"Po'bs, we need an engineer up here," ordered Hu'de.

"You and every other department. SIR! I will send one when I can. We are a little busy trying to keep the engines running. SIR!" responded Po'bs with a heavy emphasis on sir.

If the situation were not so serious, Jeanne would have laughed. It took everything she had to hold it in. Seeing Hu'de blushing, well, she thought he was blushing, was something to see.

Ten minutes later, Hu'de countermanded his earlier commands. "All departments come out of battle stations; I repeat, come out of battle stations! At'Se, bring down our shields. Ie'Wa, disarm the weapons. Po'bs, take us to half speed."

285

Hu'de looked at Zeke imploringly.

"Perfect, Hu'de, you did it perfectly."

No sooner had the ship come out of battle stations than Te'ln, upon a nod from her father, sent out a prerecorded Chohish encrypted message she had received from the Lucky Strike.

"*Sovereign Thizae, this is ship X207B; we are running system checks as ordered. We have encountered several areas still heavily impacted by the battle with the rebel Kolqux. We will continue working on our repairs. We will run additional system checks as we replace or repair defective systems.*"

The radio was quiet until swarmed with reports from the rest of the fleet.

"*Sovereign Thizae, this is ship B983S; we are running system checks as ordered. We have identified multiple parts that are showing potential failure. We will be running additional system checks as we replace or repair defective systems. We will do these while in transit.*"

"*Sovereign Thizae, this is ship B963S, we are running system...*" on and on as ship after ship reported in.

Standing, Zeke clapped his hands until he had everyone's attention. "Well, I think it is going pretty well. Don't you?"

The laughter from Jeanne at the stunned expressions on most faces did nothing to relieve their fears.

ONSLAUGHT

THE SHIPS KEPT up their testing, bringing up the shields, weapons, and increasing engine output as they made the trip to the slipstream. Progress by the engineers was slow but steady.

Bored on the bridge, Zeke and Jeanne grabbed a pot of coffee and disposable cups before walking to the engineering department to check on Jax and his group. One of the Kolqux engineers guided them to an access panel in a hallway near the front of the ship, where they found the trio bathed in sweat and dirt. The half dozen Endaens and Kolqux grouped around him were in no better shape.

Seeing Zeke, Jax tiredly waved for them to join the group.

"How is it going, Jax? Will we be able to get the work done on time?" asked Zeke.

"It will be close, but we will get it done. The Endaens are marvelous engineers and able to pass on what needs to be done to both their people and the Kolqux engineers," Jax responded while filling a cup of coffee.

Handing the coffee to the other two engineers from the Lucky Strike, he started to wolf it down, only to spit some out when it burned his tongue.

"You look tired. Maybe you should take a break?" asked a concerned Jeanne.

"Not if you want us to complete everything on time." Waving away Jeanne's concern. "This is normal for engineers when the shit hits the fan. No one remembers us before the battle."

Pretending he was shocked, Zeke stepped back and pointed to himself while mouthing, "not me; I always keep you in mind."

"Well, thanks for the coffee, but I need to get back to the group. The support structure to hold our modified device and tank has been completed. We are about to do the critical part, connect all the parts, and run our tests. Give me a few hours, and we will know if all this works."

"If it doesn't, I am not sure any of us will be around to care. We will not have time for a second try," lamented Zeke. "We will be on the bridge if you need anything. Don't hesitate to contact us. What you are doing is the lynchpin between success and our death."

"Glad you are not putting any pressure on us. Then again, that seems to be a habit with you." Waving them away, Jax rejoined his group.

More hours passed as the fleet limped to the slipstream. Tests on each ship continued with reports sent back to 'Sovereign Thizae.'

Meanwhile, the Kolqux fleet at the main planet and station started shifting around, and communications from the fleet indicated they were on the move.

They were only half an hour away from arriving at the slipstream when Jax contacted Zeke.

"Captain, we have finished our work. We ran all the tests we could, but until we turn on the unit fully, we will not know for sure. Can we turn it on?"

"Negative Jax, we will only get one opportunity to activate it. It will either work or fail," replied Zeke.

"Understand, Captain, we will run more tests on what we

can, but we think you are good to go." With that, the connection disconnected.

The end of Jax's call was like an omen. It was only a few moments later that a connection request from the Chohish came through.

Signaling Te'In to accept the call, the voice of Ukan came across the speakers.

"Sovereign Thizae, I have been monitoring the messages regarding your fleet's repair progress. What is the current status?"

Again, Te'In entered the commands to respond with a pre-planned recorded message.

"Sovereign Ukan, I believe we have resolved most, if not all, the problems identified. However, to be sure, I ordered the engineers to do a fleet-wide test on all systems. So I want permission to execute this test within the next hour. I must know the status of each ship's capability."

"You have my permission to run your tests. In the meantime, you are to merge your fleet with mine. I have sent several destroyers midway to the planets to track the rebel fleet movements. They have reported the rebel forces are mobilizing. Intercepted communications indicate the rebels are planning an attack on us here at the slipstream."

There was a break of several seconds before Ukan resumed. *"Stupid Kolqux, they made small changes to the communications protocol and thought we would not be able to debug it. Stupid, that is why we ruled them for thousands of years. We are going to go into a standard defensive posture. Place your forces appropriately."*

The end of the communications was abrupt without waiting for any confirmation.

The forces around the slipstream slowly spread out into a half-circle. The cruisers were in front, followed by the destroyers, with the battleships at the rear.

The Kolqux fleet broke up with the cruisers sliding into open spaces next to their counterparts. One Kolqux cruiser next to a

Chohish cruiser. Same for the destroyers. But the battleships passed by the other battleships to form up behind the Chohish battleships.

"Hu'de, are the Chohish ship's shields still lowered?" whispered Zeke. Almost as if he said it too loud, they would hear him.

Running to the scanning station, Hu'de muttered with the technician before bobbing his head positively at Zeke.

Sitting strapped into a strange man at war, Zeke was about to risk the lives of thousands on a crazy scheme. If this did not work, millions, maybe billions, would die.

What made it most challenging of all was that the one he had come to depend on more than anyone else was not here with him. She was sitting in her fighter next to her fellow Irracans, ready to fly out of the bay.

Every eye was on Zeke as he nodded to Te'In.

Upon Zeke's nod, a nervous Te'ln sent out the final message prepared by LS1. *"Sovereign, Ukan, this is Sovereign Thizae; we are ready to do our final test."*

A single word came in reply. *"Proceed."*

Hu'de mirrored the earlier commands that were now given on all the Kolqux ships.

"General Quarters. All hands, man your battle stations. At'se, bring up our shields. Ie'wa, arm the weapons."

The words that they were waiting for came across from Vopengi. *"All systems, I repeat, all systems are up and functional on all ships, Sovereign Thizae."*

"Fire all weapons, launch all fighters," yelled Hu'de.

The Kolqux battleships rocked as they fired the deadly linoleum-powered laser positioned at the tip of the battleships along with every laser and missile that worked.

The cruisers and destroyers fired all their weapons at the same time.

Over sixty RGN and Irracan fighters flew out of multiple bays, followed by ten bombers led by one pilot yelling, "For Spencer."

But they were not the only fighters. Close to three hundred pilotless Kolqux fighters flew out of the seven carriers. But these, unlike their RGN and Irracan counterparts, did not do any unique flying but headed straight toward predetermined targets.

Most Chohish battleships were hit in the rear by the linoleum-powered laser, which went right through the least protected part of the ship and the engines into the central part of the warship. If that was not bad enough, secondary lasers and missiles pounded the warships from all sides.

Some battleships exploded outright, others erupted in flame, and many vented air and bodies. Still, nearly a dozen were unaffected by any deadly fire from the Kolqux battleships.

These battleships started turning while bringing their shields online. But the Kolqux fighters made their presence known before their shields were fully enabled. Multiple fighters rammed the warships and exploded. All the fighters were loaded with high explosives. The fighter's computer flew it to a target determined by an algorithm put together by the most competent computer in the system, LS1.

Within a few moments, all the Chohish battleships were out of action. But that was just the beginning.

The Kolqux cruisers and destroyers had unloaded on their counterparts. Destruction of the Chohish warships was rampant. Energy weapons impacted unshielded warships boring deep inside. Air, debris, fire, and bodies erupted from these ships.

But it was not total. Chohish warship shields were brought online on dozens of ships before the missiles could arrive. While they were hurt, they were not out of action. As a result, they wasted no time firing on the Kolqux warships.

The battle raged on. Then another presence made itself known.

The remainder of the Kolqux fighters rammed into Chohish cruisers. The cruiser's shields were overwhelmed between the fighters, energy weapons, and missiles. Cruiser after cruiser went silent.

The Chohish destroyers were the least impacted, with the numbers on their side. They were hard-struck, but as the battle raged on, they overwhelmed the Kolqux destroyers.

Into this battle came the RGN and Irracan fighters. Fighters roared down onto the destroyers. Missile after missile slammed into the Chohish shields. And when the shields failed, one more wraith appeared. The missiles from the bombers ravaged the Chohish warships.

Within an hour, the battle was over.

Not even the inexperienced Kolqux needed to be instructed on what to do next. Rescue shuttles were out as soon as the battle ended. Over a dozen Kolqux destroyers, eight cruisers, and three battleships were destroyed or made inoperable. All of the Kolqux fighters were used and destroyed. Half a dozen RGN and Irracan fighters were lost, but fortunately, the pilots ejected safely in their life pods.

Ejection pods were all over the battlefield. The shuttles would pick up their maximum capacity, return to their home base, unload, and head back out again. Speed was of the essence.

While this progressed, a conference between all the major players was in operation.

Sitting on the bridge with Hu'de, Zeke listened to the damage reports. No video was involved; too much was happening to bother with that.

Zeke sent a general message only when the critical reports slowed down.

"This is Captain Kinsley, I hate to interrupt, but I believe our time here has to be very short. Another Chohish force is on the way. It could arrive at any time. We need to finish up here and get back to the planets."

"Any ship with engine problems needs to be abandoned and destroyed. Nothing is to be left that the arriving force can use. Same for all Chohish warships; they need to be made unrepairable. That needs to be done now while we unload the Kolqux warships crews. All available ships need to assist in this, starting now."

"All fighters and bombers need to land on the carriers. Once completed, the carriers need to head back at maximum speed. Once back, they need to be rearmed and refueled. And yes, Roy, I know, you have no more missiles. No need to refuel the bombers; it may make sense to drain them as fuel is now in short supply."

In a sad voice, he finished with, "I know we lost a lot of personnel today, but we cannot stop to honor them at this time. Later, if we survive, we can honor everyone that lost their lives so others can live free."

REINFORCEMENTS

IT HAD BEEN a week since the battle. Repairs on the ships were going without pause. The injured were recovering. The dead were mourned. New ships were coming online. Kolqux missiles were being replenished. Defensive platforms were being built in space and on the ground. The stations were in the process of being upgraded with more lasers and better larger missiles.

Every Kolqux individual on the three planets in the system was furiously working on something to defend themselves.

But all knew survival was doubtful if a force as large or larger than what they had just fought arrived before the RGN showed up. So if the Chohish went after one of the other two Kolqux systems, they would be forced to intercept them with an inferior force.

Then one event brought hope. The Jackal came flying through the slipstream.

When the shuttle carrying Captain Lance Henry landed at the station, he was greeted by a large group anxious to hear what he had to say.

"Wow, I knew I was popular but never thought I was this popular, " Lance said.

"It will depend on your telling them whether they love or hate you. Jeanne and I know what you will say, so, we will head back to the command center. We have work to do," announced Zeke.

"How the hell do you know what I am going to say?" exclaimed a surprised Lance.

"You told us when you stepped off the shuttle, " said Jeanne, walking away with her arm wrapped in Zeke's.

A puzzled Lance looked around, hoping someone could help him understand what they were discussing.

It was Hawke who gave him a hint.

"When you were walking down the ramp, you were smiling. If you had not met up with the reinforcements, you would not have been smiling. You could not contain yourself. Besides, the crew from the two shuttles sent out by the Admiral are standing behind you."

"Damn!" uttered Lance.

"When will they get here?" asked Hawke.

"Within the hour. I came ahead to let you know." Then smiling again, he finished with. "You know I have the fastest ship in the entire fleet."

It was a good thing Lance was as quick at moving as his ship; otherwise, he would have been hit by the heavy work gloves that Meghan and several others threw at him.

Living up to Lance's word, warships started transitioning through the slipstream in just over an hour. First through were a dozen frigates that turned around and went back through. Then the main warships began showing up. The images from the probes positioned around the slipstream were clear and concise.

The first group of over a hundred battlecruisers of different designs emerged simultaneously. It was pretty evident the RGN fleet was not taking any chances. This group would have pulverized any waiting forces. The majority were of the RGN design, followed by Sorath and Irracan.

Battleships came next, mixed with cruisers and destroyers. One group after another came through. Last were the carriers, troop ships, supply tenders, tankers, medical ships, and frigates. The numbers of ships were too many to count.

What surprised all those watching on the large monitors in the cavernous bay was the last group that emerged. Even though they had seen them in the Pandora system, they never expected to see them here. Two dozen dreadnaughts came through with a substantial protective group of cruisers and destroyers, all of Sorath's design.

Several near Hawke had to step away when he mimicked an old earth gesture. A fist pump, although no earthmen did it, in combination with a pair of wings. The mood in the bay was joyous already, so when they saw Hawke's antics, laughter was loud and heartfelt.

As Zeke and Jeanne stood in the control room on the station, Zeke knew they had decided to come here rather than watch the fleet's arrival in the bay. Then, as warships transitioned through the slipstream, tears of joy ran down many Kolqux faces. Others just sat on the floor, unable to stand as they shook so much. So many just hugged each other in happiness.

A few, Uv'ei, Uv'ek, Hu'de, and Te'ln, came to stand by Zeke and Jeanne in silence. Then, after the last RGN ship had transitioned through, Uv'ei whispered, "My friends, how can my people ever thank you enough? Without you, we would still live in fear, pain, and despair."

Jeanne answered in a deep serious tone, unlike her usually cheerful voice. "You can thank us by never forgetting the pain and suffering you experienced and lived through. Make sure it cannot happen to your children and your grandchildren. Nothing like that must ever occur again. This force you see here cannot remain forever; you will need to be able to protect yourselves."

Turning to look at the Kolqux directly. "Remember Hawke?"

Zeke answered the puzzled expressions on the Kolqux faces. "He is the one with the wings. Hawke's people, the Sorath's, fought the Chohish two thousand years ago. Millions died; entire families died; several planets had to be abandoned. But they stopped them, barely. They never forgot. They spent several thousand years making sure it would never happen again."

"If you look closely at the ships that arrived, the ones with the odd sloping on their backside, they are Sorath's. The easiest way to see it is to look at the largest ships that came in last, called Dreadnaughts. The sloping is to honor their love of flight. The firepower from those largest warships is something you have to see to believe. Each one is more powerful than this station. And this is just a small portion of Sorath's forces. They will never leave their worlds unprotected."

"That is what we should do, can, and will do for ourselves. But you risked your lives for us. You risked everything for us. Your people have died for us. Many were injured severely." Uv'ei paused as he thought of a particular marine still in a medical pod fighting for her life.

"They did not have to risk so much; they could have sat back and waited for a force like this before fighting the Chohish. How do we thank someone for risking their lives for strangers?" an emotional Uv'ek stated.

"Would being our friends be too much to ask?" asked Zeke looking at them sideways.

The next thing they knew, all the Kolqux present were bending down onto one knee.

A low murmur from Uv'ei started, soon joined by the rest that gained volume. "We, known as Kolqux, make a vow. The personnel on the Lucky Strike, the Fox, and the Jackal will be our friends for their entire lives, families, and generations to come. We will regard these individuals the same as our own. They may call on us, even if it means our death. No less than what they did for us."

Standing, Hu'de explained. "This is our custom. It started when the Chohish arrived and killed indiscriminately. Many died so others could live. The payment is due forever."

"We are honored, my friends. My family has something similar but nothing as far-reaching as yours. Then again, different customs for different reasons. I cannot speak for all my people, the Irracans; only my uncle can do that. But I can speak for my family. So let your custom become one with mine," declared Jeanne.

"All of this is a bit overwhelming. I can only speak for myself. I have come to consider all of you my friends. You know what I will do for my friends. There is no more need for me to speak more" avowed Zeke.

"But now, we, you, need to go meet the task force. Time to meet the people that are here to end this war." As one group, they all made their way to the fighter hanger.

When they arrived, they merged with the mob that had gathered. It was a party atmosphere shared by multiple races.

Looking around, Zeke saw Nkosana sitting on a melted slag of scrap metal that was a Chohish fighter at one time. Will, Isolde, and Hawke stood, leaned, and sat around him. Without the insignias on their collars, you would never have known they were officers. Their uniforms looked worn and covered in grease and dirt.

Seeing them, Zeke was surprised as everyone looked no better, including himself and the group with him. Everyone's clothes bore the same wear and stains. Glancing down at his hands, he could see grease and fuel embedded in the cracks of his calluses.

It was hard to believe he had almost forgotten the hell week before the arrival of the RGN fleet. Everyone, officers included, worked around the clock, improving the defenses on the three

298

stations and the three planets, repairing and building new ships, missiles, and lasers.

Besides ensuring the food supply was plentiful, everything else was put on hold. The entire population on three planets had one immediate goal, survival. Armies, space navies, defensive platforms, and many more were being created or improved. The pace had been hectic; no one knew when, if, the RGN would show up.

One other critical, tragic item was also being done without pause. Rescue and recovery at the cities bombed by the Chohish. Injured, still being found, were sent to medical facilities worldwide. The quality of these facilities was not very good, but it was all they had. The Chohish did not believe resources should be spared in saving Kolqux's lives. Bodies, where able, were placed in cold storage to wait until time permitted to identify and send back their families if any survived.

"Well, Admiral, I expect you will be reuniting with Admiral Katinka Chadsey. I hope your trip with us gave you the needed information?" Zeke asked as he merged with the group, finding a seat on the metal slag. He hadn't realized how tired he wasn't until he was seated with Jeanne leaning against him.

"Yes, Admiral Chadsey has already told me I will stay with the force she is bringing wherever it is headed. And she ensured I would not argue about staying on the Lucky Strike. So she brought my wife with her."

Snorting, Nkosana continued, "Admiral Chadsey knows her people and how to motivate them. Me, it is my wife. You, your ship, and your crew. The lady is one cranny lady. I must say it has been intriguing, to say the least."

"If not for my wife being here, I would have asked for more time with your group. Even though it was short in duration, my time here has been exhilarating. There are times I am sorry that I did not follow Roy's career path," lamented Nkosana.

"It is a good thing you didn't; the RGN needs competent officers at the top. Unfortunately, you and Admiral Chadsey are an exception to the norm, " Roy stated. He was squatting behind Isolde chewing on a piece of wire, barely visible.

"Damn it, Roy, quick sneaking up on me like that. After all these years, you would think I would look for you before saying anything like that," exclaimed a startled Nkosana.

Roy just shrugged with indifference.

It would be hours before the reinforcements arrived, so Zeke suggested they should all clean up and change. Surprisingly, Nkosana told them they should go as they were.

When asked why, he said the arriving force should see what it been truly like, not a sanitized version. Too often, wars are glamorized. Men and women in the media look like they just walked off a movie set. Hair is exquisitely done up, perfectly tailored clothes that fit like a glove, and no sign of dirt or bruises; in other words, fake, made up. They need to see reality. The innocents' deaths, pain, anguish, and the fighters who shared that trauma.

They were never given the option to clean up, though, as they received word they were requested to meet Admiral Chadsey immediately. Like a request from a Fleet Admiral is anything but an order. They were to board a shuttle and head toward one of the battlecruisers.

Sixteen shuttles were necessary to take all the personnel Nkosana thought should go.

Entering the dreadnaught fighter bay, the shuttles were directed to land, where an honor guard waited with Admiral Chadsey. Her senior staff members stood behind them. Off to one side were the press members with camera crews up on platforms so they could get an unrestricted visual.

As they exited, they were asked to wait until all were together in one group. The Kolqux and Endaens were a little taken back.

Hundreds of marines with a mixture of RGN, Sorath, and Irracan were dressed in full marine armor with plasma rifles resting on the floor. The longer they waited, the more concerned they were that they had rebelled only to give their freedom to another conqueror.

The loudspeaker announced the following loudly throughout the bay when they were all finally offloaded from the shuttles.

"ORDER ARMS!" After which, the marines who had been standing relaxed. They then slammed to attention with a smash of sound when the butt of hundreds of plasma rifles smacked against the fighter bay metal composite floor.

The sudden movement and the sound caused even more consternation from the Kolqux and Endaens. Several put their hands on their weapons. After a pause of several seconds…

"RIGHT ARMS!" Now the marines grabbed their rifle to rest them on their right shoulder.

Breathing became short and constrained for many; more individuals rested their hands on their weapons. Again, after several seconds, another command came loudly through the speakers…

"PRESENT ARMS!" The marines using both hands, presented their rifle vertically in front of the body, with the muzzle upward and the trigger side forward.

Confusion now reigned among the Kolqux and Endaens as this position was not an offensive move. This put the marines at a disadvantage.

"ORDER ARMS!" The marines now slammed their rifles back to the floor of the fighter bay.

Panic was now rampant in the group, except for the relaxed humans who helped calm the group. They explained to the Kolqux and Endaens that it was all a ceremony of respect for visiting officers or dignitaries, nothing to be worried about.

After the order at arms, Admiral Chadsey and her senior staff members made their way through the marines to mingle with the group.

"Evening, Captain Kinsley, I am relieved that you were able to return my Admiral Okeke to me in one piece. A quick review of his report showed it was a close call several times. I would have dreaded telling his wife that she made this long trip for nothing. She would have been distraught for me wasting her time." Admiral Chadsey stated while shaking his hand.

Turning to a tall, svelte beautiful middle-aged woman standing next to her. "Wouldn't you?"

"Most assuredly so," responded the woman.

Standing next to Zeke, Oksana belted across to grab the woman into his arms where… well… enough said.

Admiral Chadsey then walked over to Uv'ei and Uv'ek. "You must be Uv'ei and Uv'ek. I have heard so many good things about you and the Kolqux."

Glancing around, she was apparently looking for someone in particular." I recognize many here but do not see the two with which my Captains went to the Oxtaria Pulsar System. Where are you… oh… there you are. Get over here where I can meet you if you would."

Walking from behind the group were the two who had been shying away from all the unexpected attention. Hu'de and Te'ln cautiously made their way to stand in front of the Admiral.

"And finally, where is Vopengi Edoetti. Ahh… there you are… get over here, please," she requested of the Endaen. Vopengi grabbed the sleave of another Endaen to walk with him.

Standing at attention in front of the group, Admiral Chadsey addressed them. "I am Admiral Katinka Chadsey of the Royal Galactic Navy. You may hear us referred to as the RGN. I am in charge of this task force and includes contingents from the Sorath and the Irracans."

The Admiral started walking, where she patted the shoulders of each of the Kolqux and Endaens as she passed them. "From what I have heard, you have all been busy. Very busy indeed. Seems that we all have a similar problem. If you would be kind enough to follow me, I will take you to a conference room where we can start planning how we all will eliminate that problem."

Turning, she patted the shoulders while talking to them, addressing each by name as she walked back through the group. Once separated, she continued toward the exit, surrounded by a personal guard that surrounded her.

The Kolqux and Endaens stood rooted to the spot spellbound. They did not start moving until Zeke and Jeanne with their crew walked past. "Amazing woman, isn't she. Intimidated me the same way the first time I met her. Well, don't just stand there; follow me. I sure am not going to cover for you being late."

With Jeanne's arm wrapped in his, Zeke led the group, now well over a hundred strong, as he was followed by the commanders and crews from over a half dozen ships, seven planets, and stations.

Even though this dreadnaught was not the Majestic, the layout was the same, so he knew where the conference room was.

As they reached the conference room, they were met by Sorath's security, which was very similar to the Majestic. Same as then, they recognized Zeke and Jeanne and went through the same motions. Although having Hawke by his side may have made it easier for them.

The embarrassing part was that the Kolqux and Endaens all asked for an explanation as they were afraid of upsetting the Soraths if they missed some type of social protocol.

After the fifth explanation, they finally entered the conference room. It was packed with officers standing several deep in the back and sides. Not seeing empty seats, they kept making their way toward the front.

When they finally reached the front, they were making their way around to the side when they heard a cough before Zeke was addressed.

"Captain Kinsley, if you please."

Looking around, Zeke could not spot who was addressing him. It wasn't until Jeanne tapped on his shoulder and pointed to the raised stage. Then, turning around, he saw Admiral Chadsey standing impatiently at the platform's edge.

"I told you to follow me. I was unaware you had a wound that impacted your walking ability. I would have sent for a wheelchair if I had known, " the Admiral sarcastically. "But you are here now. Please collect your group and bring them up on the stage. Some attendants will help direct where everyone is to sit."

"Don't you dare? Jeanne, this is not the time or place. Oh crap..." begged Zeke just before Jeanne burst out laughing.

"I like that woman; I really do," she said between laughs.

The meetings went on for four hours. Each Kolqux and Endaen were introduced before the meeting got down to the main focus. Three questions to start it off.

First: Who are the Chohish?

Second: Where are their home systems?

Third: Where to attack next?

Walking out with his officers along with the Kolqux and Endaens, Zeke could not remember when a meeting had been so exhausting. At least they had an idea of what they would do next.

They had sent probes through the slipstream after the victorious battle with the Chohish. It revealed a pair of super planets so far from the sun that they were frozen giants. No indication of any permanent structures or Chohish presence. Their limited scan reports showed only one other slipstream in that system.

While most of the other ships headed to the fighter bay to catch a shuttle back to their vessel, they headed toward the cafeteria, anxious to try some Sorath food.

After Hawke tried to describe what was in each of the different options, all finally agreed to just get a lot of everything. They had brought a few electronic food testers to see what each race could eat. So it ended up being more fun than they expected. Food was delicious, and the vast majority found they could eat everything brought out. And they tried.

Sitting back, stuffed after eating a second helping of a broiled fish whose name he would never remember, Zeke wondered how the Sorath stored all of this fresh food. Then, about to ask Hawke, he was pinged with a priority communication.

Checking on his message, he saw that Jeanne was getting pinged herself.

"A large Chohish fleet is transitioning through the slipstream. You and Captain de Clisson are to report to the secondary conference room at the top of the hour. Per order of Admiral Chadsey."

Checking the time, he saw he had less than five minutes.

"Oh, come on, damn it, again?" both Jeanne and Zeke vented simultaneously.

"I'll get everyone home. You go to where you need to be," Will stated. "But first, we are going to stay here and have desert. Then, I will bring something back to the ship for you two."

They had a few choice words they wanted to impart to Will, but time was limited.

Entering the conference room, the group present was much smaller than the last time they were here. Instead of a packed room, there were only three others. The two admirals, Admiral Katinka Chadsey, and Rear Admiral Nkosana Okeke and his wife.

"Captains, sorry to call you back so soon, but we have a situation. The Chohish fleet you expected has arrived," explained Admiral Chadsey. "It is substantial, close to seven hundred warships, not counting the carriers. The makeup is not what we are familiar with; there are more cruisers and destroyers in the mix and fewer battleships. But they made up for that, over fifty carriers."

"The makeup is probably because the ships from this system were to make the difference. But over fifty carriers, now that is different. Hawke said they rarely used them. They must have pulled close to everything they had. That is going to be one massive fighter group." lamented Zeke

"Shouldn't be a problem; my brothers brought two Irracan carriers," voiced a smiling Jeanne. "Each of those carriers holds two hundred and fifty fighters. Irracans prefer fighters than the larger warships."

Looked at her with surprise. "Five hundred fighters against what must be close to six to seven thousand if you include the fighters from the other warships? Really?"

"These are Irracan fighters; these pilots are nothing like the normal fighter pilots you are used to. These pilots have been flying since they were large enough to fit in a pilot seat. They are the Irracan's best. They will roll over the Chohish like they didn't exist. I know most of these pilots will be mad when they see the skill of the Chohish; they like a challenge."

"I am not worried about their fighters; besides the Irracan carriers, we brought plenty of our own along with a large contingent from the Sorath's. And as good as the Irracans are Jeanne, the Soraths are much better. Trust me on that," voiced Admiral Chadsey.

"We requested your presence because we will attack the Chohish while they are still regrouping. We want to dictate the battleground," conveyed Nkosana. "My wife, Bridgette, is a Major in Intelligence. Her research indicates that the Chohish are being stretched beyond their capabilities to maintain."

"You may not know that the Soraths, with a large RGN contingent, have opened a second theatre of war. That fleet, larger than this one, is attacking through the original slipstreams that the Chohish attacked the Sorath. Our goal is to bleed the Chohish dry," updated Bridgette. "The Endaens equation about several home planets rebelling adds a new twist, and the addition of the Kolqux was totally unexpected."

"We want to eradicate this force. We want to keep the Chohish rocking on their heels. Now the question is, how to take out that force. Any thoughts?" asked Nkosana.

Seeing Zeke and Jeanne look at each other and smile, he knew they had already been thinking about it.

"Jeanne and I always knew that the Chohish would send a large force here. When the last force we destroyed did not attack the Kolqux planets but waited at the slipstream, we figured the one on the way had to be much more substantial. We thought the Kolqux system was the Chohish gathering location for attacking us. After gathering, they would stop at the destroyed station to refuel and rearm if necessary. If you count the Kolqux warships from the other systems, they would have put together well over a thousand warships to attack the Pandora again," spelled out Zeke. "Although we think there is another one on the way before they would have left here."

"Why do you say that?" asked Bridgette.

"After what they experienced in the Pandora System, we believed they planned on putting together enough forces to overwhelm any force standing in their way. After losing several hundred, they would not go small. An added incentive for an enormous force would be the honor to whoever destroys the Lucky Strike and the Fox."

"Now, as far as our thoughts on attacking the...."

ENGAGEMENT

A FEW HOURS later, Zeke sat in his command chair on the Lucky Strike. Rubbing the arms, he realized how much he had missed it. This was where he belonged.

The battle plan ended up having little input from himself and Jeanne. Admiral Chadsey, in conjunction with her planning group, had projected that something similar to what existed would occur. It was much better than what Zeke and Jeanne had come up with since they did not have all the available data on the forces.

There was one exception, though, that the Admiral agreed upon enthusiastically. To this end, the Lucky Strike, the Fox, and the Jackal led a task force of fifty ships, a mixture of cruisers, destroyers, and three carriers.

They were in the process of swinging around Shisarmel, the main Kolqux home planet, to use the planet's gravity to build up their speed.

The fleet had left hours ago, headed toward the Chohish, and the dreadnaughts had left even earlier with their escort ships.

The Chohish was still sitting idle at the slipstream.

Hours later, the dreadnaughts started slowing down. They were only going at quarter speed when they reached their maximum missile range, where they fired hundreds upon hundreds of missiles.

The Chohish, shields up and weapons armed, started moving toward them. It would take a while before they could reach their own missile range. As their speed picked up, the Chohish carriers unloaded all their fighters. Afterward, they made a half circle and headed back toward the slipstream.

The missiles from the dreadnaughts reached the Chohish ships before they had even reached half speed.

The destroyers, leading the group, destroyed many missiles, but there were just too many to get them all.

And these were enormous missiles that packed a wallop.

Detonations blossomed.

Ships floundered.

Destroyers disappeared off the sensors.

More and more missiles arrived, and more and more ships were impacted.

Thousands of fighters now joined in the effort to take out the missiles rained down on the men of war. Explosions rocked the Chohish ships as they raced forward.

Energy beams now made their presence known. Shields floundered; wreckage littered space. Ships died. But now, the Chohish had reached maximum speed and were still a force to be reconned with.

They barreled toward the dreadnaughts, who had slowed even more without reducing the fire. Half of the RGN battlecruisers, battleships, and cruisers following at a measured speed were far behind the dreadnaughts.

Behind them were the fighters, and thousands of Sorath fighters were leading RGN fighters, both looking for revenge.

The other half of the battlecruisers, battleships, and cruisers were behind the fighters. They were rocketing forward at maximum speed.

The RGN destroyers were kept back, with the carriers returning to the station. They would be part of a protection force for the other ships along with the Kolqux fleet, which was formidable in its own right. They would be even more so once they had some training.

Before the Chohish entered the range for their ship's missiles, they were struck by a massive wave from the RGN and Sorath men of war.

The numbers could not be blocked even with the fighter's help, and sometimes suicide runs to take out the missiles.

Making it even worse, the missiles were not fired randomly.

Whole groups of missiles were directed at individual warships. The targets in the first wave were primarily the battleships. And they paid the price. Shields failed, and ships shattered. Debris rained through space.

Aside from the lost warships and fighters, many of the Chohish were able to launch their missiles, and they got one volley off before they were hit by a second and third wave.

The Chohish tracked their first set of missiles, massive in its own right, head straight toward the dreadnaughts. They got a second set fired, but it was second-rate compared to their first volley. They lost many warships after absorbing two successive waves of missiles and constant laser fire.

The Chohish Sovereign, commander of this fleet, watched the human fleet sitting in his command chair. He had watched as many Chohish warships were destroyed before damaging even one of his enemies. But what concerned him the most was what ships were being targeted, Battleships.

The decimation of the majority of their missiles gave rise to doubt that the Chohish would be able to beat this enemy. It also brought a new sensation, fear.

Some got through, but only a few ever caused any severe damage. The second Chohish wave had even less of an impact. Being limited in available options, the Sovereign sent in the fighters before he was ready.

The meeting between the two fighter groups was drastically one-sided. The Chohish fighters were no match for the pilots they faced.

The Chohish never had much use for fighters hence inadequate pilot training. The fighter pilots they faced, especially the ones with the short sloped wings, emphasized the difference between the two groups.

And who would have known that the Soraths, a minor foe from a long-ago war, would be allied with these humans and weld such mighty forces? The feeling he was now experiencing was growing.

The other half of the RGN forces swept around the sides of the battle in a wide loop. As the center of the action raged, they attacked in a pincer movement.

The Chohish Sovereign watched all this movement on his screens with dread as his battleship rocked with missile hits. Looking at his fleet's remaining icons, he knew they would not survive this meeting.

He doubted that his ships would survive long enough to reach the dreadnaughts. The slow movement of the enemy now made sense. Now, even ramming would not be possible. But he was going to try. About to give his order, he died from the bridge exploding.

While that portion of the battle continued, fifty ships continued to the slipstream at breakneck speed. The gravity speed boost flung them past the struggle.

"Prepare for transition" rang through the ship. Zeke listened as Caspian gave the warning, but his attention was centered on the icons of the fleet. The fleet was now his responsibility, not the Lucky Strike. He had given that burden to Will.

311

The weight of that responsibility was overwhelming. Commanding several ships was expected from all cruiser captains as a pair of destroyers were typically attached as part of any mission. But being responsible for so many warships and three carriers was intimidating.

Again, he wondered if he and Jeanne had made the right call for the thousandth time. And not having Jeanne by his side during this crazy plan was even more maddening. Jeanne was back in the Fox to finish the campaign in case of the Lucky Strikes' demise.

"Entering the Slipstream" came Caspian's strong voice. Only seconds later, the odd effects of being on the slipstream hit him. Nausea started slow but built up rapidly. Concentrating on keeping the contents of his stomach where they belonged became even more difficult as a blinding pain burst behind his eyes.

This was the second time they had entered a slipstream faster than usual. And from observing the other crew members, not just himself, he could see they were affected more than expected. Speed did seem to affect the weight of the severity when transitioning. If he survived this crazy excursion, he would have to look at it more closely.

"Exiting the slipstream" rang through the bridge, but the voice was unrecognizable as the pain in his head was so stark. "Probes deployed."

As soon as the pain cleared, he ordered to put the status of the Chohish carriers on the center screen. It was not immediate, as not everyone had recovered from the transit ordeal. Still, within moments the screen displayed the carriers escorted by destroyers with a few cruisers mixed in.

"You were right, Captain; they do escort their carriers. How did you know? We found those other three carriers unescorted," asked Will.

"I believe the destroyers we destroyed later were their original

Attack Chohish War

escorts. They were relieved once in the station sphere of influence. The only plausible reason they would have for being there," explained Zeke. "How long before interception?"

"I estimate about twenty-three minutes. Attack pattern?" Will inquired.

"Wedge-shaped. I want the carriers protected at all costs. Once the fighter carriers unload, they will spin-off, keeping a pair of cruisers and destroyers with them. I passed the command on to their commanders and escort ships before transition. One carrier, a marine transport, will stay with the cruisers."

"Captain Farren, since this ship is under your command, maybe you can clarify what it would take for me to get a cup of hot java?" questioned a smiling Zeke.

"The prior captain had such an archaic, slow process in place before my assuming command, mind you, that we are still in the process of revamping them. Yet, I will see what we can do," riposted Will with joviality.

Zeke could not contain the belly laugh that ensued, followed by many others.

Sipping his unsweetened black coffee, he had to admit that whatever Will had done, his coffee tasted better than usual. Then again, maybe it was due to having something familiar in hand that was helping to relieve the stress of commanding so many lives.

Regardless, securing the top on his coffee, he calmly placed it in his command chair's arm holder. It was time to engage the enemy.

"If you will, Captain Farren, please connect me with all ships in the fleet."

At a signal from Isolde, Will reported, "You are connected Captain to all ships."

"Carriers, launch all fighters. Follow the plan as previously reviewed. For all captains, the protection of the carriers is paramount. Once the fighter carriers have removed themselves from

313

the battle zone, attack the enemy cruisers and destroyers. Do not, I repeat, do not close with the enemy unless necessary. Let's do what damage we can do remotely."

Pausing, as what he was about to order was reprehensible and vile, he could not allow them to get away. What he was about to order would cause Endaen's death. Before executing the order, he looked at the pair of Endaens sitting on the bridge at workstations. They nodded in confirmation. They knew he had no choice.

"The smaller carriers have been confirmed by the Endaens as Chohish troopships. We will allow them to surrender. Any that refuse are to be destroyed. We cannot allow them to escape. The larger carriers we will attempt to capture. Gear up your marines" ordered Zeke.

While speaking, fighters were being ejected from all the ships present.

Five hundred Irracan fighters came racing to the front line.

The third carrier, full of marines, stayed close to the cruisers for protection. These were going to be supported by close to another hundred fighters from the cruisers and destroyers.

But first, the enemy cruisers and destroyers needed to be eliminated. And for once, Zeke outnumbered the enemy by a significant margin.

After a few missile salvos, he knew it would be easier than expected. These cruisers and destroyers must have been older models as they did not have near the shield strength he had been dealing with.

But you have to give it to the Chohish; they never abandoned the carriers even though they were getting picked off regularly. So it only took thirty-some minutes before the last one succumbed to the missile barrage.

Now was the tricky part. Getting a hold of the carriers. It had been decided that these carriers could be instrumental in bolstering the Kolqux forces. Alleviating the RGN from having to place needed resources in the Furalla Eaara Star System.

Gesturing to Will, he waited while he signaled Isolde to send out the prepared message in Chohish.

"This is a message from the Royal Galactic Navy. Your escort has been destroyed. We have no desire to do the same to you; surrender, and you will be treated fairly. Resist; we will show no mercy. If you want to surrender, lower shields and shut down all engines and all power. It is your decision. You cannot outrun us. Means nothing to us if you resist; it will only cost us a few missiles. You now have five minutes to decide before we resume fire."

Surprisingly, more than half lowered their shields and started slowing before powering down. The rest continued on at full speed. Even more surprising, two of the carriers were the Chohish troopships. Zeke did not think any of the eight troopships would surrender.

Detailing a third of the force to stand watch on the ones powered down along with half of the fighters, he took the rest to chase after the rest. He did not trust that the carriers were not planning to send out fighters or shuttles filled with troops even though powered down.

Dogging the fleeing fleet, he sent a few of the cruisers and destroyers escorted by a group of fighters ahead to get in front of them. Then he gave the order he dreaded. "Fire at will."

One by one, the carriers were pounded into oblivion. It took a while, they had excellent shields, but it was inevitable without a sizable escort. When half had been destroyed, most of them being the troop transports, the rest shut down their shields and powered down.

Now the real work would begin. The RGN carrier, at a signal from the Lucky Strike, unloaded the marines onboard in shuttles. These made their way toward where the enemies' landing bays were located. Probes were sent in to check for power indications and a view of the interior.

One group of shuttles flew into a landing bay on the closest Chohish troop transport, devoid of any atmosphere as the shields were down.

The carriers Zeke was most concerned about were the pair of troop transports. Attempting to pacify thousands of armed Chohish could go wrong in many ways. Sitting tensely in his command chair, he waited anxiously for a report. It took an agonizing half-hour before he got the first report.

"This is Sergeant Yoel Arsenius; we have entered the carrier. The dimension of this thing is humongous. There are hundreds of shuttles. No contact with the enemy yet. We are breaking up into three groups. Each group will proceed to a separate entrance."

The sound in the background was of a man drawing in air overlaid by the heavy pounding of his armor on a metallic surface. The sudden sound cutoff had Zeke sitting on the edge of his chair, and the silence reigned for a few moments.

"Back. Sorry, had an issue. We had to blow one of the hatchways; it had no power. We are now entering a hallway... HOLY HELL... what the... We have stumbled on the enemy."

Silence reigned for half a dozen minutes before the sound of rapid movement could be heard, along with the sound of heavy cursing. "We will not be able to proceed down this hallway. Instead, we are turning back to try another entrance."

"Isolde, get me in touch with that Sergeant, cut out the rest. We need to know what he found," commanded Zeke.

Isolde entered a few commands in her terminal before swinging her arm around to point at Zeke.

"Sergeant Yoel Arsenius, this is Captain Kinsley. Please report on what you found."

"Sorry, Captain, I should have been more descriptive, but it surprised me. And few things take me by surprise anymore. I was trying to figure out if it was a trap. The hallway was filled with Chohish dead. They were stacked on top of each other and must have been two or three deep. And it was pretty recent as they did not have rigor mortis yet. There was not enough elbow room for us to tread without possibly encountering a booby trap. Captain, there must have been three or four hundred in that hallway."

Zeke looked over at the Endaens, who indicated they had no idea what had happened.

"Understand, Sergeant, we encountered something similar before. Can you tell what type of wounds they had? How were they dressed? Armed?"

"None, Captain, that is what was so strange. No wounds were present at all. Nor was it decompression; there would have been some sign of it. They were just dead. Almost like they had been standing there before they died. Normal military uniforms based on prior encounters. No heavy arms, some had a bladed weapon, but they were all sheathed in a scabbard."

"Thanks, Sergeant, keep me updated. Go check out another entrance. Captain out."

Turning to the Endaens, he waved them over. Meanwhile, reports were coming in from the same carrier of similar encounters.

Unbuckling from the safety harness, both crossed over the squat by Zeke.

"Any ideas?" he asked.

"None whatsoever," replied Vopengi. "The Chohish do not break out their soldiers into different groups like you. They keep their armor, breathing gear, and weapons in the shuttles to speed up deployment and save on shipboard space. They have lost their atmospheric shields several times. Hence losing whole contingents as they are not wearing any air-breathing gear until they put on their gear. To minimize this, they line their soldiers up in the hallways leading to the shuttle bays. Once the hatches open, they run to their assigned shuttle."

Scratching his arm, he finished. "You have to understand, Captain, the Chohish do not put much value on their own people except for the Sovereigns. Safety was not worth the extra cost; death was common. But I have no idea what could have caused something on the scale-like your Sergeant reported on."

Trying to understand this almost made him miss one of the other communication links.

"Power, there are massive power indications in that landing bay. Abort landing the marines," yelled a pilot.

"Irracans, the following groups are to join me. Champions, Protectors, and the Cleavers follow me in. It looks like they are trying to launch their shuttles. You are free to fire at will. The rest are to protect the marine shuttles." commanded Jeanne.

The sound of fighter lasers and missiles combined with pilots yelling and screaming soon filled the line, and the sound of battle ensued.

A bad feeling came over Zeke; had he made the correct call? Regardless, he knew he had to let it go. He had other concerns to worry about. He would have to let Jeanne manage the issue herself. Would this be the last time he ever heard from her?

Meanwhile, Gunner flying in his fighter near the other carriers, alerted his group that one of the carriers was showing power. "Ok, people, I'll bet they have some fighters. Stay alert and be ready. Change that; I register a bogey exiting the carrier."

No sooner said than a pair of fighters came flying out of the carrier in question. Another team followed them, with three more trailing behind.

Pushing his fighter into a steep turn, Gunner hit his afterburners once lined up with the first pair, and Librada was in lockstep with him.

Attack Chohish War

The two Chohish fighters headed straight toward them, firing a pair of missiles. Then, getting a missile lock on the fighter on the port side, Gunner sent two fire and forget missiles.

Pulling a sharp, twisted spiral, Gunner lost contact with Librada. "Librada, I am blind. Can you see me?"

"Roger, Gunner is visual. I am off to starboard, be back in a few," Librada answered.

Ejecting dozens of electronic countermeasures, Gunner slammed on his port side directional engine while continuing his spiral. Between the sharp turns and ECM, the pair of missiles racing for him lost track.

Gunner made a loop where he flipped his fighter when he reached the end. He was now facing the Chohish fighter on his tail, going backward. This fighter pilot must be pretty good to have evaded his missiles, or this one was entirely different.

Getting a lock, he fired his lasers to see them miss while he took several hits on his shields. "Damn, he is good." Then watched as the enemy fighter blew apart.

"Saving your ass again, Gunner, this is getting to be a habit."

"That is why I keep you around, Librada. You are so good at it," replied a laughing Gunner as they swung back to their group.

Seeing no enemy fighters or missing icons from his group, Gunner asked for a status update. It seemed that he and Librada had destroyed the only three that had a decent pilot. The rest were eliminated within minutes of leaving the carrier.

As for the carrier, it was destroyed by the cruisers.

Back on the Lucky Strike, Zeke checked on the status of the other carriers. The troop carrier that had tried to deploy the shuttles had been destroyed. All the shuttles had been eliminated with no loss of Irracan fighters.

It was reported, but not confirmed, that a black and red-trimmed fighter had swung their fighter sideways to slide outside the bay entrance of the troop transport. Then, sliding less than two hundred feet away, it emptied its missiles and plasma into the hold filled with shuttles trying to fly out. Only a dozen made it out; they only got a short distance before being destroyed.

Concerned about the other troop transport, he was about to order it destroyed as he had no intention to storm it when Will pinged him.

"Captain, you may want to see this."

Unbuckling, he approached Will, looking over Isolde's shoulder at one of her screens.

"The task force sent multiple probes to each of the carriers. Four on the outside and another four on the inside. Between all eight, we can get a clear power status and visual. Look what we are showing outside the troop transport."

Isolde increased the size of the image flowing beside the carrier. As it became more prominent, the appearance of a Chohish Sovereign became focused. With softly flowing gold-threaded robes, his significant figure majestically floated in space without a space suit.

"I think we may have a revolt going on. So Isolde, I need you to send out a message to them and see if we get a response? Do not alert the other carriers if possible."

"Chohish troop transport, can you hear us? This is the Lucky Strike of the Royal Galactic Navy. We have observed a situation outside your carrier. Can you explain?"

A deep, heavily accented synthetic voice replied back. "I am Omaw, group leader of the mighty Ostraron. We do not wish to die. We are tired of fighting. We just wish to go home. But we will not be treated like animals; we will fight to the death before we let that happen."

"If you surrender, you will be treated honorably, better than your fellows have treated the humans and Soraths. But any resistance, no matter how minor, will mean your immediate destruction."

Attack Chohish War

Vopengi sidled up next to Zeke. "Ask what the name of their home planet is."

"Omaw, this to Captain Zeke Kinsley, commanding this task force. Where is home? What planet is yours?"

"Why would I answer that?" an angry Chohish answered.

"Because you said you wanted to go home. How can we determine if that can be done if we do not know where that is?"

"We are from the mighty world of Yajf'ard. I am the fifteenth and youngest son of Empress Rinu."

"That is one of the Chohish worlds revolting. This group may have left before the revolt, but this Empress Rinu that he speaks of is one of the instigators of the revolt. He was probably brought up under her tutelage," whispered Vopengi.

"I will send a team of our soldiers over to your carrier. They will take control of your bridge and engineering sections. We will take you back to the Furalla Eaara Star System, where you will be treated as a prisoner of war. All will be treated fairly and with respect. I cannot make any more promises than that. Is that agreeable?"

"It is. Send your soldiers; there will be no resistance. You have my word," agreed Omaw.

"Their word is their life," stated Vopengi.

"We will see. Isolde, please notify the commander of the Marines of our intentions. They are not to take any chances; they are to get out if they encounter resistance. Make sure they have a secure path out."

Reports flooded in that they were now encountering surrender on all the other carriers. It appears that all were part of the Ostraron group. When Omaw gave his word of no resistance, he spoke for all. Even though they were powered down, the carriers must still have a communications link.

In four hours, they had all the ships secured. The Chohish troop ship was the trickiest. They ended up going with the

321

recommendation from a marine sergeant. Secure the landing bay with a company of battleoids. The shuttles had been checked and confirmed they were still stocked with weapons. The battleoids could ensure these weapons were kept out of Chohish's hands. The critical areas of the ship were locked down with a minimum of a platoon supplied with heavy plasma weapons and an auto railgun.

The first two parts of the four-part plan have been completed, and only two more are to go.

Part one: Elimination of the Chohish fleet.

Part two: Elimination or capture of the carriers.

Part three: Get the captured carriers back in one piece.

Part four: To be determined, Zeke was not sure they would survive that one.

SNOOPING

BACK IN THE Sorath dreadnaught, Zeke and Jeanne were standing around a large conference table with the two Admirals, the officers from the Lucky Strike, the Fox, the Jackal, the leaders of the Sorath, the Kolqux, and the Endaens. And, of course, Major Bridgette Okeke, who was leading the meeting.

Most were sitting, but others, like Zeke and Jeanne, preferred standing. Jax, Hawke, Jamie, Gunner, Isolde, Will, and Jamie stood next to them on both sides. Mixed in with them were the Kolqux and the Endaens. The rest of the command staff from the three ships took up most of the seats in front of them.

Major Bridgette Okeke noticed that the commands for all three ships were grouped together. She expected one ship's crew to stick together; that was expected due to the time they spent together.

Seeing all three groups clustered together, though, was unique. And add the Kolqux and Endaens into the mix, more so. This lent credence to what her husband had told her, which was suitable for their plans.

"I am glad to see everyone was able to attend the meeting. Everyone here met our new guests yesterday, so we will skip introductions and proceed. We will quickly review recent events since most already know what has occurred. And then we will spend most of our time on the next action for this group," explained Bridgette.

"Let's start with our losses. We lost half a dozen major warships, and many more were damaged. Some will require a naval shipyard, and others can be repaired locally. Thousands of lives were lost."

"With that in mind, their sacrifice was not in vain. The Chohish force was destroyed in total. We captured several dozen warships besides the carriers that Captain Kinsley in his group caught. These ships will be a great addition to building the Kolqux fleet here. We are unaware of any ship escaping our battle, but we cannot be sure. A relief force may be on the way, or one may have been sent before the battle began."

By clicking a small control device in her hand, Bridgette turned on the Four-D viewer in the center of the table. The image showed a system with four planets, one looking to be habitable. Then, circling around the planets were stations and ship-building facilities similar to what existed in the Kolqux system.

"These images were found in the database of the captured troopship carrier. We believe this system is located several systems over from this one. As you know, we have been unable to get reliable data on the Chohish history, manner of government, life expectancy, and where they are located. The Endaens helped fill in some of those details. But the Endaens that live here do not have system coordinates that we can use. They were kept in the dark; all the personnel on all Chohish ships are, so if any are caught, they cannot pass it on."

Bridgette clicked once more where the image now zoomed in to one of the stations circling the unknown planet. "Vopengi Edoetti walked us through the process the Chohish use to update the warship's guidance systems. Using that data, combined with details from captured databases, we may have a method of getting that information."

"We believe... and remember, most of this is just a hypothesis. The Chohish scrub the warship's databases when they enter this system you see here. They then download only enough coordinates to get them through the next few systems or to complete their assignment. The station you are looking at is one of a half dozen such for all system-capable ships in this quadrant of the Chohish empire. They have all the information about traveling anywhere in the Chohish-occupied systems. Including their home systems. Those stations are protected with the best armament the Chohish possess."

Bridgette leaned over the ensign in front of her and put her hands on the table. Staring at Zeke and the group around him, "We need to somehow invade that station and get that database. But first, we need to run a secret surveillance of the system. We need some spies. The data on the captured databases could be decades old as far as we know."

"I'll go."

Bridgette looked around, surprised at hearing a volunteer. "Who said that?"

"I did," Hawke replied casually with a raised hand.

"Oh hell, I knew that damn Sorath was going to get me killed at some point. Oh well, it might as well be now as later," complained Zeke, raising his hand. "Major, I figured you wanted us to go based on how you looked at us. But I wanted to know more before I was ready to say yes. But my friend here was ready before he even walked in here. But I will not ask my crew to go; they have done enough. I will only take volunteers."

"Speaking for the entire crew of the Lucky Strike, they have volunteered. We thought the captain might try something like this, so we discussed this over the past few days. The crew wants to see this to the end. They have paid in blood, pain, and lives; they have a right to ask no... it would be more accurate to say they need to go. The captain mentioned it before; nothing has changed. So I took a vote before I came over. Ship and crew are ready to go," confirmed Will.

The smile Hawke was wearing must have been contagious as the group around him mirrored it.

"The Irracans volunteer, Major. The Fox can leave immediately," volunteered Meghan.

"If you want to wait that long, they are your ships. But if you want the fastest ship in the fleet, then the Jackal is ready and waiting," spoke up Lance.

A soft squeaky voice spoke up. "The Kolqux insist on being represented. New ships are ready for deployment. As second in command, I will lead a group with my daughter, Te'In."

"We are not many, but the Endaens feel they need to be represented. If the Kolqux let us assist on their ships, we would be honored," said Vopengi, unsure if the Kolqux would agree to have Endaens on board their ships.

"We would be honored, my friend; you can ride to glory or death with me. Ha! These humans and Soraths cannot have all the fun. We are going together," stated Hu'de. Even though the top of his head was barely at the height of the tabletop, his voice left no doubt he was not to be denied.

"Amazing, just amazing. We had planned to have the Lucky Strike go alone since they have the most experience humans have with the Chohish. But now, we had a plan that would give us a lot more data on what we will face, but we hesitated to use it as we were not sure we could put together the right mixture of forces."

Bridgette leaned in even further, "So if you all are insistent, here is what we came up with."

Two weeks later, an odd fleet of starships was racing toward an unknown slipstream. They had gone through three other slipstreams before this one. As expected, all the other systems had been devoid of planets or Chohish from probes the RGN had completed before they set out. This odd fleet comprised two dozen Kolqux warships, two RGN, one Irracan, and three Sorath warships.

"See, Hawke, you should have waited until you had all the detail before speaking up. This hair-brained scheme is something I would have liked to have had some input on," voiced Zeke sitting in his command chair with his head in his hands.

"Oh, come on, you are upset they would not let you change it. Get over it; I actually like it."

Said Jeanne happily.

"That is why he has his head in his hands; it's got so big, his neck cannot support the weight," explained Hawke.

"But how did I come to be in overall command? Nkosana decides to stay back with his wife at this time. Really?" complained Zeke.

"Suck it up, buttercup," laughed Jeanne. "We are about to enter the slipstream. It will either work or be an unmitigated disaster."

As they entered the slipstream twenty-four minutes later, Zeke thought about all the conference calls he had with the commanders of the other warships. Did he miss something?

The Endaens supported the Kolqux in managing their ships while members of the RGN fleet were there to help with any needed movement or combat assistance. All agreed that Zeke was required to be on the Lucky Strike while commanding this operation.

The Kolqux fleet exited the slipstream near the center. In contrast, the two other groups left at opposite ends using stealth protocol. No communication would happen until this was over. Everyone knew what was expected and their roles. So be it.

Bolting away from the slipstream, the RGN group scanned to see what was in this system. The system matched what they had been told existed. Seven planets in total. Two were gas giants, one frozen midrange in size, and three small to tiny planets near the sun, all with no life on them.

The last planet was the one that they were interested in. This was heavily populated and showed signs of heavy activity. That was about all they could detect at this range.

The Soraths exited the slipstream only to sit there.

While the other two groups went their way, the Kolqux limped away from the slipstream. With shields and weapons up and armed at their slowest speed possible, several ships were leaking lendolium. Preset communications went out unencrypted in Chohish, asking for help.

Replies returned immediately, demanding to know who they were and what had happened. Then, using the name of Sovereign Ukan from the defeated fleet, the Kolqux pretended to be the remnants of that fleet.

Long-range scans showed a small Chohish fleet of cruisers and destroyers heading away from the planet. They could not detect any additional signs of warships present around the planet. Not that they weren't there, but without probes, they could not get that granular without an energy signature.

It would take hours before the Chohish fleet could reach the Kolqux.

Without having to give a command to Will, the Lucky Strike and its two escort ships headed toward the largest station hanging over the planet.

The Soraths, on the other side, had not moved and waited at the Slipstream.

"Hawke, if you do not mind, could you explain why you did not join the Sorath fleet?"

"My uncle gave me leave to stay with the Lucky Strike. That is not something so casually given during a time of war. Once given, if I had rejoined my people and abandoned you, I would have dishonored my uncle," explained Hawke, who finished in a sarcastic tone. "Besides, they do not need me, while you most certainly do."

As they neared the planet, they shut down their engines to reduce their energy signature. Then, coasting closer, they prepped the unique probes into half the ejection tubes.

"All probe tubes are locked and loaded." Came through the speaker by Isolde.

"Caspian, any detection of any defense platforms or ships in our vicinity?" asked Will.

"Negative, Sir. Nothing is showing up on our scans. Without probes, we would not see them until they powered up and only then, if close by."

He resisted the impulse to give an order as much as he wanted to. With Jeanne and Hawke sitting in their fighters, it was difficult to stay silent.

Suddenly, the Sorath fleet shot away from the slipstream with communications blasting and engines flaring hotly.

The Chohish increased speed and headed toward the Sorath, who went in the opposite direction.

Meanwhile, the Kolqux continued on.

"Caspian, let me know when we are in position," commanded Will.

"It will be another fifteen minutes until the Chohish will be far enough away, Sir."

"*This must be what Will felt like when he had to sit idly while I gave all the commands. Hmmm... wonder if I can go work the weapons... damn, that won't work if called upon, I would be compromised...*" thought Zeke.

The next fifteen minutes seemed like hours later before Zeke heard Will give the command.

"Caspian, if you would please."

"Probes away. Normal probes fired toward the planets and stations. The special probes fired without any engine thrust in the same trajectory."

Claxons blared; lights dimmed; red lights flashed; warnings sounded.

"Multiple defensive platforms are coming online. We are also detecting some energy signatures powering up around the station. I count half a dozen warships with more coming online," reported Isolde. "Many more."

"Damn, I thought it had been too easy," exclaimed Zeke. "Well, we accomplished what we came here to deliver. Will, get us the hell out of here."

"Missiles fired" yelled Caspian. "Time to arrival in eight-point three minutes."

Those defensive platforms had been placed much further out than he thought they would have positioned them.

The Lucky Strike made a sharp turn in a close circle, bringing groans from most at the g's being pulled. The two sister ships matched their turn.

The Chohish warships chasing after the Soraths slowed down, where they began a turn toward the heading the Lucky Strike would enter the slipstream.

"Captain, any suggestions would be helpful," suggested Will.

"Isolde, get me the Soraths on the line. Get the Kolqux on but make sure they know they are not to respond, only listen," ordered Zeke.

Within seconds, Isolde reported all the parties were online. "Captain, I have Sorath Captain Ajeet on a secure link. I cannot pronounce his actual name, so we went with this. Hu'de is also online. He is aware not to speak."

"As expected, we have run into some difficulties. The payloads were delivered. It is time to go home. But we will need to work together to make that happen. The main issue I see is the fleet closest to the slipstream. They could delay us long enough for the second force to arrive. That force is now close to eighty warships and gaining more every moment. The defense platforms act as probes, so we cannot just go silent or try to evade them. This is what I want us to do...."

The first set of missiles was destroyed or misdirected. They hadn't been enough to worry him, well, not too much. But now, he was running from two sets of missiles from several platforms.

It was easy to see what they were doing. The defense platforms were forcing the three RGN warships toward the Chohish fleet.

Notwithstanding the pounding they were getting from near misses, some being very close, they were working their way toward the slipstream.

The Chohish warships were heading to the exact location.

The Kolqux sounded alarms warning the Chohish they had severe damage and minimum offensive capabilities. They would not be able to be of any assistance even if they were in the same area. Until the conflict was resolved, they would withdraw back through the slipstream.

The Chohish concurred with more than double the ships that the RGN had and would let them know when they had destroyed the puny humans.

The Kolqux started slowing down and made a sharp turn toward the slipstream.

The Lucky Strike and its escort were out of range of the defense platforms. But now, they were nearing the Chohish fleet.

Meanwhile, the second Chohish fleet, not having to swerve to escape the missiles, had closed the distance. If the Lucky Strike was forced to slow down to fight, the Chohish second fleet would be in a position to join the fight.

"Ready when you are, Will."

"Engineering, this is Lieutenant Commander Farren; execute command 'afterburners.'"

The Lucky Strike was soon followed by the Fox and Jackal, who doubled their speed.

The intercepting Chohish fleet swung toward the new entry point to the slipstream for the RGN fleet.

This took them past the Kolqux fleet, who was now heading back toward the slipstream close to full speed though still leaking lendolium now at a prodigious rate.

Whoever was in charge of the Chohish fleet realized something was different. *"Sovereign Ukan, our sensors indicate that you are no longer experiencing engine issues. Explain!"*

The response they got was not what they expected. Instead, the Kolqux fleet let loose a whole barrage of missiles at close range before they entered the slipstream.

The Chohish fleet heading across the slipstream did not have time to return fire.

Next came another unexpected round of missiles from the Sorath fleet that had been ignored until now.

The Chohish Sovereign raged in anger and confusion. Interception of the ships that had become a pariah to the Chohish was no longer an option. Now he had to evade the dozens of missiles racing down on his small fleet. The glory he would have received from taking out those two ships were no longer possible.

And to add one final insult, the Lucky Strike and the pair of destroyers with her unloaded their own missiles against them. The Chohish sent a swarm after them, but their missiles were not going to reach the RGN ships before they entered the slipstream.

The Chohish fleet suffered damage but successfully evaded, destroyed, or redirected most missiles without losing any ships. They were soon joined by over ninety other warships, most of which were battleships.

The Chohish Sovereign, still in a rage, would not let this insult go unpunished. Instead, he was going to take command of all warships. Then he would chase down those ships. The lendolium leakage they had detected let him know those ships could not go far without significant repair.

Regrouping the fleet into one large fleet, they charged through the slipstream at the location their prey escaped from them at full speed.

What awaited them on the other side let the Chohish Sovereign know they had been suckered into a trap. They would not have time to turn around before they were forced to engage the force that had been waiting for them.

And they would only have a few moments to prepare as missiles were already on the way. Thousands upon thousands of them, volley after volley.

CHOHISH PRISONERS

RAISING HIS FORK, Zeke speared another piece of chicken. Well, it looked and tasted like chicken. Not sure what animal it was on whatever planet it was raised on. He could not interpret the Sorath name and did not want to show his ignorance to Hawke. The sauce, though, was definitely honey garlic. He knew he was wrong on that too.

"What do you think they will do with all the Chohish prisoners?" asked Hawke between bites of something that resembled calamari.

The question stopped the movement of the fork. "I don't know," responded Zeke.

Twirling her fork in the pasta on her plate before raising it onto her spoon, Jeanne asked, "If your people could, they would push them out of the carrier on into space, Hawke."

"My people have long memories, Jeanne."

"Zeke, you look conflicted. What is bothering you?" asked Will.

"What to do with the Chohish. I had terrible feelings toward the Chohish when we started this engagement. Now? I am not so sure."

Sitting at the end of the dining room table, Isolde asked what had changed for him?

"The Endaens," Zeke replied and finally put the meat in his mouth. "what is the saying? *'l'ignoranza non è una scusa valida'*"

"Ahhh... *'Ignorance is not a valid excuse,'*" interpreted Gunner.

"Did not know you knew Italian Gunner?" asked Zeke.

"His mother has Italian in her ancestry, many generations back, but she insists Italian be taught to all her children. His mother believes Italian is the proper language for the world of art and culture," replied Isolde.

"Back to you, Zeke. What is bothering you?" asked Meghan.

"How will this war end? Are all Chohish guilty? Even their children?" mumbled Zeke talking around his chewing. "Humans do not have a guilt-free history. Horrendous atrocities, like Niflhel, are not uncommon in our past. Are all humans bad?"

"What can we do, Zeke?" asked Mason. "We do not know their society."

Sitting back, Zeke responded, "Maybe it's time we do. I think I will go talk with Omaw."

Jeanne looked at Zeke like he had grown another head. "You're kidding, right?"

The look she received confirmed he was not.

The following day, Zeke and Jeanne were standing in the Chohish carrier.

It had been decided to let the Chohish reside there. Putting them on a Kolqux planet soon after gaining their freedom from the Chohish was not considered wise.

The carrier had been searched for weapons before the Chohish were let loose inside. The fighters and shuttles had been given to the Kolqux to bolster their fleet. Having the Chohish stay on their carrier removed a problem for the RGN on how to feed them.

Moving past several crewed battleoids, Zeke headed toward a group of Chohish.

It was easy to identify Omaw; he was taller and more significant than the other Chohish.

Omaw was wrestling with another, surrounded by a group of onlookers.

As they walked up, growls could be heard. When hearing the sound, Jeanne, wearing a cutlass and poniard, grabbed their handles.

Two of the Chohish turned toward the pair with a snarl.

Pushing her front foot straight forward, Jeanne bent both legs, pulling the cutlass and poniard.

"Go ahead, just try it," Jeanne warned the Chohish as she bent the arm holding the cutlass forward while moving the poniard behind her.

The pair of Chohish looked ready to fight when Omaw pushed forward between them.

"Why you here?" he asked.

It was odd to Zeke how the interpreting device embedded in his ear translated the language while speaking. First, it would let the user start talking in their language. The small AI unit would identify the language and translate it.

It was not perfect, there was a slight delay, but it works. Usually, an individual learns the language after a short time unless the language is too complicated to understand. Hawkes language is an example.

Every race Zeke has come in contact with has something similar, including the Chohish.

"To talk. And I would tell your buddies to back off. She is a fencing expert, and they would be dead before they moved two feet," Zeke calmly replied.

"And that is only true if the six large battle units behind us do not do it first," he said, pointing behind them. "Her loyal guards replaced the regular crew in them before we arrived."

Turning to the pair, Omaw gestured to the units Zeke mentioned.

When they turned toward Jeanne again, Omaw growled at them and raised clenched hands.

That seemed to browbeat them as they walked away with angry looks.

"Talk," said Omaw.

"Not here; let's go somewhere more private," asked Zeke.

Jeanne slammed her cutlass back in its scabbard. Twirling the knife, she slid it into its sheath without even looking at it.

Omaw led them to a far corner where they could be alone. Sitting on his haunches, he waited for Zeke to explain why he was there.

Sitting cross-legged, Zeke looked at Omaw closely. What he saw showed no signs of anything flashy. He was wearing simple clothes, a breechcloth covered by a flowing robe. His feet were covered in soft leather-looking sandals.

Seeing Jeanne still standing with her hands on the hilts of her weapons, Omaw flicked his hand toward her in a questioning manner.

"She does not trust you. Previous meetings with your race do not suggest putting your guard down. Chohish has killed her relatives when defenseless without warning."

"Curs, they have no honor," Omaw exclaimed vehemently. "They were not of the Ostraron. I cannot be responsible for the curs of another coterie."

"Question Zeke, what is a coterie?" Jeanne asked.

"Similar to a community, a group of individuals with a unifying common interest or purpose. My uncle used that word to describe our cocoa farmers." Zeke answered.

"Omaw, I am perplexed about how we can resolve our differences. Many hate you for what your race has done to them. They want to eradicate you."

"You do not. Otherwise, you would not be here,"

"I do not; maybe if I understood why the Chohish attacked without provocation," answered Zeke.

"Because we are bigger and stronger, humans are weak. The strong should rule."

"If we defeated you without weapons, you would let us rule you?" Zeke asked.

Zeke could see the question perplexed Omaw; he doubted any Chohish had been asked.

"A human could never defeat a Chohish without technology or a weapon," responded an indignant Omaw.

"I could," dared Zeke, not moving when Jeanne asked what the hell was he doing.

A sound came from Omaw that Zeke assumed was a laugh.

"Pick your top fighter, and I will meet him in unarmed combat," responded Zeke.

"When? Where?"

"Now, or at a time of your choosing," replied Zeke. "Here, in this bay somewhere. It won't take long."

"Arrrgghh…. What about the machines? When you die, will they kill us?"

"No, they will sit out," answered Zeke. "Unless they have reason to believe there is cheating in the fight."

"Do not insult me, human; my tolerance has a limit," growled Omaw. "Let me find one for fighting you. It may take some time as all will want the pleasure."

"One hour then, where we met you when we came in," Zeke stood, walking out with Jeanne, who still had her hands wrapped around the hilts." The walk back was done in silence. Once they reached their shuttle and the ramp closed, Jeanne grabbed Zeke's arm and twilled him around.

"What the hell was that crap? You cannot fight them unarmed; they will kill you," she yelled angrily.

"I will, I must. My conscience will not let me do anything different, my dear. But, please, don't try and stop me," pleaded Zeke.

Dropping to the seat, Jeanne wrapped her arms around her knees. "Damn you, why?"

Sitting next to her, he pulled her close. "I remembered what my father told me when I joined the navy. He said he knew I would be keeping the peace that would require people dying. He asked me to never forget one thing."

"What? What could make you want to sacrifice your life?"

"Do not blame the sons for the sins of the father. He said, '*The son shall not bear the iniquity of the father, neither shall the father bear the iniquity of the son.*'"

"What does that even mean in this case?" asked Jeanne.

"Should you be held responsible for crimes your father committed? Should the children of the Chohish be guilty of the crimes of the Chohish adults today?"

Seeing the conflict in her face, Zeke continued. "I do not want to be a part of killing children. That would occur if we attacked the Chohish homeworlds. I need to find out if it can be avoided."

For the next hour, they sat hugging each other in silence.

"Jeanne, I need to be able to concentrate. I need to go alone," begged Zeke. The eyes on her face were a sight he would never forget. The hurt and despair displayed broke his heart.

Standing, he stipped down to just his pants and shoes. Grabbing some tape, he taped his knuckles and wrists.

Walking out of the shuttle, he took several deep breaths to relax. As he told Omaw, this would not take long. Either he won quickly, or he would lose. And if he lost, he had no doubt he would not survive.

He took his time as he walked to review what he needed to do and what to expect, stopping along the way to stretch.

Reaching where he first met Omaw, he saw several Chohish there, with Omaw being one of the two.

There was no talk. Omaw just moved aside to show a lone Chohish waiting. He was much larger than Zeke. The Chohish was only wearing a breach cloth.

Further back by several dozen yards, the Chohish lined up to watch. No sounds came from the crowd, but there was no doubt in Zeke's mind; they were gleefully expecting his death.

Turning, he saw that Jeanne had come, but she hung back the same distance as the Chohish. Around her, RGN, Irracan, and Sorath personnel were gathering. The battleoids had moved closer with power lights indicating they were fully shielded and armed.

Kneeling, he took several minutes to get control of his thoughts and relax his muscles.

Meanwhile, on the bridge of the Lucky Strike, Isolde, bored, started flipping through the different cameras in the Chohish captured carriers. It was fascinating to see alien architecture.

She paused when she saw a group gathering in a Chohish carrier. If she remembered correctly, it was where the one that housed the Chohish troop prisoners. What was going on?

Zooming in, she saw two large groups standing apart from each other. The Chohish crowd was massive, while the human one was small but growing. She hovered over the human group with a woman wearing a hat she recognized. What was Jeanne doing there?

She saw a lone human on his knees with his head bowed between the two groups. He was shirtless, not wearing anything to indicate who he was. With growing dread, she had a feeling she knew who he was.

"Will, come here," she yelled in panic.

Rushing over, Will stood behind, putting his hand on her shoulder as Isolde pointed to the lone figure on her screen. Will and Isolde glanced at each other with foreboding.

"Caspian, the ship is yours. Isolde and I have to leave," yelled Will as they raced out of the bridge.

Caspian swirled around in his chair to look around the room. Everyone stared at him in puzzlement. Running over to Isolde's workstation, he saw the camera focused on the lone figure. Working the controls, he soon knew what was happening. By this time, he was surrounded by the remained crew. All watched in dread as they watched their captain stand.

The scene on the Fox bridge was a bit different. Only one person still resided. Jeanne had contacted her sister and informed her of Zeke's pending fight. The entire crew, except for one, had left for the Chohish carrier a while ago.

The Jackal was not to be left out. Lance had led all except for a skeleton crew from the Jackal around the same time as the Fox. Meghan had contacted Lance about the situation as soon as she found out.

Word spread quickly; Kolqux and Endaen were rushing to stand in front of a monitor.

On a certain Sorath dreadnaught, Hawke stood on a large bridge watching the spectacle with a forbidding feeling. Hawke knew when he was notified by Isolde that he could not reach the carrier in time. He had been visiting his fellow countrymen when the call came through.

Now he stood there with no room to move as once the word spread, every Sorath ran to a location where they could watch. He watched as Zeke stood.

Standing, Zeke could feel his muscles quivering in anticipation. Then, moving to stand in front of the Chohish he was going to fight, he spent a few moments looking at his opponent.

The Chohish was significant, but there were some telltales from how he stood. He leaned slightly to the right, which meant he favored that side. Many scars covered his body indicated plenty of fights and lots of fighting experience. Zeke expected that; he guessed Omaw would send the best besides himself.

341

Looking carefully, he saw a large scar on the Chohish's left ankle. Possible loss of mobility on that side? And was that right eye discolored? All conjecture but probable.

Tension filled the air; he could feel it from both sides. Even though he wished a crowd would not gather, he could see it growing fast.

Raising and dropping his hand to signal that he was ready, he kept his eyes on his opponent. Then, as he expected, the Chohish rushed straight at him, roaring his hate.

Everything slowed as he concentrated on what Khalessi had spent the last six months teaching him. The first thing she taught him was how to evade. Then, going to the left, he dropped low.

He was right; the Chohish favored his left foot while swinging wildly with everything he had with his right hand. If that punch had hit, it would have been all over.

As Zeke slid under the giant fist, he jabbed with his knuckles into the area just under where a human's groin would be. Khaleesi had Doc take all kinds of scans on Chohish corpses to identify the muscle layout. Then she tested what she believed were weak areas on live subjects, all to prepare her marines if they were ever in a situation like he was now.

As his knuckles made contact, he could feel the Chohish muscles contract while he also heard a grunt. Khalessi said to pay attention to sounds like that, so he knew when a punch was effective. Once he slid past, he lowered his left foot with the pressure on his toes, so he could swing around quickly, using his weight for leverage.

Jumping, he aimed his next punch at the base at the back of his neck. Then, using all his weight, he punched straight down, hitting the nerve juncture. It had taken months of practice to perfect this move. Khalessi had mocked up a set of marine armor to emulate a Chohish. One of Jax's engineers had installed sensors so it would replicate the effect on the wearer of the armor.

The punch had the desired effect; the head of the Chohish swung around in pain and partial paralyzation. But he was not out of action.

Zeke was grazed in the head by a wild swing of the Chohish's left arm. He tightened his neck muscles as soon as he felt the thick arm connecting. His head rocked sideways.

Only the neck strengthening exercises that Khaleesi insisted on saved him. She had told him most knockouts from a head hit were due to the head's swing where the brain bangs against the inside of the skull. So he needed to build strong neck muscles to stop the head swing.

But this was not the end for Zeke; the Chohish twirling in desperation had swung a right fist at his face. Knowing he could not get completely away, Zeke pressed his tongue up to the roof of his mouth, clenching his jaw while rolling out. The hand skimmed Zeke's face hard but did not take him down.

While the Chohish was off balance, Zeke ran inside the Chohish's reach. Jumping with as much push-off as he could, Zeke hit the Choish's equivalent of the trachea with his elbow. The Chohish slid backward, gasping for breath.

Not pausing, Zeke stepped forward, hitting the center of the Chohish's chest as his front foot hit the deck, transferring his weight to go through the target. As Khalessi identified, the location was the same as a humans solar plexus.

The Chohish was stopped in his tracks. Zeke repeated the hit as hard as he could. The Chohish, gulping loudly, rolled his eyes and dropped senseless to the ground.

Breathing heavily, waiting, Zeke felt blood trickling down his face from the glancing blow to his head. Seeing no movement from the Chohish, he headed toward Omaw.

Halfway there, he heard a tremendous roar. Turning quickly, Zeke saw the Chohish had risen and was rushing toward him. Off balance, Zeke knew he would be unable to put up any defense in the few seconds before the Chohish reached him.

From the corner of his vision, he saw a large body interpose between the raging Chohish and himself. Omaw, roaring his rage, hit the charging Chohish hard in the face, dropping him again. From the bent angle of his neck, Zeke doubted he would rise again.

Suddenly, from the crowd of Chohish, two appeared with their version of swords and attacked Zeke. Before Zeke or Omaw could respond, a blur flashed past Zeke.

The slim form, yelling '*Ye lily-livered cowards!*', swung a cutlass whose edges glowed in an upward swing that sliced right through the arm of one of the Chohish. Not stopping, did a return horizontal through his chest. The Chohish fell, bleeding profusely.

Jeanne ran past the body to jump high, where she took the second Chohish by surprise and rammed the poniard in his ear. Then, using the Chohish's dropping body as a springboard, she flipped backward, landing next to Zeke in a guarded stance.

Standing over the prone body of the Chohish he had taken down, Omaw roared his displeasure at the rest of the Chohish. "I gave my word. Who dares break it? Come forward and face my wrath."

None of the Chohish moved. It was as if they were shocked at seeing an unarmed man defeat one of their champions, followed by a smaller one killing two bearing swords even faster.

Omaw turned back toward Zeke when none of the Chohish challenged him. Striding to Zeke, he glared at him with inquisitive eyes.

"I would ask how but will not dishonor a clean fight." Glancing at Jeanne, still in her defensive stance, he rumbled what Zeke thought was a chuckle.

"It seems your warning held truth. The little one is fast and deadly. Your mate?" he asked.

"Yes, I am fortunate that she has graced me with her love. I would be a lesser man without her."

"Something tells me you both would be. Now that you have proven your point, what is it that you want of me?"

"Talk mostly. I do not want to make war on your children but will not allow the Chohish to make war on mine. The question I need to be answered is, how can we both come to a satisfactory resolution," responded Zeke.

"Talk we can do, but know, I lead the Ostraron, no more," stated Omaw.

"Understood. But that is a good first step," Zeke replied while putting his arm around Jeanne. "I guess telling you to stay behind was foolish, no?"

"You have done several foolish things today. That just being one," Jeanne snarked. "Don't do that again."

All three turned around to see a dozen battleoids standing in a line near them. Standing next to them were Commander Anne Dieu-Le-Veut, Jeanne's sister, and Mason, her husband, both holding plasma rifles.

"Seconds, Chohish, we were only seconds away from starting to blast away," Anne articulated with a frosty voice. "Anyone who threatens my sister or her mate must deal with my Irracans."

"And the RGN," voiced Will with several dozen marine commandos walking up in full armor.

A lone Sorath sidled up where he just smiled. "You have met us before, dog; the situation has changed. We are not so weak anymore. If you had harmed these two, Hawke, in temporary command of our fleet, ordered all Chohish to be returned to their maker, in pieces."

Turning back to Zeke and Jeanne, Omaw looked at the pair in a new light.

"Are you sovereigns? That would explain much," he asked.

He was a bit startled at the deep laugh that erupted from both.
"No, just simple, Captains. These though," pointing around him,
"are our friends. We don't care for someone hurting our friends."

Taking a long sweeping glance around, Omaw said the following as he walked away. "We will have to talk more about what a
friend is. Chohish does not have friends. Something I would like
to know more about, maybe experience before I expire."

A few hours later, with Jeanne and Zeke back in their room on
Lucky Strike, Zeke was stripping to get ready for a much-needed
shower when Jeanne asked a question he knew was coming.

"I am going to ask the same question as the Chohish wanted to
ask, Omaw, was it? How did you do it?" asked Jeanne.

"The reason is the same as I already told you. I need to understand the Chohish but do not know how I could do that if we
never talked. So I had gone to Khaleesi to beg she train me to fight
one without weapons. I figured that would appeal to their honor
if they had any."

"Khalessi was already working on the same type of training
for her marines. She has been strength training me for the last six
months while teaching me what areas to strike. And how. She had
several of her marines gear up in special armor to mimic a Chohish
to test against."

"Why not let Khaleesi do the fighting? I am sure she would
have had the same, if not better, results?"

"I needed to build trust with Omaw. When he surrendered
the carriers, I hoped he may be a Chohish we could deal with. But
now," a naked Zeke said as he walked toward the bathroom, "I
need a shower."

A stripping Jeanne laughed as she said she had worked up a
sweat before racing ahead to see if she could beat Zeke into the
bathroom.

EPILOGUE

LIFTING THE PORT glass so he could swirl the port wine, he watched as the dark red wine swirled around in the crystal glass. He could still smell the ripe musky berries scent wafting from the glass.

"Where did you get this? More importantly, where do you store it? I may have to raid it sometime. This is excellent," exclaimed Nkosana.

"I am not always in agreement with my husband, but this wine is one of the best I have ever had," agreed Bridgette.

"Let's just say my family was able to procure a case of the stuff when I was made a one-star Admiral. They kept half for themselves and gave the rest to me for special occasions," responded Katinka. She sat in her office chair with her own port wine, forgotten in her left hand.

"I asked the two captains to join us, but they gave me their regrets. They insisted they had other duties that took precedence. I did not order them as much as I wanted to, as they deserved this more than all of us," she lamented.

Still looking at the swirling port wine, Nkosana asked what could be so crucial as to refuse an invitation from the fleet admiral.

"A wedding. Isolde and Gunner have decided it is time to take their relationship to the next step. I was informed that they were attending unless I ordered it."

"Ahhh… about time. Both are good people and excellent at their jobs. Have you thought about the promotions for them that we discussed?"

"Yes, and they both deserve it. Although I have serious doubts either will take it. I do not believe Gunner would voluntarily leave Zeke's side. I was curious, so I checked Gunners' records more thoroughly. There seems to be more to their unique relationship than a casual review would show. I believe they love each other like brothers who are willing; hell, what am I saying? They have both sacrificed career advancements to stay together. Look at the risks they have both taken to save the other."

"And Isolde, she would never accept separation from Gunner, nor him from her," interjected Nkosana. "They would both resign from the Navy before separating. The Navy would be the big loser if that happened. I could tell that from the short time I spent with them."

A giggle from Bridgette grabbed the attention of both admirals. "You are two of the smartest people I know. Yet you cannot see what is so obvious even though it is right in front of your faces."

In answer to both puzzled glares, Bridgette turned on the giant 4D viewer on the conference room table. A recording popped into existence, floating several inches above the polished wood surface.

It showed the main central square of the capital city of Sobolara. The city was huge, but nothing like a human city. Where a human city would have clean, gleaming modern structures that rose high in the skies, the buildings in this city were short, dark, and dreary. Many of the buildings show structure defects and crumbling due to neglect.

In the streets, though, the throngs of Kolqux showed no signs they were embarrassed. Even though the Kolqux wore threadbare clothes, they were shouting and jumping in joy. Adjusting the image, Bridgette pulled back to get a larger view of just how many Kolqux were present. There must have been millions.

Adjusting back to a more manageable view, they watched as a procession made it's way slowly toward a huge ornate government building that showed severe battle damage. Pockmarks from laser and plasma fire marred the surface, and huge craters from some type of explosion. Dark stains caused by fire overlayed it all. This used to be the government building the Chohish ruled the planet from, but now the Kolqux used it until a new facility could be raised.

Leading the procession was Uv'ei with his bother Uv'ek. Both wore the dirty oversized human marine armor they had worn on the station. Every now and then, they would stumble on the pants that dragged on the ground they were so long. No one in the crowd laughed but cheered them on.

The medical pod containing Major Khaleesi Richards was between the Kolqux, riding on an antigrav unit. On top of the medical pod was a life-size 4D image of Khaleesi in her bloody battle armor, carrying her plasma rifle. The 4D image of Khalessi would fire her plasma rifle every now and then into the sky. It was just a light show, but the crowd did not care. Khalessi was a hero in their eye, their hero, and every time the rifle fired, the crowd roared.

Behind Uv'ei, dressed in his full Irracan-powered armor, was Sergeant Jan de Bouff, with one hand resting on the pod. He walked tall, all in armor, fully armed with a plasma rifle connected magnetically to his back.

Rolling behind them came a procession of medical pods and wheelchairs carrying injured RGN and Irracan marines, army, and pilots. These were followed by thousands of wounded RGN, Irracan, and Kolqux helping each other walk, some on crutches.

Intermixed were the medical staff from the three human warships. And, not to be left out, a chef or two.

The crowd noise was so loud that Bridgette had to turn down the volume almost too off it was so overwhelming. Even then, the volume increased to nearly unbearable levels when the following groups made themselves known.

Marching in marine cadence came to the rest of the marines in full battle armor. Leading them were marines in battleoids, with all the battle stains and damage evident on every unit. The heavy stomp of their foot pads was loud and metallic.

Yet, even the cheers for the battleoids were overwhelmed. This by the yells and screams of cheers when the rest of the marines marched by. Marching in their full-dress uniform, twirling their rifles and tapping the ground in loud clacks reverberating throughout.

But the crowning piece had to be what followed. As loud as all the prior cheers were, it was nothing to compare with what followed. The crowds just went ballistic.

Here came a mixture of humans, Kolqux, and Endaens. In the center strode Zeke and Jeanne, waving her hat with its long feather at the crowd. Each time she did, the crescendo rose.

On either side of them marched Hu'de and Te'ln and Vopengi Edoetti. Behind them came Meghan and Lance with their command crews.

Last, thousands of personnel from the three warships, the Kolqux warships, and stations mixed in. They filled the street for miles. The sound was so loud Bridgette had to mute it for several moments.

When she put the sound back on, they could hear a ribald Irracan song joined in by the RGN crew members. That caused Nkosana to choke on the sip of wine he was taking.

"A song you recognize, my dear?" asked Bridgette innocently.

"Ok, we have seen the parade before. Not sure what you are trying to point out. What did we miss?" asked Katinka.

"The interaction between the RGN and Irracan personnel. Even though the RGN and Sorath have been allies, we never acted as one. We always maintained our own forces and command structure. That is not true here. Irracan pilots flew and interfaced on RGN ships. Personnel from the Lucky Strike have been staffed on the Fox since the beginning. Have you forgotten that their commander is in a serious relationship with an RGN officer?"

"I doubt any of the officers on those three ships would accept a promotion if it meant they had to separate. I believe they would resign their commission. They have bonded like family and want to keep it that way. I speculate the RGN officers would resign and join the Irracan Navy if forced."

"Oh my god, I think my wife is right. I should have seen it. It was always on display right in front of me. The crew interacted more like family than strangers."

"Are you aware who planned the parade procession? Not scheduling one. That was all Uv'ei. But in what order and who would be in it? You only get one guess, and it wasn't Uv'ei or his brother," hinted Bridgette.

Seeing that neither of the puzzled Admirals would answer, Bridgette answered her own question.

"Our two, now infamous captains. Uv'ei wanted to find some way of honoring the RGN and Irracans on the three ships. The Kolqux never had a parade themselves, but the Chohish held them often as a sign of superiority. Uv'ei did not know what else to do to say *thank you from a grateful people.* The Kolqux had nothing of value to give them."

"Zeke flatly refused. Zeke suggested that the Kolqux hold their own parade for rising up and freeing themselves."

Bridgette remembered the adoration on Uv'ei's face as he told her all this when she congratulated him on such a wonderful parade.

"Uv'ei said he could not do that without honoring the sacrifices made by all the humans. Zeke put his hands on his shoulders and leaned down until their faces were only inches apart. *'Then, my friend, let's create one that honors all. But not one that honors one person or race above the other.'* Uv'ei said Zeke told him."

"I cannot. Not until Major Richards has recovered enough to join it. She, so much more than myself, deserves it. All her marines do."

"'Uv'ei, that is not the Major's or marines' way. She and they did what they had to because it was what was right, not for any glory. Someone had to stand in the Chohish's way. Khalessi would be horrified if she found out you thought you owed her anything for her actions. She considers you her friend. She would risk everything for a friend. I know a way, though, on how she can still participate in the parade.' Uv'ei said Jeanne whispered in his ear."

"Uv'ei, Uv'ek, Zeke, Jeanne, Vopengi, Hu'de, and Te'ln, developed who, what, when, where, and how the parade would go. Those two captains have turned out to be international and interspecies heroes. In other words, they are rock stars in this quadrant."

"Then what do you suggest, Bridgette? What do we do with them? You must have something in mind knowing you," asked Katinka, now paying closer attention to her wine. She needed a drink after that revelation.

"Create a new unified command group to manage a combined RGN, Irracan, Kolqux, and Endaen fleet. Use them as advanced scouts to flush out the Chohish. At the end of the war, we can revisit what to do with them whenever that would be," advised Bridgette.

"That may lessen the impact of what we learned from the spy satellites they placed over that planet."

"I am not looking forward to telling the Kolqux and Endaens

about that. To think the Chohish created a world populated by both Kolqux and Endaens. Two races ground into the dirt to serve" agonized Katinka. "The images of what we discovered have me sweating at night."

"Well, that is one good thing about being an intelligence officer. I do not have to be the one to pass that type of information on to them," sympathized Bridgette. "I only have to give it to the one in command."

The hand gesture Bridgette received in response from Katinka brought a laugh from both of the Chadseys.

Made in the USA
Las Vegas, NV
27 November 2024

12766423R00215